Praise for *Crash*

"A riveting, must-read story that
couldn't be more timely!"
—Ward Larsen, *USA Today* bestselling
author of *Assassin's Revenge*

"Sex, violence, suspense, intrigue, drama,
catastrophe, the end of Wall Street (almost)
as we know it—what's not to like?"
—James Grant, editor of
Grant's Interest Rate Observer

"A frightening doomsday scenario."
—*Publishers Weekly*

"A grade A thriller."
—*Booklist*

ALSO BY DAVID HAGBERG

*Kirk McGarvey adventures
*†Kirk McGarvey ebook original novellas

ALSO BY LAWRENCE LIGHT

Too Rich to Live*
Fear & Greed*

WITH MEREDITH ANTHONY

Ladykiller

NONFICTION

Taming the Beast

SHORT STORIES IN:

Alfred Hitchcock's Mystery Magazine
Ellery Queen Mystery Magazine
Thriller 2
Wall Street Noir

NONFICTION PERIODICAL ARTICLES IN:

Barron's

Bloomberg Businessweek

Chief Investment Officer

Columbia Journalism Review

Financial Planning

Fortune

Investopedia

HuffPost

Money

TheStreet.com

The Wall Street Journal

Yahoo! Finance

*Karen Glick thrillers

CRASH

DAVID HAGBERG

AND

LAWRENCE LIGHT

FORGE®

A TOM DOHERTY ASSOCIATES BOOK
NEW YORK

This is a work of fiction. All of the characters, organizations, and events portrayed in this novel are either products of the authors' imaginations or are used fictitiously.

CRASH

A Forge Book
Published by Tom Doherty Associates
120 Broadway
New York, NY 10271

www.tor-forge.com

Forge® is a registered trademark of Macmillan Publishing Group, LLC.

ISBN 978-1-250-26870-9

Our books may be purchased in bulk for promotional, educational, or business use. Please contact your local bookseller or the Macmillan Corporate and Premium Sales Department at 1-800-221-7945, extension 5442, or by email at MacmillanSpecialMarkets@macmillan.com.

First Edition: April 2020
First Mass Market Edition: January 2021

Printed in the United States of America

0 9 8 7 6 5 4 3 2 1

This book is for Judy.
And for Meredith, beloved muse and so much else.

Also: To Fred Cuppy, a friend and savvy trader;
thanks for your help and kind words.

ONE

ONE

OPENING BELL DAY ONE

1

Ben Whalen had known for the past two weeks that something was eating at his girlfriend, Cassy Levin, and he was almost certain it had to do with her work on the cybersecurity floor at Burnham Pike, the nation's premier investment bank. But he had mostly left her alone about it, figuring that sooner or later she would tell him.

As a former Navy SEAL lieutenant he had learned by combat experience how to face any problem head-on. Not that he appeared very aggressive. At five-ten and a lean 170 pounds, his blond hair and open blue eyes made him look more like the appealing boy next door than a highly trained killer.

"My hero," Cassy had called him from the first moment they'd met at Toni's, a bar on Long Island.

She was thirty, petite, with a pretty face and a nice figure, and he was turning thirty-two next week, and sometimes, like this Thursday morning, looking at her lying in bed beside him in their third-floor loft in the Village, he could only marvel at his good luck. They'd lived together for nearly a year now, and on the fifteenth, his birthday, he was going to ask her to marry him. And it scared the hell out of him that she might say no.

She'd been moody lately, which wasn't like her. She was usually feisty and spirited, but something was bothering her. Yet every time he'd brought it up, she'd just smiled and looked away for a moment. "It's work, but I can't talk about it right now. Okay, sweetheart?"

"When?" he'd pressed two days ago as they were having lunch at the Old Town Bar on Eighteenth Street.

She'd started to object, the corners of her mouth turned down, but he'd kept going.

"Is it like Murphy Tweed?"

"Don't push it, Ben, please."

"Is there an intrusion?"

"Could be," she'd said, and she'd abruptly tossed down her napkin. "I'm late." She'd gotten up, pecked him on the cheek, and left.

At her previous job over at Murphy Tweed, a small investments firm, she had worked as a cybersecurity analyst and designer. On her first day of work she'd prepared a detailed report for the brass informing them that their data system was woefully out of date and prime picking for hackers. She'd recommended a complete overhaul of the system, which at her best estimate would take as much as a half million dollars to put in place.

She was voted down, and less than a month later, the company's system had been hacked and mined for the user names and passwords of nearly one thousand customers. The stolen money had been channeled to overseas private banks where no one could find it.

In less than ninety days the company had gone belly up, the execs had been bailed out with golden parachutes, and Cassy had been blamed for the entire mess. She'd found herself out on the street with no job, no money, and no real prospects.

Until Francis Masters, a research chief at Burnham Pike, had recognized her talent and almost literally plucked her off the street.

"I would like you to do for us what you tried to do over at Murphy Tweed," he'd told her in his office. "You have the chops, Wharton and Harvard. I went to MIT myself. And believe it or not, MIT's old VP Tom Foley gave you the best recommendation of all: 'Hire her and listen to her.'"

"Malware," she'd told Ben, later that night at home. "Someone put a program into our system that can steal passwords and user names, like at Murphy Tweed, and create all kinds of other mischief."

"I know how to blow up stuff, and shoot bad guys, and seek and find."

"Macho man."

He'd shrugged. "I didn't have Wharton or Harvard, but I did have the SEALs, including hell week," he said. "But you know how to stop it."

She'd tilted her head to one side—a move that meant she was agreeing with him and thinking at the same time—a move that had turned him on from the get-go. "I think I do, and now it's up to me to convince Francis so he can convince his boss, the chief technology officer."

"O'Connell?"

"Yeah."

"Well, they hired you to improve their cybersecurity operation, so you'd think they'd listen to you."

"We'll see."

For the last week or so he'd watched the worry lines grow at the corners of her eyes and mouth, and heard her laugh, which had always been light and musical—one of her many fabulous attributes—go south.

"Screw it," he'd said at their apartment yesterday after work. "Your systems are in place, let's take a month off. Paris, get a little efficiency on the Left Bank, walk the Quai, spend the afternoons at sidewalk cafés, maybe take in a museum or two here and there. Versailles, Mont Saint-Michel, maybe a canal barge in Burgundy."

"Not now," she'd said.

"Later?" he'd asked.

"Promise."

He was going to propose in Paris. All he had to do was get her there.

2

Cassy came awake slowly, as she did most mornings. He watched her with pleasure as she stretched, arching her back, tasting her lips as if she were testing the air, just like a cat did, smiling, almost purring. Her shoulder-length dark hair was tousled, the sheet down, exposing one small breast.

Her eyes opened and she looked up at him, propped up on one elbow, watching her. "What?" she asked, smiling.

"I can't stop looking at you."

"I'm a wreck at this hour."

"My wreck," he said, and he reached for her.

She pushed back the covers and scrambled out of bed, stepping back. "Not this morning."

"We have time," Ben said, and he shoved back his covers and started to get up.

"Benjamin, no," she screeched, backing up.

They both slept in the nude, and in his eyes every square inch of her body was perfect. And again, as he did just about every hour of every day, he said a Hail Mary to his luck. He was a kid from the wrong end of a steel plant/iron-ore-mining town, and she was a New England privileged blue blood.

"Just a shower together. One reason why not."

"I'll give you two. You're taking the shuttle down to the Navy Yard in D.C. first thing, and in the meantime the roof might cave in on me this morning, so I have to be on the floor ASAP."

"Come on, Cassy. It's me you're talking to. What's going on?"

"Something. I'm not sure. But big."

Her narrow shoulders slumped, and for just a moment Ben thought that she was going to cry.

He got out of bed, and before she could turn away, he took her in his arms. She was shivering, and he held her without saying a word for a long time until she calmed down. When they parted, she looked up at him.

"I'm afraid."

"Don't be. I'm here."

"Just be here for me, Ben. Please. Promise me that no matter what happens in the next twenty-four hours or so, be here."

"Promise," he said, and he was more concerned than he'd ever been in a combat situation, where the SEALs' number-one Murphy's law was: *Incoming rounds have the right of way.*

3

Clyde Dammerman, the number-two man at Burnham Pike, was the last of the four to arrive at Kittredge, the hundred-year-old private club on Fifth Avenue. He was a tall man with a bald head, a beak of a nose, and dark, angry eyes that suited his personality. This morning, an hour and a half before the opening bell on the NYSE, they were the only four in the oak-paneled dining room on the third floor.

Reid Treadwell looked up. He was BP's chief executive officer, a trim, dapper man in his fifties with gray hair. The joke was that he was so natty he even went to bed at night dressed in a three-piece suit, the tie correctly knotted. Handsome and debonair, he radiated a charisma that landed Burnham Pike a lot of high-fee deals—and aided his almost insatiable quest for women. Always calm and composed in public, he never raised his voice even when he was irritated, like now. "You're late," he said, his tone icy but even.

Dammerman, whose idea for the crash had come to him in a dream eight months ago, took his seat. "Sorry, Mr. T, traffic."

"We're betting the fucking farm on this thing, so you could at least be on time."

"We're on point, trust me. By noon tomorrow all four of us will have become heroes, and we'll all be on our way to collecting several-hundred-million-dollar payouts. And let's not forget, the grateful thanks not only of BP, but of the few clients who will have listened."

"And screw the NYSE, and every other market across the country and the pond," Spencer Nast said, a smirk on his pinched, narrow little face. His hair was thin, his frame was thin, and so, in everyone's opinion, were his morals. Everyone, that is, except for President Roland Farmer, the multibillionaire businessman who'd hired Nasty, as Spencer was widely known, to be the White House chief adviser on economic affairs.

"Start a business, get into the markets, take a risk, and sometimes you win, sometimes you lose," Dammerman said. "This time we win, guaranteed."

"Lots of people are going to get fucked," Nasty said.

"But not us," Dammerman replied. "Not us, not this time."

Treadwell, who had listened without comment, sat forward. "Julia, we're down to the actual wire here, what's your take? Go or no go?"

Julia O'Connell was BP's chief technology officer, and without her brilliance, the Plan, as the four of them had come to call the scheme, wouldn't have a chance of working. Pleasant but socially maladroit, like many tech geeks, she was obviously trying to assume a tone of bravado among all these high-testosterone males.

"It's risky," she said. At five-two, just over one hundred pounds, with dark hair cut in bangs, she epitomized the computer whiz. She'd been a nerdy genius since she was seven years old, when she first discovered that she understood the cyberworld. She knew what computers and complicated programs were thinking. Even what they were feeling. Her babies were pure in her mind, angelic. The gods of a new age. They could do no wrong if they were handled with a velvet glove. *Garbage in, garbage out*. The mantra for the new age.

"Is it a go?" Treadwell repeated.

"Abacus is a go," O'Connell said. "A better virus than Stuxnet—the one that crashed Iran's nuclear program—less traceable because it leaves no footprint, and so deadly complicated that even the best heads won't be able to come up with the cause, let alone any solution that'll work. When we crash the market—and I mean *crash* it—they'll have to start over again. From day one, at tables under a tree on Wall Street."

"It'll effect just about every other market here in the States—Nasdaq, American Exchange, Chicago, Over the Counter—plus Tokyo, London, the Euronext, Shanghai," Dammerman said. "Thank you, Amsterdam." He raised his coffee cup, and the others, including Treadwell, did the same.

"Amsterdam," Treadwell repeated.

The fact of the matter was that when it came to serious cybersecurity issues, the most talented hackers were mostly young, disaffected people—almost hippies—who lived in communities in the slums of Amsterdam. The Russians went to them for help, as did the Chinese, the Brits, everyone. Including Dammerman, who with O'Connell's help designed the parameters for Abacus, then handed the project over to the whiz kids.

And now, within twenty-four hours, or a bit more, Abacus would be a reality, the final phases inserted into the NYSE's computer system. Markets across the world would crash, disintegrating people's faith in the system and triggering defaults of debt in an overextended world financial system. The entire planet would plunge into a mind-numbing depression the likes of which hadn't been seen since the 1930s.

Treadwell raised a finger, and instantly a waitress appeared to take their breakfast orders. Omelets or easyover with ham or bacon for everyone except O'Connell, who ordered oatmeal with half-and-half, plus yogurt and a dish of cut fruit.

"Thank you, Denise," Treadwell told the waitress, who blushed. He was a born salesman, who knew everyone's name.

"Who the hell do you think you are, Hank Paulson?" Dammerman asked, laughing. Paulson, who'd been secretary of the treasury in 2008 during the collapse of the subprime mortgage market, had famous planning breakfasts with the president of the New York branch of the Federal Reserve, the chairman of the Fed, and the comptroller of the Currency, as they hustled to stem the crisis. He ate oatmeal every day for breakfast.

"I'm glad he isn't here," O'Connell said.

No one laughed, because it was those four people who'd averted what would have amounted to a collapse of the entire American economy and almost certainly the economies of every industrialized nation. They bailed out the big banks.

"There'll be no bailout this time," Treadwell said. "Too big to fail? We won't give them the time to react. When they realize what has hit them, it'll all be over." He smiled. "I wonder what they'll call it once the dust settles?"

"How about the debt bomb," Nast said. He liked to lecture people about economics. "It's the real reason the shit storm is coming, and there's nothing anyone, and I mean anyone, can do about it."

There were four types of people in the financial world—in places like Burnham Pike, the markets, and especially the White House: dealmakers, like Treadwell, who was the driving force at BP and a smooth operator. Traders, like Dammerman, with his blue-collar background, the same as most of the market makers who manned the posts on the floor of the NYSE. Geeks, like O'Connell, who understood computers better than she did people. And wonks, like Nast, who were the numbers jockeys, the guys who analyzed company finances, figured out elaborate market algorithms, and wrote economic forecasts—everything he'd done for BP when he'd worked for the firm, and now did for POTUS.

"And we're going to make a killing by getting into cash, because we know it's coming," Dammerman said with a smirk.

"Because we made it happen," O'Connell agreed.

"Abacus is just the spark that's going to light a fire that would have come all on its own," Nast said. "And that's the beauty of the thing. The world will go to shit, and there'll be no one to blame. Especially not us."

"The 'debt bomb,'" Treadwell said. "I like it."

"It's easy," Nast said. "The world is in too much debt. Pushing the quadrillion-dollar mark. Hell, most countries will never be able to pay it back; they're having a hard time just keeping up with the interest.

"Here at home our debt is almost one hundred percent of the GDP—the gross domestic product. When Social Security was put into place in the thirties, there were forty-two workers for everyone who collected their monthly payment. Today it's three to one, and that ratio is shrinking. Americans are living longer, and Medicare's costs are spiraling out of control. So how do we fund it? More debt.

"Since the last crisis, corporate debt has gone through the roof. Companies right now owe more than six trillion dollars plus because the Fed lowered interest rates, which added more fuel to the fire. But instead of expanding production and research, building new factories, hiring more workers, they're funding stock buybacks to make their investors happy.

"State and municipal pension plans are so underfunded there's no way in hell employers will be able to meet their obligations to their retirees, and that's already here, right now, in the short run.

"Household debt is in the stratosphere. Credit cards, houses, cars, college loans. Put together, that adds up to another thirteen trillion dollars and counting.

"And just about every other country is in the same condition or worse. China is choking on debt. Greece is going down the tubes. And Latin America's debt to us? Forget them ever—and I mean ever—paying it back. Most of those countries are starting to default just on their interest payments."

Nast stopped for a moment. "Crash the world economy—starting with the NYSE—convert to cash, and we'll make our fortunes, all right," he said. "And live like kings."

"Our virus, Abacus, will start the fire," Treadwell said, "but how do we know it can't be put out somehow? The NYSE has an off-site backup computer system. If the main servers on the floor fail, they can go to the second set."

"I have it covered," Dammerman said. "Trust me. No backup computer on the planet will save the market once we pull the pin. And our Russian friends will even plant a terrorist bomb on the backup computer just as a diversion."

He laughed, his voice loud in the normally staid dining room.

Breakfast was served by four waiters, and when they were gone, O'Connell spoke up.

"But we may have a problem," she said.

"What problem?" Treadwell asked.

"A woman in my department, a data scientist named Cassy Levin, is suspicious that something is wrong. She came to me last week, damned near on the verge of exposing Abacus."

"Isn't she the dumb ass who brought down Murphy Tweed?" Dammerman asked.

"Wasn't her fault," O'Connell said. "And trust me, this gal is bright, very bright."

"Put Francis Masters on it," Treadwell said. Masters was BP's number-two cyber-research chief, a onetime hacker himself. The in-house belief was that the man would stomp his own mother to death if Treadwell told him to do it.

"I'm just saying we need to be careful," O'Connell said.

"Maybe she'll have an accident," Dammerman said.

4

It was a full hour before the opening bell on the floor of the NYSE and a half hour before Burnham Pike's DCSS—data center security suite—was officially open for business, but Cassy had been at her workstation for twenty minutes. And what she was seeing made her even more worried than she had been all week. Something was desperately wrong and getting worse.

The DCSS, located in a sub-basement beneath the firm's tower on Nassau, just up the street from the Federal Reserve Bank, was fully staffed for only eight hours per day. Nine to five, unlike the trading floors two dozen stories above.

Up there, deals were struck; down here, problems were predicted and handled before they came up.

Upstairs was where money was made for BP's clients—mostly institutional investors, such as pension funds, insurance companies, mutual funds, college endowments, charities, and family offices that handled the money of the very wealthy.

Down here was where the investments were protected from foul play.

Nothing obvious was showing up on her three monitors, and yet at least two trades that were in the process of being put together upstairs for offering once the market opened in an hour were showing minor anomalies. Most trades were done in even lots—multiples of hundreds, thousands, tens of thousands. Odd lots were trades that somehow ended up as one hundred one, or one thousand one. A minor computer error? But Cassy had a bad feeling that it was more than that, because stuff like this had been popping up for more than a week now.

Donni Imani, her nineteen-year-old super-nerd friend, slid into his seat at his station next to hers. "How's that boyfriend of yours doing this morning, Cassy?" he asked. He was well built, almost to the point of being muscle-bound, and so handsome he was pretty. And he knew it. But he was also very smart.

"He's out of town for the day," Cassy said, her eyes on the screen to her left. An offer from the Dubuque public workers trust fund in Iowa to trade five thousand and one shares of Amazon at $2,107.50 per share was on BP's list for this morning's projected trades.

Imani and his girlfriend, Tanya Swift, who worked on one of the trading floors at Bank of America, had had dinner with Cassy and Ben a few weeks ago.

That was on a Saturday evening. The next Monday Imani had declared to anyone on the DCSS floor, which was about the size of a big-city-hotel lobby, that he was henceforth and forever madly in love with Cassy Levin—and the hell with Ben Whalen.

"That guy of yours got himself a secret lover stashed away somewhere?"

"Shut the hell up, Donni, we have a problem here."

Imani leaned in closer so that he could look over her shoulder. "Another one of your odd-lot bogeymen?"

"A PW trust fund in Dubuque."

"Maybe they do it differently in Iowa."

"Not like this."

Imani moved back to his station and brought up Cassy's screen. He shifted to a history mode, which showed the trades that the Dubuque PWF had made over the past three months, then six, nine, and a full year.

Cassy moved closer so that she could see his left screen as well as her own center display, on which she was searching for other anomalies.

"The odd lots just started showing up two weeks ago," Imani said. "Give O'Connell the heads-up."

"I talked to her about it two days ago, she said it was nothing. Anyway, she's not here yet."

"Then take it to Francis, he just walked in the door."

Cassy looked up. Francis Masters was number two in charge of cybersecurity, reporting to O'Connell. He was a chunky, plump man in his late forties with acne scars on his face. He almost never wore a jacket, and went around with his shirts untucked to help hide his paunch. He had a doctorate in cyberscience from MIT—a fact he was fond of telling anyone who would listen—and he was arrogant and petulant, which was an unpleasant combination. But he was also seriously smart. Smarter than anyone else in the room, he'd like to brag. And no one ever contradicted him to his face. Except for his boss, Julia O'Connell, who was smarter than Masters and a lot nicer.

"We need more," Cassy said.

"Look at the history. They've never made odd-lot trades in the past year. It's just not done."

"Please," Cassy said, trying not to laugh. Imani was young, even for his years, and cocksure; he thought *he* was the smartest person in the room, but she loved him for it. "But I've been seeing them pop up for different buyers."

Imani grinned. "You'd think someone was practicing for something."

Cassy looked at him, her worry spiking. "Almost," she said half under her breath. Appearing to be one thing, when in fact you were another. Like Ben.

More people were coming in, powering up their workstations, even though trading wouldn't start for another half hour. They were mostly young, much younger than Cassy, and they loved what they were doing. In fact, she thought, most of the people she knew in the business loved it.

"Spending other people's money by the basketful is a kick," one of the kids had told her last month. "I mean, it's bitchin' cool! Like a video game."

For just a moment she wished that Ben were with her right now. Or, better, that they were in Paris walking along the Seine. She had an idea that he was going to ask her to marry him. And she'd known for a long time now that when he did, she'd say yes. Unreservedly yes.

The night they'd met, she and her friend Janice were at Toni's, a roadside dive on Long Island. They were playing eight ball on one of the three tables, a game Janice, who worked as an analyst on one of the trading floors over at Goldman Sachs, had introduced her to, when four monstrous, leather-clad bikers with tattooed necks and bushy beards swaggered in as if they owned the place. They came straight over to the pool table.

"Our turn," the largest of them said. He wasn't wearing

a T-shirt under his leather vest, his hairy belly spilling over the tops of his dirty jeans.

Cassy had looked up. "When we're done, mutton chops." At that moment she'd hadn't been in the mood to listen to some lowlife's arrogance.

"I said *now,* bitch," the biker roared, and everything in the place stopped dead.

A man who was much shorter than the bikers, with blue eyes and light hair, came up behind her. "The lady has a point," he said, his voice soft, not demanding.

Cassy turned and looked at him. Her first thought was that he was going to get his ass seriously kicked, and her second was that he was movie star cute.

"Who the fuck do you think you are, asshole?" the biker demanded. "Get the fuck outa here."

"Tell you what, how about I buy you and your friends a beer? And when the ladies are finished, I'm sure they'd be happy to give you a chance to play a game against them."

The biker started to say something, but then he stopped. He looked at Cassy and Janice, then at the man whom he towered over and outweighed by at least one hundred pounds, and his face began to fall, a degree at a time.

"That's okay," he muttered. "We'll play another time."

He and his three friends turned and walked out the door.

"Who are you?" Cassy asked the man who'd stared down the bikers.

"Name's Ben," he said, his smile lighting up the entire room for her. "And you?"

"Cassy," she said, almost tongue-tied. "Cassy Levin."

5

Masters had got a cup of coffee and was sitting at the break table in a corner across from the foosball table the kids used on their downtime, or when they were trying to figure out a tough coding problem.

Cassy walked over, got a cup of coffee, and sat down across from him.

He looked up from working on his iPad. "Good morning. You're early."

"I think we might have a developing problem, Francis."

"The odd-lot trades you told me about the other day?"

"It seems to be spreading."

"What do you mean?"

"I'm not sure. But if I had to guess I'd say that we've picked up a bug. Almost acts like a cyberworm, except . . ."

"Except what?"

Cassy shook her head and looked away for a moment. "It's like something in incubation. Something in the system that's growing."

"Fix it. What we pay you for."

"I have to get a handle on it first."

"Then do it."

"I think we should take this to Julia."

"Take what to Julia?" Masters asked. "Exactly?"

"I want to play a game with it. But I'll need some help, and it might take a few hours."

"Do it."

"I'd need to suspend or at least delay Burnham Pike's trades for today."

Masters laughed out loud. "Give me a fucking break," he

said. "Do you know how many millions of dollars the firm would lose? Now get back to work. Find it and fix it, and when you come up with something that makes sense, we'll take it to Julia. But not until then."

6

Reid Treadwell stood on the floor of the New York Stock Exchange a few feet away from the post that would trade the initial public offering of Rockingham Corporation, a Burnham Pike client. It was a few minutes before the opening bell at nine-thirty.

O'Connell was fidgeting off to his left, while Treadwell's attention was completely on Heather, the twenty-five-year-old daughter of Keith Rockingham, the founder of the company, who was now up on the rostrum with a half dozen of his executives.

"This is like a dream come true for my father," Heather said, almost gushing. She was a full head shorter than Treadwell, with long blond hair, a pretty oval face, green eyes, and a fabulous body, and wearing a sheer white blouse, a sharply tailored dark suit jacket, and trousers.

"I hear that you've made a lot of strides in the company's marketing department," Treadwell said. "A lot of movers and shakers have already sat up and taken notice."

She touched his arm. "I don't know how to thank you for all you've done for us, Mr. Treadwell."

"Please, no formalities. I'd be happy if you would call me Reid. My dearest friends do."

She was a little uncertain, but she nodded. Treadwell was the JFK of Wall Street. *Don't ask what Burnham Pike can do for you, ask what you can do for Burnham Pike* was the bank's unspoken mantra. "Okay, Reid," she said.

"That's better."

The floor was busy this morning. CNN had wanted to do a live interview with Treadwell, but he had declined, patting the reporter on the shoulder. "Later in the week, okay, Mark?"

"You bet, Mr. Treadwell," the man said, and he and his cameraman headed away.

Heather looked at him with open admiration, but then turned to look up at her dad on the rostrum with only minutes to go. "I've never seen an IPO go to market before," she said. "This is exciting."

Rockingham Corporation, founded thirty years ago by Heather's father, specialized in rugged outdoor wear for extreme sportsmen and -women. It had carved out a respected niche in the market but had never hit it big. At least, not until three years ago, when Burnham Pike enrolled the company as a client.

In order to make money, you have to spend it was another of Treadwell's self-serving mantras.

To start out with, BP floated $100 million in debt for the company so that it could begin a massive expansion program. And now the company was going public, hoping to raise another $25 million, this time in stock. Rockingham would be able to build a new factory in Vietnam, where labor was cheap, embark on a major ad campaign, and expand the products and equipment it offered.

"I would love to pick your brain about marketing," Heather said, pressing closer. "Reid."

Treadwell smiled. "That's right—you're Rockingham's marketing director. Are you free for lunch today, after the opening hubbub subsides?"

"Absolutely."

"Basel's," he told her. "It's a little Swiss restaurant just a few blocks from here." It was just around the corner from one of the apartments he kept at this end of town for clients and other pursuits. And sometimes, like now, he was almost ashamed of himself for how easy it was. Almost.

A middle-aged woman whom Heather introduced as an aunt showed up all overjoyed and gushing, embracing her niece in an encompassing hug.

O'Connell was at Treadwell's side. "Do you really want to do this today?" she asked, keeping her voice low.

"Stress relief," Treadwell said. "You should try it."

"I'm wasting my time here. We have that potential problem we talked about."

"Stay here and try to act like you're enjoying yourself. When the shit hits the fan in the morning, let it be remembered that we were here and enjoying Rockingham's little bullshit IPO."

The opening bell was on the verge of ringing. The rostrum was crammed mostly with Rockingham execs, including the old man himself, the company's name and logo on a banner on the wall behind them.

"Those poor bastards," Treadwell muttered half under his breath, and he had to grin.

The aunt had left, and Heather was looking up at him. "What?" she asked.

"Your family is going to make a lot of money," he said.

Heather was smiling. "You betcha, Reid, and so are you."

On the rostrum, Rockingham, a large, barrel-chested man with a thick shock of perfectly white hair, pressed a button, and the brass, saucer-shaped bell just below where he and the others stood began ringing. Four other bells around the floor's periphery rang at the same time.

Heather moved forward to applaud her father.

Rockingham pumped the hands of his execs; the well-wishers below applauded with abandon as just about everyone on the floor did at every opening bell.

"How long's their lockup period?" O'Connell asked.

"Six months," Treadwell said, his eyes on Heather, who was beaming up at her father and the others.

"Wasn't for Abacus they would actually make some money. It's a good company."

"Shut the fuck up, Julia," Treadwell said, just loudly enough so that O'Connell could hear what he was saying over the noise, but no one else could.

Rockingham and his entire executive team got a big allotment of newly public company shares for free, while a lot of friends and family had been issued special blocks that they could buy at the offering price of $7 per share. Which was a good deal, because after an IPO, the price sometimes rose dramatically, providing the company stayed healthy and the market didn't tank.

The only problem was that IPO stocks issued to execs or purchased by friends and family were locked up for a period—in Rockingham's case, six months. This meant that for a full half year they couldn't sell. That was too bad if the stock price cratered in the meantime—which sometimes it did. And by tomorrow it certainly would.

"They have an interest payment due next month, don't they?" O'Connell said.

"Five percent," Treadwell replied absently. "Now get off the subject."

The $100 million BP had raised for the company was in the form of seven-year bonds, which were sold to investors at 5 percent, paid yearly. At the end of seven years, and there were six to go, the company had to redeem the bonds and repay the borrowed money.

Rockingham's executives left the rostrum and began filtering onto the floor, while the old man himself came down, shook Treadwell's hand, kissed his daughter on the cheek, then went over to the trading post handling the IPO.

The round structure, of which there were a half dozen on the floor, was about thirty feet in diameter with banks of computer monitors and keyboards around the periphery. The market makers, as they were called, who manned each post, each with different-colored jackets—this one green—were already busy on phones and tablets. They were talking with brokers who delivered orders in person. A constant babble of voices surrounded each post. The feeling on the floor was electric.

A CNBC reporter and camera crew came over and did a brief interview with Rockingham then moved off. The old man turned and gave Treadwell a nod and a big grin. This was his day.

In Treadwell's estimation it was actually a waste of time being here, but he had to admit that it was exciting. Got his blood stirring, especially with Heather Rockingham at his elbow.

She turned to him, a huge smile on her face. "Isn't this wonderful?" she said. "My dad is so happy. But tell me something: I thought that most stock trading was done by computers. So why all the people here?"

"You're right about one thing, most of it is done by computers. Eighty percent of the New York Stock Exchange's trades are done digitally, in fact. But the exchange likes to have some live humans—market makers—at the posts who make trades, especially the more complicated ones. Trades where the guys in the bright jackets get the feel for the deal. They can haggle sometimes, and they have an instinct for what they can get in a trade. Computers don't have instincts. Just numbers."

"And all the TV cameras," Heather said. "It's almost like we're on a movie set in Hollywood."

Treadwell had to smile. "Yeah, and just about everyone here knows it."

An exciting murmur went up from a number of Rockingham's execs who were staring at the monitors on top of their post.

"We're not trading yet?" Heather asked.

"New issues like yours start trading around eleven, in an hour and a half. Right now the market makers are dickering among themselves about the opening price. A lot's going to depend on the market's direction. But everything is up to this point, which should help you."

"Fantastic," she said. "I bet the farm—my farm—on our stock. Daddy said it was too risky, but I put everything I had—a hundred thousand—into it." She looked up at Treadwell. "I believe in Rockingham, and I believe in Burnham Pike," she said. She rose up on her tiptoes and kissed him on the lips. "I have to mingle. See you at lunch."

O'Connell was at his shoulder. She nodded at a passing TV camera crew. "Aren't you worried that Bernice will see you kissing some young girl on the flat-screen?"

"My wife hasn't gotten out of bed yet," Treadwell said. He spotted Seymour Schneider just a few feet away, and he gestured for the man to join them.

Blue-jacketed Schneider, a Burnham Pike broker who'd been a fixture at the NYSE for more than twenty years, was one of the old men in the business. A couple years ago a Fox News analyst made the comment that "What Schneider doesn't know about the market isn't worth knowing."

The nearly bald man in his mid-fifties, with a look of mild surprise etched on his round, pale face, as if the world had just taken off on some strange tangent, came directly over, and he and Treadwell shook hands.

Schneider had an intuitive feel for the market and had predicted the dot-com bubble's bust in 2000, which had led to a recession and the subprime mortgage collapse of '08, which in turn had led to the Great Recession.

He looked like he was in a funk.

"So how is it shaping up this morning?" Treadwell asked.

"Like a house of cards."

"The market's up," Treadwell said.

"It's the debt, like a plague. And I don't have to tell you how fast it's spreading. But something's just around the corner that's going to send us past the point of no return. War, some earthquake or something, or maybe just someone screws up somewhere, and we'll be swallowed whole."

O'Connell went pale and was about to say something, but Treadwell held her off with a gesture at the same time he spotted Spencer Nast, who was here visiting old friends and, like Treadwell, wanted to be seen cheering on a healthy market. Earlier that morning Nast had been telling them about the same thing that worried Schneider.

"Okay, Seymour, you have my attention," Treadwell said. "Talk to me."

"Do you need me to tell you how many trillions in debt we are in, just in this country, let alone the entire world market—Europe, Russia, hell, China? The amounts are staggering. It's a debt we can never pay, and the market's not going to like it. Could be a crash is coming."

"But the market can't crash," O'Connell said, which Treadwell thought was one of the dumbest things he'd heard in a long time, especially now when Abacus was ready to be released.

"The market's too high," Schneider said. "It could be a repeat of '29 when overnight it lost, what, a quarter of its value? Everyone was poor in an instant. Guys jumping off the roofs of their office buildings. The banks were carrying too much debt, and when people went for their money, it wasn't there. Almost like the subprime mortgage crisis in '08, only no one in 1929 thought to save the banks like we did. Too big to fail? Well, they did."

Treadwell had an ominous thought that Schneider knew about Abacus.

"And don't count on the circuit breakers, if this happens," Schneider said.

To prevent panic selling, the Securities and Exchange

Commission required that when the market dropped 13 percent, trading on all exchanges had to stop for fifteen minutes. If the slide were 20 percent, all trading was canceled for the rest of the day.

"Things aren't going to get that bad," Treadwell said. "Trust me."

"From your lips to God's ears," Schneider said, and he turned and walked away.

"Do you ever feel guilty about what we're going to do?" O'Connell asked.

"Never," Treadwell replied.

"Well, I think of all the misery that's coming to ordinary people and I . . ." She stopped, realizing she had said too much.

Treadwell gave her a stern look. "Are you going soft on us?"

"No," she said, clasping her hands together.

"The entire world economy is teetering on the brink, and it's going to collapse anyway. You heard Schneider, and you heard Nast. We're just speeding it up a little."

"And making a profit from it."

"Yes, and making a profit. We'll be the last investment bank left standing in the ruins. It'll be up to us to guide the economy back to health, so why shouldn't we profit from our foresight and ingenuity? We'll be saving the world."

"After we destroy it," Julia said. But then she smiled and nodded. "But I see your point."

"We're not ordinary people, as you call them," Treadwell said, leaning closer. "Never forget it. We're more like gods."

7

The Mesa Airlines shuttle from LaGuardia to Washington's Dulles Airport was prompt, as usual, but by the time Ben Whalen's cab passed through the gate at the Washington Navy Yard on the Anacostia River, a stone's throw from the Washington Nationals Stadium, the opening bell had already rung at the NYSE.

He'd thought about Cassy and wished that she'd been able to be more open with him about what had been troubling her for the past couple of weeks. It was big, he guessed that much, but beyond that he was at a loss. He'd wanted to help, but he didn't know what to do.

On the other hand, she'd been funny last night when she'd laughed and said that she'd trade her BP secrets for his work at the Yard.

Lieutenant Commander Chip Faircloth, an old friend from ten years ago on a couple of top-secret missions to Somalia—up around the city of Harardhere, north of the capital, Mogadishu—was waiting in his office in what was called Warehouse 7A. The cavernous building, which was one of the classified facilities, had for the past year and a half been the final test and certification site of the navy's latest top-secret littoral project.

Faircloth was the project director, and Whalen was the chief SEAL design adviser even though he was no longer on active duty. But he was damned good.

Once Whalen had passed through the three-layer security posts to get into the building and was allowed upstairs to the office overlooking the construction floor, he found Faircloth hunched over a table studying a series of blueprints.

"What's the issue now?" Ben asked.

Yesterday Faircloth had sounded stressed on the phone; now it seemed worse. "We've got troubles," he said, without looking up.

"W's failed the pressure tests again?" Whalen asked. The project was named W after President George W. Bush, who'd authorized the one-billion-dollar price tag in 2008. And they were over budget by half that amount with no real end in sight.

"We send your people to sea, and before they get where they're supposed to get, they're dead. Drowned."

"Where this time?" Whalen said, joining Faircloth at the table.

"At the forward and aft hatches, but we expected that, and the engineers promise the problem can be fixed. But the ballbusters are the four exhaust tubes. Soon as we hit fifty percent drive power the seams open up."

"At what depth?"

Faircloth looked up. He was a compact man, handsome in a rodeo cowboy way, narrow hips, a lot of lean muscle, and an angular jaw like W's anti-radar profile, almost the same as the B-2 bomber's. Riding low on the surface of the water, the forty-meter stealth vessel was completely invisible to ground- and sea-based radars, and from the air, all but indistinguishable from sea clutter.

The *all but* had been the sticking problem almost from the beginning. The ship had been designed to slip just under the water, like a submarine, for short periods of time. Long enough to land a SEAL team ashore completely without detection.

But then deep-sea-penetrating radar had been developed, so the operational depth for W had been extended to twenty meters, something over sixty feet.

"The Chinese S2 system can see to one hundred meters."

"Jesus Christ," Whalen said. "The pressure hull isn't that strong."

"Look, we just found out three days ago, so I ordered the increased pressure tests, and the hull is fine except for the hatches. No problem. But it's the MHD drive tubes."

MHD—or magnetohydrodynamics—was a type of propulsion system that used magnets to electrically charge a medium such as seawater that could be pumped out rear vent tubes to push the ship forward. The advantage was that the drive system made absolutely no noise. Perfect for a stealth ship. The problem now was that at only half power the tubes leaked badly.

Whalen stared at the blueprint sheet open on the table, then went over to the plate-glass windows that looked down on the construction/test floor where W was up on chocks— all 130 feet of her.

Four techs surrounded by scaffolds were concentrating on the underwater profile of the aft end of the ship. Two of them were welding what looked to Whalen like patches around the MHD drive vents.

Faircloth joined him.

"Patches, for Christ's sake?" Whalen asked.

"Brightman thinks the fix will work." Donald Brightman was the chief designer, and now he worked as chief of the sea trials and certification team.

Two boats had been built. One was outside, partially submerged in a special pen in the Anacostia River. This was the dummy model on which fixes for problems found in number one would be designed and put into place for testing.

"Like patches on the life preservers our guys used in 'Nam. The ones that killed more SEALs than incoming enemy rounds. Remember the after-action reports we read?"

Faircloth smiled, but without humor. "'Our equipment is brought to you by the lowest bidder.'"

"This is the same old shit, Skip. It's a design flaw that

needs to be fixed before I'll sign off on the boat. I'm not going to recommend we send our guys three hundred feet down with those bullshit fixes."

"They're on my ass about the cost overruns."

Whalen turned to face his friend. "What's a life worth?"

"I'm all ears, Ben. What do you want to do?"

Whalen went to the blueprints and stabbed a finger at where the MHD drive itself connected with the drive tubes. "Let's take a look."

They got white coveralls and hard hats from a locker and took the stairs three stories down to the floor, where Faircloth gave a throat-slashing gesture to the foreman in the aft scaffolding. The welding stopped almost immediately.

"We're going inside to look at something," he shouted up to the man, who nodded.

The boat was designed to ride low in the water when it wasn't submerged, and had a very small conning tower, rising less than six feet above the deck. There were underwater hatches to allow the SEAL teams to get out of and into the boat, but the main entry was through the conning tower.

Whalen and Faircloth climbed the scaffolding stairs to the deck and then the temporary scaffold to the convex conning tower hatch, which was open.

Whalen went in first, but Faircloth hesitated for just a moment. "I'll build these things, but I sure as hell wouldn't go to sea in one."

"When someone's shooting at you, drowning becomes the least of your worries," Whalen said.

Below, and a couple of feet aft, the control room was designed to accommodate only three people: the skipper, the dive officer, and the sonar operator. Forward were accommodations for six SEAL team operators. Aft was the three-man crew quarters, plus the galley, and the head.

Below were the equipment spaces for weapons and explosives the SEALs would need ashore, along with electronic equipment.

Just forward and aft of amidships the next deck down held the underwater gear, including three battery-operated sleds that would each carry two fully equipped operators up to three kilometers, six meters under the surface.

In the center was the MHD drive itself, in a completely enclosed space. No maintenance at sea was possible, which would be a moot point in any case. There was no room in the design for technicians who could understand a problem *and* the equipment and spare parts to make repairs.

It was another design flaw, in Whalen's opinion, but one on which he was overruled.

Faircloth opened a hatch that led to the lowest deck, with not enough room in which to stand, and they both dropped inside.

Whalen went first, crawling on hands and knees to just aft of the center line, where the four drive tubes angled down from the MHD unit aboard.

He sat down and shone his flashlight on one of the titanium struts holding the fourteen-inch-diameter tubes. The problem was obvious.

Halfway between where the struts came from the drive unit and connected with the base of the tubes, hairline cracks were visible.

"Son of a bitch," Faircloth said. "Stress loads we hadn't anticipated. No way it can be fixed."

"Because you guys never thought of harmonic vibrations," Whalen said.

"And?"

"We start the run-up tests all over again. My guess is these stress fractures only occur at certain sustained power levels. Find out what those levels are, and either run above or below."

"Problem fixed," Faircloth said.

"I wish everything were that easy," Whalen muttered, his mind still on Cassy and whatever was bugging her.

8

Cassy stood at her workstation, her eyes constantly switching between her four large computer screens as she inputted the first elements of a game she was trying to play with the system in order to trick the virus, or whatever it was, into showing itself.

She was mimicking a buyer whose normal trades were showing up as odd lots. So far the virus-detection program she'd designed was showing nothing. The system was working the way it was supposed to work.

But she knew better, and she was frustrated.

"I'm not liking this, Donni," she muttered half under her breath.

But he'd heard her, and he moved over from his workstation next to hers, and studied her screens for a few moments. "Start with an even-lot trade, and see what happens."

She did it, but the buy came up as normal. "The same as when I do the odd lots."

"Can't be," Donni said. He nudged her out of the way and inputted an odd-lot trade of 1,013 shares, and almost instantly it came up as a normal trade. "It can't have it both ways."

"That's what I'm trying to tell you, and I'm getting a really bad feeling about this. It's like the damned thing has a mind of its own."

"Acts like a virus."

"I told that to Francis and he blew me off."

"So what do we do?"

Cassy switched to the screen on her right and brought up a recent history of trading from Dubuque regarding a grange holding company, which came in at lots of 1,001. Next she shifted to Danzig Capital in San Francisco, which came in at 1,002.

"Numerical order," Donni said.

"I picked them at random," Cassy said. "EconoMax, a trading firm in Minneapolis, came in at 1,003. Francis Retirement Fund, from a chain of hospitals in Gainesville, Florida, came in at 1,004."

"Artificial," Donni said. "Can't happen."

"But it is."

"I see it, but someone is manipulating the system. Has to be."

"Someone or something," Cassy said. "My guess is that the odd-lot trades are symptoms, like when your nose runs when you get a cold. A virus has gotten into our system. And the sequential odd-lot numbers are the giveaway."

When she'd found evidence of a data breach at Murphy Tweed, it had been similarly subtle and yet obvious to her. Apparent if you knew where to look and knew what you were looking at. But her boss back then hadn't believed her any more than Masters had earlier this morning.

"Okay, what do we do?" Donni asked.

"Find the coding behind each trade."

Donni slid over to his station. "I'll take Dubuque."

"I have Danzig," Cassy said. She brought up the trade on one side of her center screen, and the BP account on which the company's trades were managed on the other side. As soon as the programs got deeper into the code it became obvious that there were differences. Slight, but hardly insignificant.

She moved over to Donni's station. He was coming up with the same anomalies.

"Not enough here to see how any difference could show up in the actual trades," he said.

"Try to delete the last line of the code," Cassy said.

Donni's fingers danced over the keyboard, but when he hit *enter,* nothing changed. "We're locked out."

"Penicillin," Cassy said. At her keyboard she set up a series of commands that would seek and destroy whatever was locking them out—like an antibiotic for an infection.

An instant after she'd hit *enter,* nothing changed.

Norman Applebaum was one of the bright kids who last year, at the age of twenty, had dropped out of MIT because he thought that he was smarter than the professors. He wandered over from his station and looked over Cassy's shoulder. "You have a worm," he said.

"Duh," Cassy said.

Norman shouldered her out of the way and entered a series of commands on her keyboard. He was a runt, with a prominent Adam's apple and red hair in a ponytail.

Nothing changed, and he looked over at Donni's monitors for a longish moment before he shook his head. "Garbage in, garbage out," he said almost disdainfully. "You guys gotta clean up your act before you can find anything meaningful." He turned away and wandered toward the foosball table.

"I'm going to Francis again," Cassy said. "Maybe he'll listen this time."

She headed over to Masters's workstation, visions of a repeat of Murphy Tweed strong in her head. Only this time she knew that she was right, and she was going to be heard.

9

"How bad is this?" Masters demanded when she was finished showing him what she and Donni had found. "And how many times are you going to bring me something that's still a work in progress?"

Norman had found a partner at the foosball table, and they were playing a noisy game.

"Bad," Cassy said. She wasn't going to be intimidated by the bastard, who in her estimation was as blind as her boss at Murphy Tweed had been, even though it had been him who'd hired her.

"Okay, I'll take it."

"I can handle this, Francis." After the Murphy Tweed debacle, she had pledged that such a thing would never happen again.

"Then what are you doing bothering me?"

"I'm just making you aware that we could have a major problem."

"There's some brilliant research that you might not have seen on the eradication of well-protected intrusions that just came out of MIT," Masters said, once more reminding her that he had graduated from that institution.

"This is what I'm being paid for, remember?"

Masters's acne scars reddened. "I'm taking over," he shouted. "Do you understand, Ms. Levin?"

The foosball game stopped and everyone looked up from their workstations. Cassy felt the heat rise up from her neck.

"Has Julia returned from the exchange yet? Maybe we should loop her in on this."

"Who the hell do you think—?" Masters shouted, but he suddenly cut off in mid-sentence.

"Is there a problem?" Dammerman asked from behind Cassy.

"Nothing important," Masters said.

"Everything," Cassy said, turning around.

"From what I'm understanding, you may have uncovered a possible breach in our system."

"Yes, sir. And it's one that could really slam us."

"Like Murphy Tweed?"

"Not exactly, but the end results could be the same."

"Let's get a coffee, and you can tell me what you've found."

"I'll just come along," Masters said, but Dammerman gestured him off.

"We'll take care of this," Dammerman said.

Cassy followed BP's number two toward the elevators. Like a politician, he shook hands and had a few words with the geeks, mostly young kids who looked up at him in awe. And he made small talk with the people riding up in the elevator, who for the most part could only nod sheepishly.

BP's building, with a white atrium that soared twenty stories, was one of the newer ones in the Financial District. They got off at the floor for the cafeteria, which this time of the morning was still serving breakfast before switching over to an extensive lunch menu.

Dammerman was one of very few wearing a suit and tie. Everyone else was in business casual, the norm on Wall Street these days to make the millennial talent feel comfortable.

A stocky, broad-shouldered man with an oak-thick neck materialized beside them as they got off the elevator. He was Butch Hardy, a former NYPD cop who was head of BP's security division.

"We'll take espressos," Dammerman said, not breaking stride on the way over to a table, and not bothering to ask Cassy what she wanted.

Hardy scuttled across to the coffee bar, and Cassy had to wonder how Dammerman could get away with treating his top security man like a servant.

"Masters is a dickhead who sometimes thinks he's a hell of a lot smarter than he is," Dammerman said.

BP staffers who usually milled around the cafeteria laughing and joking fell silent, some of them getting up from where they were sitting and moving away, giving Dammerman a wide berth. They were mostly traders and wonks, more socially astute than the geeks downstairs who didn't know to be afraid of him. He had the reputation of sometimes firing people on a whim.

"Now, tell me what you think you've found," Dammerman said as they reached a table and sat down across from each other.

"I think it's a computer worm in our system," Cassy said.

"How's that different from a virus?"

"A virus needs to be attached to a program before it can spread. It can get into a network from a corrupted file, like when you click a free Florida vacation link to what turns out to be a hacker's site. It can spread only if someone then opens the file. But a worm can get to work right away. It hides better, and it's much, much harder to detect."

"Wasn't it something like that put the screws to Iran's nuclear program?"

"Yes, sir. It was a worm called Stuxnet, and it went after the centrifuges used to enrich uranium to a bomb-grade level. It caused them to spin out of control and destroy themselves. Thing is, no one detected the worm until it was too late, and even then they couldn't do anything about it. Rumor is that the Americans and Israelis were behind the intrusion. Knocked the Iranians out of the ballpark."

"You ran into a worm at Murphy Tweed, right?"

"I did, but management didn't believe me. The breach let the bad guys suck brokerage accounts dry in a matter of minutes. These were accounts protected by user names and passwords, as well as a two-factor identification routine where the customer had to text a code if they wanted to make a major trade."

"Like if they wanted to liquidate their account," Dammerman said.

"Yes. But the worm went right around it."

"So if you're right, and we have a worm, it'll be powerful."

Cassy nodded. He'd understood. "I think our worm hasn't been designed to empty accounts. I think its goal is the destruction of our system, or at least to freeze us from doing business."

"Freeze?" Dammerman barked.

"What's worse, since all trading floors worldwide, including ours, are connected in one way or the other, is the possibility that the infection could spread from us to other investment firms and banks, and even exchanges."

He was silent for several long beats, an expression of malevolence, even hate, on his face. "The entire world?" he said quietly.

"This has the look of something the hackers over in Amsterdam are capable of doing," Cassy said. "The geeks and nerds living like hippies in the slums whose only life is messing with computer systems anywhere in the world. The bigger and tougher the better."

Hardy appeared with the espressos. Cassy thanked the ex-cop, but Dammerman didn't dismiss him. He remained standing off to one side.

"How do we stop it from damaging our system? Or is it even possible?"

"I think if I can make a copy of the worm, I can turn it inside out and feed it back into the system, neutralizing the code."

"Just like that?" Dammerman said, and if Cassy hadn't

known better she would have thought he was being sarcastic instead of relieved.

"It's what I could have done at Murphy Tweed if they had let me. But I have to go back downstairs to run some diagnostics. And if I'm right, I'll be able to follow the worm everywhere, even to an infected exchange on the other side of the world, and kill it."

"You can kill it?" Dammerman said, his voice low and menacing. "Aren't you the smart one."

Cassy was taken aback. It was Murphy Tweed all over again, and she was floored. Completely lost. He was acting like this was her fault. "What would you like me to do, sir?" she asked.

"Your job," Dammerman said.

"Yes, sir."

"Butch," Dammerman said without taking his eyes off her, "keep your eye on our computer genius here, would you?"

TWO

MID-MORNING

10

The twelve directors of Burnham Pike clustered around the boardroom table on the top floor of the fifty-four-story headquarters building just past 10:30 A.M. Its glass walls offered a magnificent view of New York Harbor. The Statue of Liberty lifted her torch in the distance. The Staten Island Ferry trailed its wake as it churned away from the Battery. Numerous boats, small as toys from this perspective, cut through the calm water. The sky was a heavenly blue.

A perfect day, Treadwell thought as he entered the boardroom.

The board members applauded him, and he held up a hand in welcome and gave them his best Cary Grant smile. Everyone was happy. BP stock had risen 20 percent so far this year, and it was heading higher this morning. All of it due to his genius.

Technically, the board's job was to be the advocate for the firm's stockholders, and that included the directors themselves. It was the big leagues, because board members got a lush BP stock grant, worth $1 million per year on top of their $750,000 salaries, which gave them a powerful vested interest in how their shares fared.

The meeting space was nothing like the mahogany-paneled boardrooms of the past. It was bright and airy, with a modern long white conference table that had a calligraphed place card for each director. A briefing book sat at each spot.

Treadwell glad-handed his way among them. Like a seasoned politician whose constituency happened to be the upper 1 percent of the richest people in America, he gave each a personalized greeting, asking after wives, children, grandchildren, and old friends by name, and sprinkling comments about the directors' wealthy pursuits.

I heard Tommy got accepted to Stanford. Congratulations.

You bought the old Stuyvesant place in Newport, from what I heard. A coup.

We saw Kay Kay at the Schwarzmans' in East Hampton two weeks ago. She's as lovely as ever. Sorry you were in Japan, you missed a nice party.

He sat down at the head of the table as he regaled them with the good prospects for Rockingham's debut stock. "Our record with IPOs so far this year beats everyone on the Street," he said, and everyone smiled. They were the captains of industry, and Treadell was the commodore.

Given Burnham's fat profits, the board had already voted Treadwell a 20 percent across-the-board pay raise. Last year he'd made $23 million in total: $3 million in base pay, $7 million in a cash bonus, and $13 million in BP stock. *Forbes* estimated his net worth at $2.5 billion. That gave left-wing agitators, some of them in Congress, plenty of ammunition. They branded him as the embodiment of Wall Street greed. The real median American household income was $61,000, they said, and household net worth only $11,000. Many Americans were only one paycheck from living on the street.

"What do you hear about the China situation?" Dennis Wilson asked. He was the no-nonsense retired CEO of the nation's largest freight hauler.

"A few things, Dennis," Treadwell answered. "I'll cover them in my remarks."

"You've been recommending that we go to cash," Sarah

Cummings, the head of the largest soft-drink bottler in the world and the lone woman on the board, said. "Are you still recommending that course?"

"I'll cover that too, in a few minutes, Sarah."

Dammerman walked in and took a seat to the right of Treadwell. "Sorry I'm late, but business waits for no one."

As BP's COO, he was the number-two man in the firm, so he got a few chuckles at his disingenuous remark, but no one on the board liked him. He was too rough around the edges, and had none of Treadwell's polish and political skills.

But Treadwell trusted him, and that was good enough for the board.

"Everyone, please take your seats," Treadwell said.

In addition to being CEO, he had from the beginning maneuvered himself into the position as chairman of the board, the body that was supposed to oversee the company's operations—and the CEO's decisions. And he had hand-picked each member, all of them Treadwell cronies, more than happy to get the benefits that BP doled out to them as long as they went along with the CEO.

And only one of them had any real financial expertise, other than running their own companies, so they couldn't mount any realistic challenge to Treadwell's policies even if they wanted to.

That exception was Charles Callaway, who managed the Tobias hedge fund and was married to Treadwell's sister. But he viewed his major function as acting as his brother-in-law's cheerleader.

Treadwell took his place at the head of the table, the harbor behind him and the glow of the morning sun bathing him in an almost holy radiance. By design. In his mind, these meetings were mostly theater.

Flanking him, besides Dammerman, was the chief financial officer, Todd Penniman, a thick-necked wonk with thinning, prematurely gray hair and round Charlie Brown eyes, who had climbed up through the ranks mostly because he was a bootlicker. A devoted yes-man, he could be counted on to make the numbers look good no matter what.

A sprinkling of other BP executives sat along the walls, waiting to answer any questions the boss might have for them.

"Fellow board members," Treadwell began. "We have a problem."

Smiles around the table faded.

"A crash is coming, and maybe sooner than any of us had expected," he said, his voice as stern as a righteous preacher's. "I'm sure that some of you saw the news on the internet earlier this morning. CNN was all over it. Numerous banks in China are about to collapse. This will almost certainly cause a panic, perhaps sending markets around the world into a free fall. It'll make '08 seem like a day at the beach."

"Might cause a panic?" Dennis asked.

"We've anticipated what's going to turn out to be a mess," Treadwell said. "You may have heard the rumors that we've been moving to cash, and it's true. We've kept the news out of the media and denied it when *The Wall Street Journal*'s Tony Langley asked one of our PR people about it two days ago."

"Okay, Reid, what's 'going to cash' mean in this context?" Sarah Cummings asked.

"Over the past month we've discreetly sold off the majority of the stock and bond holdings in our own account. I have done so for myself as well, and I recommend the rest of you follow suit. But quietly; we don't want to be the root cause of the coming panic. When it comes—not if, but when—it will send the prices of our securities plummeting. If word were to get out, we would be hard-pressed to make anything on our own trades."

Treadwell paused a moment for effect. "If we'd unloaded

our holdings on the NYSE or any other public exchange, we wouldn't have been able to mask our sales. We avoided this by using our own dark pool and those of a few trusted allies."

"Brilliant, Reid," his brother-in-law said. "Dark pools, good move."

Everyone around the table nodded in agreement, but Treadwell figured he could count on one hand how many of them actually knew what a dark pool was. They were businesspeople, not traders.

Dark pools were trading platforms that substituted for public exchanges such as the NYSE, and allowed big players like BP to make substantial trades with no one the wiser. BP had its own dark pool, and yet from time to time used other, similar platforms because of the volume of securities they wanted to move.

"At this point we've successfully liquidated more than ninety-five percent of the firm's invested capital, and it's sitting in a very large number of FDIC-protected banks around the country."

The Federal Deposit Insurance Corporation covered deposits up to $250,000. No depositor would lose any money up to that amount.

Jack Perkins, CEO of the number-one tire manufacturer in the U.S., raised his hand. "Sorry, Reid, but I just did the math. There are about five thousand banking companies in the U.S. That means we can only shelter just under 1.25 billion dollars of our capital. But BP's invested capital is around five hundred billion."

Treadwell now regretted appointing the man, whom he'd thought would be easy, to the board. But in the past six months or so the old bastard had become a pain in the ass. He'd never been a financial whiz, but he was sharp.

"We've managed to do it through thousands of dummy companies we set up. And none of them have any overt links to us." Again Treadwell paused for effect. The board was with him. "Once the shit hits the fan, and I believe it will sooner than later, we will be covered."

"Is this even legal?" Perkins pressed the point.

"Our legal beagles have signed off on the strategy. We're good."

"Don't we have to report this to the SEC? What we're doing is a significant corporate event."

"Unbuttoning our fly to the Securities and Exchange Commission would defeat the whole purpose of the exercise," Treadwell said glibly.

By law, changes in a publicly traded company needed to be announced because the value of the company's stock could be affected. "According to Hank Serling this technically isn't a corporate event that rises to a mandatory disclosure." Serling was BP's chief attorney and another of Treadwell's handpicked people.

"Hank said that?" Perkins demanded. "Doesn't sound kosher to me."

"The board knows that I have never made a move without the ironclad guarantee that it's in the best interest of Burnham Pike."

"Why not put our money in U.S. T-bonds, instead of this cockeyed bank scheme? Treasuries were the safe play in '08. Everything else went to hell then, except T-bonds. Backed by the government, what could be safer?"

"Buying that amount in Treasuries would send up a red flag that trouble was on the wind. You can't hide something that big."

"Reid's never steered us wrong before," Charlie said, and the rest of the board murmured their agreement.

Sarah spoke up. "Okay, but the bigger question is: Is the situation in China so dire that we need to go this route? Why will there be a crash? How bad will it be? And how do we—you, Reid—know for certain it's coming?"

Treadwell nodded. "Good questions," he said. "All of you know Spencer Nast, our former chief economist. We're honored that he's now serving as the head of the National Economic Council, and in the White House as President Farmer's chief economic adviser. Once he's finished in Washington we hope that he'll be returning to us. He warned me three months ago that he had reliable intelligence sources that bank collapses in China were imminent. And this morning we met briefly, and he said that he believes the Chinese bank meltdown may occur as soon as today. Overnight, our time."

Perkins sat forward all of a sudden. "Can he legally share something like that with us?"

"It falls into a gray area," Treadwell said.

Almost all of the board members were agitated.

"Why exactly would the failure of banks in China affect us here?" Wilson asked.

In Treadwell's view the question was especially stupid, considering Wilson had once run an international freight hauling company.

"As you know we live in a global economy, totally connected," he said. "China's gross domestic product is second largest in the world behind ours. Their system is a mix of communism and capitalism, but what's coming will overwhelm even Beijing's total control."

No one on the board of BP said a word.

"Their banks have made enormous loans to projects that have no intrinsic value. Highways, tunnels, and railways to nowhere. Ghost cities with massive blocks of apartment towers with every unit empty."

"So why are they doing crap like that?" Alan Friedman, the CEO of a very large advertising agency, asked.

"The companies borrowing the money were ordered to do so by the government. The point was to stimulate the economy. Construction workers get paid, and suppliers of bricks, concrete, asphalt, and water and sewer pipes, you name it, are at the trough too."

"Okay, I can see where you're taking this, Reid," Wilson said. "We trade with them in a big way. But big enough so that if their economy collapses, it would hurt us as badly as the subprime mess did in '08?"

"It will be worse than 2008," Treadwell said. "Every indicator I have studied shows that our markets will sink like a brick, and the effect will cascade around the world. In the past the trade conflicts we've had with China have hurt us. This will be ten times as bad."

"So what can we do besides taking a cash position?" Sarah asked.

"It's already being done," Treadwell said. How he would love to tell them about Abacus.

11

Dammerman had been seriously pissed off that he hadn't heard from O'Connell all morning, ever since they'd returned from the stock exchange with Treadwell. She hadn't answered his phone messages or texts, and no one downstairs in the data center had seen or heard from her either.

Just before the board meeting, he'd ordered Masters to find the chief technology officer and if need be, drag her back into the light.

"She outranks me," Masters had sniveled.

"I don't give a shit. Just do it."

Now Dammerman sat impatiently at the conference table. Board meetings, in Dammerman's estimation, were a total waste of time. But Treadwell insisted that BP's COO be present at every one of them. "We need to show the flag, it's as simple as that."

"It's theater bullshit," Dammerman had retorted.

"You're damn right," Treadwell had agreed. "And you will be there at my side, and fucking well like it. Understood?"

"You're the boss."

"Yes, I am."

Dammerman's phone vibrated in his jacket pocket. It was a text from O'Connell.

I'm back.

Dammerman thumbed his reply. *Meet me in the DCSS in five minutes, and don't vanish again.*

He leaned over to Treadwell, who was listening to Perkins flap his gums. "Gotta go."

Treadwell nodded.

Dammerman pulled his bulk out of his chair and turned to go, but Perkins stopped him.

"Are we boring you, Clyde?"

Dammerman smiled. "I'm hanging on your every word, Jack," he said. "But I have to put out a fire. Nothing serious, it just needs tending to." He nodded toward Treadwell. "Listen to Mr. T. When he says it's time to dive into the bomb shelter, we dive. Am I right, or am I right?"

12

Hardy was waiting for him outside the boardroom, and they walked across to the private elevator. Despite the casual dress style and other crap that BP affected to seem more egalitarian, the top executives did retain some of the old privileges, like their own elevator.

"Are the Russians ready for our pre-strike meet?" Dammerman asked, keeping his voice low, though no one else was in the corridor.

"Locked and loaded," Hardy said. Like Dammerman,

BP's security chief had grown up in working-class Queens. As a cop he'd accumulated a lot of citations for valor, along with a number of brutality and excessive force charges, all of which were dropped. In one of the cases the supposed victim had simply disappeared.

The Russian team of former Spetsnaz operators had shown up in New York three days ago, where they had gathered the needed material for their strike on the NYSE's backup computer. Dammerman hadn't had a face-to-face yet, leaving the recruiting, initial briefing, and first significant payment in dollars to Hardy. But he was a hands-on person, and he wanted to see for himself who these guys actually were.

They got on the elevator. The shaft was glass that allowed a spectacular view of the atrium, with gardens that rose as high as the eighteenth floor and offices on the other side of the soaring open space. It wouldn't stop until it reached the floor the exec who had pushed the button wanted to go.

"We're all on board?" Hardy asked.

"Yeah, except that Reid's decided to chase some skirt today, of all days. He's a horny son of a bitch, but at least he's got good taste."

"We'll have eyes on him, in case you need to get in touch," Hardy said.

"Even if he's in the saddle?"

"Especially if he's in the saddle." Hardy chuckled. "Who is it this time?"

"Rockingham's daughter and head of marketing. And she's not going to let Reid fuck her unless she gets something in return."

13

The elevator opened at the data center, a place full of geeks and nerds who thought they were superior to just about everyone in the building, including the top-floor execs.

Dammerman was comfortable around the traders and dealmakers and even the wonks, who understood what real power was all about—and had respect. But the kids down here respected nothing and no one except their bullshit computer games.

O'Connell was at a desk in a far corner of the room, her long, delicate fingers trolling across her keyboard like a concert pianist's, oblivious to everything and everyone, including the foosball game in full swing just feet away and Dammerman's approach with Hardy in tow.

As one of BP's top executives, O'Connell had never behaved like the rest of the tech heads down here. She understood that Dammerman could fire her at any time just for the sheer hell of it, so she had been as deferential as any of the investment bankers on the thirtieth floor and above.

Until she had become a key player in Abacus. Now the woman knew that she was dismissal-proof and had become cocky.

Or at least she thought that her job was safe, but starting now Dammerman was going to teach her to think otherwise.

"Hey, Julie," Dammerman said. It was a name O'Connell hated with a passion.

"Almost done," she replied, not looking up.

"I'll wait for you, okay? But in the meantime, why don't you un-sert your head from your ass?"

O'Connell looked up, startled but still self-assured. "I'm trying to track what the Levin girl is up to. Francis and I are looking down her track to get a handle on just what the hell she's been doing, and what she's already guessed."

Cassy's workstation was across the room and out of earshot for normal-level conversations, but Dammerman didn't bother lowering his voice.

"I know what the bitch is up to, she told me while you were out fucking around," he said.

"I had to call our people in Amsterdam; we need a couple of last-minute tweaks, and I didn't want to use an in-house phone," O'Connell said. "And don't call me names."

"I'll call you whatever I want," Dammerman said, raising his voice.

"Okay, Clyde, you can do this stuff, see just how far you get. Okay?"

Dammerman was at a momentary loss for words.

"You want to push it, let's take it upstairs to Reid and get his take," O'Connell continued, her thin voice rising. But then she got control of herself. "Look, Clyde, we're all in this together. So why not just play nice? It'll be a done deal in less than twenty-four hours."

The racket rose from the foosball game. "Tell them to tone it down, Butch," Dammerman snarled. "We're paying them to work, not play games."

O'Connell gestured for Hardy to stay. "These kids are the people who make the system work. Without them we're screwed. So leave them alone. Trust me."

Hardy ignored her and went across to the table. He said a few words, and the kids filtered back to their workstations, glaring at Dammerman as they filed past.

"We have no rec rooms upstairs on the trading floors, do you understand?" Dammerman said. "Our people are too busy making money to play games." He changed tack. "You've talked to Francis and you know the score. Can Levin screw us, or is she just tilting at windmills?"

"She's onto something, or at least she thinks she is."

"Can she get to Abacus in time?"

"I don't think so," O'Connell said.

"Or don't you want to think so? Because if you're wrong, we could be fucked."

O'Connell spread her hands.

Dammerman leaned in closer. "If need be, we'll throw you under the bus, and you can take the fall. Tell me what the fuck is going on. Is she good enough?"

"She's got Donni Imani helping her. And except for her, he's just about the best we have."

"He's the nineteen-year-old kid, right?"

O'Connell nodded and looked up as Hardy returned. "Right. And between the two of them they might figure it out."

"And then what?" Dammerman asked. He'd already had Cassy's take; he wanted to hear it from his top tech.

"She's good enough on her own to come up with an anti-virus program."

"Which means what?"

"A computer worm that could get into the system and find and destroy Abacus."

Dammerman turned and looked toward where Cassy and Donni were standing side by side at her workstation. "Let them be," he said. "Just let me and Butch know if she suddenly gets up and leaves, and the problem will be solved."

"Earlier this morning you said that if anyone got too close they might have an accident," O'Connell said. "I thought you were joking."

"News flash," Dammerman said, his voice low. "I'm never joking."

14

Seymour Schneider had been keeping an eye on the monitors around the floor since the opening bell, when about twenty minutes ago the market started to trend down. Flat-screens tuned to CNBC and other channels were all alive with coverage of the latest bank woes in China.

Rockingham was taking a sharp decline. Schneider wasn't surprised to see the company's CEO himself making his way across the floor. He turned away from the post making BP's trades, but it was too late.

"Where are Treadwell and the other BP people?" Rockingham demanded. He was clearly agitated.

"Reid had a board meeting, and O'Connell had to get back to her office. They got you started, and the rest is up to the market. It's how it works."

"Why the hell is the market taking a nosedive?"

This was the part of the business that Schneider hated most, dealing with BP's clients, many of whom had no idea in hell what the market was all about, how it worked. "China, Mr. Rockingham."

"China?"

"Yes. A number of their banks are on the verge of collapse. We got the news less than a half hour ago."

"It's not fucking fair. The traders have priced our stock too low for when we actually do start to trade. And what the fuck are we paying you guys for?"

"Your product is popular in China, we know that. And you have factories there, some of which you want to move to Vietnam. But in the meantime some investors might be feeling that the Chinese bank situation will hurt you. At least in the short run."

"It's not fair."

Nothing in life is fair, Schneider wanted to say. "Look, market gains are never in favor of the nervous investor. Hang on, it will get better, it always does." *In the long run,* he wanted to say, but he held that comment off too.

"How stupid can it get? Most of our product is sold right here in America."

Schneider was in no mood to hold the son of a bitch by the hand; there were other things going on right now that were a hell of a lot more important. "The market doesn't always work with logic. Sometimes it's emotions, you know? Pure gut feelings. Go with it, trust me."

"My daughter put her entire savings into our stock. A hundred grand. What the hell am I supposed to tell her?"

"A hundred thousand?" Schneider said. "You can give her that much as a gift to replace whatever she lost, and it'll be tax-free because it's under the threshold. But you have a solid company, your stock will come back."

"We paid you people big money to make our opening happen," Rockingham said, his voice rising. "For what?"

"I'm sorry you feel that way," Schneider said. It was one of the brush-off lines he'd used more than once. What he wanted to say was: *If you don't want to gamble, stay out of Vegas. Or at the very least learn something about how the system works before you jump in.* "I'm only one of the guys who trades stocks on the floor. You should talk to Reid."

"We have to do something," Rockingham demanded.

Schneider had had enough. He stepped closer. "Why don't you take all your clothes off, to get everyone's attention, and then run around shouting that what the world needs now is some good, rugged clothing, so that your company will become a long-term winner?"

"I'll have your fucking job for that, you little prick," Rockingham shouted, but his voice was lost over the hubbub caused by the latest China news: Five more major banks had just taken a dump.

"I hope you enjoy it," Schneider said. BP had already extracted all of its IPO fees from the company, which meant Rockingham could do nothing to them. In any event, Treadwell would never fire him. "I'd love to chat more with you, Keith, but I have a meeting with Betty Ladd in five minutes." Ladd was the president of the NYSE.

15

Schneider took the elevator up to the seventh floor, leaving the noisy trading floor in exchange for the peaceful, even reverent hush of where the real business of the market was conducted. Downstairs was theater; up here was the nerve center.

He'd always loved the sense of history about the entire NYSE building, which had opened in 1903. A lot of care had gone into the architecture, from its fine Corinthian columns on the façade, to the expanse of the trading floor and the elegant rooms above. Pockmarks still remained out front from an anarchist's bomb that went off in 1920, killing thirty-three people and injuring four hundred.

The upper rooms had the studied care of a museum and had memorabilia like Jimmy Page's guitar, which the Led Zeppelin founder had played on the floor when Warner Music went public in 2005. And a framed letter from Thomas Edison, who had perfected the telegraph system, called the ticker, that delivered stock prices. Also, housed in a cylindrical case of unbreakable glass, the original signed agreement that founded the exchange under a buttonwood tree a few blocks down Wall Street in 1792.

He went down the hall to the 1792 restaurant, the exclusive enclave for NYSE employees and people from exchange-listed companies. One wall featured a large mural of the signing of the Buttonwood Agreement. Another had a framed menu from 1943, on which the most expensive item was a lobster salad for $1.25.

The breakfast rush before the opening bell was long over, leaving only a few of the tables occupied. Betty Ladd was seated alone in a corner, thumbing a message on her cell phone. She was an attractive, well-put-together woman in her early fifties with stylish medium-length auburn hair, her trademark pearl earrings, and a dove-gray expensive suit with a white silk blouse.

She had joined the exchange thirty years ago as an intern right out of college—when there weren't any ladies' rooms on the seventh floor.

As Schneider approached, she looked up and smiled. "Have a seat, Schneider," she said, laying her phone down.

She often referred to people, especially men, by their last names as one small way of asserting herself in what was still a male-dominated profession. And she always drank super-hot coffee, to make another point that she liked her coffee the same way she liked her men. Her boyfriends were uniformly handsome and accomplished. Divorced, she didn't seem to want to settle down, no matter how nice the men were. She had only been in love once, and it had ended badly. The man had turned out to be a rat.

After an early stint with the exchange, she'd become a trader at Salomon Brothers, where she thrived as an "honorary dick" among the hard-charging male traders, known as "big swinging dicks."

She had become a tough woman in a tough profession, and no one screwed with her.

"You called, I came, Betty," Schneider said, sitting across from her. "What's on your mind?"

"I hear that Reid was on the floor this morning for an IPO. A little unusual, wouldn't you say?"

"He doesn't always play by the rules, everyone knows that."

"The word is he even turned down a CNN interview."

"He has his shy side," Schneider said. They were both playing a game, and both of them knew it.

"Bullshit, Seymour. He's teasing the network guys, so what's he really up to?"

"He was busy with Rockingham's daughter. She heads the company's marketing department, and the word on the Street is that she's pretty good."

"So, he's chasing another skirt, what's new?" Betty said.

Ten years ago, she'd had a brief affair with Treadwell, joining a legion of women he'd bedded. The affair had broken up her marriage, but not his. Treadwell's wife was a society doyenne, who'd never bothered herself with her husband's flings. He was making a lot of money, and that was sex enough for her.

"Is that what you want to talk about? Reid's sex life?" Schneider asked.

Hidalgo, 1792's headwaiter, brought a skim cappuccino, the only thing Schneider ever ordered up here.

"Rumor is that BP is cashing out a good share of its proprietary accounts, a lot of the trades on a number of dark pools. He's even spreading the money around in small bits to banks to get in under the FDIC's limits."

"I'm a simple trader on the floor."

"He's taking a large piece of BP's capital and squirreling it away like hiding it in a storm cellar with a tornado on the way. That's a disaster scenario, Seymour. Drastic, wouldn't you say?"

Schneider shrugged. "Rumors are a dime a dozen. Why don't you ask Reid himself?"

"We don't talk."

When she'd announced over dinner with Treadwell and a few Street friends at Delmonico's that her husband had left her when he'd learned about the affair, Treadwell had dumped her then and there in front of everyone. She'd supposedly reacted by tossing her whiskey sour in his face and storming out.

"I can't discus BP policy," Schneider said. "You know that."

She sipped her scalding coffee without flinching. "You and I both know that China is going to rise up and bite us in the ass. And you've been the town crier, telling everyone that the worldwide debt load is going to come crashing down on us."

"I'll own up to that much," Schneider said. "And when it comes—not if, but when—it won't be pretty."

"Reid's a shrewd man. He's a bastard, but he knows his business. And he has to know what's really going on in Beijing; he has ears everywhere, including Spencer Nast, who I was told was also on the floor this morning. He was one of your guys, and right now there's no doubt he has some damned good intelligence sources."

Schneider knew exactly where she was coming from, because he was asking himself almost the same questions. "Above my pay grade, Betty."

"Really," she said, giving him a small, vicious smile. "You're the old man of the sea on the floor. You know everyone. You hear things."

"Do I?"

"Here's the trouble for BP, and trouble for Reid and for you, personally. Your company is taking its capital off the board—money it uses to trade and make deals for its own accounts."

"And the trouble is?"

"You guys have a legal responsibility to safeguard your clients' money. If Reid suspects that hard times are coming and protects the firm's money, but not its clients', it could be construed as a violation of securities law and exchange rules."

Schneider said nothing. There was nothing meaningful

he could say. He was in a corner, and Reid Treadwell had put him there.

"If BP goes down, you will too, Seymour. Do I make myself clear?"

"What do you want?"

"For now I want your take on how a Chinese bank collapse is even possible. The Communist Party controls everything. If the People's Bank of China sees commercial banks folding, it would take them over and print more money to recapitalize them. In the trade wars we've had with China, the PBOC was always there to keep the banks in good shape."

"You're right up to a point," he admitted, his voice lowered even though no one was close enough to overhear. "But what I'm about to tell you never came from me. Deal?"

"Deal."

The waiter came, poured more super-hot coffee, and withdrew. Ladd drank without letting it cool down.

"I won't confirm that this came from the White House via Spencer, or from anyone else connected in any way with BP."

Ladd held up a hand. "I got it. Maybe a little bird told you. What are you saying?"

Schneider sat back and gathered his thoughts. "We think of China as the monolith, which used to be true. But Hua Biao is weak, while Liu Feng is smart and one tough son of a bitch." Hua was the chairman of the Communist Party, and Liu was the new governor of the People's Bank of China.

"Common knowledge."

"What's not so common is that the PBOC used to be a puppet of the regime. But Liu has his own ideas."

The PBOC was much like the Federal Reserve in the U.S., with the authority over bank supervision, interest rates, and if necessary, the creation of money. After Mao

Zedong's death in '76, the Party turned to a hybrid system of Marxism and capitalism. Commercial banks, overseen by the regime-controlled PBOC, lent money at a wild pace to private as well as publicly owned corporations to build the economy as rapidly as possible. And they succeeded fabulously. In a very short time China became the second largest economy on earth behind the U.S.

"But the commercial banks made a lot of very bad loans, at the regime's request," Schneider said. "Loans that are going into default; companies are not even making interest payments, let alone paying off the loan when it's due."

"The PBOC will bail them out same as always," Ladd said.

"Maybe not this time," Schneider said. "If they freeze up, which might be starting to happen, their entire economy could collapse, bringing tough times for everyone else."

"Including us."

Schneider nodded. "And that's not all. Liu is demanding that Hua step aside and let him take over the Party as well as the central bank. But Hua, and almost certainly the Politburo, has ordered the PBOC to continue bailing out the banks. Liu is saying no, so that if the economy takes a dive, which it will and very soon, it'll be on Hua's head."

"Power politics," Ladd said.

"At the highest level. And that's what Reid is trying to guard against. If China goes down, everyone will get burned. Emerging countries supply them with raw materials. Germans sell them cars. We sell them soybeans and a lot of other foodstuffs. If all of that goes south, a lot of people will get hurt."

"It's like Reid knows the other shoe is about to drop," Ladd said. She shook her head. "Talk to me, Seymour. What's he thinking?"

"As I said, Betty, it's above my pay grade," Schneider told her. But Reid did know something the rest of them didn't.

And it had something to do with an abacus, the Babylonian calculating instrument of beads strung on wires that had been important in early Chinese history.

On the floor earlier this morning, O'Connell had mentioned it to Reid, who got angry, which he never did. Schneider, standing nearby and unnoticed, had overheard. Whatever the "abacus" was, it was important enough to scare the hell out of both executives.

THREE

THE RUSSIANS

16

Location Alpha, where the Russian team had been holed up for the past three days, was on Platt and Gold streets in a moderately new high-rise condo with underground parking. Its location near South Street Seaport, north of Wall Street and the Financial District, was an upscale address. The Russians, understanding this, were well dressed when they were out and about. They were Spetsnaz professionals and knew how to blend in.

It was also within walking distance of Burnham Pike, so Dammerman and Hardy were on foot.

"Do you think this is for the best, you coming here in person?" Hardy asked.

"What the fuck's that supposed to mean?" Dammerman demanded.

"You're BP's COO."

"No shit."

"You shouldn't be seen hanging out with these scumbags. I hired them, it's my job."

The street was busy with traffic, a lot of people surging across at every corner, minding their own business. Even the street people, set up on cardboard mats close to the buildings—especially those with overhangs to help protect them from the rain, or snow in winter—minded their own business. Their hand-printed signs bore pleas like: *Hungry. God bless for your help.*

"Do you think anyone gives a shit, Butch?" Dammerman

asked. "We're terrorists, right?" he said, raising his voice. No one noticed them. "Really?"

Hardy shook his head. "Your call, Clyde."

The building was 301 Gold, and inside they approached the concierge's desk. "Mr. Anderson for John Dugan," Hardy said.

"Are they expecting you, sir?" the man in a dark blue blazer and white shirt asked.

Dammerman wanted to reach across the desk and break the bastard's neck. He didn't like flunkies talking down to him.

"Yes, we're associates," Hardy said pleasantly.

The concierge made the call, and he nodded and hung up. "Thirty-one A, gentlemen. The first elevator on your left."

Yuri Bykov, the group leader, dressed in sweatpants and a white T-shirt, was waiting at an open door a few feet down the hall, his left hand concealed behind his back. He was short, slightly built, unremarkable-looking, with thick dark hair, a narrow face, and startling black eyes. But he was smiling.

Dammerman, who'd been a boy of the streets, instinctively understood that Bykov was a killer. The man had the look.

"Do we have a problem?" Bykov said.

"No, just a slight change," Dammerman said.

"Who the fuck are you?" the Russian asked. He brought his left hand around from behind his back, revealing a deadly looking pistol.

Dammerman started to respond, but Hardy held him off. "He's my boss, the money man."

Bykov hesitated.

"Without him, there's no deal. *Ponimayu?*" *Understand?*

Bykov stared at Dammeran for a long beat, then nodded and lowered his pistol. "*Da*," he said in Russian and turned back into the apartment.

Hardy followed first, Dammerman, now not so sure of himself, right behind.

The two-bedroom-with-study apartment was sparsely but well furnished, with great views south toward the East River. Three men, similarly dressed to Bykov, were playing poker at a table in the kitchen, at least a couple of thousand in one-hundred-dollar bills in the middle. Bykov's hand was lying facedown.

They looked up. All of them were similar in appearance to the team leader; well groomed, closely shaved, prosperous-looking, with absolute confidence in their eyes and in their manner.

For the first time in his life, Dammerman felt outgunned; he was not in charge of the situation. It was like standing next to a half-million-volt power line; *look, but don't touch.*

"You gentlemen are ready for tomorrow morning?" Hardy asked.

"We were ready two days ago," Bykov said. "We're ready now."

"Do you want to go over the timetable with me?"

"Why?"

"It'd make us happy."

"The diesel fuel and hydrogen canisters are packed in the panel van downstairs. Just before nine-thirty we'll park it in front of three twenty-five, set the timer, and walk away."

Three twenty-five was the number of the building that housed the NYSE's backup computer, across the river in Union City, New Jersey.

One of the poker players laughed. "Boom," he said.

In that moment, Dammerman was suddenly not intimidated by the four of them. They were boys, in his estimation. Highly trained with weapons and explosives and almost certainly hand-to-hand combat, but they were kids, experienced in only two things: how to kill people and blow up shit. But they had no finesse. They weren't even Americans.

"We have another issue that we want you to take care of for us," Dammerman said.

Bykov looked at him as if he were an idiot.

Dammerman nodded to Hardy, who took out an iPad. He brought up a picture of Cassy at her workstation. She was talking to Masters and had just turned to look back at her computer when Hardy had taken the picture from across the room. He held it out so Bykov and the others could see it.

"Her name is Cassy Levin," Dammerman said. "She works for us, and she could be a problem."

"A problem for whom?"

"For me, and therefore for you."

"Explain," Bykov said.

The other Russians were watching the interplay, faint smiles on their lips. Dammerman was the money man, so they couldn't be openly contentious, but he was a civilian.

"She may have information that would be a hindrance," Dammerman said.

"How so?"

"She has information about the four of you," Dammerman lied. "Your photographs, your dossiers, even this location."

One of the operators at the table pulled a pistol from the waistband of his sweatpants and started to rise, but Bykov held him off with a gesture. "How?"

"I don't know. But except for her, you and this operation are secure."

Bykov thought about it for a moment, then nodded. He turned and said something in rapid-fire Russian to the three at the table, who immediately started to rise.

"We're leaving," Bykov said.

"Five hundred thousand if you take care of the problem," Dammerman said.

Bykov stopped.

"She'll be leaving the Burnham Pike building at some point this morning, maybe for lunch."

"How can you be sure?"

"I'll make it happen," Dammerman said. "And when she leaves the building, she'll be followed, and you'll be told of her route."

"And?"

"She'll be carrying a file or files. Most likely a flash drive."

"And?" Bykov said again.

"Take her off the street and get the flash drive."

"And?" Bykov said for a third time, as if it were the only word in English he knew.

"Kill her or fuck her," Dammerman said. "I don't give a shit what you do first. But get the drive, and stay on schedule in the morning."

"We're not going to do it," Bykov said.

"Bullshit."

"We have some Russian mob friends in a place you call Brighton Beach. We'll call two of them who are experts at this sort of thing."

"When can they be here?"

"One hour."

"Call them."

"Two million for that, including our part," Bykov said.

Dammerman only hesitated for a beat. "Done."

17

Standing in front of the Federal Reserve Bank of New York, pedestrians flowing around him on the broad sidewalk, traffic heavy as usual for this time of a workday, the title "secretary of the Treasury" kept popping up in Spencer Nast's head.

His name had been mentioned by the president, but he didn't want the job. Never had. Too much politicking for his tastes. But Don Pennington, president of the New York Fed, was just the opposite, and in Nast's opinion the bastard was nothing much more than a cheese brain.

The bank was just a short distance from the exchange, and pausing in front of what had become an iconic structure—it was the bedrock of the American economy—Nast had to congratulate himself. He was a White House insider. A man of even more financial importance than Reid Treadwell.

In his days as the chief economist at Burnham Pike, he'd already been well known in the financial world. Almost a superstar even then. He had appeared on a weekly basis on CNBC, and reporters from *The Wall Street Journal, Forbes,* and a dozen other print-media outlets had come to him for his opinions.

And now as the chief economic adviser for the president of the United States, his celebrity had expanded almost to the moon and back. He was famous, and he loved every minute of it. No longer was he just some schmuck from Jersey, he was the right-hand financial man for POTUS.

The Federal Reserve was the world's most powerful bank; it was a government institution that rode herd on the nation's money supply and worked to keep the economy on a good footing.

Other central banks, like China's PBOC, were little more than knee-jerk extensions of the country's rulers. On the other hand, the Fed was independent of the White House because its decisions were supposed to have nothing to do with elections.

The Federal Reserve was based in Washington, but there were twelve regional banks, and the New York branch was the largest and most influential of them all. New York was where the country's monetary policies were conducted—

for the most part, trading Treasury bonds and dollars, and setting interest rates. The Fed's policy makers in Washington made the decisions; New York carried them out.

Looking up at the neo-Renaissance pile of limestone blocks, its windows protected by wrought-iron grilles, Nast almost had to laugh. Besides being the beating heart of the world's money culture, the edifice also harbored the world's largest depository of gold. Far below street level, behind a nine-foot-thick door, was the New York Fed's vault, which held bullion bars worth a quarter of a trillion dollars.

It was one of the reasons why the building, which had opened in 1924, had been designed to look like a fortress; a physical statement that the American economy rested on a solid foundation.

And yet the place was as fragile as a sand castle. Just about every man, woman, and child on the planet was about to find that out after the opening bell tomorrow.

Secretary of the Treasury. Nast couldn't get the thought out of his head.

Inside he was met by a young man in a blue blazer. "Good morning, Mr. Nast," he said. "Mr. Pennington is expecting you."

The ornate arched hallway was busy with people, most of whom turned their heads as he and the kid headed to the bank of elevators. In one of the cars, another young man in a blue blazer waited to escort the Washington man to the top floor. No one here was going to make the president's economic adviser wait in some anteroom.

Upstairs an attractive young receptionist opened the door to Pennington's inner office. "Good morning, Mr. Nast," she said brightly. "Mr. Pennington will see you now."

Nast nodded, and he could imagine exactly how Reid would react to her.

Pennington got up from behind his expansive leather-topped desk and came around to pump Nast's hand, his smile as pompous as his silver-streaked hair and five-hundred-dollar haircut.

At Yale he'd been the rush chairman at Alpha Delta Phi, one of the most exclusive fraternities on campus. They had turned down Nast, who'd been an awkward, ugly kid on an academic scholarship.

"Will we be seeing you and Mildred at the thirtieth?" Pennington asked. "We Elis have to stick together." Mildred was Nast's wife.

"I wouldn't know, Don," Nast said, his tone even. "I was too busy studying to socialize much." He'd graduated summa cum laude, while Pennington had skated along with gentleman's Cs. "Reunions aren't my thing."

"You were always our academic star," Pennington said. "And look where it's taken you."

He escorted Nast over to a pair of Queen Anne chairs that everyone knew came from the Pennington family mansion on Philadelphia's Main Line.

"Not to Alpha Delta Phi."

"Our mistake, for sure, Spence," Pennington said. "Now, what brings you over here this morning?"

"This isn't about me, Don, it's about you. Word is that you want to be the next Treasury secretary."

"I've thought about it, but Bob Nichols has been doing a bang-up job down there. And to tell the truth, I'm happy right here."

"Nichols has told the president that he wants to step down at the end of the year. And naturally your name came up."

Treasury secretary was on par with the chairman of the Fed, Pennington's boss. It was a quantum leap above the president of the New York branch.

"That's interesting," Pennington said, his tone nonchalant. "I'm a fan of President Farmer, of course. A fine fellow. I'll mull over the idea."

Nast was irked. The bastard was up for a major promotion—to top dog in the financial world—and he was being cagey. It was as if he were saying: *Naturally I deserve it, but I don't know if I want the bother.*

"I brought your fucking name up, it wasn't the president's idea," Nast said. "A simple 'thank you' would be appropriate."

Pennington blanched. "Sorry, Spence. I mean it. I was just taken aback, is all. Of course I'd consider it an honor just to be mentioned."

"Of course it is," Nast said, setting the hook and yanking on the line. "But you gotta earn it, Don. Play ball with us, and the job is yours."

Pennington's left eyebrow rose. "I don't know if I understand exactly what you're saying."

"Saving this nation from the debt bomb."

"You're talking about the PBOC."

"What else," Nast said. And he was tempted to add: *You overbred asshole.*

"I have it on good authority that their central bank is ready to bail out regional banks that are on the edge of failing," Pennington said. He didn't seem overly concerned.

But he never had to be concerned. He had risen to the top of JPMorgan Chase, thanks to his charm and connections, the same qualities that brought him to the New York Fed. He was a major party donor and a world-class networker, and the sec Treasury job would be another easy step.

In Nast's judgment, Pennington was another Treadwell, but without the intelligence and ruthlessness. Reid, a penniless kid from a small Ohio town, had fought inch by bloody inch to get where he was. There'd never been any high-end family or friends to open doors for him until he married into money. The man had battered them down by sheer will, and Nast was in awe of him, as well as in fear.

"I don't know what good authority you're talking about.

Liu and PBOC are going to stick it up Hua's ass. There'll be no bailouts. If the little banks are too stupid to manage their affairs, too bad."

Pennington shook his head. "That makes no sense whatsoever. I'm friends with both men, and both of them are just as concerned about their nation's welfare as we are about ours."

But they don't have Abacus, Nast wanted to say. "Don't be naive. The PBOC is going to serve Beijing a pile of horseshit. It was Chairman Hua and his predecessors heading the government who pushed the commercial banks into making those stupid loans. It's even worse than our subprime fiasco in '08. Now they're going to have to pay for it. And when the system goes south, Liu can blame the chairman and bump him aside."

"That makes no sense either. Their entire economy would collapse. Real people would suffer, big-time."

"Don't be so gullible. China's power structure has never given a damn about its people. Mao starved and murdered millions of his loyal subjects, his own people, to get what he wanted. It was power, and Liu is no different."

"Assuming what you say is true—"

Nast interrupted. "No assuming. And that's why we're heading to a major economic meltdown."

"Right here?" Pennington demanded. "So we can't sell the Chinese our soybeans or buy their cheap toys and clothes for a while. So what?"

Nast tapped his forehead. "Is there anyone home?" he asked. "You're the president of the New York Federal Reserve Bank, for Christ's sake. Think!"

Pennington puffed up. "No need to be rude, Spence."

"There's no need to be ignorant, either. 'Cause when the shit hits the fan, which it will, we'll be in danger of going down the chute, Don. And it won't be just the soybean farmers, it'll be our entire economy. And would you like to hear why?"

"Yes," Pennington said, his voice so soft now it was barely audible. He knew that he was in trouble; it was clear by his expression and by how he held himself stiffly erect.

"Our national debt is out of control," Nast said. "Everyone knows it. We've been selling T-bonds like they'd never go out of style, often fifty billion dollars in each auction. Record amounts, Don. We've reached the point where investors around the world wonder if they should keep buying. We spend more than we take in from taxes. And nothing can keep going up forever. A day of reckoning is coming."

Pennington said nothing.

"In fact it's here."

"Why's China the bellwether?" Pennington asked.

Nast couldn't believe what he was hearing. "They hold two trillion in our T-bonds, because we've never defaulted, never refused to redeem our bonds when they came due, and never skipped an interest payment. But right now it's getting a lot harder for us to keep the pledge. Maybe impossible sooner than we'd like to think."

Pennington continued to hold his silence.

"Are you with me so far?" Nast asked.

"Yes."

"The PBOC will almost certainly not bail out the commercial banks. And how will the government react to that? Without the PBOC's help, Hua is going to start unloading every T-bond of ours that he can get his hands on so that the central government can save the banks. But dumping all those bonds on the open market all at once will cause the price to drop into the cellar overnight. Too much supply, too little demand."

"Trouble," Pennington muttered.

Nast, who'd been a college professor, felt like he was

lecturing an Economics 101 class. "Our Treasury bonds back an enormous amount of private-sector debt in the U.S. Mortgages, business deals, interbank loans, you name it. They've always been great collateral—past tense. When their value drops, all that debt will be called into question. Lenders will want their money, but borrowers won't have the cash. Catastrophe."

"Okay, you have my attention. What does the White House suggest we do?"

"We need to pull the economy back from the brink, and the Federal Reserve will be at the center of it. But first we'll have to slog through a big mess."

Pennington was actually frightened.

"Look, I wanted to give you the heads-up, but I don't want you to worry. We can cover it if we work together."

"Okay," Pennington said, but he wasn't convinced yet.

"I have a couple of suggestions, and if we stay the course, everything will turn out okay. When the dust settles, after all the heavy lifting gets done, you'll come out the hero and the Treasury secretary of the United States. The man who saved the nation."

"I'm on board here, Spence."

"Another thing, first," Nast said. "Some Wall Street firms are going to be in trouble when the crash hits, which it will. But some are going to come out of it okay. Once it's over, people will want to punish the guys who were smart enough to survive. The Fed has a big role in regulating the Street, but we don't see a need to penalize success, do we?"

"I agree," Pennington said. "I'm totally on board."

"Good," Nast said. "Mr. Secretary."

18

After the board meeting, Treadwell went down the hall to his glass-enclosed office, his mind going in a dozen different directions, most of them good. In less than twenty-four hours, he thought, Abacus will have taken effect, the markets here in the States will have crashed, and the domino effect will have spread around the world nearly at the speed of light.

The computer scientist downstairs who somehow had gotten onto the virus would no longer be a problem by the end of the day, according to Dammerman. Treadwell wanted to believe it, but it was one of the worries nagging at him.

What they had put in place was about as foolproof as any complicated scheme could be, and he had a great deal of confidence in his people that by tomorrow he would be a rich man—even richer than he was at this moment—plus, he would come out smelling like a rose. The hero of the crisis. The man who'd saved not only Burnham Pike but also the investors savvy enough to have listened to him.

His secretary, Ashley Coburn, looked up with a broad smile when he walked in. "How'd it go, boss?"

"Like taking candy from a baby," he said. At thirty-one she was beyond cute, with a great ass, and more than once he'd thought about fucking her. But mixing pleasure with business at home plate was just a bad idea in any book, including his.

"They know a good bet when they see one."

"Clyde should be showing up soon."

"I'll buzz you and send him right in."

"Why don't we say the hell with it, and take my plane down to Acapulco for a long weekend?" It was a running joke between them.

"Say the word," Ashley said.

He laughed and went into his sanctum.

Glass-walled offices and open spaces where everyone could see just about everyone else all the time—total transparency for a new age, the architects were calling it—was the new thing in just about every financial institution in New York City. Except his office was soundproof. Anything said inside could not be heard beyond the confines of the glass walls.

Treadwell's office was laid out like a miniature trading floor. A flat-screen television was usually tuned to CNBC, but with the sound off. The chyron display crawling along the bottom of the picture showed breaking market news. Next to his white enamel desk was a Bloomberg terminal that accessed market data in real time, and unlike Dammerman's desk, Treadwell's held only a laptop, a telephone, an appointments calendar, and a few papers neatly arranged.

"An uncluttered workspace for an uncluttered mind," he'd told a visitor once.

His cell phone pinged. He took it out of his jacket pocket and brought up the text icon. Heather had sent him a message.

19

Looking forward to our lunch. XXOO

He was about to send a reply when Ashley buzzed him, and he picked up.

"Mr. Rockingham is on the line."

Treadwell knew what the old man wanted. He'd been expecting the call. He picked up. "Hi, Keith. What's up?"

"Not our stock, I can tell you that much. The traders are underpricing us."

"That's something that happens," Treadwell said.

"We paid you good money, goddamnit. What are you going to do about it?"

"Nothing can be done. It's the bad news from China that's hitting everyone hard—not just you. But you have a solid company, and your stock, along with just about everyone else's, will be back as soon as the craziness has passed. Happens all the time. Part of the business."

"That's what your asshole in the blue jacket told me. Name of Schneider."

"Seymour is giving you good advice; he knows what he's talking about because he's been on the floor forever. Patience."

"Patience? Do you know what the bastard told me?"

Treadwell had a good idea. Seymour was a colorful character. People either loved or hated him, but everyone respected his opinions. "No."

"He told me to take off all my clothes and run around the floor telling everyone how good my company was. I want you to fire the bastard!"

"He's a trader, and they're all like that. But he's one of our major assets, so there's no way I can fire him. How about we do dinner tomorrow night? My nickel."

"I'm going home this afternoon. But Heather tells me that you and she are having lunch today."

"She wants some business advice, and I'm happy to oblige. It'll help your bottom line in the long run."

"I've heard you're a ladies' man."

"I've been married for ten years, Keith. Happily. And breaking bread is part of my job."

"How about if I tag along with you two?"

"Fine with me, but we'll be talking about marketing, not the stock market."

"I may put in a word or two, but I'll let you two talk," Rockingham said, a different edge to his voice now. The bastard was old but no less shrewd.

"Listen, whatever you and your daughter decide is fine with me."

Ashley buzzed.

"I have someone on the other line," Treadwell said, and he broke the connection.

"Mr. Schneider is on the line," Ashley said.

Treadwell picked up. "Seymour, how is trading going?"

"Up and down. I expect that Rockingham is going to call you sometime this morning."

"Just hung up with him. 'Run around the floor with no clothes'?"

"It's a wonder the idiot ever managed to put together a decent business," Schneider said. "But we might have a bigger problem coming our way." He summarized the high points of his talk with Betty Ladd. "She's pissed off, and she'll do anything to stick it to you."

"Poor loser."

"She's head of the NYSE, and she can make bad stuff happen, you know this. If we didn't tell our clients to take their proprietary capital and cash out like we've been doing, we could end up doing serious time."

Less than twenty-four hours . . . "I'll take care of Betty. She and I are old friends."

Schneider chuckled. "If you say so, Reid. In the meantime, what the hell is 'abacus'?"

Time suddenly stopped, and Treadwell felt as if he'd been kicked in his solar plexus. It took him a moment to get ahold of himself. "I don't know," he said. "It's the thing with beads that you can use to add and subtract. They teach it in fourth grade or something."

"On the floor this morning, Julia said something about an abacus that was going to put the brakes on Rockingham, or something like that, and you told her to shut up."

"I have no idea what you're talking about, Seymour."

"Well, I heard the two of you."

"I'll be seeing her later today, maybe she can jog my memory," Treadwell said. "Maybe it had to do with our earlier conversation about teaching Rockingham how to add and subtract before he got himself involved in the market."

20

Dammerman came barreling into Treadwell's office at the same moment Ashley buzzed to say the COO was on his way.

Treadwell motioned for him to close the door.

"The Russians are set to rock and roll—" Dammerman said, but then he stopped short. "What's wrong?"

"I just got off the phone with Seymour. He said he heard Julia bring up Abacus on the floor this morning, and he wondered what it was."

"What'd you tell him?"

"I said I had no idea what he was talking about, but I'd talk to Julia later today and maybe she could jog my memory."

"She's got a fucking big mouth."

"No problem, trust me. But Betty Ladd could be a problem, at least in the short term. She and Seymour had a chat about us going to cash, and she warned him that if we were protecting our own positions without doing the same for our clients, we could go down."

"She's got a hard-on for you."

"I'll take care of it," Treadwell said. He buzzed his secretary. "Give Betty Ladd a call, tell her I'd like to have a little talk in her office sometime this morning."

"Will do," she said, and Treadwell hung up.

"She's not going to want to meet you face-to-face, given your history. Just give her a call. Unless you think she still has the hots for you."

"I said I'll take care of it, Clyde. Now, what about the Russians? Are they one hundred percent?"

"Butch dug them up, and he knows the score. They're good. Anyway, they remind me of the wiseguys I grew up with in Queens."

Butch Hardy had been a tough cop, about as corrupt as they came, and Treadwell had hired him on Dammerman's advice.

"Will they handle the problem with Cassy Levin as well?"

"They're outsourcing it to some Russian mob hard cases out in Brighton Beach."

"The Spetsnaz guys will be out of the country before noon tomorrow, but the locals might be traced, and it could come back to us."

"These guys are good, and we're paying them two mil to make sure her mouth stays shut."

"It should have been part of the original deal."

"We didn't know enough about what the woman was up to when Butch hired the demolition crew."

"The extra two mil comes out of your pocket," Treadwell said.

Dammerman chuckled. "After tomorrow I'll be able to afford it. Bykov vouches for the shooters, and so does Butch. So let's just play it as it lays."

"Are we sure we even need to go that far?" Treadwell asked. "Are we sure that Cassy can stop us?"

"Julia has her doubts. She thinks that no one can crack her program, especially after the Amsterdam nerds spiced it up. But just in case she can, I say let's eliminate the problem permanently. Cassy Levin disappears. Has an accident, ends up in the East River with all the other trash."

"What about family, maybe friends who might miss her?"

"She's got her young pal working with her downstairs, but she's the real brains."

"Do we need to make him disappear as well?"

Dammerman spread his hands. "I don't think it's necessary. One of our people ending up in the East River we can get away with, but two who've worked side by side would be too much of a stretch."

"I don't want any of this coming back at us," Treadwell said. He was more concerned about this issue than Schneider's bringing up Abacus, or Betty Ladd taking a shot across their bow.

"Cassy Levin might have the chops to stop the virus, but her pal Donni Imani sure the hell doesn't," Dammerman said. "Abacus goes into the system before opening bell tomorrow, and the shit will hit the fan globally, making us the heroes. The rich heroes. BP corners the market. Reid Treadwell—Robin Hood and Sir Galahad rolled into one."

"I suggest that you make some side bets. I will."

"You mean short the market? Already done," Dammerman said.

"I put ten mil to short a bunch of S&P 500 EFTs through one of my banks in the islands."

"I did the same with twenty mil."

"You son of a bitch," Treadwell said with a sort of backhanded admiration. His COO was rough around the edges but cunning.

Treasury had cracked down several years ago on offshore accounts because wealthy Americans used them to avoid paying taxes. Major banks in important nations like Switzerland, which had sheltered these secret money stashes, had gone along with the new rules. But banks in places like Hong Kong and Panama had given Treasury nothing more than lip service.

Treadwell and Dammerman were using money from those island accounts to wager that the entire market would plummet. The banks furnished phantom investors to do the trades. Basically they were borrowing shares of investment pools, called exchange-traded funds, or ETFs, that held the stocks of the S&P 500, which covered 70 percent of the U.S. market.

They would sell the borrowed ETF shares, wait for the S&P 500 to tumble, then buy back the shares at the much lower level. Their profit would be the difference between the higher price they sold for and the lower price they paid to reclaim the shares.

"O'Connell doesn't know how to do short, and she's too worried about her nerds downstairs. And Nast is under the microscope in D.C., and doesn't dare," Dammerman said. "More for us."

Treadwell's secretary buzzed. "Ms. Ladd will meet with you at 1792 right now," she said. "And . . ."

"And what, Ash?"

"She wanted me to tell you something else."

"Yes?"

"She said that she was going to cut off your balls and shove them down your throat."

FOUR

WARNING SIGNS

21

Don Pennington was mulling over how to treat the warning from Spencer Nast when his secretary buzzed him. He couldn't possibly ignore the president's chief economic adviser but the man was a sleazy, uncultured prick and hadn't changed since Yale. And he had the balls to waltz in here and hold the secretary of Treasury job like a carrot in front of a donkey.

He hit the key. "Yes?"

"Ms. Ladd is on one for you, sir."

"Thanks," Pennington said and picked up his phone, hesitating for just a moment before pressing 1.

In his estimation Ladd was a smart, efficient woman who'd done a good job keeping the NYSE relevant when electronic trading had all but put the exchange in a back corner. They'd known each other since business school at the University of Chicago, and had bumped into each other numerous times at tony social events in the Hamptons and here in town.

Some of the old-school Wall Street types didn't like her take-charge leadership style because she was a woman. But Pennington didn't give a damn about any of that; he just didn't care for her because he felt she didn't respect him as the chief of the New York Fed.

"Hey, Betty, lovely to hear from you," he said with a warmth that both of them knew was not genuine.

"I just had an interesting visit with Seymour Schneider," she said.

"I didn't think either of you ever left the floor during trading; does he have a bee in his bonnet?"

"You could say that," she said. "He thinks that we're on the brink of a meltdown even worse than '08."

Pennington sat up straight. She had his attention. "What'd he have to say?"

"He's like a crystal ball, and he's never wrong."

"Seymour is a good man, no doubt about it."

"Even though he works for BP," Ladd said. "But I called to find out if you've heard any rumblings from anywhere."

"A word or two here and there," he said, though he had no intention of going into any of the details that Nast had warned him about.

"It's me you're talking to, Don, so cut the bullshit."

Pennington held off for a beat or two. "Nast came to see me just a little while ago."

"Oh?"

"He brought up the China problem, especially the PBOC's probable response if some of its banks start to go down, which he thinks is a very real possibility."

"Shit, Seymour was right," Ladd said. "But just a word of caution: If Spencer promised you something, don't believe him. He's in Reid Treadwell's pocket, even though he's the president's man. And you know what they call him, don't you?"

"Nasty."

"Yeah. And Reid is a quantum leap above that, and I do know what I'm talking about."

Everyone knew about *the* romance, and how he'd dumped her. But just about everyone else in the business gravitated toward Treadwell. He was a superstar. A few called him the JFK of the market because of his looks, his charm, and his savvy.

But Pennington had also heard the story from a couple of different sources that BP's boorish COO, Clyde Dammerman, was drunk at a party in Palm Beach and said something to the effect that when you peel away all the Cary Grant savoir faire crap, Reid made Attila the Hun look like Mr. Rogers.

"I'm not going to make any sudden moves," he said.

"I understand, but I'm smelling something bad here. It's why I called. And my suggestion would be to have a chat with Miller." Joseph S. Miller was chairman of the Federal Reserve.

"About what, exactly?"

"If things actually do go south the way Seymour and Nasty suggest they might, then you need to be at the table making decisions, the same as your predecessor did in '08. Call Miller right now."

22

Joseph Miller looked and acted like a chairman of the Federal Reserve should: snow-white hair, haughty bearing, sonorous voice, and the florid vocabulary of a first-class pedant. He was at his enormous desk in his enormous book-lined office studying a spreadsheet showing the latest flow of money into various international funds when his assistant rang.

"Mr. Pennington has called with a question, sir."

As far as Miller was concerned, Pennington was a lightweight. Unlike most of the top people in the Fed, Don Pennington wasn't a Ph.D. in economics, and in serious meetings it was obvious that the man didn't know what was being discussed.

By law a committee of the Wall Street establishment chose the head of the New York Federal Reserve Bank, and Pennington was a golfing buddy with a lot of them. In addition he had contributed heavily to Farmer's presidential campaign, and under pressure from the White House, Miller had reluctantly rubber-stamped the appointment. Now Don Pennington was the second-most-important figure in the Federal Reserve hierarchy.

Miller picked up the phone. "Good morning, Don. You have a question for me?"

"Spencer Nast stopped by to have a chat this morning, Mr. Chairman."

"What for?"

"He warned me that another financial disaster is coming our way, and it'll probably be a lot worse than '08."

"If that scumbag called on a rainy day to warn that showers were likely, you'd be hard-pressed to believe him," Miller said. "Did he give you any details?"

"He's worried about the Chinese debt bomb. Said it's about to explode. He had the numbers and frankly, Mr. Chairman, he sounded very convincing."

"He always does."

"What should we do, if anything?"

"I'll make a few calls, see if anyone else is coming to the same conclusion. If it comes to anything, I'll give you the heads-up on what the New York Fed's response will be. Meanwhile, don't share this with anyone else. Just keep a lid on it, Don. Please."

"I'm part of the decision-making loop. How can I help?"

"Go to lunch," Miller said. "You're good at that." And he hung up.

23

Miller used his cell phone to speed-dial Secretary of the Treasury Robert Nichols. The Fed techs had assured him that their phones were hackproof.

Nichols answered on the first ring. "Good morning, Joseph, how's Marge?"

Marge was Miller's wife, and they were close friends with Nichols and his wife, Judy. "Looking forward to seeing you guys at the club Friday night. But that's not why I called."

"What's on your mind?"

"Have you been getting any rumbles from the White House about a financial crisis hitting the Chinese, and maybe spreading our way?"

"Practically every day, depending on who's talking."

"Don Pennington called and said Spence Nast paid him a visit to warn him about the China thing, specifically Liu Feng's supposed plan to block the PBOC from bailing out the small banks whose debt load has become critical."

"That's common knowledge. What else did he say?"

"He thought that it was imminent," Miller said.

He had a lot of respect for the secretary of the Treasury, who had earned his economics doctorate at Princeton and during the last financial crisis had served on the Fed's board of governors in Washington. Most of what happened to save the American economy in '08 and '09 was his idea. It had helped that Nichols's specialty was economic slumps. His book, *The Great Depression,* had won the Pulitzer Prize.

"Well, if it actually comes to the point where they start reneging on their bond payments to us, yes, it would become a hell of a mess."

"Maybe we should think about mobilizing right now, in

case the worst does happen. And Congress just might have to become involved like it did the last time."

"Reluctantly."

"Yes, but Paulson was convincing, just like you can be," Miller said.

Nichols had a plain-speaking style that helped him get along with the politicians on the Hill, unlike Miller, who was thought to be capable but aloof and sometimes arrogant.

"I'm sure as hell not going to take this to the White House. Nast would fuck it up royally."

"I agree, so it'll have to be like '08 and '09 again when Hank Paulson, Ben Bernanke, and Tim Geithner took the lead in the bailout," Miller said.

"It means you and I will have to step up to the plate, and I'll leave it to you to tell Pennington what to do," Nichols agreed.

"If it comes to that."

"God forbid," Nichols said.

"By the way, Bob, is there any truth to the rumor that you want to quit as secretary next year?"

"Nast is running around telling that to anyone who'll listen. But even if it were true, which it isn't, I'd stick around to see this thing to the end."

"You're the expert on depressions," Miller said. "If Hank and the others hadn't taken charge in '08, what would have happened to us?"

"Unemployment, to start with. In '08 it peaked at ten percent. In the thirties it hit twenty-five percent. But what worries me most is what would happen if we had to spend as much as Roosevelt, or for that matter, Bush and Obama, to pull us back from the brink of a total economic apocalypse."

"I think I know where you're going with this, and it gives me a massive migraine."

"Our debt is way up, greater than in '08 and a hell of a lot bigger than in the thirties. The question is: What if we couldn't afford to pay off all the unemployment claims or bail out the banks so they wouldn't fail? What happens if we couldn't borrow more money because no one would trust us to repay, on top of all the other debt we've accumulated? That's what gives me the sweats."

"This won't be easy, no matter what," Miller said.

"If China does go down, and our debt load is already at the limit, let's hope that nothing else happens."

"It'd better not, Mr. Secretary," Miller said. And he couldn't help but feel that they were adrift at sea with an impossibly heavy anvil around their necks.

24

Yuri Bykov hadn't liked the BP money man whom Butch Hardy had brought over earlier, and he tended not to trust men he didn't like. It wasn't until the first half of the two million promised showed up as an electronic transfer to their Cayman Island account that he made the phone call to Brighton Beach.

A man whose voice he didn't recognize answered. *"Da?"*

"I want to talk to Leonid."

"Who the fuck is this?"

"Ne tvoye delo." None of your fucking business. "Put Leonid on."

Leonid Anosov, an old friend from boyhood outside Vladivostok in Russia's far east, came on the line a minute later. "Who the fuck wants me?"

"I have a job for you, unless you're too lazy these days to work."

"You old bastard, are you here in the States?"

"Just across the bay from you," Bykov said, and he gave

him the address. "Ask at the desk for John Dugan. I'll call and let them know that Mr. Olsen is expected."

"When?"

"Within the hour. Can you be here?"

"Is it a *mokrie dela*?" Anosov asked. It was the old KGB's term for "wet work"—the spilling of blood, assassination.

"Da," Bykov said. "I'll need you and one other operator. Two-fifty large."

Anosov hesitated. Like Bykov he had been trained as a Spetsnaz operator, where one of the first rules of engagement was to trust no one.

"Two-fifty U.S. for *each* of you," Bykov said.

"I'll take the whole thing and divide it my way. Agreed?"

"Soglasvano," Bykov said.

"Do you have the equipment?"

"Bring your own."

"Valentin Panov will be my number two."

"I don't know the name."

"He came a few years after us," Anosov said.

"Can you trust him?"

Anosov laughed. "With my mother, but not my girlfriend."

"Bring your account number, and I'll transfer the money."

"Cash," Anosov said.

"As you wish, *tovarishch*," Bykov said, and he broke the connection.

25

Arkadi Zimin, who had come out of the bathroom as Bykov was making the call, was grinning. "We'll make another tidy profit on the side bet, and Leonid gets to do the real work."

Bykov smiled. "If you can't fuck your friends, who can you fuck?"

He phoned Butch Hardy's personal cell phone number. "The help we need from Brooklyn will be here within the hour."

"Can we trust them?"

"I wouldn't subcontract to anyone else," Bykov said. "If the broad tries to leave before my people get here, slow her down."

"No sweat," Hardy said.

"I'll need the pictures of her before then. And I'm going to need an extra five hundred thousand."

"We agreed on half of the two million, which has already been paid into your account in the blind, and half when the job is done."

"These guys will only work for cash. I need five hundred now. Send it here by runner along with the photographs. One hour."

Hardy hesitated for a beat. "I'll see what I can do."

"Just do it," Bykov said, and he hung up.

He called his people into the kitchen, where he poured each of them a chilled vodka in small glasses. "Gentlemen, *nostrovia,*" he said and drank his down, slamming the glass on the counter.

The other three did the same.

"Our next drink will be on the plane back to Moscow," Bykov said. "Do we understand each other?"

They were professionals who'd been together for a number of years, working mostly out of Moscow and mostly for mob bosses who wanted someone eliminated, or an establishment blown up with all its employees inside, and there was no need to tell them something like that. But it was ritual, and they all nodded.

"Let's go over the drill one last time. Two operators from Brighton Beach will be arriving within the hour. It will be their job to handle the woman from the bank. How they deal with her will be their problem, and we will not get involved."

"Will they be bringing her here?" Zimin asked. He was their bomb expert.

"No," Bykov said. "And a word of caution: They know that we are here to do a job, but they will not ask what it is. If they do, say nothing. In any event they'll only be with us for a short period until the woman is on the move."

No one said a thing, waiting for Bykov to continue.

"We'll leave here at 0830. Viktor will be driving the van, with Arkadi in the rear taking care of baby." Viktor Kolchin had come up the ranks in Spetsnaz a couple of years behind Bykov, and his was a steady hand. He and Zimin made a competent team.

"Work traffic will be heavy at that time of the morning, but most of it will be coming into the city, so there should be no problems in the Lincoln Tunnel to New Jersey. Alexei and I will be right behind you in the Mercedes for the pickup once you're in place."

The New York Stock Exchange backup computer was located in Union City on the second floor of a nondescript office building, the first floor of which was the World Wide Destinations Travel Agency.

"Viktor will park in front at 0930. Once Arkadi has set the timer for 0945, the two of them will dismount and walk one block south to the corner, where Alexei and I will be waiting. We will drive immediately to JFK for our 12:10 flight home," Bykov said. "Questions?"

"What if we're stopped by the police?" Kolchin asked.

"No reason for it to happen, unless you drive erratically or exceed the speed limit."

"It's not as bad as Moscow, but everyone speeds here," Alexei Mazayev said. He would be driving the Mercedes. He'd been a military intelligence junior officer before transferring to the Spetsnaz, where he'd come to Bykov's attention. The two of them had become friends over the past several years, and had been mistaken for brothers because they looked so much alike.

"Go with the flow," Bykov said. "Just don't stand out."

Kolchin, who at six feet and just under a stocky one hundred kilos was the hothead of the group, started to raise his hand, but Bykov cut him off.

"We will do everything within our power to avoid getting into a gun battle with the local cops."

"I won't leave my weapon here," Kolchin said.

"None of us will. All I'm saying is that I want this to go down easy and clean. But if we're backed into a corner, we will defend ourselves, and if need be, separate and execute the exfiltrate plan."

Kolchin nodded.

"You have your kits including money and papers, as well as alternate airport routes. You know the escape, evade, and disperse drill."

No one said a thing.

"Once we reach the parking garage at JFK, we'll leave the weapons in the trunk of the car, along with all of our secondary papers in a burn bag that will be set to go off if tampered with.

"Inside the terminal we'll separate and go through security at our planned intervals. At no time will we attempt to communicate with each other until we're off the plane at home."

Still no one said anything.

"Are we clear, *tovarisches*?" Bykov asked.

"*Yasno.*"

FIVE

PROJECT W

26

After an hour and a half spent working on corrections to the problem with W, Ben and Faircloth went across to admin, where they were immediately admitted to Rear Admiral Paul Huggard's office. The two-star was in charge of the Navy Yard overall, but at this moment in time, W was his top priority by a very wide margin.

Faircloth was carrying several sheets of blueprints under his left arm, and Ben had brought along his rough drawings and calculations in a copybook marked TOP SECRET on the front cover.

The admiral, his jacket off, was seated behind his desk when the two men walked in, came to attention, and saluted crisply. Huggard returned the salute and smiled.

"Civilians don't salute," he said.

"Old habit, sir," Ben said. "But we have a problem."

Huggard, who was one year shy of retirement, was a silver-haired bear of a man, standing well over six feet and weighing 220 pounds on a good day. But he still put in a credible workout at the base gym, often beating men half his age.

"I figured as much," he said, his smile fading. His career-capping goal was to see W operational. And each time Ben and Faircloth showed up in his office with what he called "the look," he could see his goal fading.

"Maybe we should go into your conference room so we can spread out the blueprints, sir," Faircloth said.

"Big problem or little problem?"

"Big problem," Ben said.

"Shit."

"But I think that it can be fixed."

"Oughta be fixed, can be fixed, or must be fixed to save the boat?" the admiral asked. His Ph.D. from MIT was in naval engineering, and he was damn good. Among the best in the navy, which was why he'd been picked to manage this project.

"Must," Faircloth said.

"Ben?" Huggard said.

"I'm in complete agreement."

The admiral reluctantly got to his feet, and the three of them went to the adjoining conference room, which could seat eight comfortably. In the past year he had come to call the place the Hemorrhage Palace, because every time Ben and Faircloth came over with a problem, the navy would end up hemorrhaging money, and the blame would fall on his shoulders.

"Okay, what is it this time?"

Faircloth laid out the first page of the blueprints, and Ben held them in place with four ship's coins he'd brought over for the purpose.

"The drive tubes," the admiral said. "Or the drive it-self?"

"The MHD unit works per specs, but it's the tubes," Ben said. "Stress fractures."

"We expected it."

"Which is why we specified hardened titanium for the support struts."

"So?" Huggard asked.

"At two specific frequencies, each covering a narrow band of less than fifty cycles per second, we think that a harmonic wave is induced into the struts. From there it's transferred to the drive tubes, and the tubes open up."

"A hole in the hull?"

"Holes in the hull, collectively big enough to sink the boat," Ben said, pointing out the eight places along the tubes that he'd marked with a yellow highlighter.

"Are you suggesting we scrap the entire project?" the admiral asked.

"No, sir," Faircloth said. "Ben has come up with a couple of fixes."

"I'm all ears, gentlemen," Huggard said. "Impress me."

"The cheapest fix—in fact the one that would cost almost no money—would be simply to reprogram the MHD's operational computer to bypass the two frequency ranges that cause the problem."

Huggard saw the issue immediately. "The operational capabilities would be impaired."

"But not seriously," Ben said, though he didn't believe it.

"We couldn't know that until we had precision sea trials. Under simulated battle conditions."

"Yes, sir," Ben said. "Evasion maneuvers in which speeds would have to be randomly and quickly changed to confuse the enemy's targeting computers."

The admiral took only a moment to make his decision. "That's out. We're not going to send personnel to sea putting their lives at risk because of a design flaw."

"Yes, sir," Ben said, very glad that the navy had seen fit to send the right officer to administer the project.

"You mentioned two fixes."

"Ben came up with it, and it's ingenious," Faircloth said.

"Ingenious as in how many tens of millions of dollars?" Huggard asked.

"Actually I'm thinking more like eight hundred—" Ben started, but the admiral interrupted him.

"Eight hundred million?"

"No, Admiral. Eight new struts at one hundred thousand dollars each. Eight hundred thousand total, plus maybe one month for the retrofitting, and then we'd be ready for sea trials."

"Show me."

Ben opened his copybook to the sketches he'd made, along with the underlying calculations, and laid it on top of the blueprints.

"The solid titanium struts go into harmonic vibrations at the two frequency ranges we talked about. I'm suggesting we use thick-walled but hollow struts and fill them with nitrogen gas at pressure to dampen the harmonics."

The admiral looked at Ben's math. "At what pressure?" he asked. "If it's too high the struts themselves could pose a danger of exploding, sending shrapnel though the boat's hull."

"I did some of the math in my head on the way over. But we'll need to run a simulation on the mainframe to check me out."

"As I said: Impress me."

"I'm thinking in the range of twenty-five to thirty-five psi."

"Pounds per square inch. The same pressure in an automobile's tires," the admiral said. "I'm impressed."

– – –

On the way back to the warehouse Faircloth was upbeat. "Impressing an admiral is not an easy thing to do, pal. But you sure as hell knocked it out of the ballpark."

"We did," Ben said absently. He'd been thinking about Cassy.

Faircloth stopped. "Okay, Ben, it's me you're talking to. What's up?"

"I'm a little worried about Cassy."

"Do you think that she's running around on you? I mean, you're bright and all that, but frankly you're not much to look at."

Ben had to chuckle. "It's nothing like that. But something is going on at work, and I think it's got her . . ."

"Worried?" Faircloth asked.

"Frightened."

"Call her right now, and then let's have some lunch. Arguing with a two-star has always made me hungry."

– – –

Cassy's cell phone rolled over to voicemail after five rings, but it wasn't terribly worrisome to Ben. A lot of times she switched her phone to silent mode when she was deep into a new project.

He called her shift supervisor, Francis Masters, who answered on the second ring.

"Masters."

"It's Ben Whalen. I've tried to reach Cassy, but she's not answering her cell. Can you ask her to give me a call whenever she's free?"

"Sure thing, but it'll have to wait until after lunch."

"She's busy?"

"She's not available," Masters said, and he hung up.

Cassy had said her immediate supervisor was a jerk, and this confirmed it. Ben's worry went up a notch. Something wasn't right. He could feel it in his gut.

SIX

CONFRONTATIONS

27

Reid Treadwell spotted Betty Ladd sitting at her usual table in 1792. Motioning the maître d' away, he went across to her, curious but not particularly concerned why she wanted to see him so urgently.

She was texting someone, and she looked up, a neutral expression on her face. Despite himself, Reid still thought that she was a fine-looking woman, and he almost regretted dumping her. Almost. And he smiled thinking about how she had reacted.

She put her phone down. "What are you all smiley about, Treadwell?" she demanded, the famous Ladd frown lowering the corners of her mouth. "Isn't the world economic order on the highway to hell?"

Treadwell sat down across from her. "That's what Seymour thinks."

"He's hardly ever wrong."

The headwaiter came over, and Treadwell ordered coffee.

"Well, if he's right this time, Burnham Pike will do what it can like we did in '08."

"The word is that your people are expecting the Chinese to implode over a brouhaha between the government and the PBOC."

"Who told you that?" Treadwell asked, masking his surprise.

She smiled faintly. "Manhattan is a small town after all. Especially this end of it." She drank some still-steaming coffee. "I've also heard that you people have been converting your in-house capital into cash and have sprinkled it around to FDIC-insured banks. Of course by law, you'd need to publicly disclose such a big move."

Treadwell shrugged nonchalantly. It was his signature gesture in tense situations. "If such a thing were true—and I'm not saying it is or it isn't—we'd be within our rights not to disclose it until we filed our quarterly with the SEC. And that's two months from now."

"Sounds like some more of Hank Serling's doublespeak," Ladd said. She leaned across the table, venom in her narrowed eyes. "Just for the sake of argument, let's say you were pulling a stunt like that. You have clients who've invested billions with you. If you *were* making a move to protect the bank's assets, you'd be required to offer the same protection to your clients."

Treadwell's coffee came, and he took his time stirring four packets of Splenda in the cup.

"Quit stalling, Treadwell. I want some answers that make sense, or I swear to Christ I'll nail your fucking hide to the front door downstairs as a warning to other pricks like you."

Treadwell continued stirring. "Sorry, Betts, but I like my coffee sweet, just like my women." It was a riff on Ladd's old saying that she liked her coffee hot, just like her men.

She didn't rise to the bait. "Treating clients' money differently than your proprietary capital is against securities law, as you damned well know. We could kick you off the exchange, the SEC could put BP out of business, and you would end up in jail."

Treadwell grinned. "I hope it won't come to that," he said. "I'm told that prison coffee isn't very good." He looked around at the nearly empty room. "I'd miss this, you know." He looked directly at her. "Especially you."

She ignored his flirting. "I remember the stunt BP pulled

in '08. I wasn't in charge of the exchange then, but if I had been, you assholes would have been swinging on the gallows."

"Just like you, I wasn't the boss then either."

"But you were part of the inner circle. I'd guess one of the engineers behind the slippery short sales."

In 2008, the subprime mortgage market was burning down. Amid the housing boom leading up to the crisis, banks had issued truckloads of mortgages to people who couldn't afford them, called "liar's loans." The banks didn't bother insisting that borrowers document their ability to pay even the interest, because the surge of subprime mortgages was jacking up home prices right through the roof. Everyone was getting rich.

Treadwell's favorite story about those days was of the Las Vegas stripper who had no savings but had financed five houses, which she planned to flip at a higher price to avid buyers on the hot real estate scene. It was like playing at the slots, only this was a sure bet, she—like just about everyone else—thought.

Her plan was to pay off the loans and pocket the difference. But she was too late. The housing market collapsed, and she was out in the cold.

The smaller banks didn't care that the loans were as rotten as last week's fruit basket. They made their money by selling them to the big firms on Wall Street, such as Burnham Pike, which packaged hundreds of the loans into bonds, called mortgage-backed securities, and sold them to investors with no savvy.

When mortgages, by the thousands, defaulted, the bonds became worthless, the investors got screwed, and the financial crisis was in full swing.

Treadwell smiled. "What we did in '08 was perfectly legal, and even you have to know it."

"That's open to interpretation, Treadwell," she said

sharply. "You people conned your investors like old-fashioned carney barkers. You knew damned well that the bonds were going into the pits, so you bet against your own customers. Doesn't get sleazier than that."

Burnham Pike had sold the bonds short in '08, just as Treadwell and Dammerman were doing now with the S&P, waiting for the Abacus-fueled inferno. The company had made billions on those bond-shorting trades, and technically speaking it was legal.

When BP's CEO and the company's legal counselor were called before an irate congressional committee the next year, Treadwell's predecessor claimed the shorting was a "routine hedging tactic" that all smart investors employed as insurance in the unlikely event that a trade went bad.

But Treadwell wasn't about to tell the president of the New York Stock Exchange, or anyone else, for that matter, that he and his COO were shorting the primary stock market index using secret offshore accounts in an expectation of a Wall Street wipeout.

Nor would he tell her that BP would be the last, or among the last, investment firms able to mint a fortune in the ruins with little or no competition.

Nor that he, Dammerman, and O'Connell would enjoy huge bonuses in addition to the short-selling profits they would make. Nor that Spencer Nast, who'd leaked them CIA secrets about China's possible troubles, would get his super-bonus once he rejoined the firm after his Washington stint.

Ladd was visibly angry, and it did Treadwell's heart good to see a woman he considered an ice maiden losing control. "You're not being very nice this morning, Betts," he said, goading her.

"My name is not Betts, and no, I'm not nice," she said loudly enough for the few other pre-lunch customers to overhear. But they looked away, no one wanting to offend two feuding Wall Street gods.

"Well, Ladd, don't think for one minute that Burnham Pike would fail to give its clients the heads-up on a possible financial catastrophe."

In fact, this one was covered. To withstand some official inquiry from Congress or the SEC or whoever down the road, Treadwell had personally directed BP's client services department to warn the wealthy people, the pension programs, the university endowments, the charitable foundations, and all those who entrusted the firm to run their money.

They would start today after the market closed. By then, of course, it would be too late, unless the brighter clients acted immediately in the overnight markets.

By opening bell tomorrow, Abacus would be a done deal; the crash would begin and ripple across the entire planet.

"Knowing you like I do, your clients will get the word, but not until BP's capital has been safely tucked away."

She was right about at least that much. BP wasn't about to let panicky clients rush to sell, disrupting the market while the firm was disposing of its own assets.

"We're positioning the firm to help our clients and the entire investing community. You know damned well that a strong Burnham Pike is good for Wall Street and good for America. We won't become another Lehman Brothers. Nor will we hold our hand out for a bailout if things do go south."

"My ass," Ladd said, pointing a long-nailed finger at Treadwell. "You smug son of a bitch. Whatever you're trying to pull, I'm going to find out, and when I do, I'll cut off your balls and shove them down your throat."

"As you told Ashley," Treadwell said. "Crude, but charming as usual."

"Fuck you, Reid!" Ladd shouted.

Everyone heard her. The headwaiter started to come over from his station but then thought better of it and turned back.

Treadwell worked to keep his voice even. "Sounds like there's more to this than BP's business practices. Like maybe that I broke up with you. Get over it, Betts. That was ten years ago. At least have a little self-respect."

"You told me that you loved me, you prick," Ladd said, trying to control her voice.

"Ancient history, Betts."

"I was a fool to believe you, and an even bigger fool to fall in love."

Treadwell finally had his fill. "How could anyone love you? Even your husband took advantage of our little fling as an excuse to get out of a marriage to you. And I can't blame him, it just took me a little longer to dump you."

Ladd shot up. "You fucking bastard," she said as she headed for the door. "Watch yourself, Reid, because I am."

28

Donni Imani was watching over Cassy's shoulder as she finished the last bit of coding in her anti-virus program, which she had decided to call My Fair Lady after what Donni had told her many times was his all-time favorite musical.

"There," Cassy said half to herself, but Donni heard her.

"Done?" he asked her.

She nodded.

"Now take it to the brass," he said.

She looked at him, then glanced over where Masters and O'Connell were in deep conversation across the room. "They're not going to like it," she said, visions of Murphy Tweed running through her head.

"Who cares? You're going to save the firm. You'll at least get a raise."

Norman Applebaum came over, took one look at Cassy's screen, and lit up in a goofy smile. "You finally solved it, without my help. Outstanding."

"I'd rather be outstanding than standing out," Donni said with obvious dislike.

Norman was socially challenged, like a lot of the post-adolescent geeks in the business. But Cassy felt a little sorry for him, a feeling that was mixed with awe. The kid was a genius.

"We have a cure, I think," she said.

"Then what are you waiting for?" Norman asked. "Put it into the system. That's what we're being paid for."

"I need a go-ahead," Cassy said.

"From Masters? With the way he feels about you, good luck."

"What do you mean?" Cassy asked, but she knew exactly what he meant. Masters had hired her, but in the past few months his attitude had changed.

She glanced over again to where he and O'Connell were standing. Butch Hardy had joined them, and it gave her a chill. Ever since Dammerman had told the chief of security to keep an eye on her, that's exactly what he had done. Every time she looked over her shoulder he was there.

"This morning when Dammerman's goon broke up the foosball game Theodore and I were playing—you know, to clear our heads—Masters didn't say a word."

"What's your point?" Cassy asked.

"He shoulda stuck up for us, but he didn't. So I reversed his phone; maybe I could catch him saying something stupid and give it out to everyone. But it's way better than that, and I have it recorded."

"The suspense is killing me," Donni said sarcastically.

"It's just like the movies. I'm the spy, and I bugged him."

"Okay," Cassy said. "Tell us."

"Only if you go out with me tonight."

Cassy was floored. She was seven or eight years older; he had a schoolboy crush on her.

"Be careful, lover boy," Donni said, smirking. "She has a boyfriend. And this guy is a Special Ops super-commando, Rambo-killer dude named Ben. The first time they met he stared down a motorcycle gang trying to hassle her. He was just like the Grim Reaper in person, and they bugged out, no questions asked. *Capisce?*"

"Never mind," Norman said, and he turned to go, but Cassy put out a hand to stop him.

"Let me listen to what you recorded," she said. "Please?"

Norman brushed off her hand and walked away.

"Prima donna asshole," Donni said. "Now either put your program into the system or walk it over to Masters. With O'Connell standing there you're bound to make points."

"Come with me, I could use the backup."

"Not on your life," Donni said. "Didn't you know that my favorite color is yellow?"

"Mine isn't," Cassy said, and she turned and started to where Masters and O'Connell were still talking. But Hardy had moved off to the left to where he had a clear line of sight to her workstation, and she felt a little shiver of fear.

Word was that when he worked as a cop for the NYPD, he'd killed a man who had supposedly accused him of being on the take with a couple of mob bosses. It was a wonder to her why BP would hire a man like that if the rumors were true.

Theodore Brightman caught up with her, and she pulled up short. "Norman's pretty hacked."

"Why?"

"You hurt his feelings. He was just trying to warn you that Masters has been shadowing you all day."

"How could he know something like that?"

"He told you. He bugged Masters's phone."

An uneasy tickle traveled up Cassy's spine. "Tell him I'm sorry," she said, and she went the rest of the way.

Masters and O'Connell broke off their conversation. Neither of them looked happy to see her.

"I've figured out how to neutralize the worm from our system," Cassy said.

"Good for you," Masters said, but he didn't sound sincere. "Send it to me, and I'll beta test it myself before we go any further."

"I think that we should do it right now. This thing could go critical at any minute."

"I'll take care of it," Masters said.

"Well, at least let me be part of the test. It's my program."

O'Connell offered a weak smile. "Francis is right. It's better if upper management takes over from here. But we want to thank you for being on the ball. This is not going to be another Murphy Tweed, I promise."

"If this worm kicks in, it would crash trading not only for us, but for every trading desk on the planet. Including the NYSE."

"If your program pans out, which knowing your abilities I'm sure it will, we'll input it after the closing bell. If we did it now, it could have some unintended consequences."

"Believe me, this thing I found is super-toxic, and I saw what something like this can do to a firm. It destroyed Murphy Tweed in less than a year."

"And we appreciate that you want to make sure nothing like that happens to us," O'Connell said.

"As I told you, I'll take care of it," Masters said. "Now get back to your station and send me the goddamn program."

Cassy wanted to tell him to go screw himself, but she held her temper in check and turned back to O'Connell, whom she'd thought of as her mentor from the beginning. "With all due respect, Julia, I should be in on the beta test."

"We'll take care of it," Masters said, his voice rising.

Cassy had her fill. "You're shadowing me, Francis," she said sharply. "Why?"

"You cloaked your station to block our access. That's against company policy, and you damn well know it."

"I isolated my station because I didn't want whoever is behind the worm to watch what I was doing to defeat it."

"You should have come to me before you started screwing around," Masters said. "That's what I'm here for, to help my people do their jobs."

O'Connell was saying nothing, and Cassy didn't understand.

"All right, I'll give it to you. But I'll put it on a flash drive, instead of sending it through the network, in case anyone else is shadowing me."

"Good," Masters said.

"I'll personally handle the beta test," O'Connell said. "And both of you can get back to work."

It wasn't what Cassy wanted, but it was better than she expected. "It'll take a little time to get it onto a flash drive."

"Just send it up to my office when you're ready," O'Connell said. "And believe me, Cassy, I appreciate what you've done and continue to do for the firm. You'll get full credit."

"If it works," Masters said.

"It will," O'Connell said. She patted Cassy on the shoulder and left.

"Well, get to it," Masters said.

- - -

Back at her workstation Cassy was fuming, trying to get her temper in check.

"That didn't go so good," Donni said without looking away from his screens.

For just a moment she wanted to bark at him, but then she had to laugh. "I don't think Francis likes me, but at least Julia listened."

"So what's the upshot?"

"They want me to put the program on a flash drive and send it upstairs."

"I think I hear a *but* in there," Donni said.

"Listen, I'm going to need your help."

"Okay," Donni said after a hesitation. "With what, exactly? Just remember that my favorite color is still yellow."

"I'm going to make two flash drives. One with some junk on it that will take time to decipher. And the other with the real anti-virus program we cooked up."

"No need to guess which one you're going to send to O'Connell," Donni said. "But what about the real one?"

She glanced over her shoulder in time to see one of Hardy's security people, this one a tall, beefy woman who looked like another ex-cop, join him.

Cassy took out her phone and scrolled through the contacts list, finding the number of a friend of her parents that they gave to her when she first moved to New York. *She's someone you can trust,* they'd told her. She'd never used the number, and she didn't even know if it was still active, but she hoped it was.

"We're going to have lunch together, and you're going to carry the real flash drive out the door."

"No way I'm putting my ass in a sling."

"I need your help, Donni. They're bound to search me when I try to leave. That's why Butch called in the woman next to him."

"They might search me."

Cassy couldn't help but smile. "I seriously doubt it. It's me they're after."

Donni nodded. "I'm going to regret this, but maybe Ben will let me be his best man at your wedding."

Cassy laughed, though her insides were roiling. "I'll put in a good word for you."

"Deal," Donni said.

29

Bykov stood behind the apartment door, his Glock G26 subcompact pistol raised shoulder-high, as Kolchin looked through the peephole. "It's a woman, carrying an attaché case."

The buzzer rang again.

"Anyone else in sight?" Bykov asked.

"No. But the concierge would have let us know if she brought someone with her."

"Unless the man had a gun pointed at his head."

The buzzer rang a third time.

"Let her in."

Kolchin unlocked the door and opened it. "May I help you, miss?" he said in decent English. His accent was the least heavy of the four of them.

"Your concierge called to tell you that I was on my way up. I have something for you from Mr. Hardy." She was of medium height and compactly built, but she looked and sounded like a cop.

Bykov nodded, and Kolchin stepped aside to let the woman in.

Once she had cleared the doorway, Bykov pushed the door closed.

Kolchin took the attaché case, handed it to Bykov, then turned the woman around. "Hands on the door, please."

She did as she was told, and Kolchin quickly and efficiently frisked her, running his hands over and between her breasts, then under her skirt, front and back between her legs.

"Clean," he said, stepping back.

The woman turned around. "Get your jollies off, asshole?" she asked.

"I'm sure he did," Bykov said, sticking the pistol in his belt at the small of his back. "Would you care to join us for a drink?"

"No. I was told to wait for you to count the money and acknowledge that it's correct."

Bykov handed the case back to Kolchin, who took it to the dining room, opened it, and counted the money. It took several minutes.

"Five hundred thousand," Kolchin said.

"Photographs?"

"Several, some of which we've already seen, but a couple of new ones."

"You may go now," Bykov told the woman, and she started to turn. "One question first. Are you a police officer?"

"I used to work with Butch, but that's been a couple of years now."

"Fly then, little bird."

"I don't know what's going on, but I hope to fuck I never see you guys again," she said, and she left.

"She was sweet," Kolchin said. "I would have fucked her."

"You would have fucked a goat if it spread its legs," Bykov said, as the others laughed.

— — —

Bykov phoned Hardy's private number, and the man answered on the first ring.

"It's Dugan," Bykov said.

"Did my courier show up?"

"She just left, and everything is as it should be. Is our subject still there?"

"Yes, but something is going on, and I don't know how long I can keep her without arousing some suspicion."

"What something?" Bykov demanded.

"It's about the program she's working on. She's sending it upstairs to management, and there's a good possibility she won't be carrying it out of the building."

"You said it could be contained on a flash drive, is that right?"

"Yes."

Bykov couldn't imagine how a man as stupid as Hardy made it through a normal day without getting lost. "Maybe she made two, one bogus and the one she will keep in her possession, the real thing."

"We've considered just that, but whatever the case may be, our deal still stands. I'll call you when she leaves, hopefully not until lunch, and I want your people to pick her up and dispose of her."

"Assuming she leaves the building with something damaging to your company, where is she taking it?"

Hardy hesitated for a beat. "I don't give a shit, because you're going to stop her."

"What door will she come out of?"

"Nassau Street," Hardy said. "Are we clear?"

"Yes," Bykov said, and he hung up. But the real question in his mind was why were they willing to pay two million dollars to blow up a building, and another half million to assassinate a woman? And he was a man who'd never liked unanswered questions.

30

The concierge called, and Bykov answered. "Yes?"

"Mr. Olsen and an associate are here to see you, sir. Shall I send them up?"

"Please do."

A couple of minutes later the two operators from Brighton Beach showed up, and after identifying them through the peephole, Bykov let them in.

Anosov was short, lean, and dark, originally from the south in Uzbekistan, and Panov was much larger, with a barrel chest and the look of a Far Easterner, either from Mongolia or Siberia. Both of them were dressed in laborer's clothes—jeans and loose-fitting khaki shirts, the tails out to conceal pistols.

Anosov and Bykov hugged. "Good to see you again, my old friend. Life is treating you well?" Anosov said.

"Tolerable."

Anosov introduced Panov, and Bykov introduced his team members, and after they'd all shaken hands and sat down at the dining room table, Anosov went immediately to business.

"Are we late?" he asked.

"No," Bykov said. He spread out the photographs of Cassy. "This is your target. She works for an investment firm, so she shouldn't give you any trouble."

Anosov studied the photographs and showed them one at a time to his partner. "Good-looking woman. What's the problem, is she stealing from the company or something?"

"She may be carrying a flash drive that contains information the company wants returned to them."

"Why don't they just ask her for it?"

"They want her to disappear. Permanently, I'm assuming, because the information they want is on a flash drive, but it's also inside her head."

"Why don't you handle it yourself?" Anosov asked. "You have the muscle."

"We have a second op."

Anosov took a photograph of Cassy peering over her shoulder from what looked like a workstation with several computer monitors. People were standing at similar stations on either side of her.

"Where is this place?"

"Burnham Pike; it's on Nassau Street, not far from here."

Anosov looked up, a faint smile on his narrow lips, almost as if he were getting ready to enjoy a nice meal. "We will have a free hand?"

"I want the flash drive today as soon as you've secured the woman. Send one of your people over with it. How you proceed after that is your business."

Anosov started to say something, but Bykov held him off. "Our deal stands as it is, Leonid. We're old friends, don't fuck with me."

31

An unmarked Lincoln Navigator driven by a stern-looking FBI special agent took Spencer Nast from his Tribeca hotel to the Jacob K. Javits Federal Building on Foley Square in the Civic Center district in Lower Manhattan.

The beefy man in a plain blue blazer with the Bureau's insignia on the left breast had met the president's economic adviser in the hotel lobby, and without a word had chauffeured him over and escorted him to an unmarked door on the forty-first floor that was equipped with a retinal scanner.

But the door lock buzzed open before Nast could look into the scanner.

"I'll just leave you here, sir," the agent said, and he turned on his heel and was gone.

The suite of offices belonged to the National Security Agency's New York Operational Center, and its presence here was classified. Only those with the need to know were admitted, and Nast was one of them.

Inside, a pair of security officers were there to check

credentials, take a driver's license or some other form of picture identification, and require a sign-in, none of which was required for someone from the White House.

A young woman in a plain gray skirt and white blouse appeared. "Good morning, Mr. Nast, we're already set up for you," she said.

"Who's waiting for my call?" Nast asked, following her down the hall of what could have been any minor government bureaucratic office: worn carpeting, drab green walls, scuffed desks, people going about their business with little or no noise.

"Mr. Kolberg."

Samuel Kolberg was the president's chief of staff, a dour man who had little time for anyone except his boss.

The teleconference center was behind a steel-reinforced door that the young woman opened by entering a seven-digit alphanumeric code on a keypad. Inside she seated Nast at the head of a small conference table that faced a large flat-screen monitor and CCTV camera.

"When you're ready, just give your name," she said, and she left.

The agency was best known as the major U.S. intelligence-gathering organization whose headquarters was in a black monolith of a building just outside Washington, from where it monitored as many as a trillion phone and computer messages worldwide every day. But the NSA also gathered satellite and drone intel, as well as provided the means, such as this office, by which federal officials up to and including the president could communicate with absolutely no fear of being surveilled.

Nast identified himself, and the monitor came to life, showing the president's small desk and book-lined private office. The chair was empty at the moment. But Kolberg, no jacket, his tie loose, his collar button undone, came into view.

"Good morning, Mr. Nast, the president will be with you momentarily," he said. "Please stand by." And he left.

Nast was always nervous in the presence of the president, but he was especially jumpy at this moment, considering what he and the others were about to put into place.

Farmer, in a pinstripe suit, showed up and sat down behind his desk. At six-three, the president was an imposing man even when sitting. He had a square, granite-hard jaw, wavy gray hair, and shrewd eyes. During his campaign the media had dubbed him as a man "bucking to join the other four at Rushmore."

"Okay, Spence, what's the latest bullshit about China that has you all het up?" Farmer demanded. He sometimes affected a cornpone folksiness that made him sound like a dumb Texas hick. But he had a sharp intelligence, and was a master at sizing up the people around him. In addition, he was a student of history, an expert in both constitutional law, and in the politics of raising money for his campaigns. But he knew very little beyond the basics about economics, and that left an opening for Nast.

"It's grim and could very well get worse, Mr. President," Nast said.

"I'm listening."

"You've no doubt read the intel brief about the feud that's building up over there, and you've heard my take on what we're calling the debt bomb. Our objective at this point should be to prevent the U.S., and the rest of the world, for that matter, from getting screwed by the Chinese mess. If their banking system went down, it would almost certainly trigger a massive recession, maybe even worse than the one that started in '29."

"Explain to me why on God's green earth this could become our problem? If China goes down, then our trade deficit would be solved."

"The worst-case scenario is that once the PBOC refused to bail out the smaller banks, Chairman Hua would have to start unloading his U.S. Treasury bonds to step in. And that's a lot of money, more than two trillion dollars. But all sorts of loans are backed by our T-bonds—home loans, business loans, even car loans. Once the collateral shrank, the lenders would need their money back so they wouldn't go down the tubes.

"Trouble is, our entire society is in debt up to its gills. People wouldn't be able to repay their loans, and this thing could cascade into an even worse recession than the one that the '08 subprime mortgage crisis created, and as I said, even worse than '29."

"Herbert Hoover had the bad luck to be president when the Great Depression started," Farmer said. "They named shantytowns after him: Hoovervilles. A Hoover blanket was a newspaper. A Hoover flag was empty pockets turned inside out. And I can tell you that I don't want to hear about Farmervilles. No thanks."

Nast wasn't the least bit surprised that Farmer was thinking more about his reputation than the health of the country. A typical fucking politician.

"I agree, Mr. President," he said. "Which is why we need an action plan to get ready for the worst. And as it turns out, I've got one ready, which I can send to you immediately." He had to stop from grinning, because once Abacus hit, any federal backstop would fall apart like a house of cards. But whatever happened he would turn out to be the hero. Or at least *a* hero.

Farmer sat back, nodding. "Okay, I like a man who warns me about a problem but then tells me that he has a solution. I wish I had more like you on my staff."

Nast brought up his proposal on his cell phone and transferred it to the connection with the president. "It's coming your way now, sir. We essentially use the template from the '08 financial crisis and its aftermath. Bailouts for important financial institutions from the federal government to prevent their failure. Then the Federal Reserve would buy back as many bonds as possible to stop them from going bust. Plus, there's a unique funding arrangement to turn to if no one is buying our bonds anymore and we need money to fund our program. And so forth."

"And so forth? What about the innocent people who get laid off, who get their loans called, who lose their houses, who can't afford to put food on the table for their families? Who end up living in a Farmerville?"

"If the banks are saved, Mr. President, they can renegotiate the busted loans with their customers."

"Vultures aren't kind by nature," Farmer said, and he spread his hands. "After '08, banks came out smelling like a rose, while real people went broke. But it was the banks that caused the problem in the first place. Quite a racket they had going. Instead of drinking in front of bars they should have been behind bars."

"Perhaps, sir," Nast said. "But look at it this way. Banks are like the engine of a car. Remove the engine, and the car doesn't go anywhere. Banks circulate money through the economy. Anyone you pay, or anyone who pays you, does it through the banking system."

"What I don't understand is how we got into this mess in the first place. Sure, big debt has always been a problem, like an ugly wart. But now it's like a cancer, eating us alive."

Nast hesitated. "Well, sir, in all candor, one very big reason is that politicians promised more than the government's revenues could deliver."

"I'll cop to that," Farmer said. "I've done it myself. Gotta slop the hogs or they get ornery. Right now our debt is as much as our gross domestic product, I get that too. But in

World War Two, wasn't the national debt even more than it is today?"

"Yes, sir," Nast said.

"We seem to have skipped past that without a problem. The debt shrank like a five-day-old tomato in the fifties. And by the nineties we were running a surplus, as I recall, and the national debt went down again. How come?"

Nast always liked it when the president wanted a tutorial, because he could show off his intellect and deepen the man's reliance on him. "It's true, we did run up a large debt in the war. But the postwar circumstances favored us. Europe and Asia were in ruins, so our companies swooped in to rebuild and provide them with our goods. We had no competition.

"In the fifties we enjoyed a surge in affluence. Our factories were humming at capacity. Everyone was buying new cars. And new technologies, like television, were creating new industries. A torrent of fresh tax revenue from all this business activity and consumer spending meant we didn't have to borrow as much, and the debt naturally went down, like that tomato."

"And in the nineties?" Farmer asked.

"Another explosion of new technologies. Suddenly the internet and advanced computers delivered a new leap in economic productivity. But then it ended."

"Why?" the president asked.

"It reached a saturation point, which happens after a technology expansion. The railroads and the telegraph in the 1880s were powerful economic boosts. Then things plateaued. Today we have further technological innovations, sure, but they don't deliver the big bang we saw in the nineties."

"You're tiptoeing past the part the politicians played, like yours truly."

"I appreciate your honesty, Mr. President," Nast said. He

loathed buttering up people. Most of them weren't as smart as he was, and they didn't deserve civility, let alone flattery. Still, he made exceptions for his superiors in rank, such as Farmer and Treadwell.

"In the Reagan era, and again with the second Bush and Trump, taxes were cut, mainly for the wealthy and for corporations, on the theory that the extra money in their pockets would juice the economy."

"But it didn't happen, did it?"

"They expected more factories, more research and development, more productivity, and it did happen to some degree. Mostly, though, the rich and corporate America pocketed the tax savings. Companies preferred to spend money on buying back investors' stock, and pleasing the well-off crowd, rather than plugging it into research and development and the like, which would take a while to pay off."

"Everybody's hooked on debt," Farmer said. "More addictive than heroin."

"Private equity firms borrow tons of money to take over companies, fire a lot of the workers, then sell off the remnants for a big profit. Nothing is created, just paper profits for the takeover guys and misery for everyone else."

"And it's firms like your old employer, Burnham Pike, that lend the pirates the money they use for their takeovers."

Nast always got uncomfortable whenever the president brought up BP. But he ignored the remark, hoping Farmer would drop it. "Corporate power has grown; unions have become a joke, so workers have no bargaining power. Plus U.S. companies automate factories or ship American jobs overseas to countries where labor costs are dirt cheap. So in inflation-adjusted terms, people are making less money than they did ten or twenty years ago. That's why consumer debt has gotten out of control. Average people borrow to bridge the gap between what little they can earn and what they need."

"Government's been spending the long green on other stuff too."

"Yes, sir. For starts we've beefed up the military. The Iraq war alone cost us $2.4 trillion, which was a waste if you ask me. We've made all kinds of promises to the public with Social Security and Medicare, which cost more and more as our population ages, with fewer young people to feed the system. To combat the Great Recession, we had to lay out additional trillions."

"Some of it to bail out Wall Street," Farmer said. "Now, I love you like a brother, and that's a natural fact. But let me ask you this. You were the top-dog economist at Burnham Pike before we made an honest man of you and hired you to serve your country. BP's a bank too, so your old buddies like Treadwell will benefit from any bailout we might offer. Right?"

"Yes, Mr. President, Burnham is an investment bank. Its main focus is on financing corporations and managing people's investments."

"Big companies and wealthy people."

Farmer, who gladly took donations from Treadwell and his one-percenter buddies, also had a populist streak. Nast understood this. In public he was a friend of the little guy, while he held his other hand out to take money from the big players.

"That's true, sir," Nast said. "The big commercial banks like Chase and BOA have large retail branches that offer the public checking accounts. BP doesn't do that. But in the eyes of the law, it's still a bank."

"And it would take a sweet bailout from the Fed if they got themselves into trouble."

The debt bomb, with Abacus to light the fuse, would

leave just about every bank in tatters, with the exception of Burnham Pike, which would come out the hero.

"This time the bailouts would have to be bigger—if it came to that," Nast said. "I'm just saying, Mr. President, that we should be prepared in case things do start to go south."

"Tell me, Nast, does your proposal recommend who would be in charge of the rescue operation? You, perhaps?"

"No, sir. But someone would have to put it to the key people on the Hill. Probably Bob Nichols and Joe Miller."

"No shit. You'd be about as welcome in Congress as a whore in church. No offense."

"None taken, sir."

Farmer was silent for several beats. "I want you back here as fast as possible. I'm going to call a meeting in the Oval Office as soon as you get back. The more heads we can put together on this thing, the better off we'll be."

It was called spreading the blame, in Nast's estimation. Diluting the situation so that the president would come out the savior of the nation if it worked, or if it didn't, at least he would go down fighting as the champion of the underdog.

32

Treadwell had a lot of New York restaurants that he loved, but Basel was the best for seduction, and it was within walking distance of his pied-à-terre. The restaurant was dark, with lots of wood beams and tasteful frescoes on the wall, and it was usually sparsely populated at lunch.

Heather was already seated at a table in the corner when he walked in, and before Marcelle, the maître d', came over, he went to her. She had changed into a sheer white silk

blouse, with no bra, and a short plaid skirt that rode halfway up her well-shaped thighs.

She smiled brightly as he bent down to give her a kiss
on the cheek. But at the last second she turned so their lips
met, and she held the kiss for a moment before parting.

"Were you waiting long?" Treadwell asked, sitting next
to her.

"Just a few minutes," she said. She placed a hand on his
leg. "I didn't want to be late."

"This is one of my favorite places, especially for lunch.
It's never too busy."

"More intimate," she said. "I like it."

"I'd hoped that it would be just the two of us."

"If you mean my father, he won't be joining us. Our stock
is down over the Chinese rumors, and he's in one of his
moods. He's somewhere drinking Jamesons and sulking.
He'll fly back home later today."

The old man had become a pain in the ass, and Treadwell
was glad for more than one reason that he hadn't shown
up. "It happens sometimes with IPOs. But the stock will
come back because Rockingham is a solid company, and
from what I understand you're doing a damn fine job of
marketing."

"Maybe not if China goes south."

"There are ways around something like that if it
happens—and I do mean *if*."

"My hundred grand is taking a hit, but if we don't raise
the twenty-five mil we were counting on, we'll have to scale
back our expansion plans."

"Like I said, there are things we can do," Treadwell said.
He wasn't liking where this thing with her was going.

"For instance?" she asked.

"We could always do a secondary offering once your
price-per-share rebounds, which it will."

She smiled, but it was more mischievous than warm. "Well, no matter what, BP will do okay."

"We might be able to lower your fees," Treadwell said. "BP likes to take care of its customers."

She smiled again, this time the warmth back, and she touched the back of his hand. "I like being taken care of, Reid."

"Can do," Treadwell said, returning her smile.

Marcelle came over with a flourish as usual. "Mr. Treadwell, welcome, welcome to you and your lovely lady. May we start you with a cocktail?" Over the years Treadwell and other Burnham Pike execs had spent a lot of money here.

"I think a bottle of Chasselas Ilex Grand Cru would be nice," Treadwell said. The white wine came from one of the best vineyards in Switzerland.

"Excellent choice, sir," Marcelle said, and he hurried off.

"I agree," Heather said.

"You're young to be head of marketing for a company the size of Rockingham. How'd you get there?"

"Do you really want to know?"

"Actually I want to know everything about you, and your background is a good start."

"MBA from the University of Wisconsin four years ago, top of my class. Two years at Lee, Johnson and Ballard and then over to Daddy's company, where I took them from a stodgy old man's fly-fishing clothing company to a younger demographic into anything having to do with the outdoors, from mountain climbing to skateboarding."

LJ&B was the largest marketing company in Chicago and the fourth largest in the entire U.S. Treadwell was impressed, and he told her so. "No wonder you've done so well," he said. Left unsaid was that it helped to be beautiful, rich, and Rockingham's daughter.

"My motto from the beginning has been 'Balls to the

walls, boys,'" she said and smiled again. "So what about you, Reid? Is everything I've read in the tabloids true?"

"They like to make up stories, and the more outrageous, the more papers they sell," Treadwell said. "But wasn't it P. T. Barnum or someone like him who said, 'I don't care what they write about me as long as they spell my name right'?"

"Some people said it was George M. Cohan, or W. C. Fields, but I've always preferred to believe it was Mae West. I think I'm something like her."

"When it suits you."

"They say that you take no prisoners."

"Business isn't a kid's game."

"I particularly liked the story about Ted Partridge, who it was said had the inside track of becoming BP's head of senior client investing but instead ended up being indicted for front-running. He went to jail, and you got the job instead."

"He was a crook, and I found out about his scheme and reported it."

"One of the financial newspapers hinted that you set him up. That he wasn't guilty."

"And when I threatened to sue if they couldn't come up with the proof, they retracted the piece."

"I read about that too. But you were on the way up, and no one was going to stop you," Heather said.

"Just like you?"

"Just like me."

In fact Partridge was innocent, charged with the crime of front-running, which meant using secret, inside information from his Burnham Pike job to buy shares of stock cheaply just before big positive news about it went public, and cleaning up when the price surged. But the evidence that Dammerman had planted was so well done and so overwhelming that no one had believed the man.

Marcelle brought the Chasselas, made a show of uncorking it, and poured a sample for Treadwell.

"Superb," Treadwell said.

Heather studied him the entire time, with such an enigmatic smile on her lips that he had to wonder what her game was.

Marcelle filled both of their glasses, left menus, and when he departed, Heather raised her glass. "A toast to you, Reid."

"Why?" Treadwell asked.

"For being a man I admire a great deal."

"I'm glad you said that."

"My father taught me that to get ahead you sometimes had to break a few heads. It's something we've both done."

"Why would you need to do something like that when your father is the boss?"

"Are you kidding?" Heather said, her laugh harsh. "The old guys who were with my father from the beginning had reached their shelf life. They blocked every idea I came up with, so I convinced Daddy to offer them buyouts. These guys were stubborn but they weren't stupid, so they accepted. All but one of them."

"What happened to him?" Treadwell asked.

"Supposedly he was dipping his finger in the till, and when he was arrested, he died of a heart attack." She drank some wine. "He didn't have what it takes. *"Tant pis,"* she said in French. *Too bad.*

"Entendu," Treadwell said. *Agreed.* He raised his glass. "To Heather Rockingham, hard-nosed businesswoman definitely on her way to the top."

33

An hour later, after they'd finished their lunch—blackfoot chicken in morel sauce for him and dry-aged Swiss pork in sherry sauce for her—and were drinking their port, she pressed her knee against his.

"I'm going to need your help," she said.

"You have my attention," Treadwell said.

"I've taken steps to clean out the board of directors, who were getting as old as the execs I forced out. The new board is solidly on my side. Sound familiar?"

"I've done the identical—"

"I know you have. Now shut up and listen, there's money to be made in what I'm going to tell you. Money for both of us."

Treadwell sat back and nodded. Lunch was definitely looking up.

"My father wants to stay in place as CEO until he dies. We've made some real strides, but I want a lot more. I want to take on more debt—something he definitely doesn't want us to do—to buy up our top three competitors, so we're number one. And right now Justice under Farmer doesn't give a damn about antitrust. Plus all that extra debt will mean big fees for BP."

The kid had no idea that after tomorrow Rockingham wouldn't be able to pay its electric bill, let alone become the champ of down jackets. Or that the money BP was going to rake in as one of the sole survivors of a worldwide economic meltdown would make the fees she figured BP was going to make nothing but chump change.

But Treadwell smiled and nodded. "First things first. What to do about your father?"

"I'll have the board impose an age limit of sixty-five for

our CEO. Daddy just turned sixty-five three months ago. He'll fight it, of course, because he won't think it's fair—which it won't be. But I'll want you to back me up when it comes to a knock-down-drag-'em-out."

Treadwell raised his glass to her. "Done."

"Then let's go to that apartment I've heard about. I need to tear your clothes off."

– – –

The weather was pleasant, and Treadwell decided to walk the couple of blocks to his apartment, his limo driver following a discreet distance behind them.

"Anticipation, is that what this walk is all about?" Heather asked. She wasn't happy.

"You'll get what you want, sweetheart, but indulge me this time," Treadwell said. "It'll be worth it."

"If you say so."

His cell phone vibrated in his pocket. He glanced at Heather. "Excuse me a sec, I need to take this." He answered the call. "Yes."

It was Julia O'Connell. "Sorry to bother you, Reid, but this is important."

"I'm busy, make it quick."

"The woman I mentioned this morning from my department by the name of Cassy Levin says she has created a countermeasure to what she thinks is a worm in our system. It's Abacus."

Treadwell held himself in check. "How credible is this?"

"She's loading it on a flash drive for me to beta test."

"Is Hardy ready?"

"Yes."

"Then get the material and make the problem disappear."

"Christ," O'Connell said. "Abacus is one thing, but what I think you're suggesting is something completely different."

"I don't care. I want you to make it happen. Now. This afternoon. Do you understand me?"

O'Connell hesitated.

"Goddamnit, Julia, just make sure Butch takes care of it."

"I'll see what we can do," she said and hung up.

"A problem?" Heather asked.

Treadwell smiled. "Just business as usual."

SEVEN

GLIMMERINGS

34

Joseph Miller's secretary buzzed him a couple of minutes before noon. He had just been thinking about heading over to the Hay-Adams for lunch, alone this time because he had a lot on his mind after his chat this morning with Bob Nichols.

He answered. "Yes."

"Mr. Nichols wishes to have a word with you, Mr. Chairman."

"Put him on."

"No, sir, he's here in person."

Miller was flustered for just a moment. This wasn't good. "Send him in," he said.

Nichols barged in, out of breath, his face red. He tossed a sheaf of papers on Miller's desk and sat down across from him. "It looks like it might be starting sooner than we thought."

Miller held up a hand for him to stop as he scanned the papers, which appeared to show the early result of an auction in progress of $50 billion in ten-year notes.

He looked up. It was unusual enough for the secretary of the Treasury to show up unannounced, but what he had brought with him was over the top. "Can this be accurate, Bob?"

"I'm afraid it is. But it just came out of the blue."

"Isn't this what we talked about this morning?"

"Yes, but goddamnit, that was theory, this is fact, and it's happening a lot sooner than I'd feared."

"Not enough bidders," Miller said half under his breath. "Has anything like this happened before?"

"No, Mr. Chairman, not even during the Great Depression. Our bond auctions have always been oversubscribed, never under."

"Well you wrote the definitive work on depressions. So what do you suggest? Do we call off the auction?"

"It's in progress, no way to stop it now. But no matter what, it's going to be a major embarrassment for us. You never see undersubscriptions except in small, emerging-market nations. Places like Tanzania, Ghana, or lately, even Greece."

At that moment Treasury was auctioning off the block of bonds, the money from which was needed to finance the operation of the U.S. government. In the past such offerings had never failed to attract hordes of bidders from around the world—including China, which was the largest holder. But now, if Miller was reading the preliminary summary report correctly, only half the usual number of bidders had made offers, which was depressing the value so seriously that it seemed unlikely the auction would raise the $50 billion needed.

It was a clear signal that investors no longer accepted the full faith and credit of the American government, of the largest economy on earth. They didn't trust the U.S. to pay the interest on the bonds, much less repay the debt when the bonds came due.

U.S. securities were issued for terms ranging from four weeks to thirty years, with higher interest paid the longer the maturity stretched. The ten-year Treasury note was the linchpin of the entire debt market. Corporate bonds, city and state municipal bonds, home mortgages, and many others used the ten-year as a benchmark. And many employed the T-note as collateral for other borrowings.

The secretary of the Treasury and the chairman of the

Federal Reserve looked at each other, each wanting the other to say something. But nothing was to be said. The situation was what it was—unprecedented.

Miller's secretary buzzed him. "President Farmer has asked that you speak with him on video."

"Me?" Miller asked.

"No, Mr. Chairman, you *and* Mr. Nichols."

– – –

Miller and Nichols went into the adjacent conference room, which was also used for video links, a large flat-screen monitor on the wall facing the head of the table with seating for twelve. The image of the president's study came up, and Sam Kolberg, his chief of staff, came in view.

"Is there any truth to what we're hearing over here?" he asked.

"Afraid so," Nichols said.

Kolberg moved away as President Farmer, in shirtsleeves, showed up and sat down behind his desk. "Glad I caught the two of you together. So what the hell is going on with our market?"

"To this point only half the number of bidders we needed to sell out the bond issue have shown up."

"Are you suggesting I'm going to shut down the government because we've run out of cash?"

"No, Mr. President," Nichols said. "We're good for several months yet. And our revenue stream from payroll withholding is steady."

"Give me the long run."

"We could be in trouble, Mr. President," Miller said. "But we've weathered other storms, and I expect that we'll weather this one, if it comes to that."

"I'm up for fucking reelection in sixteen months; what do you want me to tell the good people of Iowa? That I've bankrupted Washington?"

"We'll sell what we need to sell if we offer higher interest rates," Nichols said. "Right now the ten-year is at three percent. We can bump it to four."

"Maybe even five percent, if need be, Mr. President," Miller said.

"We kick the can down the road, and pay the piper later," Farmer said, his voice rising. "Is that all you guys can come up with? You want us to start acting like some fucking banana republic?"

"It may be our only recourse at this point, Mr. President," Nichols said.

Farmer looked away for a moment, and when he turned back to the camera he had visibly calmed down. "How did this happen to us?"

"Our debt, which used to be around seventy-five percent of our gross domestic product, has doubled in recent years," Nichols said. "Investors are becoming concerned."

"We're the richest, most powerful nation on the entire planet."

"Yes, sir, but a huge number of baby boomers are retiring. They're starting to draw on Social Security, which ran out of money last year. We used to be able to pay it from payroll deductions, but the boomer generation is so large that its need for Social Security is overwhelming the system. Added to that, Medicare is in the same boat, and there's no end in sight."

"Maybe we should start killing off our senior citizens," Farmer said, but then he passed a hand across his forehead. "It's a goddamn joke."

"Used to be that we could count on a demographic of age expectancy," Nichols said. "But modern medicine is keeping people alive much longer so that they can continue collecting Social Security and Medicare."

"Maybe we should start killing the doctors instead,"

Farmer said half under his breath, but he waved that away too.

"That's not the problem right now, Mr. President," Miller said.

"I'm listening."

"The word is circulating that the Chinese might start dumping the two trillion in our bonds they're holding to bail out their commercial banks if Liu and the PBOC refuse to do so."

"Liu is a power-mad son of a bitch. And trust me, I can spot one a mile away. He'd throw his country, not to mention the entire world, in front of the bus. Marcus is trying to make contact with Hua in Beijing, plus Liu, but there's been no response so far." Marcus Conwell was the U.S. secretary of state and a tough but respected negotiator.

"We're in a serious situation, Mr. President, there's no doubt about it," Miller said. "But I think we can manage through."

"How, Joe?" Farmer asked. "We're playing with boys who don't give a damn about anyone except themselves." He looked off-camera for a moment. "Spencer is up in New York. I'm getting him back down here pronto, and the four of us are going to put our heads together to figure a way out of this mess. A shit train is coming down the tracks, gentlemen, and we need to stop it before it gets here."

35

Butch Hardy was just finishing his report on the extra money he'd sent over to the Russian team with Charlene along with the photographs of Cassy Levin he'd included on Dammerman's orders when his phone rang.

He picked up. "Yes?"

"Meet me at the Nassau Street door," Dammerman said. "We're going for a little walk."

"When?"

"Now."

"Yes, sir," Hardy said, but Dammerman had already hung up.

He printed out the brief report, erased the file from his computer, and put the hard copy in his locked file cabinet before he grabbed his jacket and went upstairs to the reception desk on the main floor.

"Good morning, sir," one of the big men at the desk said, nodding respectfully as he passed. The entire security crew in the building, including the guys on reception, had been his hires after he'd thoroughly vetted them.

It was nearly a year ago when Dammerman had called him into his office and ordered the replacement of everyone on security.

"Sure thing, sir," Hardy had said. "But can you tell me why?"

"Security is shit around here. I want it tightened up. Good enough?"

"You're the boss."

"And never forget it," Dammerman had said darkly.

And Hardy hadn't.

Dammerman seemed to be in another of his dark moods, which had been happening more frequently over the past month or so, when Hardy joined him at the front door.

"Let's go," BP's COO said. He headed up Nassau Street at a brisk pace, and Hardy fell in beside him.

It was just past noon and time for lunch, which was what Hardy figured this meeting was all about—going to lunch to discuss things too sensitive to cover in the building. Later, if or when the shit hit the fan, they would have plausible deniability: *We never had any discussion of that nature in either of our offices so far as I can recall.*

Time was when Wall Street players would take a break for long liquid lunches. That wasn't done much anymore. A mostly sober, stay-at-your-desk work ethic reigned. Even the traders on the floor, who were rough-around-the-edges frat boy types, no longer hit the bars during the day.

In the digital age nobody dared to be away from a trading terminal—everything happened in split seconds. If you didn't notice a price aberration and act on it at once, you could lose millions for your firm. Even going to the john was a high-risk proposition for a trader.

Of course Dammerman was above any such restrictions. He'd spent a lot of high-stress years at the trading posts as a swinging dick, bellowing profanities and trading at a manic speed.

"Trade or quit, I don't give a fuck, just get out of my way!"

But right now, as number two at BP, he was the master of his universe, and everyone, including Hardy, knew it.

36

The dimly lit bar was called Mongo, and at this hour it was beginning to fill up, but a table for four in one corner was empty, and Dammerman steered them over. As soon as they were seated, a beetle-browed bartender came over with a double scotch-rocks, which Dammerman drank down immediately, and the bartender took the glass.

"For you, sir?" he asked Hardy.

"A Diet Coke."

"Why don't you get a real drink?" Dammerman demanded.

"I'm still an on-duty cop at heart," Hardy said, after the bartender left. "And we've got a big day tomorrow. I'll drink later."

"Suit yourself," Dammerman said. "Did you have Reid and the Rockingham broad followed like I asked?"

"They left the restaurant early and went to the apartment about thirty minutes ago. Looked chummy, my man said."

"Okay. What about Levin?"

"O'Connell is waiting for her to deliver the flash drive. Soon as that happens she's almost certainly going to leave the building for lunch somewhere. It's what she usually does. And as soon as she clears the building, my Brighton Beach people are going to grab her."

"She never has lunch at our cafeteria?"

"I'm told not," Hardy said. "Anyway, why do we need to make her disappear? Just asking."

"She knows something she shouldn't," Dammerman said. "And I don't want her shooting off her mouth to the wrong people."

"She'll disappear."

The bartender returned with their drinks, and when he left, Dammerman leaned forward. "Permanently."

"The Brighton Beach guys are ex–Russian Special Forces. They'll get the job done."

"I don't trust fucking Russians. They've got no respect for us."

Hardy almost laughed out loud, but he thought better of it. "Trust me, these guys are the best. Highly trained, good with explosives, weapons, hand-to-hand combat, and no conscience. They do what the money tells them to do."

"And afterward? What's to keep them from opening their mouths and fucking us?"

"When they're done, they'll walk away until another job comes up. They won't want to screw up their own reputations. I'm telling you, these guys are pros."

This time Dammerman sipped at his drink, obviously weighing all the angles. "Any of these guys ever fuck up, go down?"

"We busted a few now and then when I worked anti-terrorism."

"You're not filling me with a lot of confidence here, Butch."

"The guys who went down were stupid. They made mistakes. Somebody ratted them out for chump change. Some babe they were fucking and slapped around because she pissed them off called the cops. Shit like that. But I'm telling you the people I hired are the best."

"I don't want any problems coming back at us, that's all."

"They won't," Hardy said.

Dammerman was silent for a long beat or two, working at his drink. He was worried, and it was a rare sight to Hardy, who was thinking that he liked it.

"What about the Levin broad, do you think she believes something is going on?" Dammerman asked.

Something big *was* going on, Hardy was sure of it. But he shook his head. "She's as clueless as all the other geeks down in the DCSS," he said. "But I'll tell you the one who really worries me."

"Yeah?"

"Julia O'Connell. I don't think that she sees the real world for what it is. She's another geek, and if there's a weak link it might be her. Just saying."

37

Julia O'Connell hurried out of the BP tower and crossed Broadway. Zuccotti Park was busy at lunchtime on nice days like this one, and she hoped that no one from the firm would be here to see her.

She stopped for a moment to look for any familiar faces, but so far as she could see there were none, and that was a good thing. But for some reason *Joie de Vivre*—Joy of Life—the massive sculpture of two bloodred twisted steel beams, made her feel anything but joyful.

Betty Ladd had phoned from her office at the NYSE and asked to meet at the park. Masters had just told her that Cassy was still putting the finishing touches on her anti-virus program.

But he'd also told her that Butch Hardy had disappeared without a word, though he'd left one of his security people to keep watch on the young woman.

All of it was getting to be too much for Julia, and in some ways she wished that she were shed of the entire Abacus scheme, but it was too late for that now. And she had a dark feeling that Betty's call had something to do with the insane scheme.

When she came around the right side of the sculpture, she spotted the NYSE president seated on one of the park benches, a Starbucks coffee container in her left hand, and she walked over.

Betty looked up, a warm smile on her narrow face. "Thanks for coming on such short notice."

Julia sat down on the opposite end of the bench. "What's up with meeting in public?"

"I didn't think you'd want to come to my office. I get the feeling that you're afraid of something or someone."

"What makes you think something like that?" Julia asked. She was almost sorry that she'd agreed to meet.

"Just a feeling," Betty said. "Anyway, my question still stands. You're afraid of something. What is it?"

"Reid," Julia said. She had no idea what Betty knew or had guessed, but she figured that mentioning Reid's name might throw the woman off track.

Betty shrugged. "You were seen on the floor this morning. You and Reid, and of all people, Spencer Nast. I want to know what's going on."

Julia's insides were churning. "I can't discus company business, especially not with someone in your position."

"This is just an innocent question," Betty said. She reached across and touched the back of Julia's hand. "We've got history together. Just answer me as a friend."

Julia looked away for a moment. "We were supporting Rockingham's IPO, and Reid asked me to tag along. You know, show the flag."

"Oh, come on. Since when is the technology director of any major investment bank on the floor for an insignificant IPO?"

Julia had nothing to say. Betty was her cousin, twelve years older, and had been there in the early years after her parents had been killed in a car crash. She'd almost been a mother, helping with college, helping with Julia's early career.

"Everyone knows that Reid wants to screw Rockingham's daughter. But I know the bastard well enough to understand that something else is going on."

Julia shook her head, her eyes moistening. She was afraid, but she definitely couldn't tell her cousin what the trouble was. It was too late for that now, and she was sorry that she had come here.

"I don't want you to get in trouble at work. Tech and especially finance are in the men's world. But you've come nearly to the top in both."

Unspoken was that Julia would not have gotten so far up the food chain without Betty Ladd's help.

When Julia was in college she'd gotten involved with a group of boys who were ace hackers. To show them up and maybe gain a little respect, she'd hacked into the local electrical power grid and blacked out the entire town for thirty minutes.

She was good, even then, and had covered her tracks, except that the boys she'd wanted to impress gave her up.

She would have gone to prison, her scholarship in computer science revoked. It would have been the end of her brilliant career even before it started.

But Betty Ladd, who by then had been a rising star on Wall Street, persuaded the town, whose bonds her firm floated, to drop the charges as a mere schoolgirl prank. Next she talked the college into not canceling Julia's scholarship after she pledged a substantial donation. And she'd paid for a very good lawyer to make sure that the charges were expunged from the public record so that not even a hint of criminal activity would be connected with her cousin.

"Thanks to you," Julia said.

"I always know a good bet when I see one," Betty said. "But my question still stands: What's going on?"

So far as Julia knew, Treadwell had no inkling that Betty Ladd was her cousin, and she wanted to keep it that way. Betty had recommended her to Treadwell's predecessor, who'd hired her on the spot. But considering the history between Betty and Reid, if the truth came out, Julia was almost certain that Reid would dump her.

Right now she felt as if she were the proverbial idiot caught in a bear trap with the bear closing in.

"Reid wanted to get Seymour's take on where the economy is heading, and he thought coming for the IPO would kill two birds with one stone."

"He could have called Schneider into his office after the closing bell."

"Seymour has a special status with us, and he hates to leave the floor, so Reid leaves him alone. Anyway I've never been on the floor for one of our IPOs, and I asked to tag along."

"Okay," Betty said after a beat. "I'll buy that, for now. But what about Farmer's economic adviser?"

Julia shook her head. "I don't know."

Betty sipped her coffee and watched the passersby for a few moments. "I've heard that BP is moving into cash. That right?"

"Above my pay grade. Right now I have my people beefing up cybersecurity protocols for our clients."

"A little bird whispered in my ear that you had breakfast in a private room at Kittredge, along with Reid, his lap dog, Dammerman, and Spencer Nast. What was that all about?"

Betty had eyes and ears everywhere. "Nothing about going into cash."

"I didn't ask what you *weren't* discussing."

"It wasn't about BP policy, I can tell you that much. Spencer is no longer an employee, and Reid would never bring up something like that in front of an outsider."

"Give me a break, Julia. Nast is in one of those classic Washington revolving-door jobs. Once Farmer loses reelection, Nast will come tootling back up to his old berth at BP, only with a bigger pay package. BP is like the Mafia: Once you're in, you never leave."

"We talked about the 'debt bomb,' as Spencer calls it. There's nothing to prevent a fed from sounding out people on Wall Street about an important issue."

"You make Nast sound like Mr. Nice who gives a damn about what other people think."

Julia noticed a large man dressed in an ordinary business suit out of the corner of her eye off to her left. When she looked at him he turned away. He was one of Hardy's goons, checking up on her. It was exactly what she was afraid of happening.

"I have to get back," she said.

"Wait a minute, please. I think Reid is trying to pull some kind of a fast move. The China situation is scary; in fact, they could be on the brink of collapse. They might even try to dump our T-bonds. That would tear the hell out of the market. And today's Treasury auction is undersubscribed, the last I heard, which is another bad sign. I get all that. But for Reid to take BP to a one-hundred-percent-cash position is way over the top."

"Maybe he's only being prudent," Julia said. "The two of you have issues, but he's done a good job managing the firm." She got to her feet. "I really have to get back."

"Reid's taking the firm into an all-cash position has been noticed by the bond buyers. For them it's just another vote of no confidence."

"I'm a technologist, Betty, not an economist," Julia said. She glanced to her left, but the big man was gone.

Betty sat back. "You should talk to Tyler Wren. He's the reporter who dug up the dirt on Reid that he wasn't allowed to publish. In fact he was fired, courtesy of Reid. He can tell you a lot about your Mr. Treadwell."

"I'm going now," Julia said.

Betty got to her feet and hugged her cousin. "Something's up, Julia. Be careful you don't get crapped on. Reid has a habit of doing that to the people around him."

38

Leonid got up from the dining room table where he and Valentin were playing poker with Bykov's people. He was already up forty grand, but for now it was nothing more than play money; in the end the six of them would settle up. There was certainly enough money between them.

He was bored, but then he and his people out at the Beach had only been doing the few odd jobs here and there. Mostly hijacking trucks of sides of beef from the farms and selling them for twenty cents on the dollar to a local supplier, who processed the meat and distributed it to grocery stores across the river in Manhattan. Sometimes they got lucky with cartons of cigarettes, and once with fur coats that went to places upstate where the anti-fur liberals weren't so visible.

Often some of the eleven guys would chip in and buy a couple of whores for the night, but for the past three months it had been same-old-same-old, and this half mil had seemed almost heaven-sent.

His two biggest problems lately were keeping the crew reasonably sober in case something did come up, and paying the increased hush money the local cops were demanding. He wanted to kill a couple of the bastards, but that would lead nowhere except jail.

In the kitchen he got a bottle of Evian from the fridge and brought it to the kitchen table, where he had a drink, then took out his 9mm Steyr GB, unloaded it, and began checking for any signs he'd left lint behind after the last cleaning. The Austrian double-action automatic pistol, with its eighteen-round detachable magazine, was an old friend. He'd taken it from the body of an American Special Forces guy he'd killed behind a bar in Kabul about ten years ago.

After he was posted back to Moscow when his eighteen months of undercover work were done, he'd bought a suppressor from a dealer of weapons used by American soldiers.

Bykov came in, grabbed a carton of milk from the fridge, and sat down across from Leonid. "I haven't seen one of those guns in a long time," he said.

Leonid handed him the pistol butt-first, and Bykov held it in his right hand, getting a feel for the weight and the grip. "Supposed to be a good weapon."

"It tolerates bad ammunition and even a bit of mud and sand now and then."

"As long as it hits what you point it at," Bykov said, handing it back.

"Hasn't failed me yet, though it hasn't got much use lately."

The two men were silent for a bit, until Bykov leaned back. "How's it going over here for you?"

"Tolerable," Leonid said. "But I think it's getting to be time to bail out somewhere."

"Any place in mind?"

"My French isn't bad."

"Marseille?"

"It's an idea," Leonid said. "How about you? What brings you to this side of the pond? Something interesting?"

Bykov shrugged. "Not really. But our employers have deep pockets."

"I'd say. Five hundred large for a simple street grab is good. What about afterward?"

"This one's going to be short and sweet, and we'll be home before the dust settles. Could be something else in the works in Saudi Arabia I might be able to use a little help with."

"What about this crew?"

"There'll be plenty of work for all of us."

"Can you give me a clue?"

"It's an op in the desert outside Medina. A cousin of MBS is evidently about ready to try a power grab with the help of an American crew. We'd be there as backup."

"For the cousin or the prince?"

"The prince, naturally. And this one could have the backing of a player in Moscow. The president would love to get a foot in the door over there, maybe steal a few jet deals from the Americans."

"Power politics," Leonid said. "Dangerous."

"Lucrative," Bykov replied.

Leonid worked the Steyr's slide a couple of times, then seated the magazine and jacked a round into the firing chamber before laying the pistol on the table. "My guys like it here."

"It'd just be you."

"I'll think about it."

39

Bykov went back into the dining room and gestured for Zimin to break off and join him at the front door. The bomb expert folded his hand and came over.

"Yes, sir."

"We're driving across the river first thing in the morning, and I want to make one last check of the van," Bykov said.

"As you wish."

The two of them took the elevator straight down to the underground parking garage, turned left, and walked down the ramp past a dozen cars, finally coming to the plain white Mercedes transit van they'd rented from an agency on the Upper East Side two days ago.

Zimin would be doing his business in back once they arrived at the travel agency in the morning, while Kolchin would be behind the wheel waiting until the detonator circuit for the explosives was set and the two of them could get out and walk one block around the corner.

Alexei Mazayev, driving the backup Mercedes C300, Bykov riding shotgun, would be waiting for them to show up, and from there drive directly out to JFK for their flight home.

The final payment would not be deposited to their offshore account unless the bomb actually went off and destroyed the entire building, so Bykov wanted to make sure that everything was as it should be.

He unlocked the doors, and they got in. Zimin went into

the back first while Bykov locked the doors and then joined him.

The cargo space was crammed floor to ceiling, left to right—with only a narrow crawl space in the middle—with fifty-pound bags of ammonium nitrate fertilizer stacked on top of long narrow cylinders of nitromethane gas and several tubes of Tovex, which was like dynamite.

The gas, which was normally used to power racing motorcycles, had been bought from a supply company in Queens, the fertilizer from a farm supply in a small town twenty miles from West Point, and the Tovex they stole from a construction company's warehouse up in Danbury.

When the detonator circuit was activated, an electric signal would be generated that would ignite the Tovex, creating a massive explosion of the fertilizer and Tovex. It was the same combination that Timothy McVeigh and Terry Nichols had used in '95 for their attack on the Murrah Federal Building in Oklahoma City, which killed or seriously wounded nearly nine hundred people.

This time the casualty list would be much smaller, but the NYSE's backup computer would be completely obliterated.

"Once the countdown clock is set, we'll have five minutes to get out of the blast zone," Zimin explained.

"Tell me again why we just don't use a cell phone signal to set the thing off."

"Be our luck that someone makes a wrong-number call while we were close. This way is better."

"What if we're delayed?" Bykov asked. He had been around high explosives all of his career, long enough to respect their power and yet not be frightened if the proper procedures were followed. Yet he'd also had experiences—all of them had—with shit happening by dumb luck.

"We shoot our way clear, unless we want to become martyrs."

At this moment the timer was set to zero, and the positive lead on the battery was disconnected.

"Don't make a mistake in the morning, Arkadi," Bykov said.

"Be there when we come around the corner," Zimin countered.

40

Reid Treadwell was panting into Heather Rockingham's bare shoulder, and when he calmed down a little he raised his head so their faces were inches apart. "Christ, that was good," he said, and meant it.

"We corn-fed Midwestern girls can show up your refined New York ladies anytime," she said, grinning. She squeezed his hips with her thighs.

"Now I know why I like an early lunch," Reid said. He made to pull away, but she held him in place with her legs.

"Stay," she said.

He settled in. "Obliged," he murmured.

She laughed lightly. "You have a lot of stamina for an old guy."

"And you have a lot of technique for a kid." Of all the women he'd bedded, the ones half his age were always a special treat.

"I like older men," Heather said. "Especially successful ones."

"And I like you."

She laughed again. "No, you don't. You just like getting in my panties."

"I hope you'll be sticking around town for a while. I'd like to see more of you." He didn't know how she was going to feel in the morning when the bottom dropped out of the market. But he didn't give a damn. Here was here and now was now.

"Here's the deal, Reid. I'll let you recharge for a bit, but then we're going to do this again. Do you think you can handle it?"

"Easy," Reid said.

Her legs parted, and when he slid out of her it was almost painful. He rolled over on his back, and she turned to him and nestled against his chest, one leg thrown over his, and played with his chest hair.

They lay in a broad California king bed in the penthouse apartment's sumptuous bedroom, done up in a Middle Eastern theme: bright kilim rugs from Turkey, ceramic urns from Egypt, bronze lamps from Morocco.

Treadwell had always left home décor to his wife, and it amused him that she had decorated this place as a guest apartment for visiting financial dignitaries from all over the world, and not for the real purpose he used it.

The midday sun bathed the broad patio outside the door with a soft light. For a half minute or so, he closed his eyes, thinking that everything was perfect, until it suddenly struck him that his cell phone had chimed while he and Heather were making love.

"Sorry, love, I have to check my phone, crazy day in the markets," he said. "Just be a sec."

"No problem," she said, swinging her legs off the bed. "I need the loo."

He got his phone from the nightstand, and for a moment he simply watched Heather's great ass as she headed for the marble bathroom. When she shut the door, he checked the missed calls. This one was from Dammerman. He hit *replay*.

"Call me ASAP, Mr. T. I was going to have one of Butch's boys come fetch you, but I thought you'd like a call first."

Treadwell got off the bed and walked to the patio window looking out toward the Hudson River, traffic heavy as usual thirty stories below on Rector Street.

He was about to return Dammerman's call when his phone chimed, and Betty Ladd's name came up.

He answered. "What do you want? I thought I'd heard all the lovely things you had to say earlier."

"I forgot to ask you what you were doing this morning at Kittredge's with Spencer."

"Discussing economic policy, what else? The debt bomb. The Chinese situation. Spence is just as pessimistic as Seymour. Anyway, what the fuck business is it of yours?"

"You're cooking up something. I know goddamn well you are. And I'm telling you, Reid, I will absolutely destroy you if you're fucking with the markets for your own gain. I shit you not!"

"Crude as usual, Betts," he said, and he broke the connection.

He phoned Dammerman. "What's up, Clyde?"

"I thought you'd better know that Butch put a tail on Julia. She met with Betty Ladd at Zuccotti Park."

It was if an electric prod had been zapped against his balls. "Did they get any of the conversation?"

"Apparently not," Dammerman said. "I'm at Mongo's right now with Butch. He got a call that she talked to Ladd for maybe five minutes. And it was cozy, like they were old pals. But when Julia got up and walked away, she didn't look happy."

"What's the connection between Julia and Betty?" Treadwell demanded. This was not good.

"Beats the shit outa me. But Butch says that he doesn't trust Julia any farther than he could throw our building. Me, I never liked her. All those geeks are wired different than us. We needed her to get us Abacus, but now that's a done deal, she's yesterday's fish."

"Don't mention that word on the phone, goddamnit,"

Treadwell said. He could feel his cool slipping. They were so fucking close he could almost taste it. Nothing was going to screw the deal. Nothing and no one.

"Whatever, Mr. T. All I'm suggesting is that maybe we should add her to the Brighton Beach list. We don't need her now."

"We don't know that. Something could go wrong, and we'd need her help. Any of a thousand technical glitches to the system. And besides, the Levin girl claims she's come up with evidence of a virus in our system for which she's apparently developed a cure. She's supposedly delivering it on a flash drive or something to Julia today."

"So what do you want to do?"

"I'll talk to her," Treadwell said. "This is the endgame now, and I'll take care of it."

"I meant about Levin?"

"Get the flash drive. Whatever it takes."

41

Julia O'Connell was sitting at her desk, sure now that meeting with Betty had been a bad mistake, especially in lieu of what was going to happen first thing in the morning.

Her phone rang, and she nearly jumped out of her skin. It was Reid's cell. "Yes."

"Are you out of your mind?" Reid shouted. "Meeting with Betty Ladd?"

She said nothing.

"What did you two talk about? Now of all times; for Christ's sake, Julia."

"It was her idea. She wanted to meet outside of our offices. Said it was important."

"What was important?"

"You had me followed. Why?"

"It was Butch's call," Reid said. "And how the hell does a computer jock know the president of the exchange?"

"I met her years ago at a technology conference here in New York," Julia lied. "She was there to mentor newcomers, and she picked me along with a few others."

"And you've been pals ever since?"

"She's checked on me from time to time. But mostly it was years ago, ever since your . . . the incident between the two of you."

Reid was silent for a beat or two. "You know what's at stake."

"Of course I do. I can't get it out of my mind."

"What did she want?"

"She knew that you and I met for breakfast with Clyde and Spence, and she wanted to know what that was all about."

"And?"

"I told her that it was really none of her business. And then she wanted to know why all of us were on the floor, and I told her we were supporting our new IPO, and you wanted to have a chat with Seymour."

"And?" Reid demanded, relentless.

Julia felt as if she were being pounded into the ground, and her voice rose. "She wanted to know if it was true that we were going all cash. I told her that I didn't know, and even if I did, it wouldn't be any of her business."

"Ladd is like a fucking cobra, and she hates me, you know it," Reid said, his voice notching up a pitch again. "Why didn't you tell me or Clyde the instant she called you?"

"I don't know."

"Listen to me, you stupid fool. We're on the brink of the greatest financial coup in history. For the next twenty-four hours I don't want you going to the women's room without letting me or Clyde know."

Julia was mad. "I don't have to take this."

"You want out, then get out. But keep your fucking mouth shut, or I'll have one of Butch's pals pay you a visit. And believe me, you won't like it."

Julia was about to shout back, but Reid had hung up.

She slowly put her phone down and sat back, not an idea in the world what she could or should do next.

42

"That was intense," Heather said.

Treadwell spun around to face her. She was naked, a slight smile on her lips. "A staff problem, is all," he said.

"You're tough, and I like it. Just don't ever talk to me that way, okay?"

For once in his life he didn't know what to say.

"But whatever you're up to, I want in," she said.

43

An FBI limo brought Spencer Nast to the 34th Street heliport on a barge in the Hudson River near the Javits Convention Center just before one o'clock. The driver got out and opened the rear door.

A sleek white Sikorsky S-76 with civilian markings but piloted by a pair of air force officers was warming up, ready to get down to Washington as quickly as possible, as soon as Nast was aboard. The limo and aircraft were SOP for high government officials needing to get somewhere in a hurry and discreetly.

"My bag from the trunk?" Nast asked, getting out.

The driver, who was a Bureau special agent, hesitated for just a moment, but nodded. He went to the other side of the car, got Nast's bag out of the backseat, and brought it around.

Nast's phone rang. "In the chopper, please," he told the agent, and then answered the call. It was Sam Kolberg, the president's chief of staff, whom Nast had thought from the beginning of the campaign was nothing but a royal pain in the ass.

"I'm at the Thirty-fourth Street heliport ready to take off, if that's why you're calling."

"We're waiting, Spencer, and the president is running out of patience."

Nast bit back a sharp retort. Kolberg was technically his boss, but only technically. Reid Treadwell had been one of the president's main donors, and Reid had recommended Nast as the president's chief economic adviser.

Since Nast had political insulation, Kolberg could only retaliate in petty ways, like assigning the president's chief economist to an office not in the West Wing but over in the Eisenhower Executive Office Building, which was nothing but an ornate old pile of French Empire–style architecture.

"I'll be landing on the White House lawn in less than two hours. Miller and Nichols will be there, and we can hash out our next moves."

Kolberg started to object, but Nast held him off.

"It's around midnight now in Beijing, and I seriously doubt that the Chinese will be doing anything at this hour. So just hold on to your Jockeys, Sam."

The agent tossed Nast's bag in the backseat of the helicopter.

"Betty Ladd gave me a call a few minutes ago," Kolberg said.

Nast was about to start toward the chopper, but he pulled up short, his breath almost catching in his throat. "What'd she have to say?"

"You know that we're old friends," Kolberg said. "When she was over at Salomon Brothers getting her start, our law firm did business with her. In fact, I was assigned to do the work."

Kolberg's family law firm was one of the most prominent in San Francisco. Sam had gone to a third-tier school and graduated in the middle of his class, but since he was family, he got the position over law review grads from top schools such as Harvard who would have given their eyeteeth for it.

"When you were working for Betty, I was busting my hump for my Ph.D.—a real degree—at Penn State, existing on ramen noodles," Nast shot back. He was actually proud of what he called his gritty background.

"I don't have time for your bullshit class resentment," Kolberg shot back. "Betty's worried that you and Treadwell are thick as thieves, and she's convinced that he's trying to somehow make a buck off the China crisis. Is that true?"

"Give me a break, Sam."

"Any truth to it?"

"For Christ's sake, I had breakfast with Reid this morning. It's my job, you know, to keep up my contacts with people on the Street. He used to be my boss—past tense—but I'm no longer privy to his business plans. I'm the president's economic adviser, not a Burnham Pike employee."

"Word is you're going back as soon as you leave Washington. Maybe a good idea to keep your finger in the pot?"

"I don't know what I'm going to do. Maybe go back to teaching, or maybe stick around for a second term," Nast said. "Wouldn't that be nice, Sam? The two of us together for another four?"

"I'll discuss it with the president."

"He and Reid are fast friends, you know. Campaign contributions, support in lots of the right places. And it's not likely to end next year." Nast hesitated, loving this. "I don't think that Reid would care to hear that someone was spreading rumors."

Kolberg said nothing, and Nast ended the call.

The pilot opened his door. "We have clearance, sir," he shouted.

"Stand by, I need to make a call first," Nast said.

"Sir, we have onboard comms."

Nast turned his back on the man and speed-dialed Dammerman's cell. The COO answered on the first ring.

"Are you on your way to D.C.?"

"I'm at the heliport now. I just got a call from Sam Kolberg, who told me Betty Ladd talked to him about us. Frankly, what the woman is doing is getting me worried."

"Son of a bitch. How the hell does she know Kolberg?"

"They're old pals. But what's Reid's take on the situation? Are we still good to go?"

"She's got her thing for him, but she has nothing except her bullshit suspicions."

"I don't like it."

"Take it easy. She's been after Reid all day, and she even had a face-to-face with Julia."

"Jesus, Clyde, what the hell was that all about?"

"Trust me, everything is under control. Just take care of your end in Washington. Okay, pal?"

Dammerman was Nast's closest ally at BP, and had been from the beginning. They'd both come from blue-collar neighborhoods in the New York area: Dammerman from Queens and Nast from Garfield in Jersey.

Dammerman had been a street-corner tough, Nast a bookworm whose only social interaction in high school was the chess club.

But both of them had fought their way tooth and nail to Wall Street prominence.

"To tell the truth, Clyde, I'd rather stay here in New York when it all goes down. The guys around Farmer are going to have nervous breakdowns. It won't be pretty. Or safe. They're going to want someone to blame, and I'm the one in the catbird seat."

"Exactly why we want you down there. When the shit hits the fan, you need to keep your boss thinking that he's in charge, keep his people from looking our way. Once the dust has settled, the Chinese will get the rap, and we'll be home free. We just have to get past the first few hours after the opening bell. Trust me, we're going to end up heroes."

"Okay, I'm on my way," Nast said.

"What about your pals Nichols and Miller? Can you keep them in line?"

"We're all meeting in the Oval Office as soon as I get down there. Right now they're focused on the China thing, just like everyone else. I'm going to give them a plan that'll never go through but will sound good to the American public." *And make me a hero,* he thought.

"Less than twenty-four hours now, Spence," Dammerman said. "Stay the course."

44

Cassy popped the second flash drive—the one containing the real anti-virus program—out of her machine and palmed it as she glanced at Masters, who was on the phone, his back to her.

The woman ex-cop that Hardy had stationed across the room had pulled a chair over twenty minutes ago and was glancing at a magazine, looking up every so often.

"Is that it?" Donni asked. His eyes were wide, but he was grinning.

Cassy nodded. "Are you ready?"

"This is serious, isn't it?"

"Dead serious. We're going to take the remedy to someone who can help us. Outside the company. I don't trust most of our people upstairs. That's why I'm going to give Julia a fake drive."

Donni looked like a deer caught in the headlights of a car, his eyes wide. "Why don't you trust them?"

"I'm almost sure that the worm started right here in our system, not from outside somewhere."

"Is it Francis, do you think?"

"I don't know, but everyone is treating me like the enemy, not someone just doing her job," Cassy said. She looked away for a moment then turned back. "I want to trust Julia, but I'm not sure."

"Okay, I guess I'm your man," Donni said.

Cassy stepped over and hugged him, and as they were embracing, she slipped the correct flash drive in the back pocket of his floppy linen plants. Taped to the back of it was the password. "My hero," she whispered.

"Reluctant hero."

"Showtime," Cassy said.

They parted, and Cassy erased all traces of the fake anti-virus program from her machine. The two of them then went over to Masters's desk.

He turned and looked up. "Gotta go," he said and put down the phone.

"We're going to lunch," Cassy told him.

"Have you finished copying your program that's going to save the firm?"

Cassy held up the fake drive, and Masters reached for it.

"I'll drop it off at Julia's office on my way out. I need to explain a few things to her."

"Tell me."

"No."

Masters's eyes narrowed. "I'm your goddamn boss."

"And Ms. O'Connell is yours," Cassy said. "Now, do you want to argue about it, or can we get out of here?"

Hardy had come out of nowhere and was just suddenly there. "Is there a problem, Francis?"

"Yes, Ms. Levin has the flash drive with the anti-virus, and I volunteered to hand-carry it up to Ms. O'Connell's office, but she refused to hand it over."

"I need to tell her a few things about the program," Cassy said.

Hardy glanced at Donni, who shrank back. "No problem," he said.

"Well, get the fuck out of here," Hardy said, and he glanced over at the woman cop and nodded.

"We'll be back in a half hour," Cassy said.

"See that you are," Masters told her.

She and Donni headed out to the elevators in the corridor, passing the woman cop, who glared at them.

On the way up, Cassy punched 6 for the cafeteria floor, and then 23 for O'Connell's office. "Wait for me, and we'll leave the building together," she said. "Just don't lose that drive."

"Not a chance."

45

Cassy got off the elevator and crossed the carpeted corridor. Julia O'Connell, behind her desk in her glass-walled office, looked up, smiled, and waved her in. She seemed a little strained, as if she had heard some bad news.

This floor was busy but subdued, no noise, no one ever in a hurry. BP was one of the largest investment banks in the country, and everyone took their job seriously.

"You're finished, then?" Julia asked pleasantly.

"Yes, ma'am," Cassy said and handed over the flash drive.

"Francis said that you needed to tell me something?"

"It's encrypted, and I need to give you the password."

"Okay."

"You might want to write it down."

"I have a pretty good memory."

Cassy gave her the seventeen-character alphanumeric-symbol password. "Would you like me to repeat it?"

"It's not necessary," Julia said. "Is the password for this the same on your machine downstairs?"

"No, ma'am. I erased it. Just in case."

"This is the only copy?" Julia asked, holding up the flash drive.

"Yes," Cassy said, and she started to go, but Julia gestured her to sit down.

"Just a minute, please, if you have the time."

Cassy's fear spiked, but then she steadied herself. "Of course," she said and sat down.

"You got a bad deal at Murphy Tweed from what I was told. It won't happen here if your work pans out."

"Thank you."

"What I want to know is how you came across this virus of yours? What gave you the first clue?"

"It was fairly easy once we knew what we were looking for."

"We?"

"I meant *me*," Cassy said. "I was seeing a bunch of odd-lot trades across the board. Started about two days ago, but it's been peaking all this morning."

"What made you pick up on something like that?"

"I have a seek-and-identify program I use. It's an input to my main anti-hacking design-and-test program."

"I haven't heard of it."

"It's fairly new."

"You designed it?" Julia asked.

"Yes," Cassy said. "Anyway, as I said, I began picking up a lot of odd-lot trades, and when I went looking for the cause and the source, I came up with a pretty potent intrusion. Almost reminds me of the Stuxnet virus we and the Israelis used to mess up Iran's nuclear program, except this one isn't attacking industrial equipment, it's going after our market computer systems."

"Do you have a name for your program?"

"My Fair Lady."

Julia chuckled. "Why that name?"

"It's old-fashioned, but it's always been my favorite musical."

"Problem solved."

"Maybe," Cassy said. "But this thing is spreading really fast. So far it's only in our system, almost as if someone was testing it on us first before releasing it."

"Any idea who's doing it to us?"

"It has the look of something the Amsterdam tribe would cook up just for the fun of it."

"Releasing it where?" Julia said, and she seemed a little pale to Cassy.

"I don't know. But I suppose if it were someone in our company, we might send it to a rival's mainframe."

Julia sat back. "Good Lord, is that what you think is happening?"

"No, I'm not accusing anyone. I was just saying something like it wouldn't be the worst-case scenario."

"What would?"

"Sending it out into the world."

"Where?"

"Just down the street to the New York Stock Exchange for starters," Cassy said.

Julia sat still for a long moment or two. Then she picked up the flash drive. "And this would stop it?"

Cassy nodded. "I'm pretty sure, it would."

Again Julia hesitated for a second or two. "Who else have you told about this?" she asked.

"Just Francis, and Mr. Hardy was there before I left the floor. He heard some of it."

"How about any of your coworkers?"

"Most of them know I've been working on an anti-virus program, but that's what we all do every day. Keeps the firm out of trouble."

Julia smiled. "Go have your lunch now. I'll take care of this. It's what I do."

Cassy got up and started to leave.

"Thank you," Julia said. "Very much."

EIGHT

KIDNAPPED

46

Hardy was at his desk trying to think out what was apparently coming at them tomorrow. Dammerman hadn't said anything specific, but he and the top brass had been on tenterhooks for the past week or so, and especially this morning.

It was no big deal to him to take down the Levin broad—orders were orders, and it was what he was getting paid for—but it made no real sense. Evidently she had pissed off someone on the top floor badly enough to order her elimination. Whatever she had done had to have been large. Kidnapping and murder were the real deal, a hell of a lot more real than extortion, racketeering, or money laundering. People could get serious jail time.

But he had put a few things in place to cover his own ass. To begin with he'd made sure that whenever and wherever he and Dammerman had spoken there were no recording devices, and especially no wires. A few years ago a geek friend downtown had sold him a cigarette pack–size device that could detect any electronic emissions within a twenty-five-foot range.

"Just keep your voice low enough so that someone outside that range can't hear you," the kid had told him.

But in all that time, and for all the things he'd done for Dammerman and the firm, he'd never thought he needed the detector till now.

His phone rang, and he picked it up. "Hardy."

It was one of his lieutenants, the same one who'd followed O'Connell. "Levin and Imani are just leaving the building."

"Follow them, and as soon as you find out what direction they're taking, call me back. And if they take a cab, get the number and let me know immediately."

"Got it," the man said and hung up.

Like a lot of ex-cops, at the beginning of his career Hardy had been a gung-ho athlete, in fantastic physical shape. But as the years had gone by, switching from being a cop on a beat on foot to a detective sitting on his ass in a car on a stakeout, he'd gotten soft around the edges. A little paunch, a little weakness in the knees, for which he compensated with a short temper.

Lately he'd been thinking about getting out. Maybe heading down to Miami Beach, something he'd talked about ever since he could remember. Summers here were okay, but the winters were bullshit.

But the money at BP made up for a lot of snowy days and freezing-your-ass-off nights.

His phone rang. "South on Nassau Street."

It was not the same direction Julia had taken—that had been to the west—and he had to wonder if they were going to meet with the head of the NYSE, like Julia had. But it didn't matter.

"Stick with them until I call you," Hardy said.

"Yes, sir."

Hardy broke the connection and dialed Bykov's burner phone. The Russian answered on the first ring.

"Yes."

"They're on the move."

"Where?"

"On foot south on Nassau Street. Do you know where I'm talking about?"

"Of course," Bykov said. "Is the op a go?"

Military asshole, Hardy thought. "The op is a go."

47

Bykov had a map of Manhattan folded to show Fulton Street and the Financial District, the Brighton Beach operators at his side.

He stabbed a finger on the location of the BP building on Nassau Street. "They're heading south on foot."

"Are they going somewhere we can intercept them?" Anosov asked. He was the hardest of the two, and in his Spetsnaz days had been very efficient, especially in urban infiltrations.

"Unknown. But they are being shadowed in case they take a cab or perhaps the subway. I'll let you know when you're entrain."

"I want unrestricted mission orders."

"Your only order is to make her disappear, permanently," Bykov replied.

"What about her companion, the kid?"

"Him as well. But the woman may be carrying a flash drive—it's a small device—"

"I know what it is," Anosov said.

"If you find it, destroy it." Bykov looked up from the map. "It would be unfortunate if I were to learn at some date in the future that the information contained on the drive were to surface somewhere. *Ponimayu?*" *Understand?*

"Understood."

"Then *udachi*." *Good luck*. "And go with God."

– – –

Anosov and Valentin Panov took the elevator down to the parking garage, where they got their Cadillac Escalade SUV with deeply tinted windows from the guest parking spot. Valentin was behind the wheel, Leonid riding shotgun.

Before they started the engine, Leonid took out the photographs of Cassy and Donni and studied them one by one, handing each to Valentin as he finished.

"She's a good-looking woman," Leonid said, looking up.

Valentin grinned. "Be a shame to eliminate her when we're finished."

Anosov had been thinking much the same since the first time he'd gotten a look at the photos. "What do you have in mind?"

"She's a marketable commodity."

"So is the boy with her."

"We don't have a contract on him."

"So?"

"When we're done, we could clean them up and send both of them across the border to Canada—it's soft enough—and then I was thinking we might get a good price with the Saudis. A package deal?"

"A hundred thousand?" Anosov asked.

"Each," Panov said, and they laughed.

"Go," Leonid said.

Panov started the Caddy, backed out of the slot, and once outside, turned onto Platt, headed west.

"What's our play?" Panov asked.

"Get over to Nassau, do whatever you have to do to get ahead of them, and then double-park. I'll get out. I don't think we'll have much trouble with either of them, especially if I let them see my gun."

48

Cassy and Donni stopped for the light at Maiden Lane, just a couple of blocks down from BP. The streets weren't as narrow here as they were south of Wall, and traffic was heavy both on Nassau as well as on the sidewalks.

Cassy took out her phone and dialed the NYSE main number. She was frightened now, and her hand shook.

"Are you okay?" Donni asked.

She glanced at him as the number rang. His eyes were wide, and he acted as strung out as she was. "Look back and see if Hardy's got someone following us," she said.

He turned around. "Not that I can see."

The NYSE operator answered, and Cassy asked to speak with Betty Ladd.

"Who is calling, please?"

Cassy gave her name.

"One moment, please."

The light changed, and for some reason Cassy's eye was drawn to a white Cadillac Escalade with New York plates. The side windows were so deeply tinted that she could hardly see inside, and she only caught a glimpse of the driver and maybe one person on the passenger side when it passed them heading south.

Betty came on almost immediately. "Good afternoon," she said.

"I'm on my lunch hour, and I need to talk to you about something."

"Is it about work?" Betty asked, her voice suddenly sharp.

"I think so, but I'm a little confused. And scared."

"Okay. Where are you right now?"

"A couple blocks south of the office. I could be at the exchange in just a few minutes, if you have the time for us."

"Who's with you?"

"One of my friends in the DCCS."

"Okay, listen, stay right where you are, and I'll send a car for you. Okay?"

"I don't want to make a fuss; anyway, no one is following us, and we can be there faster than you could send a car to us."

Pedestrians were surging around them. Donni took her arm and as they started across the street the traffic light counted down from eight seconds.

"I'll leave word at security out front and have Jennifer waiting inside to take you upstairs," Betty said. "But for goodness sake, can you at least give me a hint?"

"I'm bringing something for you to see. It's important."

"Okay. I'll be here, but calm down, okay?"

"Okay," Cassy said, her heart racing.

49

"That was them on the corner," Anosov said.

Valentin took the next turn onto Broadway, where he headed south, and then turned west at the next intersection back to Nassau, each time getting lucky with the lights.

Anosov watched from the door mirror. "Got them," he said. He took out his Steyr, checked the load one final time, and stuffed it in his belt on the left side, out of sight beneath his jacket.

When the two were less than a half block away, Leonid got of the car and opened the rear door so that it was just slightly ajar.

He put his right hand beneath his jacket, ready to open the coat far enough so that the weapon would be clearly visible to both the woman and the guy.

Pedestrian traffic was heavy, and for a moment Leonid lost them. He stepped away from the car to get a better look.

50

Cassy spotted the same white Caddy SUV she'd seen passing them, a bulky, foreign-looking man wearing jeans, a white shirt or pullover, and a dark suit jacket standing beside it, and she pulled up short.

"What?" Donni said.

"The guy by the SUV. I think he's one of Hardy's people."

"Oh shit, oh shit," Donni said.

The man spotted them.

"Run," Cassy said, swiveling on her heel.

Donni was frozen to the spot.

"Run, goddamnit!"

"Where?"

"I don't care, just run!" Cassy said. "I'll meet you at the stock exchange."

Donni turned and sprinted away, and the man by the Caddy suddenly shoved a pedestrian aside and headed toward Cassy, who was rooted to her spot for a long moment. She managed to speed-dial Ben's number, then turned and headed the same way Donni was running.

Ben answered on the second ring. "Hi, darling, what's up?"

"A man in a white Caddy SUV was waiting for me and Donni and now he's heading my way. I think he might be one of Hardy's people, and I think he means to kidnap me."

"Listen to me, Cassy. I want you to head someplace more public than a street corner, maybe a bank lobby that will have security."

"I'm running."

"Tell me everything you can. You said a white Caddy SUV. Plates?"

"New York," Cassy said, and she gave Ben the first three numbers.

"One man?"

"On the passenger side, chasing me. Another driving."

"Describe the man chasing you."

"Dark, large, wearing jeans and a jacket. I think he's foreign."

"I have you on your GPS tracker. You're two and a half blocks south of BP; run there if you think you can make it."

Cassy looked over her shoulder. The man was shockingly close, less than thirty feet away now, and gaining. "I can't make it, Ben. He's right here."

"Stop right now. Turn around and take his picture and send it to me. Then start yelling. Cause a public scene. That will stop him."

"Ben—"

"Do what I say, Cassy, your life depends on it."

She pulled up short, turned around and took the man's photograph, and hit the *send* button.

He was on top of her.

She raised both hands over her head. Her heart was racing, and she was sure that her legs were going to give way.

An ambulance, its siren blaring, came across Nassau on Maiden Lane at the same time the man reached her. He opened his jacket so that she could see the gun in his belt.

"There'll be no trouble, Ms. Levin, if you will come with me. I promise that we will not harm you. But if you make noise, we will."

"What do you want?"

"Something that doesn't belong to you from your office."

"I don't have the flash drive. I left it with my boss."

Leonid took Cassy's arm, and turned and started back toward the Cadillac.

She tried to pull away, but he was too strong. "You son

of a bitch," she screamed at the top of her lungs. "Help me! Help!"

"We're going to the precinct station," the man said, loudly enough so that the few passersby who were taking notice could hear. "With or without the handcuffs."

She didn't know what to do.

"Then we're going to fetch your boyfriend."

51

Ben had been working on the blueprints with Chip when Cassy's call came in. She'd been abducted. But the man who had taken her had not been smart enough to disable her cell phone and to this point he was hearing everything: her screaming, his impersonating a cop, the traffic noises, and the ambulance. He'd jotted down the time it had passed Cassy's position.

Chip, knowing that something was happening, had looked up from the drawings but said nothing.

"Donni doesn't have anything to do with this, and Hardy and Masters both know it," Cassy shouted.

Ben put his hand over the phone's mouthpiece. "I need a jet up to LaGuardia ASAP, and a chopper standing by to get me over to the Hudson Yard heliport."

"You'll need a car," Faircloth said, as he made a call.

"Yes."

"A driver?"

"No, but I'll need a Beretta and a couple of mags." The 9mm Beretta 92F was the old standard-issue military pistol. It wasn't sophisticated, but it was reliable out to around ten feet, the range of most successful sidearm gun battles.

"On it," Faircloth said.

Ben heard something that sounded like a car door opening, then Cassy's voice, much calmer now.

"Where are you guys taking me?"

"We mean you no harm, Ms. Levin," the man said. "Trust me."

"You're not cops," Cassy said. "You're goddamn Russians."

"If you don't start cooperating, I'll have to hurt you. Do you understand this?"

"I understand that you're kidnapping me. But why, for Christ's sake? I don't have any money."

The sounds changed, and Ben realized that she was inside the car now.

"But if you guys are spies for the KGB or something, I don't have the flash drive. I gave it to my boss."

The Russian said nothing, but the car door was shut.

"You might as well let me go, and you can tell Butch Hardy for me that he's a fucking idiot, and I quit as of right now."

"*Yeb vas! Det telefon!*" *Fuck off! The telephone!* another man said.

"A car is coming to get you to Andrews," Faircloth said. "A crew is scrambling a V-SP, it's the best we can do on such short notice." The aircraft was an older Gulfstream designated a C-37A/V that was used for VIP transport. Cruising at nearly five hundred miles per hour, the flight time to LaGuardia would be around a half hour, including takeoff and landing.

"Bastard!" Cassy shouted, and the signal from her phone ceased.

52

The Russian in the backseat with her had used a penknife to pry off the protective case on Cassy's phone, then the rear cover. He took out the SIM card and battery, both of which he tossed out the window.

"Letat"—fly—he told the driver, who immediately pulled away from the curb and merged with traffic.

"Do we need the kid who was with her?"

"Da. He went around the corner on Maiden Lane."

Panov glanced in the rearview mirror then suddenly made a left at the next side street, angry drivers honking their horns.

Cassy was thrown against Anosov. She reared back and slammed her fist into his cheek. He hit her with his fist on the side of her head, and she momentarily fuzzed out.

"Suka!" Bitch!

Panov laughed. "Do you need some help back there?"

"Drive!"

53

Donni had never been so frightened in his entire life, not even in Montana when he was in high school and three of the jocks from the football team cornered him beneath the bleachers and were going to beat him up because he had mouthed off. A janitor had come along and the boys had left, but for the rest of that year the pressure on him had been nearly unbearable.

It wasn't until college at Stanford when he was fifteen and realized that he was very smart, and that there were others just like him in California, that he had come out of his shell.

But at this moment he knew that he was running for his life, and that the only way he could ever help Cassy was to get the flash drive over to Betty Ladd at the NYSE.

He was just a block away when he looked over his shoulder and spotted the white Caddy coming around the corner practically on top of him. He couldn't believe how fast it was happening. He'd never been much of an athlete, and right now he was running like a cripple.

The light was changing against him, and he doubled his efforts to get to the other side, his only concern the Caddy behind him.

At the last moment, in the middle of the street, he looked up in time to see a garbage truck, racing to beat the light, right there.

Then nothing.

54

Panov pulled up at the red light just as Donni ran into the street and was struck full-on by the garbage truck, going way over the speed limit. His body was knocked to the street, and before the driver could react, one of the massive front wheels ran over Donni's body, crushing the skull.

Cassy watched it happen, all the air emptying out of the world, all of her emotions completely gone, so that she could only sit open-mouthed in disbelief.

"My fault," she mumbled. "My God."

"He shouldn't have run," Anosov said. "And there is no God."

Cassy turned to him. "You unutterable bastard," she said softly.

The light changed, and Panov had to maneuver around the truck and the body. There were no sirens yet.

"What's so fucking important that he had to die? He never hurt anyone in his life."

"I don't care," Anosov said. "You took something from your company that wasn't yours to take."

"I gave it to my boss, you fucking freak!" Cassy shrieked, and she turned away.

Anosov grabbed her by the base of her skull and forced

her to face him. "I'll only tell you this one time, little girl. If you ever raise your hand or your voice to me again, I will make you wish that you'd never been born."

Cassy stared at him.

"Do you understand me?"

She said nothing.

"We're taking you someplace where we're going to fuck you. Me first, and then the others, if I give them the go-ahead, which I may not if you cooperate. Do you also understand this?"

Cassy managed a smile, and she shook her head. "*You* are so fucked, and you don't even realize it yet."

55

Nichols and Miller rode in the backseat of a limousine on the way over from the Federal Reserve to the White House. Traffic was heavy as usual, but not as heavy as the mood of both men.

"I hope he buys what we're suggesting," Nichols said.

"I hope he understands it," Miller replied.

"Spencer will be able to explain it to him," Nichols said. He leaned forward. "Is anyone following us?" he asked.

The driver, in a black suit and white shirt, glanced at the secretary of the Treasury's image in the rearview mirror. "Not to this point, Mr. Secretary," he said.

Nichols sat back, only slightly appeased. It wasn't every day that the two most powerful men in the nation's financial apparatus visited the White House at the same time. If the media got wind of it, questions that neither man wanted to answer publicly would be asked.

They were admitted through the west gate, past the Eisenhower Building, well out of sight of the press room. An aide met them at the door and escorted them to the Roosevelt

Room, directly across the hall from the Oval Office, where they took their places at the conference table.

"FDR rescued us from chaos," Miller said. "As bad as the Great Depression was, his New Deal literally saved the day."

"He didn't have the same trouble selling T-bonds as we're having right now," Nichols shot back. "And this is just the first of our problems."

"Unless we raise the rates, as you suggested."

"How high is the question," Nichols said. He was genuinely worried, more now than any time in the past. "I don't want us to come across as some third-rate Third World country. And our debt load is already so high, adding to it would put our interest repayments higher than our military budget."

Kolberg hesitated at the open door for just a moment or two before coming in. "For your information, gentlemen, this room is named after both FDR and Teddy," he said with his usual sour attitude.

"We stand corrected," Nichols said. "We have a lot to cover this afternoon. Will the president be joining us shortly?"

"He's on the phone now, but he wants you two to be point men for any crises that might develop. Spencer will call the behind-the-scenes shots."

"Nast is nothing but a Wall Street shill," Nichols said, not wanting to believe what he was hearing. He and Miller exchanged a glance.

"Not my decision," Kolberg said. "He has the president's complete trust."

"Everyone on the Hill actively hates him," Nichols said.

"And his pals at Burnham Pike are going to use him to take advantage of the Chinese problem," Miller added. "Mark my words."

Kolberg shook his head. "It may come as a surprise to

you that I agree. I heard about the bullshit he pulled at Penn State to get a tenured professorship."

"And now he advises the president of the United States on economic policy."

"As I said, it's not my decision. Nast was suggested by Reid Treadwell, who was, and still is, one of the president's strongest supporters."

"Treadwell's out for only one thing—Treadwell," Miller said. "You know how he shorted the market in the mortgage meltdown crises in '08, and BP came out smelling like a rose. It was a wonder he wasn't indicted for that move."

"Could be he's doing the same thing again," Nichols said. "Or don't you read between the lines?"

"We've heard the rumors that BP has been liquidating its stocks, bonds, anything else they can get rid of, and going to cash," Kolberg admitted. "Then spreading it around in small amounts so that their deposits are protected by the FDIC. But they've broken no laws, right?"

"You're right," Miller said. "But as a lawyer you ought to be able to see how close it comes to being outright fraud."

"Enlighten me, Mr. Chairman," Kolberg said dryly.

"The FDIC guarantees up to a quarter of a million dollars per account. But it's not tax money, the funds come from what the banks pay in fees. So if all hell breaks loose the deposits will be safe."

"I know that," Kolberg said.

Miller sat forward to emphasize his point. "You have to ask why Treadwell is taking his bank to cash right now. Does he know something the rest of us don't? Or could it be something else?"

"What are you suggesting?" Kolberg asked, obviously taking care with his words.

"All I'm saying is that Treadwell is a smart man, maybe too smart, and Spencer Nast is his, always has been," Miller said.

An aide came into the room, said something in Kolberg's ear, and stepped back.

"Mr. Chairman, the governor of the People's Bank of China tried to reach you at your office; his call was patched through to here," Kolberg said. "Would you like to take it in private?"

"No," Miller said. "Do it here and now with the three of us and the *two* Roosevelts."

Kolberg hit the flashing light on the telephone console, and Liu Feng came on the speakerphone.

"My greetings to you, Mr. Chairman," he said, his English almost without accent. He had studied at Princeton and received his economics Ph.D. from Stanford. "You are at the White House, and I suspect that you are not the only government official present. Am I correct?"

"You are, Governor Liu," Miller said. "I'm with Secretary of the Treasury Bob Nichols and White House Chief of Staff Sam Kolberg. We have been discussing what is currently happening in Beijing."

"I would be more concerned about what is happening in your own country. Namely, the failure of your Treasury bond auction. Maybe we talk freely?"

Miller glanced at Nichols and Kolberg. Chinese intel had to be damn good. News of the auction debacle hadn't broken yet in the U.S. media. "We'll figure that out. What worries me most is that the PBOC won't bail out its commercial banks that are teetering on the edge of failure, which puts your economy in grave jeopardy."

"The banks having trouble are themselves to blame, along with our own—at present—incompetent government planners. We are the People's Bank of China, serving our population, not the imbeciles who run the commercial banks. Let Mr. Hua's government repair the problem it has created."

"Governor Liu, this is Secretary Nichols."

"Good afternoon, sir."

"Won't the PBOC's noninvolvement not only cause a large number of Chinese commercial banks to fail, but possibly create a panic that would spread worldwide? Perhaps even worse than what happened because of our own poor banking practices in 2008?"

"Mr. Secretary, I believe that your immediate concern is that Hua's government will unload the two trillion dollars' worth of your T-bonds we hold. It would give the government immediate cash, but it would severely devalue your bonds even further than is happening at this very moment. The effects of that move would be worse, as you say, than the panic of 2008."

"We are working the issue, Mr. Chairman," Nichols said.

"Then we must agree that we have a common problem," Liu said. "Too much debt. Perhaps, then, it might be a good thing to go through the purgative of a global depression."

"I'd prefer that we not," Miller broke in. "Such catastrophes not only lead to much suffering but as a result of the 1929 crash and the depression of the thirties, we were led into World War Two."

"We may find out, despite our best efforts, Mr. Liu," Nichols added.

The silence hung heavy until Kolberg spoke up.

"Secretary of State Marcus Conwell has been trying to reach out to you and Mr. Hua without success."

"Mr. Conwell is a politician. He and Chairman Hua understand each other. But I prefer to speak with economists, who understand that the worldwide debt is out of hand. If we need to go through fire to be rid of it, then so be it."

Miller had no idea what to say in reply. It sounded to him that the man was talking about war. Nuclear war!

"It is the middle of the night here," Liu said. "I must get my rest."

The connection was broken.

"Jesus Christ, did I hear what I thought I just heard?" Miller said.

Kolberg got to his feet. "I'll brief the president." He'd brought a file folder with him, and he laid it on the table. "This is Spencer's plan, and it's impressive."

"You can't be serious," Nichols said. "The Treasury secretary and the Fed chairman are the ones to make those kinds of plans, the same as they did in '08. Not some Wall Street puppet like Nast."

Kolberg left the room without another word.

"We need to go to the Hill," Miller said. "Get the Speaker's attention."

"Speculative disasters have never moved Congress, and you know it," Nichols said.

"Well, something's going to give, and when it does, everything will fall into a bucket of shit, and you know that too," Miller said. "We can kid ourselves that we have the resources to prop up the system like we did in '08, but we don't. We simply don't."

NINE

THE FLASH DRIVE

56

They got off the Shore Parkway in Brooklyn and went down a street below an elevated railway that was filled with shops like the Taste of Russia, a furrier, and a nail salon. The streets were alive with traffic—every second car, it seemed, was a Mercedes—and the sidewalks were filled with people of all ages and sizes, including grandmothers wearing head scarves.

Normal, everyday families, Cassy thought, and that alone frightened her almost as much as the man sitting next to her. Bad things could actually happen even in a place like this. And she knew in her heart of hearts that even if she could manage to power down her window, stick her head out, and scream at the top of her lungs, people might look up, but they would do nothing to help her. They would mind their own business.

Come to me, Ben, she almost mouthed the words, *I need you.*

Panov turned down a broad avenue lined with five- and six-story brownstone apartment buildings, the traffic here much lighter, the sidewalks empty.

Two blocks farther, he turned down a narrower street and stopped at a tall, steel mesh gate. Behind it was the trash-filled backyard of a two-story brick building with long green awnings shading the windows on both floors.

A stocky man in jeans and a tight-fitting light green V-neck sweater, a big pistol stuck in his belt, came out and unlocked the gate, swinging it inward far enough so that they could drive through. He closed and locked it again.

Panov parked next to a low wooden shed that butted up to the back of the building, and Anosov got out on the driver's side, holding on to Cassy's arm and dragging her with him.

"So this is the *putana*?" the man in the green sweater asked, his Russian accent thick. The word meant *whore* or *prostitute*.

Anosov laughed, said something in Russian, and Panov and the man in the green sweater grinned and nodded.

"But she's a handful, Vasili," Anosov said. "Maybe you'll need help."

They went into the house, Anosov's grip firm enough on Cassy's arm that it hurt, even though she was not resisting.

They went up two steps and through the back door into a short pantry hall that opened onto a large kitchen. A half dozen men, mostly in jeans and T-shirts, were seated around a large round table, eating what looked like some sort of stew, with several loaves of bread from which large pieces had been torn, and big bottles of beer with porcelain caps.

A man was taking a beer out of a refrigerator, while a large, shirtless man with a huge belly and a massive hairy chest was at the stove stirring something in a big pot.

The odors of grease and of unwashed male bodies were nearly overpowering, and Cassy gagged.

One of the men at the table laughed. "I don't think she's going to like Mikhail's cooking," he said.

The others laughed too.

"Maybe I'll have to give her something else to eat," the man at the stove said.

"Do you want something to eat or drink?" Anosov asked.

Cassy shook her head, unable to speak.

"I'm taking our guest to the attic room, and until I give

the word, it's hands off, *gospoda*," Anosov said. "Am I clear?"

Another man appeared at the door across the kitchen, and he pulled up short, his eyes all over Cassy. He grinned. "Nice merchandise," he said. He was tall and on the slender side, a pistol stuck in his belt.

"Am I clear?" Anosov repeated.

"Yes, sir," everyone responded, obviously not liking it.

"Just relax," Anosov said. "We have the rest of this day and all night, so you'll get your chance."

His grip still tight on Cassy's arm, he led her across the room, brushing the man at the door aside. They went back through what was a dining room with a long table that could easily seat a dozen, and then into the living room with a lot of overstuffed furniture and out into the front stair hall.

All the windows in the front of the house were covered by heavy drapes, only a small amount of light coming from the outside, completely blocking anyone from seeing what was happening in here, and Cassy's despair deepened.

A chair and a side table with a half-full ashtray, a couple of Russian-language magazines, and a cell phone were set up in a corner of the stair hall. The man who'd opened the gate for them was the rear-door guard, and the man with the gun who'd come into the kitchen was the front-door guard. The place was a fortress.

She didn't resist as they went upstairs, but Anosov never let go of her arm.

A half dozen doors opened off the corridor that ran the length of the second floor, at the far end of which was a bathroom, its door open.

Halfway down the hall, Anosov reached up and pulled a cord that lowered a set of folding stairs, the spring twanging.

"Up the stairs," Anosov said, and Cassy climbed up on

all fours into an attic, with rough boards for a floor and open roof beams that sloped down to the eaves. At the front a small window let in some light, while at the other end a room that looked like a large closet or storage space with a thick door had been constructed on one side.

As Anosov came up the stairs, Cassy had a wild thought that she should kick him in the face, and then somehow make her way down to the front door and make her escape.

But she stepped back instead, and Anosov joined her.

"You missed an opportunity just now," he said. "Too bad."

"What do you want with me?"

"The flash drive you stole from your bank."

"I told you that I gave it to Ms. O'Connell. She's my boss. You can check with her."

"First I'll search you, just to make sure."

Cassy spread her arms. "Be my guest, you fucking pig."

Anosov laughed, then took her arm and led her to the door at the rear of the attic, where he undid the latch and opened it.

The room was small, less than ten feet on a side with the sharply sloping roof beams on the left, beneath which was a narrow cot with only a rough blanket and a dirty pillow. A portable plastic toilet, like campers used, was set up in the opposite corner. There were no lights nor a window. With the door closed it would be like sleeping in a coffin, and Cassy had to shudder.

"Take your clothes off," Anosov said, letting her go when they were inside.

"Are you going to rape me?" Cassy demanded, her voice a lot stronger than she felt.

"Later. Right now I want to see if you have the flash drive."

Cassy hesitated for a moment. She was frightened and angry.

"Take your clothes off," Anosov said.

She took off her blouse and handed it to Anosov, who searched the pocket and the folds of the cloth before he tossed it aside. She took off her bra, and he checked it the same as he had the blouse.

This was worse then she'd expected it would be. She was naked from the waist up, and she'd never felt more vulnerable in her life than right now.

"Everything," Anosov said.

Cassy sat on the edge of the cot to take off her gray Sketchers sneakers, which she handed to Anosov, who checked them before tossing them on the floor.

Then she stood up and took off her khaki trousers and her panties and tossed them to the Russian. "You got what you wanted, now get out of here and leave me alone."

"Not quite," Anosov said, checking the trousers' pockets before tossing them and the panties aside.

"I've got nothing!" Cassy shrieked.

"You were telling the truth, after all," Anosov said. He left the room and closed the door, the sound of the latch going home loud.

Cassy rolled over, her knees up to her chest, and she began to cry.

– – –

Downstairs, Anosov phoned Bykov. "She doesn't have a flash drive."

"Are you sure?"

"Da," he said.

57

Chip Faircloth drove Ben over to Joint Base Andrews. Once they'd presented their IDs and were cleared through the gate, he headed to the hangar where the Gulfstream's two-man air force crew were warming up the VIP jet's engines.

"What the hell would the Russians want with Cassy?" Chip asked.

"She's been having some kind of an issue at work, and whatever it is she's apparently carrying a flash drive with something on it."

"Industrial and technology secrets I can understand, but investment banking? Maybe the accounts of some heavy players they want to hack into."

"Could be one of their own, squirreling away money they want to keep from someone in the Kremlin."

"But they didn't take her cell phone until she let you know that the Russians had New York plates and were taking her somewhere—Brighton Beach is the obvious guess. It's a Russian enclave in Brooklyn. Of course you'll go running to save her, and maybe that's the real reason they took her. They want you."

Ben had thought the same thing. "W?" he said.

"You're *the* key player," Chip said. "They grab you, and they think they'd have the ship."

Ben glanced at his friend. "I'm going to find out."

Chip nodded. "I almost pity the poor bastards," he said. "But seriously, buddy, I can arrange to have some muscle back you up. A couple extra guns might come in handy."

"They'd just kill her and scatter," Ben said. "I'm doing this one alone."

"Your call. But I'm better at intel than you are, so I'm riding up with you."

– – –

The pilot was in the cockpit ready for takeoff when Ben and Chip Faircloth were hustled aboard and took their seats.

Before they were buckled in, the first officer had closed and dogged the hatch. "You guys ready?"

"Let's go," Chip said. "And let us know when I can use my laptop and cell phone."

"Give us about ten minutes to get to altitude," the man said. His name tag read SCOTT. He looked like he was barely out of high school.

They were rolling toward the taxiway before Scott even took his seat.

"Replay what Cassy sent you before her phone went dead," Chip said.

Ben took out his phone and hit *replay,* and they listened as the Gulfstream was cleared for immediate takeoff and accelerated down the runway.

Chip had powered up his laptop, and though he wasn't on the internet yet, he could take notes.

He jotted down the first three digits of the New York plate and transferred the photograph of the man who'd grabbed Cassy from Ben's phone.

There'll be no trouble, Ms. Levin, if you will come with me, the man in the photograph said.

"Definitely Russian," Chip said. "But wait, go back."

Ben backed up to just after Cassy had taken the photograph and the siren passed.

"An ambulance," Chip said. "Continue."

I don't have the flash drive, Cassy said. *I left it with my boss.*

Cars were passing, and what sounded like a truck rumbled by.

You son of a bitch, Cassy screamed. *Help me! Help!*

We're going to the precinct station.

"He's no cop," Ben said.

"Maybe not. But it's something we can check," Chip told him.

Less than ninety seconds later the sounds changed, and a car door opened.

I understand that you're kidnapping me, Cassy said. *But why, for Christ's sake? I don't have any money.*

Moments later the car door shut.

You might as well let me go, and you can tell Butch Hardy for me that he's a fucking idiot, and I quit as of right now.

Yeb vas! Det telefon!

Bastard! Cassy shouted, and the signal ended.

"Play it again, from the beginning," Chip said.

Ben did, and Chip took a few more notes until it ended. "Definitely Russians, and they are almost certainly taking her somewhere in Brighton Beach. Finding them, let alone digging them out, won't be easy."

"If we go in, sirens blaring, they'll just kill her and get rid of the body," Ben said. "I'm doing this alone."

"I agree. But not until we come up with some decent intel for you. Brighton Beach may not be that big, but two guys hunkered down with one woman somewhere will be like looking for a needle in the proverbial haystack."

"So we change the odds."

"First, who is Butch Hardy?"

"I think he's chief of security for Burnham Pike, the bank she works at."

"She mentioned giving a flash drive to her boss. Maybe we can start there."

"No."

"Why not?"

"I'm not sure, except that she was having trouble at work, and it was really getting to her. If she was afraid that the bank's chief of security had ordered her kidnapping, and his priority was getting a flash drive Cassy supposedly had on her, asking for their help could make things worse."

"Okay, flash drive means computer information," Chip said. "You've said that she works for the bank's cybersecurity division. So she might have found out something she wasn't supposed to find out, copied it on the flash drive, and was trying to get away without being caught. So where was she going?"

"She was heading south on Nassau," Ben said.

"Inside the Financial District. Does she know anyone outside of Burnham Pike? Someone working at another bank?"

"She told me once that her folks were friends with the woman who's now the president of the New York Stock Exchange."

"That's where she was going," Chip said. "We have something to work on now."

"No cops," Ben said.

"I hear you, my friend."

"Good."

"But if you want me to back off, forget about it."

"Intel, Chip, nothing more."

Chip started to protest, but Ben held him off.

"This will get real ugly real fast, and I won't be reading anyone their rights. Do you understand what I'm saying?"

Chip took a moment or two before he answered. "The Russian mob never works alone. The odds will be against you. And all it takes is one lucky shot."

"I'm not talking about just the Russians."

58

Eight minutes from takeoff, they were climbing above ten thousand feet and had turned northeast toward New York City when the copilot turned around in his right seat. "You guys are good to go," he called back.

Chip connected with the internet and began his search while Ben replayed Cassy's frantic phone call one more time. When he was finished, he brought up the photograph of the Russian kidnapper.

He stared into the man's eyes for a long time, his anger barely below the surface. Whatever happened before, starting at this instant in time the Russian was a walking dead man.

59

Heather was relentless and so wild she was nearly out of control, and at one point in their lovemaking for the second time, Treadwell was nearing some limit he'd never known existed.

When they finally parted, he rolled over on his back and tried to catch his breath. "Jesus Christ," he mumbled.

Heather laughed. "Is that good or bad?"

Treadwell had to laugh too. "Better than good, but you damned near killed me."

"I think I scratched your back. Maybe even drew some blood."

"I'm not a bit surprised," Treadwell said. "But seriously, you need to stick around town for a while."

"Our stock is going to hell, just like the market, so I might as well stay here to see how it pans out."

In the morning she, along with a lot of other stupid bastards, weren't going to be so happy at how things turned out. Except for the investors BP serviced. They'd be calling him the savior. The miracle worker. The God almighty of the market.

Heather poked him in the side. "Hey, earth to Reid," she said. "Where'd you just go?"

"Sorry. A lot going on today."

"You get laid twice, and you forgot me already?"

He rolled over and kissed her. "A thousand apologies. Won't happen again, promise. By tomorrow I'll be a different man."

She kissed him back, then drew away, a mysterious look on her face. "You have a virus in your system and a person named Levin has the antidote on a flash drive, right?" she said. "You were reading the riot act to someone named Julia—I'm guessing she's your head of IT, the one on the exchange floor this morning. And she talked to Betty Ladd, who Daddy and I met. And Betty hates you. And you threatened Julia with Butch's pals paying her a visit if she didn't keep her mouth shut. Would that be Butch Hardy, your chief of security?"

"It's complicated."

She propped herself up on an elbow. "I'm sure it is. But from where I was sitting in the cheap seats, you sounded like a gangster."

Treadwell grinned. "Macho Wall Street bullshit."

"What's going on?"

"We're in the middle of something pretty delicate. Something I can't talk about just now. Understand?"

"The bathroom door was open, and I heard just about everything. You were pissed off big-time. Sounds more than delicate to me."

His cell phone buzzed, indicating an incoming text. He

got it from the nightstand and opened the message. It was from Butch, and the news wasn't good. *Send my car,* he texted back.

"Bad news?" Heather asked.

"No, just difficult," Treadwell said, and he got out of bed. "Sorry, but I gotta go."

"You said that you're on the brink of—what'd you call it? 'The biggest financial coup in history'? So tell me about it, I can keep my mouth shut."

"I wish I could, really. But it involves a client, and sharing that kind of information with anyone is strictly a no-no."

"I can help you, Reid, and I think you know it," Heather said. "Let me in."

"I'll think about it," Treadwell said. He gathered his clothes off the floor and headed for the bathroom.

"With the right incentive, maybe I won't keep my mouth shut after all. Betty Ladd seemed like a genuine person."

Treadwell stopped and turned back to her. "That would be the biggest mistake of your life. Trust me on that one."

She just looked at him with a half smile.

In the bathroom with the door closed, he splashed some water on his face, gargled with mouthwash, and then got dressed. But it was only when he was finished that he realized he'd left his cell phone on the nightstand.

"Son of a bitch," he said half under his breath and he went out to find Heather sitting on the edge of the bed, his cell phone in hand. "What the fuck do you think you're doing?"

She turned and looked up at him, this time her smile broad. "Hardy says Levin is gone and the kid is missing. What's it mean?"

"Wall Street shorthand to keep snoopy people like you in the dark."

"I do my homework too, Reid. Hardy isn't one of your

financial whiz kids. He's a thug. An ex-cop with a question-able record."

Treadwell took the phone from her. "A word of advice: Be careful what you wish for, because you just might get it, and it won't be something you wanted after all."

60

An armored black Mercedes SUV was waiting outside the apartment building on Rector Street when Treadwell charged out the front door. He climbed in the back before the driver could get out and open the door for him.

"Let's go now," Treadwell said.

He could have walked, but this was faster and a lot more secure. From time to time a disgruntled investor would accost him on the street, but Butch always had someone covering his back, and the problem would be immediately solved.

They headed away, but as Treadwell was putting his tie on he realized that they were going in the wrong direction. "I want to go to the office."

"Yes, sir, but I'm taking a detour. There's a traffic tie-up on Broadway, and it's blocked off."

In less than five minutes they pulled up in front of the Burnham Pike tower, and Treadwell climbed out of the car and bolted across the sidewalk. Once inside, however, he slowed down and, head high, marched to the executive elevator, conscious that the security staff and others in the lobby were watching him as they did every day he came in. *So goes Treadwell's mood, good or bad, so goes the day.*

Upstairs, Dammerman and Hardy were waiting for him, and they looked grim.

Treadwell charged past them and into the reception area of his office, where Ashley looked up.

"Hold all calls?" she asked.

"Right," Treadwell said without stopping. "But get O'Connell here now."

"Yes, sir."

Inside, once the door was closed, Dammerman started, "They grabbed Levin without a hitch, but she didn't have the flash drive on her."

Treadwell took off his suit coat and draped it over the back of the chair. "Good. That means she didn't make a second copy."

"We're not so sure," Hardy said. "We sweated out one of the kids whose station is next to hers. He thought she might have made two copies."

Treadwell sat down. "Could she have given it to her friend?"

"I think it's a real possibility. They left the building together, but the Russian guy said he took off."

"Did they follow him?" Treadwell demanded.

"They said there was no reason. Levin was their primary target."

"So we don't know where he is?" Treadwell asked.

Hardy nodded.

"So if there was a second copy of the flash drive, he could have it?"

"Yes, sir."

"Then find him. Now!"

Ashley buzzed. "Ms. O'Connell is here."

"Send her in," Treadwell said.

As she came through the door, Hardy glared at her and left.

"I came up as soon as I heard you were in the building," Julia said.

"Levin may have made two copies of the flash drive, is that right?" Treadwell demanded.

Julia glanced at Dammerman, sitting to her left, and then back at Treadwell. "She gave me one, but Francis said that one of Hardy's people leaned on Norm Applebaum, who apparently overheard her and Donni Imani talking. But that's not all."

"What the hell are you talking about?" Dammerman asked.

"The drive Cassy gave to me is garbage. But the program she described to me could attack Abacus."

"And stop it?" Treadwell asked, his voice suddenly soft.

Julia nodded.

"Fuck," Treadwell said. "If you had the real flash drive, could you reverse engineer it?"

"Yes."

"Have you searched the computers at her workstation?" Dammerman asked. "Maybe you can find it there."

"It's possible."

"Then do it," Treadwell said.

Julia hesitated. "I don't know if I want to be a part of this any longer," she said. "I don't know if I can take the pressure."

"Less than twenty-four hours, Julia," Treadwell said. "And we need you. I need you to find Levin's program." He paused. "Will you help?"

Julia nodded. She gave Dammerman one last glance and then turned and left.

"Jesus," Treadwell said.

Ashley buzzed him. "Ms. Ladd is calling on one, and she sounded insistent. Do you want me to tell her to call back?"

"I'll take it," Treadwell said, and he punched *1*. "Now what the fuck do you want?"

"I'm trying to find Cassy Levin. She called and said she

was on her way to see me, but she never showed up. And she sounded stressed out."

"Who the hell is Cassy Levin?"

"She works for you."

"I don't know the name."

"Well, I do. I'm friends with her parents. But when I called her extension there wasn't an answer. I want to know what the fuck's going on, Reid."

"None of your business," Treadwell said, and he slammed down the phone.

61

Spencer Nast glanced out the right window of the Sikorsky S-76 helicopter as they passed over the Delaware Memorial Bridge just south of Wilmington. Traffic below was heavy and once again he told himself just how glad he was that he wasn't in that mess with all the nonentities.

For just a brief moment his mind was off the crap CNBC was broadcasting, but then he turned his attention back to the twelve-inch TV monitor in front of him, the sound fed to his headphones.

And nothing was good, starting with the T-bond auction that was in the middle of a gigantic meltdown. "A cataclysm," one talking head said.

"This is like learning that your solid brick mansion has suddenly started to crumble," another pundit said.

Gina Sutton, the current White House press secretary, was at the podium in the press room, holding an impromptu news conference in front of two dozen reporters. "The Treasury auction is nothing more than a temporary glitch," she said with a straight face, and Nast had to admire her composure while telling such a major lie.

"This is the result of China's debt problem, and very unikely to recur any time soon," she said, then turned on her heel and retreated inside the West Wing.

But she was nothing more than a shill, an imbecile, in Nast's mind, and just about everyone in the press corps knew it.

Of course Sam Kolberg was worse, because he didn't have the guts to ask the president's chief economic adviser what not to say before he allowed Gina to open her mouth.

Nast turned back to the small screen. Markets worldwide were tumbling. The Standard & Poor's 500—which was the prime benchmark index for the U.S. stock market—was down 10 percent. And even bond prices, in addition to Treasury notes, were in a steep nosedive.

The timing couldn't be better, in Nast's estimation. Abacus, which would be set loose by the opening bell tomorrow, would kick in about the time that the China mess was likely to surface.

As a plus point, the Treasury auction wipeout couldn't have come at a better time. He hadn't thought that something like that would happen this soon, and once again he had to admire Reid Treadwell's foresight. The man was a genius.

The pilot radioed him: "Sir, your wife has been patched through. Would you take the call?"

Nast's first reaction was to say *Hell no*. He didn't give a damn about her, but the helicopter crew would probably think it was odd, and word would get back to the media—as such things usually did. CNBC and especially ABC hated him, for some reason, and right now he wanted to stay as far below the radar as possible.

"Of course," he said into his mic.

Mildred came on. "Where are you, Spencer? What is all that noise?"

"I'm in a helicopter on my way back to Washington. What do you want?"

"I'm calling to remind you—again—that Billy's bac[
and he's coming over for dinner. Will you be home in tim[
for cocktails?"

Their son, William, had never been anything more tha[
a lazy, indifferent fool. He was back now from an Outwar[
Bound adventure in some ungodly place like the Rockie[
and there was no doubt he would spend the entire evenin[
complaining about the food, the bugs, the rain, and ju[
about everything else. He was the son of the economics ac[
viser to the president of the United States, and he never le[
anyone forget it.

"I don't know when I'll be home," Nast said.

"Well, we haven't seen him for the entire summer," hi[
wife whined. "At least you could make the effort."

Not seeing his son was a blessing. His SAT scores wer[
subpar, and Nast had pulled a lot of strings just to get th[
kid into Penn State, let alone Harvard or Yale. His intell[
gence was on Mildred's level, which said a lot for the idic[
gene being passed along.

"If you'd stop watching the soaps and pay attention t[
the real world, you'd know that we're in the middle of [
major financial crisis. And I am the chief economics ac[
viser to President Farmer. On top of that I really don't giv[
a damn about choking down another of your wretche[
dinners."

"I'm sorry, Spence, but Bill is our son."

"For the thousandth time, my fucking name is Spence[
not Spence!"

"I'm sorry—" Mildred began, but Nast broke the connec[
tion.

For a long moment or two, he simply sat there, his min[
seething. Life was damned unfair, and the problem was tha[
Mildred had never realized that she was a part of the prob[
lem, not part of the solution.

62

Almost immediately the pilot was on. "Sir, the White House is on teleconference."

"Put it on."

Kolberg's image came on-screen from the president's study, and he didn't look happy.

"I'm on my way, damnit. And if you have an issue with that, take it up with the fucking pilot."

"Listen up," Kolberg said. "We were just on with Liu, and the man said that our crisis could lead to an actual nuclear war."

"What the hell are you talking about?" Nast demanded. "Let me listen to the recording."

"The president is on his way—"

"Now, goddamnit. I know the man, I know how he thinks."

Kolberg nodded, and a moment later the recording came up.

Nast listened closely to what Liu had to say, and mostly *how* he said it, his exact wording in English. Plus his interchange with Miller and Nichols. The most interesting part was the end, after Miller recounted how the 1929 market crash and Great Depression led to World War II, and Liu's reply.

But I prefer to speak with economists, who understand that the worldwide debt is out of hand. If we need to go through fire to be rid of it, then so be it.

"He's not talking about war," Nast said. "You need to know the Chinese mind-set. He means economic devastation. Everything is about economics with them. That's how they moved up from tending rice paddies to become the second largest economy in the world. If you ask them about the weather, they'll reply in economic terms."

President Farmer came into view on the helicopter's video screen and sat down at his desk. "Hell, I know that Liu may be crazier than a shithouse rat, but the boy's not stupid. If he wants to take over the government from that empty suit Hua, there wouldn't be anything left after a nuke exchange other than a blackened bone and a hank of hair."

"Are you sure, Mr. President?" Kolberg asked.

"Yes," Farmer said. "Now, where the hell are you Spence?"

"In a chopper, should be with you soon, Mr. President."

"Well, what about Miller and Nichols, then? Or are they AWOL?"

"They had an appointment on the Hill," Kolberg said. "They'll be back when Spencer gets here."

"Let me guess, they've run off to tell their troubles to Stephanie," Farmer said. Stephanie Holland was the Speaker of the House. "They want to end-run Spencer's proposal."

Nast wasn't surprised. "Have you had a chance to look it over, Mr. President?"

"I did. And it looks like you want to spend a hell of a lot of my money."

"No, sir. The money would be coming from the Federal Reserve."

"I'm sure that Joe is having a shit fit over that one. Something else he can whine about to Stephanie."

"The auction today has shown us that investors aren't happy with our debt load. A lot of them have even started to lose faith that we can repay the T-bonds we keep peddling."

Farmer rubbed his jaw. "If Liu decides not to tap some of his PBOC reserves to bail out their banks—which are in worse shape than ours are—and Hua goes for some quick cash by dumping his two trillion bucks of our Treasuries, our ability to raise more debt goes from bad to worse. Is that what you're telling me, Spence?"

"Yes, sir," Nast said, pleased that Farmer had absorbed his tutorials. Sometimes it wasn't clear that the president was understanding or even listening to what his chief economist was telling him.

"Well, this time it's not totally up to me. I can give Congress a nudge, but the ball's in their court. And you're not the man to go over and make the argument, because you don't have friends. But Nichols is, because they like him and he's a natural-born politician, unlike Miller, who's a stuck-up prick."

"You endorse my plan, Mr. President?" Nast asked. He didn't give a damn what anyone on the Hill felt about him, because come tomorrow it would be he who was the hero, not Nichols.

"Well, if we end up sucking wind due to a worldwide economic meltdown, like you suggest might happen, then I think we should give it a try. Giving twenty grand to every citizen below the median income is radical, but desperate times call for desperate measures. And I'd like to wear the hero's medal for a change."

"You will, Mr. President," Nast said. He glanced over at Kolberg, who looked as if he'd just swallowed a bucket of raw jalapeños.

"What I don't want is a country littered with Farmervilles," Farmer said. "But you know who could do a good job selling your proposal on the Hill? Your old boss, Reid Treadwell. Now, he's the one who should have been a politician. Hell, he could talk a beggar out of his bowl. We all know he can talk just about any woman out of her panties. Fact is, I don't think there's man alive who has more need for applause than him."

"Reid is all of that," Nast said.

"In fact, I hear tell that you broke bread with him this morning while you were up in New York."

It sounded like an accusation to Nast, and his gut suddenly tightened. "I'm sorry, Mr. President, I didn't quite catch that."

"You heard me," Farmer said, his voice suddenly hard. "He may be your former boss, but I'm your boss now. I want you to cut off contact with that slippery son of a bitch. It things do go south, I'll need you in my tent, not in his. You read me?"

"Loud and clear, Mr. President," Nast said. "I'm your man." But come tomorrow it wouldn't matter what Farmer wanted.

63

Yuri Bykov was getting nervous about this simple assignment, especially after Leonid Anosov had phoned and said the woman didn't have the flash drive that seemed so important to Butch Hardy. Twice he had almost phoned the Brighton Beach number to make sure he hadn't misunderstood, but both times he'd backed off. Leonid was an old friend, and he vouched for his crew, which was good enough to take to the bank. There was no reason for him to lie.

He stood at the dining room window looking toward the East River and the traffic on the street twenty-four stories below when Zimin came down the short hall from the bathroom and joined him.

"Is everything in order, Yuri?" Zimin asked.

Bykov shrugged. "I don't like loose ends."

"The Brighton Beach guys?"

Bykov shrugged again.

"Maybe we should have handled it ourselves."

"Wasn't my call."

"Then it's not our problem," Zimin said. "Do you want a beer?"

"Later," Bykov said. His cell phone buzzed. It was Butch Hardy.

"I need some information about your Brighton Beach people."

"You hired them."

"They're your pals," Hardy said. "I want to know if the bastards are telling the truth or are they blowing smoke up my ass."

"The truth about what?"

"The flash drive the woman carried out of here, god-damnit. We want it found!"

"My people were not involved," Bykov shot back. "You hired us to do a job, which we will do in the morning, and then we'll be gone."

"You fucking well vouched for them, and we paid you a shit pot of money to do one simple job. I want it finished, do you fucking well get my point?"

"Leonid's not a liar."

"Either he is or you are. The woman left the office with a friend. Your people grabbed her and found no flash drive. It means her pal has it. But they said they didn't see him. They're lying."

"She could have dumped it somewhere," Bykov said.

"Not likely," Hardy shot back. "Get me the flash drive, or we'll want our money back. *All* our money."

Bykov wasn't impressed. Hardy was nothing more than a little man in a job that was way out of his league. "Maybe we'll just leave."

"You won't walk away, because I could ruin your fuck-ing reputation, and that's the only thing that keeps people like you employed," Hardy said. "We paid for the flash drive. Get it." He hung up.

64

Anosov was at the front-door guard post talking with Dmitri Sorokin when his cell phone chimed. He answered it. "Yes."

"It's me," Bykov said. "Can we talk?"

"Of course," Anosov said, and he went into the dining room, where he eased back a corner of the heavy drapes and looked out the window. Nothing moved on the street, but he was a cautious man, and Bykov sounded like he was troubled about something.

"I got a call from the money man who wants the flash drive the woman or her partner carried out of the building where they worked."

"Trust me, *tovarich,* she doesn't have it."

"I believe you, but what about the friend?"

"She was alone when we picked her off the street."

"*Da,* but what about when you first spotted her?"

"She was alone."

The phone was silent for a beat. "Think about this very hard, Leonid. These people have a lot of money and influence not only right here in New York, including Brighton Beach, but around the world. They could make a lot of trouble for us."

This time Anosov hesitated.

"If the woman didn't have the flash drive, it must mean her friend had it."

"She could have tossed it."

"Yes, but perhaps not," Bykov pressed. "What about the friend?"

"*Yeb vas,* the son of a bitch was run over by a garbage truck on Broadway before we could get to him."

"Any chance he survived and took off?"

"No," Anosov said.

"Then his body would have been taken to the morgue. Send someone there and search his belongings."

"I don't even know the bastard's name."

"Find out," Bykov said. "For all our sakes." He hung up.

65

Cassy was hungry, but worse than that, she was incredibly thirsty, and she had to use the toilet. She never wanted to see anyone more than she wanted to see Ben. Yet she was frightened even of that because of the number of armed men in this place. She'd counted at least nine, and maybe more. Impossible odds even for a man like Ben.

She rolled over on her side, her knees up to her chest, and began to cry softly.

The door latch rattled as it was pushed back.

Cassy turned around and sat up as the door opened and the man who had searched her walked in. He did not look happy, and she was terrified that the rapes were going to begin now. She didn't know how she would be able to take it.

"This is not going to happen, you son of a bitch," she shouted. "If you want to fuck me you'll have to kill me first and get your jollies off with a dead body."

"If need be, then that's the way it'll happen," Anosov said. "But that's not why I'm here. The people at your bank want the flash drive you stole."

"You know I don't have it!"

"Yes, but I think you gave it to the man who was with you. The one who got run over by the truck."

Cassy fought back the urge to burst out in tears. Donni had been so outrageously young and sweet, and his death was her fault.

"I only made the one copy, which I turned over to my boss."

"Ms. O'Connell, yes, I know. But I am told that one of your coworkers said you made two copies. So where is the second one?"

"There isn't a second one."

"Causing you pain would make no more difference to me than stepping on an ant. It's up to you, but in the end you will tell me what I want to know. Why not save us both the trouble?"

Cassy held her silence, but she felt as if she was going to throw up.

"All I want is the name of the man who was killed on Broadway."

Still Cassy remained silent.

Anosov took a bottle of water out of his jacket pocket. "I think you must be thirsty," he said.

Cassy looked at him.

He opened the bottle and began to pour the water on the floor.

"Donni," Cassy said, hating herself. But he was dead, so it didn't matter. "Donni Imani."

66

Ben had gone about as far as he could go without something from Chip, who had been busy at his laptop from the moment the copilot had given them the go-ahead. Ben had replayed Cassy's phone call again, focusing on Butch Hardy's name. Cassy had called him a fucking idiot. But his was the only name at BP she'd mentioned.

He got on his phone and brought up a directory for the bank. Working down from Reid Treadwell, the CEO, he found Butch Hardy under the title chief of security. He speed-dialed the number.

A man with a gruff voice and a New York accent answered on the first ring: "Hardy."

"Mr. Hardy, my name is Ben Whalen. I'm a friend of Cassy Levin's. She's been a little under the weather for the past couple of days, and when I tried to reach her number at the bank there was no answer."

"I'm chief of security, not a babysitter."

"I understand. But I was calling you just to confirm that nothing might have happened to her."

"Look, pal, I'm chief of security. Now, if there's nothing else I can do for you, I suggest you postpone your love life until after business hours."

"Before you hang up, may I be straight with you?" Ben asked.

"What the fuck do you want?"

"I'm a former Navy SEAL."

"So?"

"And the one thing you never want to do, Mr. Hardy, is piss off a SEAL. Do I make myself clear?"

Hardy laughed.

"I have a very good reason to believe that she's been kidnapped by two Russians who were driving a Cadillac."

"Kidnapped?" Hardy shouted. "What the fuck are you talking about?"

"I'll be landing at LaGuardia, and the first person I'm going to talk to is you."

"Good luck, because I'm going to be out of the city through tomorrow afternoon. Now, get the fuck out of my hair, because the one thing you never want to do, SEAL, is piss off an ex–New York City gold shield."

"I'll find Cassy, and when I do I'm coming after you," Ben said. "Count on it." He hung up.

Chip had looked up from his laptop. "I assume that was the bank's chief of security, but I thought you weren't going to call him."

"I changed my mind."

"Well, it didn't sound good to me. What's the upshot?"

"He was lying."

"If he was involved in hiring some Russians to kidnap her, you can bet that he's on the phone right now telling them that a pissed-off SEAL is on his way."

"I hope so."

"Are you considering the possibility that they'll just kill her and dump the body somewhere?"

"Not until they find out what she did with the flash drive," Ben said.

"Are you really going to the bank to confront him?"

"He's a start," Ben said. "But what have you come up with?"

"Not as much as I wanted. But the plates on the Caddy are of a sequence assigned to Brighton Beach, so at least we've confirmed what we already thought we knew. But the time of the ambulance didn't pan out, though it got me thinking about her friend that you've told me about."

"Donni Imani."

"They're close?"

"I think so."

"But I was thinking that maybe she and her friend left work together, and maybe she gave him the flash drive when she realized what was going down."

"It's possible."

"But while you were talking with Hardy, I got on the bank's directory and came up with Imani's and Cassy's workstation addresses. I tried messaging them both, but neither answered. Next I tried their phones, but again got no answer."

"Cassy's gone, and maybe Imani was taking a break."

"I called his immediate boss, a guy by the name of Masters. I told him that Donni was an old pal and we were supposed to have lunch together. He told me that Imani had already left the building."

"What are you driving at?" Ben asked.

"I demanded to know if he left alone or with Cassy Levin," Chip said. "And the guy was a natural. He said he and Cassy left the building practically hand in hand."

"Proving what?"

"Like I said, when she realized something was going down, and why, she passed the flash drive to her friend and told him to run."

"Okay, assuming Imani has the flash drive, where'd he take it?"

"To the morgue," Chip said.

"How do you know that?"

"I checked for emergency calls in the vicinity of where they grabbed Cassy. There was no nine-one-one mention of a woman being kidnapped, but there was a fatality about that time a block and a half away on Broadway. When I checked the morgue with Imani's name I got the hit. His body is there, and I'm betting the flash drive everyone seems to want is with his things."

"What about the Russian Cassy caught on her phone?"

"I sent his picture to Niklai Radchenko, who's one of the neighborhood coordinating officers in the section of the NYPD's Sixtieth Precinct that covers Brighton Beach. I got a hit almost immediately, and he wants me to call him on his direct line."

"I don't want to involve the cops."

"I sent the pic in the blind," Chip said. "The decision is yours, but I'd like to call this guy to find out what he knows."

Ben didn't like it and he was about to say so, but Chip held him off.

"I'm doing research on the Russian mob for *The New York Times,* and all I want to know is if he's connected."

"He'll check your background, and he'll want to know how you got the picture."

"It only took a minute to set up a newsroom address that'll come directly to me. But right now we're only stabbing in the dark. We need a location."

Ben looked away. "I'm afraid for her. Afraid that she's gotten in over her head. Butch Hardy seemed like a scumbag."

"Your call, Ben. All I can do is provide you with decent intel."

"Do it."

"Guys, we're about twenty minutes from landing," the copilot called back. "I'll need you to shut down your computers and phones in about ten."

"Got it," Ben said, as Chip brought up the cop's number on his phone in speaker mode.

The cop answered on the first ring. "Radchenko."

"This is Chip Anderson, I'm the one who sent you the photo."

"I know, I checked you out. How'd you get the shot, and where was it taken?"

"Downtown, and I took it. I just want to know where I can find him."

"Why?"

"I want to trade him the picture for his story."

The line was silent for a couple of moments. "I would advise you against trying to make contact with him. He's about as bad as they come, but he's well connected and for the moment we can't do a thing. No proof."

"Nonetheless I'd like to try. Guys like that sometimes are in love with the media if they think they'll get a fair story—some publicity."

Again the cop hesitated.

"Look, I'll share whatever I come up with with you. Who knows, maybe he'll slip up and give me something you can use."

"Your funeral, Anderson," Radchenko said, and he gave an address. "His name is Leonid Anosov, and he doesn't work alone."

67

It was well after lunch and Treadwell usually had a coffee at this time of the afternoon, but at the moment he was in absolutely no mood for anything. Ashley had asked if he wanted something brought up from the cafeteria, but he'd declined with a shrug.

And sitting now in full view of anyone walking past his glass-walled office, he was trying to pretend that he was busy scanning the trade data on his machine, watching the financial news feeds, and answering emails. But the missing flash drive stabbed deep into his brain, and for now he could concentrate on nothing else.

If Abacus were to fail, or worse yet, be revealed, he would be done. Maybe even have to do some jail time, a thought that was impossible to conceive. *How the mighty have fallen,* the unbidden thought came into his head. Maybe from the Bible his dad read to him when he was a kid.

His phone chimed with an incoming text. It was from his wife, Bernice, once again reminding him about the Spring Gala tonight at the Metropolitan Museum of Art.

It was something he definitely didn't want to do, especially not tonight of all times. But then again, this was another chance, like this morning's visit to the NYSE floor, to show that nothing was out of the ordinary with him or with the firm.

And he loved being noticed in public.

For Bernice, though, the season was the lifeblood of her existence. She loved the arts and arty people, and she loved the pomp and circumstance of the parties. *Be seen or be forgotten;* it was as simple as that for her.

Burnham Pike and Mr. and Mrs. Reid Treadwell were significant donors to most of the city's cultural institutions, and just like Reid, she loved being noticed by the glitterati.

Ashley buzzed him. "Mr. Dammerman on one."

Treadwell took the call. "What?"

"I'm coming up," the COO said.

"A problem?"

"Looks that way," Dammerman said and hung up.

Ashley was on again. "Mrs. Treadwell on two."

Treadwell picked up. "I just now got your text, Bernice."

"I don't care if the market is melting down or the sun is swallowing Wall Street," she said, a sharp edge to her voice. "You will show up at the Met tonight. Clear?"

"We're in the middle of something I can't leave."

"At the Met. Tonight at eight." She hung up.

His wife didn't have to remind him that despite his substantial Wall Street compensation package, she had a lot more money than he had. Or that he owed his career to her father, Thatcher Pike, whose ancestors had founded BP.

Once he had tried to disagree with her whether to fire their live-in chef, a French-Algerian from Marseille. The man's haute cuisine was too exotic for his tastes: Uzbek pickled vegetables, Laotian bamboo ginger quail, Ethiopian *kitfo*.

"Is it too much to want a simpler dish from time to time?" he'd asked.

Bernice had arched her left eyebrow. "You can take the boy out of Ohio, but you can't take Ohio out of the boy," she'd said.

They had an ironclad prenuptial agreement, and they kept the chef.

Dammerman showed up a couple minutes later, and he was obviously troubled.

"What's the issue?" Treadwell asked.

"Some guy named Ben Whalen called Butch, claimed he's a former Navy SEAL tough guy, and says he's looking for Cassy Levin."

"What'd Butch tell him?"

"Nothing."

Hardy got off the elevator and walked across the hall into Treadwell's office, closing the door behind him. "We may have an issue, Mr. Treadwell," he said. "I got a call from someone claiming to be Levin's live-in or something."

"Clyde was just telling me about it," Treadwell said. "What'd he say, exactly?"

"Said that two Russians driving a Caddy kidnapped her right off the street. And says he's on the way from some-where, and he'll be landing at LaGuardia. Says he's coming to see me."

"Jesus, what the hell is going on?"

"I don't know how he's getting his information, but what the hell do you want me to do if he actually shows up here?"

"Have him arrested," Treadwell said. "Just get him out of our hair."

"On what charge?"

"I don't give a fuck. Trespassing. The son of a bitch threatened you."

"How far do you want me to take it?"

"I don't care. Kill him if you have to."

"I'm on it," Hardy said, and he left.

"We just need to get past opening bell in the morning, and nothing will touch us," Treadwell said. He opened a drawer, took out a .45-caliber pistol, and placed it on his desk. "Maybe he'll show up here and threaten me. The only thing I could do is shoot the bastard in self-defense."

"I didn't know you were packing," Dammerman said, a slight smile at the corners of his thick lips.

"It was my dad's gun from 'Nam, and he gave it to me when I went to college at Brown. Providence had a reputation as Rhode Island's toughest town."

"Did you ever have to use it?"

Treadwell hesitated for a moment, thinking back to that other time. "Almost," he said. "My father always said that if the VC ever overran their position, and he was about to be captured, he'd blow out his brains first."

68

After Dammerman left, Treadwell tried to get back to work on a departmental spending spreadsheet when Ashley buzzed him again. "Betty Ladd is in the lobby insisting on seeing you."

"Shit."

"I'll tell her that you're in the middle of a board meeting and can't be disturbed," Ashley suggested. She and just about everyone else in management knew the story between the two of them.

"No, Ash," Treadwell said. "Send her up." Right now maintaining the illusion that everything was fine was the top priority.

He hung up, and for a moment he stared at the pistol, and almost smiled with a little thrill of pleasure thinking about the possibility of shooting the bitch between her beady eyes. But then he put the weapon back in the drawer and closed it.

Betty got off the elevator, charged across the corridor, and burst into Treadwell's office, her fists clenched on her hips as she stood in front of his desk.

Like a defiant schoolgirl called to the principal's office, Treadwell thought, and he almost smiled again.

"What have you done with Cassy Levin?" she demanded.

"I checked after your call, and I was told that she works in our data center security suite. She tries to keep hackers and the like from invading our system. Apparently she had a bigger role at Murphy Tweed and was responsible for the disaster that sank the firm. Frankly, I don't know why we hired her."

"None of it was her fault. She warned them, but no one wanted to listen to her."

"Her excuses, or yours, don't matter," Treadwell said. "So what's the issue?"

"She called me and said that she had to talk, and that she was bringing something important. She sounded frightened. And that concerns me. A lot."

"I talked to her supervisor, who said she'd left for lunch. Pretty normal, Betts."

Betty shook her head. "You're up to something, Treadwell. Goddamnit, I can feel it in my gut, see it on your fucking face!"

"I think you ought to see a shrink. Really."

"I'm watching you. If anything has happened to that girl, I'll make sure it comes back to you. And that's a promise you can take to the bank."

"Before I have security escort you out of here, I have a question for you."

"Like what?"

"I was told that you met with my technology officer today in Zuccotti Park. I was just wondering what you two talked about?"

"Why don't you ask Julia?"

"She said that you were pumping her with questions about BP's activities. But in view of your position with the

exchange, that would constitute an official inquiry, something you're required to inform us about beforehand. And
trust me, Betts, my legal people would have no compunction
about reporting your actions to the SEC."

"Stick it up your ass, Treadwell. It was family gossip,
nothing more. Julia and I are cousins."

Treadwell was taken aback, but just for a moment.
"Family or not, if I find out you talked about BP business,
I'll nail your ass to the barn door. Guaranteed."

69

It took Treadwell a minute or two to get his temper in check
after Betty was gone, then he picked up the phone and called
Dammerman. "Betty Ladd was here wanting to know what
happened to Cassy Levin, but then she left me with a little
tip about one of our top people."

"That Julia is her younger cousin?"

"How the hell did you know that?"

"I just found out. Butch is here in my office, and he's been
looking into what Julia's been up to today. Turns out that
Betty has been helping Julia for a long time. Even opened
the door for her to get a job here."

"Goddamnit, I want you to sit on Julia, and I mean sit on
her hard," Treadwell said, shouting. He very seldom raised
his voice, but this day was turning into nothing but shit.

"We're on it, Mr. T," Dammerman said.

Treadwell slammed down the phone, and when he looked
up, Heather Rockingham charged past Ashley's desk and
barged into his office.

Ashley got up, but Treadwell waved her back.

"Shut the door, if you would, Ash," he said. When she
did, he got up and went around his desk to embrace Heather.
"What are you doing here?"

"To see you, of course," she said. She wore a clingy, short, low-cut red dress that showed off her legs halfway up her thighs and a lot of her chest.

Treadwell thought she looked like a whore, but a desirable whore, and he tried to kiss her again. She held him back.

"Hold on, tiger," she said. "Before you bend me over the desk, we have some business to discuss."

"Business?"

"Cutting me in on the deal," she said. "What did you think?"

"I don't know what you're talking about."

"I think you do, Reid." She took an iPhone out of her purse. "This thing's got a great recording app. I switched it on the moment I walked into your apartment." She grinned. "I got your conversation with Clyde Dammerman, plus your text while I was sitting on the toilet." She smiled again. "Do you know that you make a hell of a lot of noise during sex? I just love it!"

Treadwell didn't know what to say. He went around behind his desk and sat down.

"You called it the greatest financial coup in history," she said. "I want in."

TEN

CLOSING BELL DAY ONE

70

Ben Whalen and Chip Faircloth landed at LaGuardia's private jet terminal a little after two in the afternoon, and the pilot taxied over to one of the hangars, shutting down when they were stopped.

The copilot came back. "What's your pleasure, guys? We can refuel and return to Andrews, or if you're only going to be a couple of hours we can stick it out here."

"Head back to the barn," Ben said. "I don't know how long we'll be here. Maybe even overnight."

Chip had gotten back on his computer once they'd landed, and he looked up now. "I suggest that if we're going to Cassy's bank we start at the top. CEO's name is Reid Treadwell. I did a bio check on him: The guy is well-connected, but he's considered one of the top sharks on Wall Street."

"I'll start with him, but you're going back to D.C."

"I'm in this too," Chip said.

"It's probably going to get messy, and you're still wearing a uniform, which means you answer to the admiral. But I'm in civvies, which means I can quit."

"Huggard will never dump us, at least not till W is certified. Anyway, you're just a grunt who's going to need some backup. So I'm staying here in case the waves start piling up."

The copilot had opened the hatch, and he turned back to

them. "Looks like whatever you guys are up to has already started to create waves. We've got company."

Ben got up as a stocky man with a salt-and-pepper mustache, dressed in a sport coat and tie, came aboard, holding up his NYPD ID wallet, a gold shield badge on his belt. The copilot stepped aside.

"My name is Sergeant Adams," he said. "Which one of you is Benjamin Whalen?"

"That's me," Ben said.

The sergeant pocketed his ID. "You're under arrest. Do I have to cuff you?"

"That depends on what I'm charged with."

"Threatening an individual with bodily harm."

"If you're talking about my telephone conversation with the chief of security at Burnham Pike, it's not how I remember it."

"You were recorded, and I listened to it," Adams said. "What'll it be, tough guy, cuffs or not?"

"I'll talk to the admiral, and we'll straighten this out," Chip said.

"I don't think we have a lot of time," Ben said.

"I'm on it," Chip said. "We're going to stick around for a bit," he told the copilot, who nodded.

"You and this aircraft will go back to where you came from," Adams said, but Chip was on the phone again, and the pilot was in his seat in the cockpit.

"Let's get this over with," Ben said.

"I said I want this aircraft out of here."

"Sorry, Adams, but you don't have the authority," Chip said, and he turned back to his phone.

"We'll see," Adams said.

He turned Ben around, cuffed him, and, taking his arm, led him down the steps and across to the backseat of a waiting Chevy sedan, another man behind the wheel.

71

Once they were clear of the airport it took about thirty minutes to cross the river into Manhattan and the Midtown South Police Precinct on West Thirty-fifth.

Adams took Ben directly back to an interrogation room with only a small steel table and two chairs. "Are you going to cooperate or will this get difficult?"

"Your call," Ben said.

"Goddamnit, you threatened a friend of mine, and I want to know what the fuck you're up to."

"A friend of mine was kidnapped by two Russians and probably taken somewhere in Brighton Beach. I came up from D.C. to find her."

"She's at lunch with another friend. Maybe she dumped you."

"Let's get this over with, okay?"

"It's not going to be that easy. A formal complaint has been lodged against you. And like I said, I listened to the recording."

"I have a recording of my own. How about we make an exchange?"

Adams took the cuffs off. "Everything out of your pockets and on the table," he said.

Ben did as he was told, and the sergeant motioned for him to sit down, then made a phone call.

"Have Sid come in," he said and sat down across from Ben. "You claim to be a former Navy SEAL, that right?"

"Yes."

"Thanks for your service. What are you working at in D.C.?"

"It's classified."

A gruff-looking young man with a scorpion tattoo on the

right side of his neck came in, and Adams gave him Ben's cell phone. "There may be a recording on this thing, make me a copy."

"It'd be too bad if something happened to my phone, even though I don't need it," Ben said.

"You're full of threats."

Ben sat forward. "Cut the bullshit, okay? I didn't come up here on a government jet to play games, nor did I want to get the police involved, because I've dealt with the kind of people who took my friend. They don't give a shit about local cops, who they think of as only minor annoyances. It's why they still operate in front of your noses. So let's get on with this so I can get on with finding her and get out of your hair."

"Tough guy," Adams said. "But even if you're telling the truth, which I doubt, what makes you think you could go up against these Russians of yours?"

"I can."

"Have you ever killed a man?"

"Yes."

"More than one?"

"Yes."

"I meant more than one at a time, on your own, with no team to back you up."

"Yes," Ben said.

Adams sat back, and after a moment or two shook his head. "I believe you," he said. "Problem is, you're not going to run around my town killing people."

"Whatever it takes to get my lady back."

"Cassy Levin, that her name?"

"Yes."

"The other problem is that my friend thinks that you could be a real threat to his safety."

"If he's involved with Cassy's disappearance, then he's right."

"So what do we do?" Adams said. "Butch told me that the young woman—who he calls a gigantic pain in the ass—went to lunch with a friend of hers, and that she's not back yet. But when she does return he'll have her give me a call."

"She doesn't answer her cell phone."

"Lots of people switch off at lunch."

Ben said nothing.

"If you're released, will you promise not to try to contact Mr. Hardy?"

"He's the first one on my list, because he knows what happened and where in Brighton Beach she was taken."

"Then I'll have to hold you overnight, at least," Adams said.

The man who'd taken Ben's cell phone came back with it and handed it to the sergeant. "Nothing on it. I think the SIM card was probably damaged."

72

The Sikorsky touched down on the White House south lawn around three, and a flight crewman hustled to open the hatch and lower the boarding stairs.

"Watch your step, sir," he said politely.

Nast just glared at him, wondering why he always had to be surrounded by complete idiots.

One of Sam Kolberg's interns, a kid with the remnants of acne, was waiting for him. "How was your flight, sir?" he asked, extending his hand.

Nast brushed past him. "Smoother than your complexion," he said, and he headed across the lawn, the intern trailing behind.

He had been thinking about Farmer's direct order to cut off all contact with Reid, which was as surprising as it was disturbing to him. Reid was one of the largest contributors to the president's war chest, but there had to have been some sort of a rift recently.

But then, as the saying went: *If you want a friend in Washington, get a dog.*

The president was in the Oval Office, his feet up on the Resolute desk, which had been crafted from the wood of a nineteenth-century arctic exploration ship, when Nast walked in. The ornate desk had been a gift from Queen Victoria to Rutherford B. Hayes, and had been a fixture in the Oval Office since.

Kolberg sat in one of the two chairs across from him.

Nast's proposal lay open on the desk, and Farmer tapped a finger on it.

"You've got balls of steel, Spence," the president said, chuckling. "Using Federal Reserve money to pay for your financial rescue plan."

Nast took a seat. "That's the beauty of it, sir. The precedent has already been set for us. After the '08 crisis, the Fed pumped money into the economy by buying T-bonds and mortgage-backed bonds. It has the power to create money. That's the key to its existence."

"But that creates inflation, something nobody wants to see happen," Kolberg said. "Prices going through the roof like in the seventies and eighties."

"In the first place double-digit inflation is no longer the problem," Nast shot back. This was his territory. Kolberg was clueless. "The world has changed since then. Technology has made most businesses faster and more efficient. And that alone tends to keep prices down.

"So does the surge in international commerce. High-paying union jobs have disappeared because they've been transferred to Mexico and Vietnam and China, where labor is cheap. Which means that our labor costs have plummeted, which tends to keep inflation in check."

"A lot of good-paying jobs have gone up in smoke," Farmer said with a bite. He was back in his populist, friend-of-the-average-working-stiff mode. "And that's a damn shame. The American worker has been fucked more times than a tied-up goat."

"But this gives us a lot of leeway, Mr. President," Nast said, pressing his argument. "In the wake of the '08 problem, Congress voted seven hundred billion to bail out the banks and another eight hundred billion to stimulate the economy, using tax credits for businesses and consumers, plus spending on public works like roads and bridges.

"That money came from the taxpayers themselves, plus borrowing from the bond investors who buy Treasuries. And on top of that was the three trillion plus the Fed created to buy those bonds."

"Why can't we do the same thing now?" Kolberg asked.

"Do you mean more borrowing?"

"Yes."

"Even you should know the answer to that one, Sam," Nast said, loving it. "The failure of today's Treasury auction would simply be repeated."

"Not if we paid higher interest."

"Pay all the interest you want, we still wouldn't be able to overcome the widespread perception that we can't afford to pay even a small interest rate because of the gargantuan debt load we're carrying. And that would be especially true if China decided to dump the two trillion in our bonds that they hold.

"Hua would get far less than the two trillion, of course, because he'd have to sell at a discount. But if he gets desperate enough, with the PBOC turning its back on him and the commercial banks falling like dominoes, he'll do it. For us, the bottom line would be a disaster. We'd never be able to raise the money."

Farmer took his feet off the desk and sat forward. "What

you're asking is that Congress create a new stimulus program plus a bank bailout if it comes to that. And a big chunk of that would be used to send half the American public a check for twenty grand. All courtesy of the Federal Reserve."

Nast nodded. "Yes, Mr. President, that's exactly right."

"Well, I see two problems right off the bat. First, we gotta get Congress to go along with this. Holland and I have had our differences, so that's a definite hard sell. And to convince that hard-assed Miller to have the Fed create abracadabra big bucks—trillions of dollars—won't be easy either."

Farmer exchanged a glance with his chief of staff.

"The Fed is independent of me. I can't tell Miller what to do. Which means we've got ourselves a briar patch to hack through."

"That's why Miller and Nichols are on the Hill at this moment," Kolberg said. "We'd be facing a lot of legal barriers to what you're proposing."

"Christ, Sam, can't you get it through your thick head that what is about to hit us will change all the rules?" Nast practically shouted. "The bolder our strategy, the better. If Joe Miller and the Speaker of the House put the brakes on our rescue program, they'd become the most hated people in the country. And you could use your bully pulpit, Mr. President, to stick it to them big-time."

Farmer turned a wistful glance out the window toward the Rose Garden for a long moment. "You've got a point, Spence. If things do go straight into the toilet, like they're looking to do, then we need to offer leadership that can save our economy and our nation."

"Thank you, Mr. President," Nast said, holding back a smirk for Kolberg.

"Sam?" Farmer asked.

"You're the president."

Nast almost laughed out loud. What the idiots didn't

realize was that whatever the government ended up doing would probably not work. But right now he was playing the role of the savior of the nation, who was trying to keep the ship from sinking.

"What if your idea doesn't work?" Farmer asked.

"Years of depression, maybe," Nast said. "Farmervilles."

"The big boys didn't starve in the thirties, and they won't this time if the shit hits the fan," Farmer said, not taking Nast's bait about Farmervilles. "And from what I know about Reid Treadwell's fancy footwork, I have a hunch that he and his Burnham Pike pals will be eating caviar and drinking champagne no matter what."

Nast felt a sudden chill. "They're in my past, sir. As you've instructed, I will have no further contact with Reid or his people."

"That best be true, because this time, unlike after '08, I will see some of those Wall Street butt wipes who game the system end up on the guillotine." He smiled. "Do you get my drift, Spencer?"

"Yes, Mr. President, I do."

73

Julia O'Connell was lost in thought, trying to figure a way out of the mess she'd been part of creating, when Dammerman burst into her office like a tidal wave ready to destroy everything in its path.

"Betty Ladd is your fucking cousin," he shouted. "When were you going to let me or Reid know?"

Julia was knocked completely off balance.

"What kind of shit are you trying to pull on us?"

Julia forced herself to get it together, because in less than twenty-four hours, win, lose, or draw, she was out of here. "Lower your voice," she said. "This is my office."

"This office belongs to Burnham Pike, not you. And maybe you should never have been here in the first place. Maybe Butch could round up a crew to move you out."

"I've had my fill of you, Clyde. Your loudmouth bullying, your low-class attitude, your wrong-side-of-the-tracks boorish mouth."

Dammerman was nonplussed for a moment.

"When it's done, I'll have all the money I've ever wanted, and delighted to never see you or this place again." Her voice was even, despite the effort it took her. "And if you and Reid don't stop with the threats, maybe you'll find out why you still need me. The hard way."

Dammerman came to the edge of her desk, his bulk towering over her. "Reid wants to know what you and Betty talked about."

"I've already told him."

"I mean about our work here."

Julia got to her feet and came around the desk to him. "I'll go up and tell him again. Maybe he's as dim-witted as you are, and he needs me to draw him a diagram."

Dammerman pushed her back. "You're not going anywhere until you start giving me some straight answers."

"Get away from me, you bastard," Julia shouted and tried to step around him, but he grabbed her arm so hard it hurt.

"She saved your ass in college after you pulled your little stunt, and now you owe her something. What is it?"

"Don't be an idiot. I'm sure as hell not going to blow the whistle on myself."

"Bitch."

The door swung open, and Todd Borman, an IT tech who'd been with her for a long time, came in. Broad-shouldered and six-three, he'd played football at Stanford starting his freshman year. He thought Julia was a goddess.

"May I help?" he asked.

"Get the fuck outa here," Dammerman said.

"I'm sorry, sir, but if you don't release Ms. O'Connell and step away, I will have to help you do it."

"You're fired," Dammerman shouted.

Todd was on him in a flash. "Yes, sir," he said, his voice flat as he broke Dammerman's grip on Julia's upper arm and shoved him away.

"You son of a bitch."

"I really don't want to hurt you, Mr. Dammerman, but I will."

Julia got between them. "Its okay, Todd. I'll take it from here." She turned to Dammerman. "I'm going upstairs now to straighten this out with Reid."

"You're staying here," Dammerman told her. "I'm ordering it."

"Order this, Clyde," Julia said, and she gave him the finger then stepped back. "How'd you like to head upstairs with me?" she asked Todd.

"Yes, ma'am."

A half dozen of Julia's IT personnel were lined up outside the glass-walled office and holding their phones up as they took videos of the encounter with BP's COO.

"I wonder what HR is going to say when I show them the videos of your assault on me," Julia said, and she and Todd marched out the door.

74

Treadwell looked up as Heather showed up at his door. Ashley came around from behind her desk to stop her, but Treadwell waved her off.

"You're back," he said when Heather came in and shut the door.

"I didn't like where we left it," she said. She sat down on the chair in front of his desk. "We need to talk."

"I've said all there is to say."

"Not a chance in hell. All you have to tell me is: 'Yes, darling, I'd love to cut you in on the deal.'"

"Okay, if that's the way you want it . . . *darling,*" Treadell said. "I don't know if you've heard the rumor, but I've taken BP to cash. I think the situation in China is going to blow sky-high, and soon. Added to that is our own government's debt. We're buried up to our ears and there may be no realistic way to pull us out of a downward spiral."

Heather said nothing.

"I don't know if you're following my logic, but this deal you're talking about is BP going to cash. Simple. And if you want us to take Rockingham in the same direction we'd be happy to offer the service."

She crossed her arms. "That's it?" she asked skeptically. "I understand what's happening to the market because of China, plus the failure of the Treasury auction. And I even understand why our stock is taking a beating today. But you taking your firm to all cash? That's the 'greatest financial coup in history'?"

Treadwell shrugged.

"The way you were talking about the deal was making money, not just avoiding losing it."

"If we can maintain our capital when all hell starts to break loose, then we'll be in a decent position to take a lot of money during the recovery. And that means your company will ultimately be the beneficiaries because we'll have the resources to not only help you expand but maybe give you the capital to buy up other companies at recession-rate prices."

Heather smiled. "Why do I feel as if you're bullshitting me?"

"What makes you think something like that?"

"Back at the apartment you told me that talking to Betty Ladd would be the biggest mistake of my life. And you said that my wanting to get in on your deal might be something I didn't want. Sounded like threats to me."

"Betty would screw you over just because you and I were together. And as far as the deal goes, we're talking about very big money. And if it goes south, which is always possible in any deal, you could get burned."

"You got a text that said 'the Levin girl is gone and the kid is missing.' And she was the one who supposedly came up with an 'antidote' to a virus. So quit fucking around, Reid. I want to know what's going on."

"Not now," Treadwell said. "I'll call you later."

Butch Hardy, along with one of his female security people, showed up. They had a word with Ashley, who had apparently called them.

Treadwell motioned them in. This wasn't how he wanted the situation to develop, but he wanted to get rid of this fool. "Ms. Rockingham was just leaving," he said. "See her out of the building, would you, Butch?"

"You bastard," Heather screeched.

The female security officer took Heather's arm. "No trouble, now, young lady."

Heather pulled away. "Don't you dare touch me!"

Hardy and the woman each took an arm, dragged Heather to her feet, and marched her out the door.

"Call *me*?" she shouted. "We'll see who calls whom!"

75

Julia O'Connell got off the elevator and crossed the hall, Todd trailing right behind her, as Hardy and one of his people marched Rockingham's daughter, screaming obscenities at the top of her lungs, out of Treadwell's office.

Julia stepped aside as they passed.

"I can blow the lid off the entire fucking deal!" Heather shouted, spittle flying from her lips. "The flash drive with the antidote. The missing girl and her friend." Her eyes locked with Julia's for a moment. "Your boss banging me! It's all recorded. Every bit of it."

Hardy and the woman cop dragged Heather onto the elevator, and then they were gone, the sudden silence on the floor almost deafening.

Treadwell motioned for Julia to come into his office.

"I'll handle this," she said to Todd, who handed her a cell phone he'd gotten from one of the ITs downstairs.

"Show him this."

"You have pictures from downstairs?"

Todd grinned. "It's already starting to go viral on Instagram and Facebook."

Julia patted him on the shoulder, then went into Treadwell's office, closed the door, and sat down across from him. "That was quite a show."

"The woman is certifiable," he said.

"Yes, but she apparently has a pretty good idea what's going on," Julia said. Her gut was on fire. "Just how much *does* she know, for God's sake?"

"Not enough to cause anything more than a nuisance."

"Well, you have another nuisance you'll have to deal with," Julia said. She brought up a video on the phone and shoved it across to Treadwell, who watched it with a stony face.

"Jesus," he said, looking up.

"What are you going to do about Clyde? Talk about certifiable. The man is an animal who needs to be put into a cage."

"I'll talk to him, but in the meantime we have to keep this among ourselves."

"It's on the internet already."

Treadwell sat back. "My God," he said softly. "Now of all times, Julia?"

"I didn't start it."

"You did by meeting with Betty."

"We talked about family, damnit."

"Why didn't you let me know you and she are cousins?"

"Because you and Betty hate each other's guts, and I don't want to be a part of that mess," Julia said. "But it brings us right back to the . . . situation. What are we going to do?"

"We're going to stay the course. Less than twenty-four hours."

"What about Cassy?"

"She's gone," Treadwell said. "Permanently."

Julia looked away for a moment. "Fraud is one thing, Reid, but murder is another."

"She was kidnapped, and all I know is that she is no longer a problem. Our hands are clean. *Your* hands are clean."

"In the meantime, what about Clyde? The bastard assaulted me, and you need to do something about it."

"Your call. All I ask is that you wait until the dust settles. After opening bell tomorrow, we're all going to be busy around here."

Julia was mollified, but just barely. "I want an apology," she said. "A *public* apology in front of my staff."

"Done," Treadwell said.

After a long moment, Julia nodded. "In the meantime, keep him out of my hair."

"What about Abacus? If Cassy really had the antidote, could it be used by someone?"

"Not off-site. Everything that goes out of here has a BP marker. Somebody would have to be on the premises to make it work."

"Are you sure?" Treadwell asked.

"Absolutely," Julia said.

76

Julia took Todd with her back to her office in case Dammerman came after her. She was frightened of not only what he was capable of doing to her but of the entire plan and her involvement with it.

When she thanked her IT tech and dismissed him, she got on her cell phone and searched for the number of the reporter Betty Ladd had told her about.

A man answered on the third ring. "What is it?" he demanded. He sounded drunk.

"Mr. Wren, I'm Julia O'Connell, and I'm trying to find out about Reid Treadwell. I think that he's mixed up in something that concerns me. You were the journalist who wrote an exposé on him."

"Treadwell? He cost me my job, my career, my marriage, my kids, everything. Now I live in a tiny shithole above a Chinese restaurant. Me and a few dozen roaches. He and his pal Clyde Dammerman framed me for insider trading. Said I was front-running a merger announcement. Hell, I never even owned a share of stock, but they faked records to show I was lying. So I served time."

"I'd like to see the material you gathered on him."

"I know who you are. You work for him at Burnham Pike. Why'd he put you up to this? Hasn't he already screwed me enough?"

"Yes, I work for him, and he'd be angry to learn I called you. But I'm leaving the firm, and I have to know what I'm dealing with."

"Even if you're telling the truth, who cares? He got a court order to seize all my material, and now it's under permanent seal somewhere. They even threatened my publisher with a multibillion-dollar lawsuit, and the coward caved, even though my proof was solid. The paper ran a retraction, took the story off the web, and fired me."

"I managed to dig up a copy. Your story documented how Treadwell framed Ted Partridge, his rival for a big job at BP, and the man went to jail for front-running, the same as you. And your story seemed solid to me."

"So what do you need from me?"

"I want to know if you came up with anything else."

"Like you wouldn't believe. The guy is smooth and classy on the outside, but it's only a cover. In fact, he's nothing more than a sociopath. No empathy for anyone. All he cares about are his good name and his career. I found out that when he was a kid—for fun, mind you—he used to blow up frogs with firecrackers. And in college he framed a professor who was bringing cheating charges against him. His climb up the path to success is littered with enough bodies to put Macbeth to shame."

He disconnected, and Julia sat back with the single thought that she was next on Treadwell's list.

77

Valentin Panov had gone on a grocery and vodka run, and when he got back, a couple of the guys helped him put the stuff away in the cabinets and fridge. At thirty-eight he pretty well figured he had found his place in the world, a situation where he belonged.

He'd grown up in a small town in Russia's wild far east, not far from Vladivostok, and from the age of fourteen he'd been a runner for the mob, helping hijack shipments by sea of just about everything from condoms to cigarettes to booze, and once even four Mercedes SUVs.

At sixteen he'd killed his first man, a security guard on the docks, and instead of traumatizing him, he'd thought it was the greatest accomplishment of his life. Thereafter he'd been a marked man, of interest to the local cops, and held in high esteem by the mob, and finally the big guys in Moscow, some who'd originally earned their chops in the old KGB.

By the time he was twenty-nine it was suggested by a friend that he get out of Russia. Some people in Brighton Beach would be waiting when he got off the plane, and they would have a job and a home for him.

He'd never once looked back, never once regretted the move, and never once missed his old friends. The U.S. was his home, a land of opportunity where the pickings for the right man were unlimited.

"Where's Leonid?" he asked one of the kitchen crew.

"Upstairs, waiting for you to get back."

Panov went up to Anosov's room, where their computer was located, and knocked once on the doorframe.

"*Vstupat*," Anosov said. *Enter.*

He was sitting at his desk, and he looked up. "Where the hell have you been?"

"Restocking the pantry."

"Well, I have a job for you, and it has to be done immediately," Anosov said. "With no fuckups. *Ponimayu?*" *Understand?*

"*Da.*"

"The guy who got nailed by the garbage truck when we picked up the Levin bitch was almost certainly taken to the city morgue. His name is Donni Imani. I want you to go over there and look through his personal possessions. He may have been carrying a flash drive." Anosov held one up. "Just like this."

"I don't know where the place is."

"It's inside Bellevue Hospital, in Kips Bay just above Twenty-third on First Avenue."

"I haven't had lunch yet," Panov said.

"Right now, and don't fucking come back empty-handed. This is important. Our entire operation could depend on it. Are you clear?"

"They only give out that kind of shit to a relative or cops."

"Tell them you're his uncle," Anosov said. "Again, the guy's name is Donni Imani."

Panov nodded.

"Jump."

78

They had decided to keep the white Caddy out of sight in the garage until they were sure that no one was looking for it, so instead Panov took the Subaru hatchback he'd used on the grocery run. He took the Brooklyn–Battery Tunnel, traffic busy as usual, then headed north up FDR Drive straight to Kips Bay.

He got lucky with a parking spot not too far from the main entrance to the hospital, and inside followed the directions on the directory down to the basement, where the morgue was located.

A heavyset woman in jeans and a man's white shirt was on the phone behind the reception desk when he walked in. No one else was present.

When she was finished, she hung up. "May I help you, sir?"

"My nephew had a horrible accident earlier today, and I think he was brought here."

"Name of the decedent?" she asked.

Panov didn't know the word. "Sorry?"

"Your dead nephew, what was his name?"

"Donni Imani."

The woman entered something on her computer. "Donald."

"Donni."

She looked up with a smirk. "No Donni, only a Donald Imani, age nineteen, involved in a vehicle-pedestrian accident, extensive trauma."

"He went by Donni, but that's him."

"Your name?"

"Tom Raven." It was the name on his New Jersey driver's license.

"ID?"

He took it out of his wallet and handed it over. She scanned it into the computer.

"Is that necessary?"

"You have a problem?" the woman asked, handing his license back.

Panov had had enough of her officious attitude. "Yes. My nephew was run over by a fucking garbage truck, and I want to claim his body. Do you have a problem with that?"

"The name of the funeral parlor?"

"I haven't picked one yet."

"Come back when you've decided," the woman said. She did something else with her computer. "You can discuss it with his parents when they get here from Miami tomorrow. In any case, they have priority."

Panov didn't know what to say, except that he wanted to strangle the bitch.

"Will there be anything else, Mr. Raven?"

"Can I at least see the body?"

"That'll be up to his parents."

"For Christ fucking sake—"

"Do I need to call the police?"

Leonid was going to blow his top, and there was nothing he could do about it.

A man in a white lab coat walked in, glanced indifferently at them, and then went through the swinging doors into the back.

"Mr. Raven?" the woman said.

Panov turned and left.

79

Betty Ladd was just getting ready to head down to the trading floor for the third time, to check what the mood was with less than a half hour to go in the session and the stock slide accelerating, when her cell phone rang.

The caller ID was for Denise Baker, a waitress at the Kittredge, who was one of Betty's informants. She'd texted earlier about the meeting among Treadwell and a few of his executives and Spencer Nast, but hadn't added much more except that they'd been deep in conversation.

The club was where a lot of Wall Street's movers and shakers met to discuss just about everything that had happened, was happening, and was likely to happen on the Street, and the waitress was a good resource who was well worth the extra two hundred in her tip envelope each week.

Betty answered. "Hi, Denise, have something new for me?"

"I was too busy until now to give you everything about the meeting with Mr. Nast and the folks from BP."

Betty couldn't help but smile. "Tell me, dear."

The day had been difficult starting just after lunch, when the market had lost 13 percent, tripping a circuit breaker that halted trading for fifteen minutes so that everyone could stop and take a deep breath. And at this moment stocks were approaching the 20 percent–loss threshold, which would shut the market down until opening bell tomorrow.

She was hoping that Denise would have something

useful to tell her about Reid. Maybe even something that was relevant to what was happening to the market.

"Most of the time I wasn't close enough to make out everything they were talking about, but I managed to get the gist of it."

"Go ahead."

"Anyway, Ms. O'Connell was talking about a virus, and Mr. Dammerman said that it could have an effect on just about every stock exchange in the world," Denise said. "It sounded crazy to me, but they raised their coffee cups to toast someone or something in Amsterdam, I think."

If Burnham Pike was afraid of a computer virus it would explain why Julia had been a part of their inner circle, which almost never included a woman. And Amsterdam, if that's what they'd said, was a well-known home base for world-class hackers.

"You sure they used the word *Amsterdam*?"

"Pretty sure," Denise said. "But the funny thing was, they seemed happy about it—about the virus."

"Happy?"

"Yeah, and they even had a name for it. Called it Abacus."

After Denise hung up, Betty sat back and tried to make some sense of what she'd just been told. Reid was up to something; she'd known that when she'd learned he'd been taking BP to all cash.

And she didn't trust the bastard any farther than she could throw the building she was in. But a virus named Abacus from Amsterdam? And Julia's meeting her in the park, and later Cassy's frantic phone call that she was coming to the exchange with something, and then her disappearance.

None of it was adding up, on top of which was the nose-dive the market had been taking since midmorning.

"I'll be downstairs," she told her secretary as she emerged from her office and headed to the elevator.

80

The floor was in near-total meltdown. Traders were shouting back and forth even though almost all of their trades were done on tablets. Television monitors were showing continuing stories on the Chinese financial mess, as well as the failure of the Treasury auction.

For several seconds she merely stood on the outskirts, trying to take it all in. It seemed like the panic of '08 all over again. She felt in her gut that somehow this was Reid's doing, and yet intellectually she knew that wasn't possible. This was simply a meltdown, not the result of some virus in BP's system.

She spotted Seymour Schneider near his post, where he was talking to someone on his cell phone—almost certainly someone at BP. She walked over, and when he looked up and saw her, he said something else and broke the connection.

"We're just about at twenty percent," he said.

He almost looked frightened, and it was something Betty had never seen before. "I know," she said, and it sounded stupid even to her own ears. "But I have a question."

"Not now."

A computer-generated voice came over the public-address system: *"Trading is suspended for the day."*

Monitors showed that Standard & Poor's had just crossed the 20 percent threshold, and a large moan went up from the floor.

"A train wreck," Seymour muttered. He took out a handkerchief and wiped his brow.

A Fox News reporter and cameraman started over, but Betty held up a hand for them to give her a minute, and they pulled up short.

"I'll make this quick," she told Seymour. "Has Reid, or anyone else from BP, mentioned something called 'abacus'?"

"Julia said something about it when they were on the floor this morning. Something to do with the Rockingham IPO, but it didn't sound good to me. Anyway, Reid seemed pissed off, and he told her to shut the fuck up."

"And?"

"When I got a chance, I asked him what 'abacus' was, and he said he wasn't sure. He thought it might have been a joke about how Keith Rockingham was so stupid he couldn't count without using an abacus. The ancient Chinese beads-on-strings computing machine."

"Did he seem on the level to you?" Betty pressed.

Seymour's eyes narrowed. "If this is about your feud with him, I'm staying out of it."

"Okay," Betty said. "I was just curious, is all."

Seymour glanced up at the monitors. "I knew we were in for a ride, what with China's debt and ours," he said. "I hate to tell people I told you so, but I told you so."

He moved off, and the Fox reporter and cameraman came over. "What happens next, Ms. Ladd?"

"I wish I knew," Betty said, and before he could ask a follow-up, her cell phone rang. It was her secretary.

"Keith Rockingham's daughter is here."

"What does she want?"

"She says she has a secret recording of Reid Treadwell that you need to hear."

"I'm on my way," Betty said, trying to keep the grin off her face.

81

Heather was waiting in Betty's walnut-paneled reception room, and she jumped up when Betty walked in.

They shook hands. "I'm sorry that your IPO had to happen on a bad day," Betty said. "But the market always recovers. Always."

"Thanks for seeing me without an appointment," Heather said.

Betty thought that the woman looked a like a whore, but she smiled. "No calls," she told her secretary, and ushered Heather inside.

When they were settled across from each other on matching nailhead chesterfield sofas, Betty asked if she would like to have a coffee or perhaps a glass of wine.

"Maybe later, but right now I want you to listen to something. And then I have a text you need to see."

"Very well."

"Some of it is . . . intimate."

"I don't embarrass easily," Betty said.

Heather played the recording of her and Reid making love—the encounter had almost certainly taken place at Reid's pied-à-terre on Rector Street—and then the calls he'd made to Dammerman and Julia. "Sorry about the noise," she said, but it was obvious she wasn't sorry at all.

Betty waved it off. So far nothing she'd heard was new or even interesting.

Heather handed her phone over. "This is the text about someone named Levin being gone and the kid being missing."

Betty quickly read through the text. She had no idea what it meant, except that Cassy was apparently missing, and she felt a chill. She listened to the recording again, of Reid's abusive language with Julia, and his mention of the "greatest financial coup in history," as well as her own conversation with him.

When she looked up, Heather was watching her, an angry expression on her face.

"He's got this big deal, and he won't let me in. And I sure as hell don't buy his bullshit about taking his bank to all cash. And did you hear how he threatened me and Julia O'Connell?"

"He has a history of doing just that," Betty said, but she couldn't get her mind away from Reid talking about a worm in their system, and something about a flash drive that Cassy was carrying, and now she was gone, which was the most ominous thing.

"This could be a blessing in disguise," Heather said. "I think whatever the bastard is up to is probably crooked, which is why I came to see you. Maybe we can help each other nail him. Send him to jail."

Betty almost smiled, except she was worried about Cassy, who had probably been so frightened she had gone into hiding somewhere. "I think you might be right about Reid trying to pull off some sort of a fast deal. And I think that we might be able to help each other, if you're willing to go toe-to-toe with him."

"You're damn right. I'm willing to do anything to stick it to him after he treated me like I was some common whore."

Betty held up the phone. "There's nothing solid here that would hold up in court, so what we need to do is rattle his chain, get him to lose his composure so he'll make a mistake."

Heather was doubtful. "I don't know if something like that would work. He's smooth."

"But besides money, his top priorities are his reputation and his social standing."

"That sounds like him."

"How would you like to go to a party tonight at the Met?"

"I really didn't bring anything formal to wear."

"Don't worry, you look fine as you are right now. Where are you staying?"

"The Grand Hyatt on Forty-second."

"I'll pick you up at eight."

"Is Reid going to be there?"

"Yes, and so will everyone in the city who counts," Betty said. "Including his wife."

82

Miller and Nichols had a very late lunch at the Hay-Adams because Stephanie Holland was on the floor riding herd on what an aide described as a crucial bill that needed her full support. At the table, they had looked over Nast's absurd plan, and it was even worse than they thought it probably would be.

They didn't make it back to her suite of offices in the Longworth House Office Building on South Capitol Street until well after three, and neither of them was happy about the delay. But they were coming with hats in hand, and it was never wise to anger the woman who was second in line to succeed the president behind the VP.

Nevertheless it was galling, especially to Nichols, who as Treasury secretary was fifth in line to the presidency. But it was all about pecking order, and Holland was letting them know just that.

The same aide came out to the anteroom. "Gentlemen, the Speaker will see you now," he said and turned on his heel and walked across the corridor, not bothering to make sure they were following until he was at the open door and stepped aside.

Holland was at her desk, her eyes glued to her computer

screen. Without looking up, she waved them to sit down in front of the fireplace, which during the summer was always filled with bouquets of flowers.

"Be just a minute," she said.

Miller and Nichols exchanged a glance, but took seats across a low coffee table from a beautiful Eames chair known as the Speaker's Throne.

After a full two minutes, she looked up, smiling. "That's done," she said, and she got to her feet and came over to them.

She was a stylish woman in her mid-fifties, slender, with soft brown hair parted down the middle—the same as her politics, she liked to say. She almost always dressed in a white silk blouse and plain skirt, medium heels, and a simple strand of pearls that accented her lovely neck.

They stood up as she came over, offering her hand first to Nichols. "Bob, how lovely it is to see you again."

"And you, Stephanie," he said, taking her delicate hand in both of his for a longish beat.

She turned to Miller. "Mr. Chairman," she said, and shook his hand for just a moment. "Sorry I had to keep you waiting, but it was the new fisheries bill, which needed a steady hand. It's been a pet project of mine."

"We understand," Nichols said.

"Please have a seat, and tell me what I can do for you this afternoon."

"We talked last week at the Kennedy Center party, and I touched on the problem we're having with debt," Nichols said. "Especially ours and China's."

"You bored me to tears," she said, fluttering her fingers, which she did when she was dismissing something she thought irrelevant. "And before you start again, I know all about Spencer's master plan to save our republic as we teeter on the brink of economic disaster."

Miller gave an involuntary grunt. How she had been able

to get her hands on Nast's crazy plan was beyond him. Except that, although she wasn't an intellectual giant, she did have daunting contacts.

"Do you have a comment, Mr. Chairman?" she said, smiling, something she always did when she was being sarcastic.

"This is not a frivolous issue, Madam Speaker," Miller said. "At this very moment, China's central bank is about to let its commercial banking system go under, which threatens to bring on worldwide chaos. In fact, we got off the phone with Governor Liu, who's head of the People's Bank of—"

"I know who he is," Holland interrupted. "In fact, we played tennis once at Merion Cricket Club outside of Philadelphia."

Miller was beyond frustration, but she held up a hand for him to allow her to continue.

"I'm not being frivolous," she said. "I realize that we couldn't sell all our Treasury bonds at today's auction, and that the stock market is in a free fall because of it. But I have to wonder."

"Wonder what?" Nichols asked.

"Wonder if it's as bad as you say it is. Nast wants to take us to DEFCON Five and have you print unlimited amounts of money to make up for the T-bond debacle. The fool wants to give just about every other American twenty grand in cash—and you have to admit that's a slick move. Meanwhile I'm told that the two of you want to go to DEFCON Three by raising the rates on Treasurys until someone buys them at a hell of a cost to us, and then ask Congress to hand out maybe a trillion dollars like we did in '08 to save Wall Street."

"Spence's proposal would ruin our fiscal standing," Miller said.

"Well then, what do you want from me?"

"Go public with your opposition," Nichols said.

"To your idea or Spence's?" She smiled. "I'll think about it."

Miller shook his head in disbelief. "With all due respect, Madam Speaker, we need to act right now."

Nichols broke in. "If and when the PBOC refuses to help the commercial banks—which is in actuality a scheme to oust Hua as head of the government—it will end up being '08 or something even worse."

"Are the both of you so sure that you've read the China situation accurately?"

"Yes, we have," Miller said. "As head of the PBOC, Liu is in a strong enough position to pull it off. He'll take charge in Beijing, and Hua will be exiled, jailed, or executed."

"An interesting assessment," Holland said. "But wrong." She let it hang for a moment. "Liu, like you, Mr. Chairman, prides himself on being an economist, *not* a politician. While Hua, though low-key, is a superb politician. Between him and Liu there is no contest. From what you told me, I think you misheard Liu on the phone today and came to the conclusion that he was talking about nuclear war."

"That's not true," Nichols said.

"When it comes to politics, both of you are out of your depth," Holland said. "If you want my advice, gentlemen, leave politics to the politicians."

"China or not, Madam Speaker, we're in trouble," Nichols said. "Our debt load is killing us, and something will have to give if we can't raise money in the bond market to spend our way out of it."

"That makes me wonder if this might be some clever ploy by Spencer's old boss, with Nast himself right in the middle of it."

"Ploy?" Miller asked, scarcely able to believe what he was hearing.

"By Reid Treadwell," she said. "I know the man well. Very well."

"You went to college together," Nichols said.

"Yes. And we were an item for a bit, if you can believe it. I got to know him before he became the big man on campus, but even then he was a scheming son of a bitch."

"Why are you telling us this?" Nichols asked. "What's your point?"

"No matter what happens in the next few days, I want you to take a very hard look at Reid and Burnham Pike and Spence's current relationship with the firm. Nast may be the president's man, but he's still Reid Treadwell's humble servant."

"I'm still not following you."

"I got a call from Betty Ladd today. She and I are what you might call members of a women's club—women who Reid has used and discarded. She said that from her perspective as president of the NYSE she's been conducting an informal inquiry into his recent business practices. He's taken his firm to an all-cash position, and she thinks that could be a prelude to some sort of an under-the-table maneuver."

"The man has a lot of friends here in Washington, including Farmer himself," Nichols said.

"Not a lot of people want to cross him," Miller added, realizing his mistake the moment the words came out of his mouth.

"Including you, Mr. Chairman?" Holland asked. "The Federal Reserve regulates the major banks, including Burnham Pike. Or does Reid have some sort of a hold on you?"

"Certainly not," Miller said. "But he is one of Farmer's major supporters."

"What about the chair that BP endowed when you were in academia? That was a million a year. And you did a stint as a consultant for the firm, which paid well, I'm told. Maybe after the Fed you might want to return."

"I don't know what the hell you're getting at, Madam Speaker. Treadwell may own Spencer, but the Federal Reserve—and that's me—is independent from everyone, bankers *and* politicians."

"I'm not insinuating anything here. All I'm saying is that Reid Treadwell is a slippery customer whose major passion in life is Reid Treadwell, because at heart he's just a frightened little boy from a small town in Ohio."

"He doesn't come across that way," Miller said.

"In school he was class president and had a Rhodes scholarship lined up when one of his professors accused him of cheating on a test. He came to me in tears saying that his life was over. He would be a laughingstock, and even his summer internships at Burnham Pike would disappear."

"What happened?"

"He called me that night and said he was going to end his problems once and for all. No one would be able to laugh at him ever again. I ran over to his dorm and found him sitting on the edge of his bed with a gun against his temple, his finger on the trigger."

"Jesus," Miller said. "That's not the Treadwell I know."

"Anyway, I managed to talk him down, and it was just a few days later that he dumped me," Holland said.

"So, what was the upshot?"

"Before we parted company, I told him that with his golden tongue, he could probably talk the professor into withdrawing the charges. But it didn't matter because he said that he had it all worked out."

"And?"

"I told him what he was going to do was unethical at the very least, but he wouldn't listen. Turns out he had a friend at Burnham Pike who told him that the professor had inherited a small sum of money and had opened an account there. Between the two of them, they doctored some trading records and reported the professor for insider trading."

"My God," Miller said.

"Supposedly the professor was front-running a pending merger deal, and he'd bought stock in the company that was going to be acquired ahead of time. Of course when the deal went through, the stock went crazy, and the professor made a ton of money."

"Let me guess," Nichols said. "The professor was arrested, the university dumped him, and the cheating charges against Treadwell were dropped."

Nichols sat forward. "Treadwell's friend at BP was a man named Dammerman?"

"None other," Holland said.

"Hard to believe," Miller said. "But in the meantime, where do we stand? We're going to need Congress to help out just like it did in '08."

The aide came to the door. "Madam Speaker, the president is on the phone."

"Line one," Holland said without getting up from her chair. "Yes, Mr. President, what can I do for you this afternoon?"

"Tell those two sons of bitches sitting across from you to get their tender asses back here on the double, we have work to do!"

83

Chip had placed a call to Huggard back in D.C. as Ben was being escorted off the aircraft, but it was a full two and a half hours before the admiral returned his call. In the meantime he had moved into the pilots' ready lounge, where he had a cup of coffee and a sandwich from one of the machines.

He'd also found out that Ben had been taken to the Midtown South Precinct, along with the names of the precinct commander and the New York City commissioner of police.

"Tell me that you and Ben are in the air and on the way back to do what you're being paid to do," Huggard said.

"Still on the ground, sir. We ran into some trouble."

"Police trouble?"

"Yes, sir. Ben was arrested as soon as we touched down."

"On what charge?"

"Threatening an ex-cop who is head of security at the investment bank where Ben's girlfriend, Cassy, works in IT."

"If I'm going to pull some strings for you guys, I need to know exactly what the hell is going on up there."

"Cassy Levin evidently stumbled on some problem at the bank—something her bosses evidently didn't want her meddling with—and she was kidnapped by a person or persons we believe are Russian and probably taken to an unknown location in Brighton Beach."

Huggard was silent for a moment or two. "How sure are you about your information?"

"She was recording what was happening to her and sending it to Ben's phone in real time until the transmission was cut off. The speaker was definitely Russian, and my guess, from the way he talked and the way the grab went down, would be that he was a former Spetsnaz operator."

"What other intel do you have, and how are you getting it?"

"We believe that she left the bank with one of her coworkers, a guy by the name of Donni Imani, and just prior to the grab, they separated. The bank's security officer said the two of them were out to lunch."

"And?"

"On a hunch I trolled the Manhattan nine-one-one logs, and found that at the same time Cassy was being taken, an unidentified male was struck by a truck less than a block away. I checked the EMT and hospital mainframes and found Imani's name as deceased. His body was taken to the morgue at Bellevue Hospital."

"And you believe that his death is connected with the kidnapping."

"Coincidental but connected," Chip said. "Cassy was evidently carrying a flash drive with information on it that the bank apparently didn't want her to take out of the building. I think that when she realized what was happening, she gave the drive to her friend, who took off and was killed."

"What else?"

"A guy by the name of Tom Raven showed up at the morgue claiming to be Imani's uncle and wanted to collect his nephew's belongings. He had no proof of kinship, so he was turned away. But I'm betting he was a Russian sent there to find the flash drive."

"Did you get the name of the arresting officer, and where Ben was taken?"

"Sergeant Roger Adams, and he's at the Midtown South Precinct."

"Hold on, I'll get right back to you."

"Do you want the precinct commander's name?"

"I'm going to call the mayor, we're old friends," Huggard said. "In the meantime, I suggest that you rent a car and get over to the precinct. I want this settled and you two back to work first thing in the A.M. Clear?"

"Yes, sir," Chip said, but the admiral had already rung off.

84

Adams was on the phone at his desk assuring Butch Hardy that Cassy's boyfriend was out of circulation for now when the precinct commander's assistant showed up.

"Voight wants to have a word."

"Be right there," Adams said, and the uniform left. "Gotta run, Butch, but whatever's going on you'd better get done with it or walk away, whichever makes the most sense."

"I owe you one, but just keep him there overnight."

"I'll see what I can do," Adams said and hung up.

Whalen was a pain in the ass, but he'd been a Navy SEAL lieutenant, which was a very big deal. Whatever it was that Butch was involved with over in Brooklyn had all the earmarks of going south at any moment.

He went down the hall to Precinct Commander Leonard Voight's office. The door was open, and Voight beckoned him in.

"Close the door, Roger," he said.

Adams did as he was told and went to sit down, but Voight held up a hand.

"This will take just a minute."

"Okay, Len, what's up?"

"You arrested a man by the name of Benjamin Whalen. And at the moment he's here in a holding cell. And you arrested him because you were told that he verbally assaulted a friend of yours."

"I have a copy of the recorded threat."

"From Butch Hardy, who was fired from this precinct just before I showed up, because he was nothing but a scumbag on the take."

"Unproven allegations. I've known Butch for—"

"I don't give a fuck if you think the son of a bitch is Jesus

Christ himself. And the reason this afternoon that I don't give a shit is because there's one thing I like even less. And that is a telephone call from the mayor, who told me in no uncertain terms to get my head out of my ass. And would you care to guess why he would say something like that to me?"

Adams held his silence.

"Because his pal is an admiral down in Washington who happens to be Mr. Whalen's boss," Voight said, his voice barely rising above a conversational level. "Now what do you suppose we should do to get the mayor off my ass?"

"I'll see to it immediately," Adams said.

"Then we never need to talk about this again."

"No, sir."

– – –

Ben looked up from where he was sitting on the edge of a cot as a deputy came to the door of the holding cell and unlocked it. "Whalen?"

"That's me."

"You're out of here."

Chip was waiting with Adams at the front desk when Ben came out. He had to sign for his wallet and other things that had been taken from him.

"I don't give a fuck who you know, tough guy, but if you so much as get within a block of Burnham Pike I'll have your ass back here," Adams said.

"It's my first stop," Ben said. "And you might want to give them the heads-up."

– – –

Outside they walked over to the public parking area where Chip had left the rental Chevy SUV and got in.

"Drop me off at Burnham Pike and then get your ass back out to the airport and take the plane back to D.C."

"If she's across the river in Brighton Beach, how are you going to get there?" Chip asked. "Take a subway? I'm driving."

"You're not getting involved, this is my problem."

"The admiral made it mine too. He wants both of us back in one piece, and the only way he knows that's going to happen is if I tag along and watch your back."

ELEVEN

CRISIS ARISING

85

Spencer Nast was waiting in the Roosevelt Room when Sam Kohlberg brought Bob Nichols and Joe Miller in, and the three of them sat down at the long conference table across from him.

Miller just nodded, but Nichols smiled. "Good afternoon, Spence," he said.

"It's Spencer."

The only people who got away with calling Nast Spence were his superiors plus Don Pennington, whose campaign contributions had landed Pennington the New York Fed presidency, and who would keep the pols away when BP emerged on top from the rubble.

"Good to know," the Treasury secretary said.

It was a wonder in Nast's mind how the idiot ever managed to write a Pulitzer Prize–winning book. "What were the two of you doing on the Hill?"

"Taking Holland's temperature, because we're going to need her help getting our rescue plan through Congress."

"You mean the one I worked out?"

"Actually, no," Miller said. "Bob and I have come up with a program that's a lot more practical than yours. Your idea about turning the Federal Reserve into a cornucopia of newly created money is . . . what can I say? A recipe for disaster? The dollar would become next to worthless in the international trade market. Our exports would suffer for sure, and our role in international finance would evaporate."

"How do you expect to bail out the banks and just about everyone else who'll go down the tubes if the market crashes? Where's the money coming from? More borrowing? The auction failure today sent us a clear message that investors are getting sick of our sky-high debt. The only possible resource at this point is the Federal Reserve."

"Over my dead body," Miller said dramatically.

Nast wanted to say that Butch Hardy could arrange an accident. Problem solved.

"Holland isn't particularly impressed by your plan," Nichols said.

"She's a politician and doesn't understand it. What do you expect?"

"You got a beef with politicians, Spence?" President Farmer asked as he came through the door.

"No, sir," Nast said as he and the others got to their feet.

"Take a load off," Farmer said and sat down at the head of the table.

The others followed suit.

"I was talking about the Speaker, Mr. President," Nast said. "She's never been known as a deep economic thinker."

"You're right, but she's a shrewd woman who gets things done. We don't see eye to eye, never have. But I respect her, and I advise that you do the same."

"Yes, sir, I will," Nast said. "But for the moment I'd like to go over some of the finer details of my plan with you."

"You've already briefed me, and I've read the thing," Farmer said, and turned to Nichols and Miller. "Now, I'd like to know why you pulled an end run on me by talking with Stephanie before we hashed things out. I expected you to stick around until Spence got here, and between us we could figure our way out of this mess—if a mess is actually coming our way, as you all seem to agree it is."

"It is, Mr. President," Nichols said.

"Bob, I could fire your ass in a New York minute if you refuse to play fair with me," Farmer said, and he turned to Miller. "You're an independent over at the Federal Reserve, but with not too much trouble I could pry you loose as well." He paused for effect. "Do we understand each other, gentlemen?"

Nichols nodded, but Miller started to object until the president cut him off.

"You'll get your chance, Mr. Chairman, because I truly want to hear what you have to say. I want every idea on the table here, even Spence's wild plan."

Nast had to keep from smiling; his *wild* plan?

Farmer swept his large hands across the tabletop as if he were smoothing a wrinkled map. "Here's the lay of the land," he said. "Back in '08, when the world financial system was going to hell, the Federal Reserve chairman and the Treasury secretary worked together to save it, with the New York Fed chief putting the program into effect. But I get that Ben Bernanke and Hank Paulson had advantages we don't have. Like a debt load that was way lower than the one we're faced with, and an unflagging demand for our T-bonds.

"I want to know what we can do this time. Pay through the nose in higher interest rates to take on even more debt than we're already choking on, like Joe and Bob want? But that'd just be kicking the can down the road, to my way of thinking. Or raid the Federal Reserve to pull new money out of the clear blue sky, which among other things would put twenty large in the pockets of the bottom half of the American public? What Spence wants."

"Mr. President, if I may have the floor for a moment—" Nast began, but again Farmer cut him off.

"Here's the problem, Spence. My original idea was that you would quarterback our rescue operation from behind the scenes, and the Fed and Treasury would carry the ball. Especially Bob, because old Miller is about as unloved in Congress as you are. But I'm having a whole lot of trouble seeing how you're all going to work together. As a team."

Nast tried to speak up, but Farmer continued, "Now, Joe, how about you give me your grand vision, and try not to bore the living bejesus out of me."

"My pleasure, Mr. President," Miller said. "And I'll try not to bore you."

"I'm a simple country boy. Get to it."

Miller launched into a complex explanation of what the debt load was doing to the government and to the economy in general, and his opinion that the situation would get worse—much worse—unless something drastic was done immediately. It was something he'd already explained, but when a president asked a question, you answered it.

After nearly ten minutes, Farmer raised a hand, and Miller stopped short.

"That was better than Ambien," Farmer said. "What you're saying is that since we've already piled on a wagon-load of debt, what's a few tons more? We need to save the economy, right?"

"Yes, sir," Miller said and he started to say something else, but once again Farmer cut him off.

"There's an important detail you're missing."

"If it's how much we'd have to shell out, Mr. President, it would be substantial. In the coming auction we'd have to raise the rate on our ten-year Treasury—our benchmark obligation—from three percent to seven. And should the Chinese catastrophe actually occur, well—"

"What's missing, Mr. Chairman, is Spence's good idea about giving the bottom half of the American public some much-needed cash. If we assume that China wrecks the world's economy, it would mean a lot of our folks would be out of work. Spence's payout would tide them over and put money back into our economy. It'd be like giving a transfusion to a weak patient."

"You're talking about socialism, sir," Miller blurted.

"I was waiting for you to trot out that term," Nast said. "Anytime Washington gives something to tide people over, you make it seem like the Russian revolution, the Bolsheviks storming the czar's palace gates. By your logic Medicare and especially Social Security are socialism too. But because they work so well and they're so popular, no one wants to ax them or even shrink them."

"They're bankrupting us already, and everyone knows it," Miller said. "Their benefits need to be trimmed right now. Cut in half."

"Not on my watch," Farmer said.

"And what will you do when the next Treasury auction at seven percent fails as well, Joe?" Nast asked.

"You think that you can just waltz in and convert the Federal Reserve into a direct-revenue source for the government?" Miller demanded. "Only taxes and borrowing can do that by law. And there are a lot of statutes that would get in your way if you tried something like that."

"We'll change them," Nast said in a rush. He knew he was on top.

Farmer rapped his knuckles on the tabletop. "Enough," he said. "We can work out the details later on. But for now we have a more immediate concern that we have to deal with."

"What's that, Mr. President?" Nichols asked.

"A possible scheme by a man we all like and distrust coming down the pike to corrupt high government officials. A man by the name of Reid Treadwell, who is a personal friend of mine."

Nast had a hard time catching his breath. It was as if all the air had suddenly left the room.

"Reid has greased plenty of palms. My election campaign

for one. Your high and mighty university chair, Mr. Chairman, was funded by Burnham Pike. And, Spence, you were his top economist and still are."

"Sir, you told me to cut off contact with Reid. It's done. And my dealings with him have been at arm's length ever since I came to work for you."

"Son, you're pissing in my ear and telling me it's raining outside," Farmer said. "Don Pennington called me and said you offered him Bob Nichols's job as Treasury secretary. The only problem is, it's not yours to give. What's worse is that Don said that the price was to 'play ball,' as he put it. Meaning don't give Wall Street—Burnham Pike—a hard time if shit goes south. Look out for their interests. I'm thinking that Burnham Pike wants to clean up like they did in '08. I can smell a Reid Treadwell maneuver rolling down the road at us. And in my book, what you tried to do to poor old Pennington was outright bribery."

"Mr. President, I never offered Don anything."

"Nasty, I was born at night, but not last night. Pennington wants Bob's spot at Treasury, but he doesn't trust Treadwell to add up two and two to get four. He ratted you out, my boy."

"With all due respect, Mr. President, it's his word against mine. He may have misinterpreted what I told him. He's a part of the bank regulatory process, and I never told him, or even intimated, that he go easy on Wall Street. In fact, I told him the opposite. Vigilance, I said, if any firm oversteps its bounds."

Farmer laughed. "You're tap-dancing faster than Fred Astaire," he said. "Thing is, I got another call about you this afternoon."

"Sir?"

"Betty Ladd, who's a straight shooter in my book, said she was sure that Treadwell was up to something no good. Could be whatever it is has something to do with a computer virus or something. This thing apparently could screw up stock exchanges around the world. At that breakfast you had with Treadwell and his crew this morning, you were all toasting it."

Nast struggled for a response.

"And it had a weird name too," Farmer said. "Abacus, I think Betty said."

86

Bykov waited a couple of hours before he called Anosov back to see if there was any good news about the flash drive after Panov's failure at the morgue.

Anosov answered on the first ring, as if he'd been expecting the call. "Yes."

"It's me, what have you come up with?"

"There's no way we're getting the flash drive from the dead guy's things at the morgue, not without causing a lot of suspicion, something I definitely don't want."

"Our employers won't give a shit about your problems, Leonid. Either get the flash drive, or come back here with the money, because I sure as hell won't pay for your screwups."

"I'll think about it. But I'm bailing out within the next twenty-four hours. I've already got just about everything in place."

"These people have a long reach."

"Listen to me, Yuri, shit is starting to go east, if you know what I mean," Anosov said. East was the direction of Siberia from Moscow. To a Russian it meant bad things were about to happen.

"*Ya ponimau,*" Bykov said. *I understand.* "If you're going to Marseille, bury yourself for a few months until things cool down."

"Canada first."

"Why?"

"I'm going to drive the woman up to Montreal. I've already been offered one hundred thousand euros sight unseen."

"When do you leave?"

"Sometime in the morning. I want to be out of the city by dawn."

"What about your people?"

Anosov hesitated for a moment. "Valentin's tagging along. He's an asshole, but he's a friend."

"The others?"

"They're sticking it out."

"Go with God, *staryy drug,*" Bykov said. *Old friend.*

"And you."

— — —

Butch Hardy was just about to leave his office to check on his security people, mainly at the front and rear entrances to the building, when his phone rang. It was an outside line.

"Hardy."

"It's Dugan," Bykov said. "There's no way we'll be able to get the flash drive without causing some serious blowback. Which wouldn't do you any good if it's something you need to keep secret."

Hardy couldn't believe what he was hearing. "Goddamnit, you vouched for those people."

"They're your people. Anyway, I was told that the kid's parents are coming for the body in the morning. Unless they're computer experts, they won't know what a flash drive is or how to use it, so your secrets are safe."

"We want our money back."

"It won't happen."

"We'll see," Hardy said, and he slammed the phone down.

87

Treadwell was in his office talking with Dammerman about Betty Ladd and her suspicions when Ashley buzzed him.

"It's Mr. Hardy on two," she said.

Treadwell put it on speakerphone. "What do you have for me?"

"It's a no-go. But the good news is that the kid's parents are picking up his body first thing in the morning, and it's highly unlikely they'll know what the thing is or even care. Anyway, it's the investment bank's business and is probably encrypted."

"What about our money?" Dammerman asked.

"It's gone, and I suggest that we treat it as an ordinary business loss and don't pursue the matter. But it's your call, and I'll do whatever you want me to do."

Dammerman started to say something, but Treadwell shook his head.

"You're right, Butch," he said. "We'll just hold off for now."

"Yes, sir," Hardy said, and Treadwell hung up.

"What do you want me to do?" Dammerman asked.

"Butch is right, we'll just leave it be for now."

88

Anosov was at an upstairs window in his room, staring down at the sparse traffic on the street below. It was a workday afternoon, and most people in Brighton Beach were on the job somewhere. By five or six tonight the bars would be filled with laughing men and their women, who by midnight

290 - DAVID HAGBERG and LAWRENCE LIGHT

would be drunk and thinking about heading home for a few hours' sleep before the morning shift.

Ordinary people leading ordinary lives, something he'd not had since his Spetsnaz training days, and especially not since he'd been given a dishonorable discharge for striking an officer. The prick had deserved it, and the court-martial board had agreed, so he wasn't given any jail time.

And now Brighton Beach was over for him. He and Valentin had plenty of money to get to Marseille, with a quick stop in Montreal, and set up shop for the next gig. But maybe not for eight months or so. Time, he thought, to take a break and enjoy himself.

He turned away from the window and went down the hall to the bathroom, where he washed his hands and splashed some water on his face.

When he was finished, he went back to the attic stairs, which he pulled down, and headed up to the woman.

Time, he thought again, to start enjoying himself.

– – –

The tiny attic room was dark except for a little light shining through the edges of the door, as Cassy tried to work the balltop hinge pin out of its sockets with her bare fingers, which were bloodied now after a half hour's work. But the pin had come loose, and she thought it would come out, when she heard the attic stairs swing down.

She stepped back, wiping her bloodied fingers on her jeans as someone came up the stairs.

It was going to start now, and she didn't know how she was going to take it. She wanted Ben more than she'd ever wanted anything in her life. And it wasn't to save her—there were too many of them downstairs for even Ben to take on—but for him to be here and tell her that he would love her no matter what happened.

The latch was thrown, and the man who had searched her came in, leaving the door half open so that there was some light.

"Take off your clothes," he said.

Cassy backed up a step. "No."

"If you make it easy, I won't have to hurt you. But I will if need be."

She backed up again. "No, you bastard!" she yelled.

He was on her in an instant, and she only had a vague notion that he had hit her in the face with his fist when she fell back onto the bed, her stomach roiling and her senses fuzzing out.

89

Hardy was just leaving his office to go downstairs and have another chat with Masters about the program Cassy Levin was working on when his phone rang. It was Roger Adams.

"You've got trouble coming your way, Butch."

"Tell me that you're keeping Whalen overnight like I asked."

"The guy's boss is pals with Mayor Young, who called Voight, who ordered me to release the bastard. I told the prick to stay away from you, but he said his first stop was the bank."

Hardy was thinking fast. "How long ago was that?"

"Half hour."

"Christ," Hardy said and hung up.

90

Chip found a parking spot on Nassau, half a block from Burnham Pike. "I'm going in with you," he said.

"Stay here," Ben told him.

"If and when you start busting heads, I'll stand back, but for now two government IDs beat one. Anyway this is an investment bank, which means it's a civilized place, filled with civil people, not macho, knuckle-dragging tough guys."

"Listen to me. I need you as a backup when the shit hits the fan. I need to keep you in reserve. I don't want anyone other than the cop who arrested me to know your face."

Chip was frustrated. "Well, I'm not going to let you go into the bank packing. In the first place they're probably expecting you, and carrying a firearm in this state carries a pretty stiff penalty. Huggard wouldn't be able to bail you out again."

"You win, but in the meantime I need you to pinpoint the Brighton Beach location where they took Cassy."

"I'm on it," Chip said. "But I assume that after we're done here, we're going over to the morgue to try for the flash drive. Could be we'll be able to find out something about the Russian who used his Raven ID."

"I'm depending on you."

"I have you covered."

"What floor is Treadwell's office?"

"Fifty-four."

Ben got out of the car, walked up to the Burnham Pike tower. Inside he approached the registration desk, where two large men in blue blazers with the firm's logo on the breast pockets looked up.

"I'm here to see Mr. Treadwell," Ben told them, showing them his driver's license.

"Do you have an appointment, Mr. Whalen?" one of the security people asked.

"No, but I think he's probably expecting me."

"Yes, sir." The agent picked up the phone and called someone. "He's here."

A woman was just getting off the elevator. Ben turned and, moving fast but not running, vaulted the turnstile that blocked the lobby from the elevators. He got to the car before the doors closed.

"Stop now," the guard at the turnstile shouted.

Ben hit the button for fifty, the highest floor it would go to, and as the doors closed, he saw one of the guards at the desk pick up a phone.

91

Hardy was waiting for the executive elevator to take him upstairs to warn Treadwell that Cassy's boyfriend might be showing up here when the security officer's call from downstairs rolled over to his cell phone.

"Whalen showed up like you said he would, but before we could stop him he grabbed an elevator, and he's on his way up."

"Is he armed?"

"I didn't see a bulge under his jacket, but he could be carrying in a holster at his back. But the guy's not big. Can't be more than five-nine or ten, and lightweight," the officer said. "Do you want me to shut down the elevators?"

"No," Hardy said, making the snap decision.

The elevator came, and on the way up he used the house phone to call Treadwell.

"Mr. Treadwell's office, who may I say is calling?" Ashley answered.

"I'm on my way up, but we have some trouble coming our way. Tell the boss."

92

Ben was just getting off the fire stairs up from fifty when a stocky man entered Treadwell's office just down the corridor. Other than that man, the corridor was as empty and as hushed as a church on a Monday afternoon.

He went down to the CEO's office, where the man was waiting for him.

"I'm going to have to ask you to leave this building at once, Mr. Whalen," Hardy said.

Treadwell was behind his desk watching them, and Ben met his eyes and nodded.

He turned back to the stocky man. "Or what?"

"I'll have you arrested."

"Didn't work the first time, and I just have one question for your boss."

Hardy reached for Ben's arm.

"I would advise you not to touch me," Ben said quietly, not moving away.

Hardy stepped back. "Ashley, please call the police department, tell them that we have a situation here."

"That won't be necessary, Ash," Treadwell said from his office door. "Please come in, Mr. Whalen. And Butch, if you'll just wait outside here for a minute, you can escort the gentleman out of the building."

He stepped aside, and Ben went in after him.

Treadwell didn't return to his desk. "Now, as I understand it, you're close to one of our employees, Ms. Cassy Levin, and you believe that she's missing."

"She's been kidnapped by a Russian or Russians and has been taken somewhere in Brighton Beach."

Treadwell didn't react. "I'm told that she hasn't come back from lunch, but if you think, for whatever reason, that a crime has been committed against her, then I suggest you inform the police."

Ben smiled and nodded. "Thank you, Mr. Treadwell, you've told me everything I needed to know." He started to turn away but then turned back. "I will find her and deal with her kidnappers. Then I will come back here with the flash drive she recorded, and we'll have this discussion again. And perhaps for your safety you might want to have a police presence. I'm sure they'll have a few questions of their own."

— — —

Chip was on his laptop when Ben got back to the car. He looked up, grinning. "You're not going to believe this."

"I'm all ears," Ben said.

"There's a central automated switchboard and recording system in the building. I trolled the numbers for Reid Treadwell, the CEO, and for Butch Hardy, the chief of security."

"I just met them both."

"Treadwell is in a dispute with a woman by the name of Betty Ladd. Turns out she's the president of the New York Stock Exchange, and she's accusing Treadwell of some sort of stock manipulation or financial hanky-panky. But I got really lucky with Hardy. He made one phone call to some-one named Dugan, who was definitely a Russian or maybe Eastern European. Anyway, Hardy broke off the call almost immediately."

"But?"

"I think he made a mistake by using his office phone to call this guy. I think he probably switched to his cell phone."

"And?"

"I'm accessing NSA's data retrieval base, phone calls in the last twenty-four hours between U.S. cell phones to people with Russian accents inside the country. We might get lucky."

"How long?"

"Minutes, hours, days," Chip said. "Anyway, my machine is chewing on it. In the meantime, let's try the morgue, and on the way you can assure me that you didn't shoot anyone yet."

93

Dammerman showed up at Treadwell's office, his fleshy face downcast. "We've got a problem, Mr. T," he said, closing the glass door behind him.

"Christ, is Whalen back?"

"No, and this is ten times as bad. It's going to hit the news any minute now, and I thought you'd want to be prepared. The media's bound to come calling for you to make a statement."

Treadwell slumped back in his seat. He'd spent the last hour or so appeasing several board members and a number of important clients who were worried about the way the market had taken a dump just before the closing bell.

"What's it mean?" had been the common refrain.

"Hold on, we're on top of it," had been his reply.

But now Dammerman's warning that something even worse was coming at them—at him personally—wasn't something he wanted to hear. "What is it this time, Clyde?"

"Farmer just fired Spencer Nast."

Treadwell sat bolt upright, as if he'd just received a high-voltage shock. "What the hell for?"

"The official version is that Spence resigned because he wants to spend more time with his family."

"He hates his wife and kid," Treadwell said. "Have you talked to him?"

"He texted me about it, and said he wants to talk to you as soon as possible."

"This is a goddamn disaster, or it will be if the idiot opens his mouth to the wrong people to save his own ass," Treadwell said. He called his secretary. "Ash, get me Spence."

— — —

Spencer Nast sat on a park bench in Lafayette Park across Pennsylvania Avenue from the White House, unable to grasp what had just happened to him. Tourists were peering through the fence, hoping to get a glimpse of the president or someone else important, but it seemed like they were from another planet, another galaxy.

White-shirted security people had escorted him out of the building and down the driveway to the Northwest Appointments Gate. His office in the Eisenhower Building would be inventoried, and anything belonging to him, and not the government, would be returned as soon as practicable.

Farmer had told him to get the hell out of his sight in front of Miller and Nichols. "You no longer work for me because I don't trust you."

Kolberg had hustled him out of the Roosevelt Room, where a pair of security officers were waiting to escort him past West Wing staffers who looked up as he passed and then either averted their gaze or openly grinned. The walk had been more than humiliating.

Sitting now, trying to work out his options, he was mostly at a loss. The only things that really mattered were the Abacus deal and his position at BP. But he wasn't sure of anything.

His cell phone chimed, and he picked up. It was Treadwell, who didn't sound happy.

"What the hell happened, for Christ's sake? I counted on you to shield us from anything that might come our way from your end down there."

"Nothing I could do about it, Reid," Nast said. "Apparently Betty called Farmer and warned him that you were up to no good. He believed her, and he's convinced that I'm still more loyal to you and BP than I am to him. I tried to tell him that wasn't the case, but he didn't believe me."

"Jesus, is that all?"

"It's Don Pennington. I talked to him about the Treasury secretary's job, and he evidently called Farmer to find out if I had been telling the truth. I never thought the moron would be so stupid as that, but Farmer threw it in my face as well."

"You told me that you had him in the bag," Treadwell said. "What else have you screwed up?"

"I can still be useful, Reid. I know all the players down here, and we still need to cover our asses after opening bell in the morning. I know which buttons to push, and I'm capable of pushing them."

"You fucked up, Spence."

"Things that can't be predicted sometimes go wrong," Nast said. He wasn't going to bring up Betty telling the president that she'd overheard them at the Kittredge this morning talking about Abacus.

The only thing he could do now was wait until the virus did its job, and he'd be home free.

"That's what you were supposed to cover for us."

"You're still going to need me as your chief economist, and I have my portion of Abacus."

"I'll get back to you on both of those possibilities,"

Treadwell said. "But now get the fuck off the phone, I've got some fires to put out up here. Shit that you were supposed to take care of, genius."

The phone went dead, and Nast hunched over in despair, letting it slip out of his hand and fall to the ground. He began to cry, something he hadn't done since he was a child. Everything he had worked for, everything that meant anything to him, was gone, and he didn't know what to do about it.

A man, obviously homeless, with a small cardboard sign that read GOD BLESS YOU, walked past. "Hey, brother," he said to Nast. "It could be worse. You could be me."

Nast looked up, took a five-dollar bill out of his pocket, and gave it to the man.

"God bless."

— — —

Treadwell had put the call on speakerphone so that Dammerman could hear. They looked at each other. "The goddamn fool."

"Look on the bright side, Mr. T. The market is down twenty percent today, trading suspended. The shorts you and I made through the Caribbean banks are paying off bigtime. And when Abacus kicks in at opening bell tomorrow, we'll hit the jackpot."

Treadwell nodded, but his stomach was in a knot. "With Betty on our ass, and now Farmer—who never had any qualms about taking my money—on board the witch hunt, we have to watch our step."

"They didn't even give the bank a second look after we made that great short in '08. The pols huffed and puffed, but no charges were ever filed."

"It might be different if this creates another Great Depression."

"Nobody can trace Abacus back to us. The Whalen

boyfriend can't prove a thing. And his girlfriend has disappeared along with the flash drive antidote. Problem solved."

"No unauthorized personnel will be allowed inside this building until after opening bell. I want Butch to be perfectly clear. It's all hands on deck starting right now."

Dammerman nodded.

"I want your men armed."

"Done. But in the meantime, what about Spence? I don't think we should give him a dime."

"We wouldn't want him to turn state's evidence."

Dammerman shrugged. "Accidents happen."

Treadwell turned away. He had a bitch of a headache coming on, something a couple of aspirin wasn't going to make go away.

"By this time tomorrow we'll have the world by the balls," Dammerman said. "If Washington wants the economy to keep going, it will need Burnham Pike to help finance the recovery. The only investment bank that didn't go up in flames."

Treadwell was lost in his thoughts and didn't reply. Too much could still go wrong.

"The funny thing is, Nast thinks I'm his friend. But I was never able to stand the sanctimonious son of a bitch."

The flat-screen television on the wall across from Treadwell's desk was tuned to CNBC. He glanced at it as the talking heads were in the middle of a discussion of how the widespread market carnage was due in a large part to the failure of the Treasury bond auction plus the bank turmoil brewing in China.

The television program switched to Gina Sutton, the White House press secretary, who was announcing that the president's economic adviser, Spencer Nast, had resigned to spend more time with his family. But she turned and left, taking no questions.

"Everyone knows that was a crock of shit," Dammerman said. "No one resigns from anything to spend more time with their family. And the typical visual would have been for the president to appear with Spence, telling everyone about how much the guy contributed and how much he would be missed."

Treadwell looked away from the television. "What if they arrest Nast, and he turns on us in exchange for leniency?"

"Then we're cooked."

"Nast has to vanish. Clear?"

"Consider it done, Mr. T," Dammerman said.

94

Dammerman returned to his office just down the corridor from Treadwell's and shut the glass door. He went to the window and looked north toward the Chrysler and Empire State buildings as he worked to get his thoughts straight.

Things were getting a little too fuzzy around the edges for him, and it gave him the willies. Especially Treadwell's melting down and ordering Nast taken out, which made no sense at all. As much of an idiot as Nasty had always been, he was a high-profile player in Washington. And making him disappear, though certainly doable, would present a number of problems, not the least of which would be a full-court press by the D.C. police and almost certainly the FBI.

Despite what he had told Treadwell, Dammerman didn't think he should give any orders right now to make Nast go away like Cassy Levin. It would be too risky.

In '08 Treadwell was *the* man, almost single-handedly bringing BP out of the subprime mortgage mess that the company had helped stoke. But now he was caving in, and maybe going to the gala at the Met this evening would help calm him down. He'd always liked the attention from the high society set that his position and his wife's money gave him.

Attention that Dammerman had always thought was pure bullshit. Personally, he'd never parted with a dime for charity. If the do-gooders wanted to raise money, why not go out and earn it themselves instead of dressing up in tuxedos and holding out their begging bowls?

No one in Queens, where he was born and raised, did silly shit like that.

In the meantime he had to take care of himself with some insurance.

He went back to his desk, where he took one of his burner phones out of a drawer and called Dieter Kristof, his alternate broker, one of the wheeler-dealers who managed off-the-grid transactions with money stashed in offshore banks and other places that the IRS didn't need to know about.

Kristof was a former BP broker who'd served three years in the medium-security federal prison at Otisville in western New York state for a number of trading violations. He'd never changed his modus operandi, but now he was doing business in Hong Kong, guzzling mai-tais and banging the local girls, whom he impressed with his money.

Treadwell had his own alternate brokers, but for security reasons and just plain common sense neither of them knew who the other dealt with.

Given the business with Heather Rockingham, the flash drive that had somehow gone missing, and Cassy Levin's ex-SEAL fiancé showing up out of the blue playing the macho man bullshit, Dammerman had decided earlier today to switch gears and reverse his order to short the S&P 500 to the tune of $20 million—betting that the market would take a nosedive.

"Honorable Ho's," Kristof answered with his slight German accent.

"Six plum wines to go," Dammerman replied. It was their code this month.

"It's a done deal. But it beats the hell out of me why you'd want to unwind this trade. The market is already down twenty percent, so even if it stays there, you'd clean up by morning."

"I've got my reasons," Dammerman said. "No footprints leading back to me."

"As usual. But it hurts to think of the serious money that could have been added to your account."

"Talk to you later," Dammerman said, and he broke the connection.

Tax havens, especially in Hong Kong, where privacy laws blocked outside taxing authorities such as the IRS from looking into their customers' affairs, were strictly protected. This was a good thing under most circumstances. But he didn't want to take any chances right now. It was just a gut feeling, but he'd always gone along with his instincts.

With the way things had been going since noon, Dammerman had decided to bail, just in case, and then try to keep Reid on track. And it wouldn't be the first time, or probably the last.

In college when they'd first met, Treadwell was a sharp customer—unflappable, self-possessed, charming, but dumb in a lot of ways. Like being caught cheating on a test. Dammerman had been working as an intern at BP, and he'd cooked up a deal that got the professor fired and Treadwell off the hook.

Since then Treadwell had cut a lot of corners, and Dammerman had been right there backstopping him.

But this time was different. Taking out Nast would be a problem. But there were others too. Julia O'Connell was definitely a weak link, especially because of her connection with Betty Ladd, who already had a major issue with Reid.

And Butch Hardy, who knew too much, but not the real reason why they were involved with the Russians.

– – –

Dammerman phoned Hardy, who was downstairs in DCSS, and asked him to come up.

"Good, I was planning on talking to you anyway. We have a problem."

"What's the issue?"

"I'll be right up," Hardy said, and he hung up.

Dammerman sat holding the phone to his ear for a beat before he could calm himself enough to put it down without going ballistic. No one hung up on him. No one.

Hardy showed up a couple of minutes later. Still holding himself in check, Dammerman waved him in.

"I can't get ahold of the Brighton Beach guys," Hardy said.

"What are you talking about?"

"I called to find out if they'd managed to get the flash drive, but they won't call me back. I was even going to offer them some extra money. A bonus. But nothing."

"You told them you wanted them to give back the money we already paid. Why the fuck should they want to talk to you again?"

Hardy spread his hands. "If you told me why the flash drive is so important, maybe I could think of something else."

"What's on it is none of your fucking business," Dammerman shouted, finally losing what little self-control he had left. Failure was never an excuse. Never.

Hardy's jaw clenched. It was obvious that he didn't like being talked down to. He was a guy from the streets, and no bullshit top-floor exec was going to treat him that way.

But Dammerman didn't care. "What's on the drive doesn't matter. Nor do I give a shit about your Russian friends. But we do have another problem that might be coming at us sometime tonight."

"Yes, sir," Hardy said evenly.

"The problem is Whalen. I think it's a good bet that he'll try to get in the building tonight. I don't want that to happen."

"I have two officers on eight-hour shifts overnight."

"I want all hands on deck, and that includes you."

"Against one man?"

"It's possible he got the flash drive your Russian pals couldn't get. I don't want it anywhere near this building."

"I don't give a flying fuck what's so important on some flash drive, but my people—me included—will need triple pay if we're going to do an overnighter."

"I don't give a damn," Dammerman shouted. "Why did we pay your douchebag Russians a shit pot full of money to get a goddamn bit of plastic from a corpse? Your people should have put a gun to somebody's head and demanded to be shown Imani's body!"

"The morgue is crawling with cops. They would have taken down our guy, or he would have told them God only knows what, which could have led back to us. Or didn't you consider that?"

"You vouched for them, you fuck head," Dammerman said. "Spetsnaz and all that horseshit. Now all you're giving me are excuses."

"Watch who you're calling a fuck head, asshole!"

Dammerman got to his feet. "I'll call you anything I want to call you. I scraped your ass out of the gutter after the department fired you. I gave you your life back along with a lot more pay and perks than you ever got as a cop. And you know what? I can take it away just like that." He snapped his fingers. "Fuck head!"

Hardy was seething with anger, but he didn't raise his voice. "Will there be anything else, sir?"

"I don't care if you have to drive out to Brighton Beach, but I want you to make sure your pals don't screw the pooch in Jersey tomorrow morning. Can you at least get that much through your thick head?"

Yes, sir," Hardy said through clenched teeth. "I can get it through my thick head."

"Then get the hell out of here. And try not to fuck up again."

95

By the time Chip had parked at Bellevue Hospital, he'd gotten no hits from the NSA search program. "This could take time," he said.

"We don't have time," Ben said. "Any way to speed it up?"

"Not without the risk that my incursion would be discovered, in which case I'd be blocked from their mainframe, and a couple of guys with guns would come looking for me."

"Stick with it, and hope I get lucky inside."

"You're going to need someone to play the role of a lawyer, so I'm coming with you this time," Chip said.

They went into the main building and took an elevator downstairs to the morgue, where a woman in jeans and a white shirt was at a desk behind the counter.

"May I help you?" she asked, getting up and coming to them.

"We're here to identify the remains of Donald Imani, who was killed in a traffic accident earlier today," Ben said.

"His sister asked if I could stop by for her," Chip added.

The woman raised an eyebrow. "The decedent apparently has a lot of friends and relatives, and I'll tell you the same thing I told his uncle: Mr. Imani's parents will be arriving in the morning to claim the body." She started to turn away.

"Excuse me, Miss," Chip said. "My name is Chip Fair-cloth. Lieutenant Commander Faircloth, Naval Office of the Judge Advocate in Washington, D.C. And actually, we're here under orders. The decedent may have been carrying material sensitive to an investigation we're involved with."

The woman wasn't impressed. "What information?"

"It's classified."

"Bring me a court order."

"May I have your name, please?"

"Margaret Singer."

"If need be, Ms. Singer, I'll order an investigation into your apparent attempt to impede a federal inquiry. I could have people here within the hour."

The woman said nothing.

Chip nodded. "Someone will be in touch with you and your superiors later this afternoon." He turned to Ben. "We're wasting our time here, Captain," he said. "Let's go."

They were halfway to the door when the woman stopped them.

"Wait," she said.

They pulled up short and turned around.

"I don't want any trouble," she said. "I'm just trying to do my job, is all."

"The same as us," Chip said.

"May I see some ID?"

They went back to the counter and Chip produced his U.S. Navy identity card.

The woman copied it on a machine under the counter and handed it back. She phoned someone named Larry, who came out a minute later in a white lab coat.

"These gentlemen would like to look at the belongings of Imani, Donald A. If they wish to take something away with them, have them sign a four fifty-one."

"Yes, ma'am," Larry said. He was a young man with

a broad smile, which Ben thought unusual in a place like this.

He led them back past an autopsy room, to the refrigerated area where bodies were kept in drawers stacked three high in a dozen rows. He opened a middle one four rows along, a puff of refrigerated fog rising.

"Take your time," he said. "I'll be just down the hall on your way out."

A clear plastic bag with Imani's bloodied clothes plus a large manila envelope were lying at his feet on top of the sheet.

Ben took out the envelope and opened it. Besides a wallet, seventy some dollars in bills and change, a small plastic holder with toothpicks, another with dental floss, there was a small black flash drive with the word SCANDISK printed on one side and SCANDISK CRUZER 408 plus some other symbols and numbers on the other side, and a narrow strip of paper with a string of numbers and letters on the bottom.

"That it?" Chip asked.

"Nothing else is inside."

"Then let's get the hell out of here, this place gives me the willies," Chip said.

Ben pocketed the device, and on the way out they stopped at the kid's desk where Chip signed for it, and then they went through the double doors to the front desk.

"Did you find what you were looking for?" Margaret asked.

"Yes, we did," Chip said. "Thanks for your help."

"You're welcome, just don't mention my name."

— — —

Back at the car Chip powered up his laptop and accessed the NSA program, but no hits had shown up yet. "What do you want to do next?"

"Bring up the call Hardy made on his landline to this Russian."

"All he wanted to know was if they'd found the flash drive, but then the call ended," Chip said. He pulled up the call and played it back.

"Again," Ben said.

Chip did it again.

"The guy is definitely Russian, and he talked like a soldier."

"We knew that already."

"What was the area code of the number?"

"Six four six," Chip said. "And I already checked, it's in Manhattan, not Brighton Beach. Could mean she's in town and not across the river in Brooklyn."

"She's in Brighton Beach."

"Are you sure?"

"Yes."

Chip glanced at his laptop screen, numbers on the NSA site scrolling up so fast they were nothing more than a blur, with pauses every now and then before the search continued.

"What now?" he asked.

Ben glanced at his watch. It was just four-thirty. "We'll find a place to hunker down until you get a hit."

"Okay, where?"

"Brighton Beach," Ben said. "But first give me the pistol."

TWELVE

RESCUE

96

Treadwell got home to his elegant old-world co-op on the Upper East Side a little after seven, in plenty of time to dress for this year's Met Gala, the theme of which was the Roaring Twenties. He loved high society parties, although putting on stupid-looking period garb was beneath his dignity. Still, he had a lot more on his mind than trying to argue with Bernice about dressing in a costume. In any event, she would already have laid out what he was to wear.

He'd brought Duke Lawson, one of Hardy's people, along for security this evening, and he intended to take the large, muscular man to the gala, though something like that was never done.

But with Whalen storming the gates this afternoon and still out there at large, plus the Russian hoods here in the city and the ones out in Brighton Beach, he didn't feel safe. He even carried his father's .45 in a holster beneath his jacket.

The doorman greeted Treadwell with his usual polite enthusiasm but didn't acknowledge the larger man, who would remain in the lobby. Bernice would never have permitted someone like him to come upstairs to their two-story digs.

"I'll be down in a couple of minutes," Treadwell told his security man, who merely nodded and stepped aside.

Upstairs, Bernice, already changed into a designer short silk flapper dress with a fringe above her knees, white gloves to her elbows, and a headband with a feather in front, was waiting for him.

She had been a spoiled, overbearing rich girl from the beginning, but Treadwell had to admit she was an attractive woman. Always had been.

"You look like your best friend, if you ever had one, just died," she said.

"The market went to hell today," he said, walking past her into their exquisitely furnished apartment. A large oil painting of Bernice's late father, Thatcher Pike—in his day the stuffiest son of a bitch on Wall Street—stared down at him in disapproval.

"Isn't it always going to hell?"

"No," Treadwell said, taking off his tie and heading back to his bedroom wing.

Bernice was right behind him. "Considering who's on the guest list, I want you to be your usual charming self. I simply won't put up with any nonsense from you."

Treadwell stopped and turned back to her. "What are you talking about?"

"For starts, the bimbo you had lunch with today, and no doubt bedded afterwards, will be there, though how someone like her could ever be invited in the first place or come up with the thirty grand admission donation is beyond me."

Not good, Treadwell thought.

"Frankly I don't care what you do with your spare time, Reid, just don't embarrass me in front of my friends."

"I won't."

"And make sure that if any of your other dreary friends— like Dammerman, who I saw manhandling one of your female employees in a Facebook video—show up, they stay away from us. People like him can't be good for the firm."

"Neither would BP taking a beating if another '08 or even '29 comes along," Treadwell said. "Right now I have so much on my plate keeping the firm safe that I can't be bothered with some domestic dispute."

Bernice gestured him away. "I don't want to be late. Get dressed," she said, and walked away.

She'd never objected to his flings before, as long as they never went public. In any event she had her own personal trainer, a handsome male model half her age, who came over once a week. But Heather at the gala was more than disturbing, especially right now with everything else that was happening.

— — —

His costume of striped trousers, bow tie, two-toned shoes, a straw boater, and white gloves had been laid out for him, and when he got dressed he met Bernice at the elevator, and she nodded her approval.

But downstairs when she spotted Lawson standing to one side she pulled up short. "Is he really necessary?" she demanded.

"Yes, but he'll stay out of the way."

"He'd better."

They'd come over from BP in the Maybach, Lawson driving, and he took them to the Met, opening the car door for his boss first.

"Stay close," Treadwell said softly.

"Will do," Lawson said.

Treadwell handed Bernice out of the car, and they followed the growing crowd up the sweep of the stairs into the neoclassical museum's Great Hall, stopping every few steps to exchange handshakes and air kisses.

Inside, as they went through the receiving line, Treadwell automatically switched on what the press once dubbed his JFK mode, delivering handshakes, smiles, and pleasant commentary about the weather, the market, the situation in China, even the upcoming elections, which was the easiest because, except for a handful of Hollywood celebrities, just about everyone here this evening was a multimillionaire—or even billionaire—Republican.

Stephen Schwarzman, head of one of Wall Street's most powerful buyout firms and longtime adversary of Treadwell's, came over, smiling as Bernice drifted off with friends. "So, Reid, rumor is that you're taking the firm to all cash. Any truth to it?"

"If there was, I wouldn't tell someone like you."

Both men laughed, and Treadwell looked to his left as Schwarzman moved off.

Heather was across the room, standing by herself, a glass of champagne in her hand. She was wearing her revealing red dress and spike heels, and she stood out from everyone else in the room.

Treadwell called Lawson on his cell phone. "I'm going to need you to take care of something for me," he said in a lowered voice.

"Should I bring the car around?"

"No," Treadwell said. "Just stand by."

He broke the connection, and as he pocketed his phone, he happened to glance to the left in time to see Betty Ladd, martini glass raised to her lips, staring at him. She was dressed like Zelda Fitzgerald and wearing a cloche hat. She looked smug to him, even from across the room.

97

Betty's phone buzzed. It was Julia O'Connell, who sounded as if she was crying.

"We need to talk, because I can't take this any longer," she said.

"Okay, Julia, calm down and tell me what's going on."

"Cassy's been kidnapped, and I think they want her killed."

"Jesus, who did this?"

"Reid and Clyde Dammerman," she sobbed, and then the rest all came out in a rush. "It's Abacus, and Cassy figured out an antidote, and they can't let her use it. And I was a part of it. And I'm so sorry, but I don't know what to do. I don't . . ."

"I don't understand what you're saying. First, where are you right now? Are you someplace safe?"

"I'm at home, I'm okay."

"Just stay there," Betty said as she moved off to the side. "Now tell me what's going on. Everything. Starting with Abacus."

"It's a virus that Reid and Dammerman want to use. If the virus is introduced into our system, it will crash your computers."

"What do you mean 'your computers'?"

"The New York Stock Exchange. They want to bring down as many trading systems around the world as they can."

"Our backup computer would switch on."

"I don't know about that. All I know is that they'll blame the virus on terrorists. Russian hackers or someone."

"I saw Spencer Nast with Reid and Dammerman on the floor. Is he a part of it?"

"Yes," Julia said. "And so was I."

"My God."

"I didn't know what I was doing. Or I never thought it out. But Abacus started as a theoretical design of mine. I wanted to see if something like that could be done. I even sent it over to some people in Amsterdam who fine-tuned it for me. Made it hackerproof."

"Why didn't you back out when you knew what they were really up to?"

"I've asked myself that very question a million times. At first it was just a fun thing, you know, like taking down the power when I was in college. And then Reid promised that I would be rich. I could retire, or open my own company."

"That's why Reid took the bank to cash. Probably even made some trades in the Caribbean to short the S&P."

"I don't know about that part, except that they kept talking about the debt bomb, which was going to explode anyway, and they were just going to help it along. It would be worse than the thirties, except we'd save our bank. We'd be on top of the world."

"If I call the FBI, would you be willing to tell them the same thing you've told me? Even if it means you might have to go to prison?"

"Yes. I'll do anything I can to help."

"Then stay where you are. I'll take it from here."

Julia started to cry again. "I don't know what to say. How to thank you."

"Try to get some sleep; tomorrow is going to be a very long day."

"Okay," Julia said and she hung up.

Betty put the phone in her purse and spotted Reid and his wife talking to someone across the room, then she spotted Heather Rockingham alone and threaded her way across to her.

She'd picked up the girl at her hotel and got her into the gala using one of the complimentary tickets that were given each year to the NYSE. Once she and Heather had arrived, they'd separated to give Treadwell the false impression that they weren't here to gang up on him.

Heather turned when Betty got to her. "Is it time?" she asked.

"Yes, we need him to make an admission, so let's rattle his cage a little and see what happens."

"Great."

"Take this and put it in your clutch," Betty said, holding out her hand.

Heather shook hands and took the device about the size of a book of matches that Betty had palmed, then turned and walked away.

98

Bernice had hauled Treadwell away to meet some fashion designer friends of hers when Heather showed up.

"So this is the wife," she said, raising her voice enough so that everyone nearby could hear her.

Bernice turned and smiled. "Yes, this is the wife," she said. "But I don't think I have to guess who you are. The current slut my husband is fucking?"

"I can see why he came to me and didn't stick it out with you," Heather said. "But I just wanted to share with you and your friends the scheme that dear Reid is about to spring on us all. It's a computer virus or something which is supposed to sabotage just about every stock exchange on the planet. But he's smart, and he and his pals will make some big bucks if no one blows the whistle in time."

Reid had stepped back a pace and called someone on his cell phone.

Bernice laughed out loud. "It's always been amusing to me to hear the fantastical stories that my husband spins in his little love nest. But this is one of the better tales."

The people around them didn't know what to say, but they were sticking around to hear how it all turned out. This was part of the gala's drama.

"I think you all may want to give your brokers a call," Heather said. "Like before opening bell."

Lawson suddenly appeared and took Heather by the

arm. "Miss, your car is waiting," he said, and he hustled her kicking and screaming out of the Great Hall. He was a powerful man, twice her size.

"Excuse me for a moment," Treadwell said, nodding to his wife, whose complexion had turned red.

"You son of a bitch," she said half under her breath, but he caught it, and so did the people next to her.

He walked away and went out one of the service doors on the far side of the room where he'd instructed Lawson to take the woman.

They stood near a fire door at the far end of the deserted corridor, Heather shouting something, but when she spotted Treadwell approaching she stopped.

"You can leave us now, Duke," Treadwell said, and the big security officer nodded and left.

"Okay, you prick, the next move is yours," she said. "What'll it be?"

"May I have your cell phone?"

"I'm not recording anything," Heather said, but she took out her cell phone and handed it over.

Treadwell took the battery out, pocketed it, and handed the phone back to her. "You want in on the deal?" he said. "Okay, you're in."

"What exactly are we talking about?"

"A significant amount of money for you."

"Abacus will do that?"

"Not quite, but something like that and more. No trading anywhere for at least a week, possibly longer. Systems will be fried. The financial world will be on its knees. But Burnham Pike will be standing tall, helping society recover. And trust me, my dear, it'll be a gold mine."

"What about Cassy Levin?"

"She's no longer a problem."

Heather smiled and shook her head. "You fucking scumbag," she said, and she raised a middle finger in his face.

Treadwell grabbed her arm and bulled his way through the fire door, shoving her nearly down the stairs.

She started to scream, but Treadwell pulled out his father's .45 and shot her in the middle of the chest at point-blank range.

"Oh," she said, and she fell backward, tumbling down the stairs, coming to rest on the first landing, her lifeless eyes open.

Treadwell cocked his head. "Oh," he said, mocking her last word.

He holstered the pistol and went back to the party, where he tossed the white gloves that would hold powder residue from the pistol shot into a trash basket. He knew that the area off the Great Hall was soundproof, so the gunshot wouldn't have traveled that far. But he wasn't so sure whether he should apologize to Bernice first, or find Betty and tell her to go fuck herself.

99

With traffic it had been nearly five-thirty by the time Chip and Ben got over to Brighton Beach, and after a quick tour of the small Brooklyn neighborhood, the bars already filling up with the afterwork crowd, they drove over to the nearby Best Western on West Thirteenth Street and got a room for the night.

By midnight they still hadn't got a hit from the NSA telephone search, and Ben was going crazy.

"This could take all night, and we still might not come up with anything," Chip said.

Ben had been at the window looking down at the parking lot. He turned around. "What else can we do?"

"Going back to the bank won't help; even if we got past security again, they'd just call the cops, and I don't know if Huggard would be able to convince the mayor to let you go a second time."

"Someone there had to have hired the Russians to kidnap her for the flash drive, and they're going to want it back."

"Even if you're suggesting a trade—Cassy's location for the flash drive—what would be in it for them? Again, they'd simply have you arrested and take the thing."

"And we still don't know what's on it?" Ben asked.

"I think it's some kind of a program, but to do what, I have no way of knowing. The thing is encrypted with an algorithm that could take months to crack. But we've got the password taped to the bottom."

"If Cassy gave it to Imani and told him to run, then it's her creation. And she's damned good."

"She'd have to be, to work for a place like Burnham Pike."

"Imani gave his life to keep the thing away from them, and they know Cassy doesn't have it, so there'd be no reason to keep her alive," Ben said. It was the one thing that kept running around inside his head, gnawing at his gut.

"But that's just the point," Chip said. "If whatever's on the flash drive is Cassy's work, then they'll need her alive to decrypt it."

"So a trade might work."

"They need her alive, but there's no way they'd let her ride off into the sunset with you."

"Then we have to find out where they've taken her," Ben said, and he turned back to the window.

"I have another idea," Chip said.

Ben turned back again. "I'm all ears."

"It's dangerous, and you'd definitely need backup."

"Get on with it, goddamnit."

"You said the bank's chief of security, the one who

made the landline call to a Russian in Manhattan, is a tough guy."

"Ex-cop, and pals with the cop who arrested me at La-Guardia."

"Maybe you can make a trade with him."

"You just said they won't be willing to trade the flash drive for Cassy."

"No, but it's almost a hundred percent bet that he hired the Russians who snatched her off the street."

"You said he called a Russian in Manhattan."

"Different guy," Chip said. "Maybe an intermediary who hired the Brighton Beach people, if that's who took her."

"What are you thinking?"

"Maybe he'd be willing to trade Cassy's location for the flash drive."

"That's it," Ben said, hopeful for the first time since they'd left Washington.

"And that's why you'd need some muscle to back you up."

"Hardy's an ex-cop, so the police wouldn't do us any good. Anyway, I have my own idea."

"Listen to me for a second, would you?" Chip said. "I'm not talking New York cops, I'm talking the FBI."

"Why the hell would the Bureau want to get involved?"

"Think it out. Cassy works for the largest or maybe second largest investment bank in the country. She works in cybersecurity. She developed some program which she recorded on a flash drive, and yet she probably didn't tell anyone in management. She and her friend just took off running with it."

"Running where?"

"Doesn't matter. What does matter is that she thought it was so important she not only had to get out of the building with it, but when she realized that she was about to be kidnapped, she gave it to her friend and probably told him to run. Which he did, and which got him killed."

"So BP was up to something illegal," Ben said.

"It'd be my guess. Now we're talking about a federal crime, something the Bureau would be interested in."

"Not yet."

"First let me get ahold of someone in the Bureau's office here, see if we can get some intel. They're going to have to run it through channels, but it might be faster than waiting for a hit from NSA."

"We're not getting the Bureau involved."

"Have you finally lost your mind?"

"I'm going in alone."

"No way in hell," Chip said.

"Alone," Ben said. "Can you copy whatever's on the flash drive to your computer?"

"Already done, thanks to the password."

"Good. Give me Hardy's telephone number."

"Goddamnit."

"If something goes south, then you can call the Bureau. But first you're going to let me handle it."

"Two problems," Chip said. "If he agrees to the trade, you and he will have to meet so you can hand over the drive. And he'll probably have some muscle of his own standing by, unless he's as dumb as you are."

"And the second problem?"

"If he gives you the actual location, he'll tip off the people holding her so they'll know you're on your way."

"Fine."

"Bullshit, *fine*. There'll be more than one of them, at least the two we know about. And you said the guy who snatched her sounded ex-military."

"Spetsnaz," Ben said. "Give me Hardy's number."

100

It was a few minutes after twelve when the last man in Hardy's usual rotating day crew of nine men and three women, most of them ex-cops, showed up to join the normal weekday overnight shift of two men. They met in the front lobby, and all of them were armed, following Hardy's orders.

"It's all hands on deck. We're looking at the possibility of a break-in sometime from now until the early day shift starts showing up at eight."

"Can you tell us what the nature of the break-in might be?" one of the security officers asked. "Is it a burglary?"

"Unknown at this point," Hardy said. "But you should expect that the assailant could be armed."

His landline upstairs rolled over to his cell phone after two rings. He answered it. "Hardy."

"Ben Whalen. I have your flash drive, and I'm willing to trade for it."

"What do you want in exchange?"

"The location of Cassy Levin."

"Where do you want to meet?" Hardy asked without thinking.

"Outside the Nassau Street entrance to your firm. I'll be on foot, alone and unarmed."

"When?"

"Forty minutes from now."

"Done," Hardy said.

101

Chip parked on Nassau Street one block down from the Burnham Pike building. The only traffic was a lone cab with a fare in the backseat that cruised past. This part of Manhattan was mostly deserted at this time of night.

Ben got out of the car. "Give me twenty minutes, and if I'm not back by then, you can call in the reinforcements."

"Careful," Chip said. "We need you."

"Cassy first," Ben said, and he headed up the street.

Hardy was waiting alone outside the building.

Ben stopped a few feet away from him, took the flash drive from his pocket, and held it up. "Where's Cassy?"

"How do I know that's the flash drive she made?"

"You saw the list of Donni Imani's possessions from the morgue, didn't you?"

"I got it earlier, after you'd been there."

"It will have listed the flash drive with the writing SCANDISK printed on one side and SCANDISK CRUZER 408 on the other, plus some other numbers and symbols on the bottom."

Hardy checked his phone, which had the inventory. "That's right," he said. He squinted at the screen. "It had a small piece of paper taped to the bottom of it. I don't see it on the drive you've brought me."

"I don't know about that. It must have come off." The slip of paper had the password, and Ben wasn't about to hand it over.

With a grunt, Hardy gave him an address in Brighton Beach.

"If she's not there, I will come back for you. Understand?"

Hardy nodded and held out his hand.

Ben stepped forward and gave him the flash drive. "Go back inside."

"If this isn't the real drive, I know how to find you. Understand?"

Ben nodded, and Hardy turned and went inside the bank building.

102

Anosov was in the kitchen having a beer with several of his crew who were waiting for a chance with Cassy once they were given the go-ahead. None of them made mention of a long scratch that was still oozing a little blood on the side of his face. The woman had fought back so hard that in the end he'd just left her alone. The Canadian syndicate with whom he'd made a deal for her would not have accepted damaged goods.

His cell phone rang. It was Butch Hardy.

"I have the flash drive, but you have trouble coming your way."

"What trouble?"

"Levin's boyfriend. And he's an ex–Navy SEAL."

Anosov smiled. "We'll be ready. What about the woman?"

"Make both of them disappear."

"Consider it done," Anosov said and hung up. "We're going to have a little fun tonight," he told his people. "Get everyone down here. Armed."

103

Ben gave Chip the address where Hardy told him that Cassy was being held, then programmed it into his cell phone. "You're going back to the hotel, and I'm going to drive myself over."

"Not a chance in hell," Chip protested.

"You're a damned fine engineer, but you're not combat trained."

"I brought another pistol."

"Which the first guy you came up against would take away from you," Ben said. "I'm doing this alone."

"This is bullshit, Ben. I'm calling the Bureau right now."

"No."

"Goddamnit."

"I'll leave my cell phone on. And if sounds to you like I'm in trouble, then you can call for backup."

"It'll be too late by then."

"It's my call."

104

Anosov's crew of ten men gathered around in the kitchen, and he briefed them on who was coming their way and why.

"The American cowboy riding in to save his girlfriend," Vasili Melnik said, and the rest of them laughed.

"I want this clean, no outside interference," Anosov said. "Which means we have to let the gentleman inside before we take him down."

"Why don't you let me and Sergei save us all some trouble?" Melnik said. "We'll wait outside—no guns—and when the stupid son of a bitch shows up, we'll break his fucking neck."

"He's an ex-SEAL," Anosov said.

"*Pizdec,*" Melnik said. *Pussy.*

"I want it clean. No noise."

Melnik and Sergei left their pistols on the kitchen table and went out the back door.

"SEALs aren't pussies," Anosov told the others. "If he should get past them, I want him to think that they were the only lookouts on duty, and that the rest of us are either asleep in our beds or maybe playing poker in the dining room."

The others were skeptical, but they nodded.

"I want a layered defense. Scatter yourselves between here and the attic."

105

Ben drove past some brownstone apartments, lights on in some of the windows, then turned down a narrower street of two-story houses. He passed one with a steel fence and a gate that led into a trash-filled backyard as the GPS on his phone announced that he had arrived at his destination.

Not slowing down, he drove to the end of the block where he shut off the headlights and made a U-turn, parking two houses up.

He waited a full minute to see if he had been spotted, but when there was no obvious response, he got out of the car and went the rest of the way on foot, holding up just inches from the edge of the tall fence.

Peering around the corner he could see a shed to the right and a back door into the house. No lights were showing from any of the windows, and nothing moved. But the white Caddy Escalade that Cassy had described in her phone call was parked to the left of the door. Hardy had not been lying to him; this definitely was the place. But it was a sure bet that the BP's chief of security had warned them that someone was on the way.

Drawing his pistol and keeping it low in his left hand, the muzzle pointed away from his leg, he moved briskly past the fence and made his way to the front porch. He sprinted up the walk and mounted the two stairs to the door framed by narrow, stained-glass windows.

He tried the doorknob with his right hand, and it turned easily. It wasn't locked. They were expecting him.

Backing away, he looked through the window on the left and spotted the vague outline of someone standing just inside. Raising his pistol he fired one shot, and the figure moved backward and fell to the floor.

At that moment he burst through the door in time to see a man appear on the stairs, and he fired another shot, hitting him center mass.

As the man tumbled forward down the stairs, two others appeared in the wide doorway to the right, their guns drawn, but before they could fire, Ben shot both of them in the chest.

He ducked back, and an instant later someone behind the two men began firing.

Waiting for a brief lull, Ben reached around the corner and fired four shots in rapid succession.

Someone grunted, and the house fell silent.

Ben stepped back to the door, and making sure that no one was coming up the walk, closed and locked it. No one was coming up on his six, at least not through the front door.

The man lying at the foot of the stairs was still alive. He had his pistol in his right hand, and Ben took it away, ejected the magazine and cycled the round from the chamber, then laid the pistol aside.

He held his breath for a long moment. The house was silent, though he was pretty sure that there were others here, probably spread around.

Pressing the muzzle of his Beretta against the man's temple, he leaned in close. "Where is the lady who was brought here?" he whispered.

The man mumbled something that Ben couldn't quite catch.

"Tell me, and I'll let you live."

The man raised his head a couple of inches so that he

could look up at Ben. "In the attic, but you'll never get her out of here alive."

Ben pushed him aside, then got to his feet and made some noise tromping up the first four steps before he silently came back down.

Almost immediately a man in the dining room peered around the corner, leading with his gun hand, but before he could shoot, Ben fired three shots into the plaster wall just to the left of the doorway.

— — —

Melnik and Sergei came into the kitchen where Anosov stood next to the dining room door, just out of the line of fire. No one else was in the kitchen.

"He came through the front door, but locked it behind him," Melnik whispered.

"Valentin's down and so are Ilya and, from the sounds of it, probably Nikolai and Yuri," Anosov said. "I don't know about the others, but this fucking guy is good."

"What do you want us to do?"

"Go back outside and cover the front door. I'll stay here."

— — —

Holding up just around the corner from the dining room door, Ben had heard at least one man come into the kitchen, but then leave. Almost certainly to go back outside and cover the front door.

Moving with care, he stepped over the Russian who was barely breathing and silently made his way upstairs to the landing, where he peered around the corner. The long hallway was very dark, and so far as he could see, nothing moved.

The attic stairs had been pulled down, but there was no noise from up here or downstairs. And there was no way for him to know how many Russians were still operational.

— — —

In the attic room Cassy had listened to the gunfight below, and she knew that Ben was here for her. Earlier the stairs had been pulled down, and she'd heard one man coming up. At that point she'd been certain that either the bastard who'd tried to rape her or one of his other assholes was on their way to try again.

She went to the door and looked through one of the cracks. The attic was mostly in darkness, but she could make out the dim figure of a man crouched next to the opening where the stairs had been pulled down.

"One man at the head of the attic stairs," she shouted. "At least eight others downstairs."

— — —

"Suka," the Russian crouched at the attic opening muttered under his breath. *Bitch.*

Keeping an eye on the corridor below, he turned toward the room where the woman was being kept, all thoughts of fucking her now out of his head. He just wanted to shut her mouth, permanently.

— — —

"Now," Cassy shouted, as the Russian pointed his gun at her, and she dropped to the floor.

— — —

Melnik turned toward the stair opening and crouched down as a man's arm, gun in hand, rose up. Instinctively he batted the pistol away with his left hand as he tried to bring his gun around.

— — —

Ben grabbed the Russian's gun hand and yanked hard as he swung to the left, halfway off the stairs.

The pistol discharged a few inches wide and the Russian came headfirst through the opening, flailing his arms as he fell to the corridor floor.

Turning back, Ben fired two shots, the first hitting the Russian in the left shoulder and the second plowing into the base of his skull.

The house fell silent again.

— — —

Cassy got to her feet. "Ben?" she said.

"Here," he answered just outside the door, and she stepped back as the latch was withdrawn, and he was there, taking her in his arms.

"Oh God, oh God," she cried. "I knew you would come."

They parted, and she looked up in his eyes.

"Are you okay?" he asked. "Can you walk?"

"With you, anywhere, anytime."

— — —

Anosov slumped against the kitchen doorframe. One of Spetsnaz's rules was that if things seemed to be going to shit they probably were, and it was time to stand down and cut your losses.

He heard Whalen and his woman in the hallway above.

"Mr. Whalen," he shouted.

"Yes," Ben called back.

"I propose a truce."

"Talk to me."

"You have what you came for, and my casualties have become unacceptable. I'm in the kitchen at the back of the house, and my remaining man is in the front waiting for you. We will withdraw him and give you a clear path away from here."

"I can't trust you."

"I give my word as a former Spetsnaz captain to a former SEAL officer."

"I still don't know if I can trust you."

"I'm going to put my weapon down and come to the front hall, where I will unlock the door and tell my man that we are going to walk away. There is a good afterhours place one block away where we will go to have a vodka."

"Do it now," Ben said.

Anosov laid his pistol on the kitchen table, then walked out into the stair hall where he unlocked the door. He didn't bother looking up the stairs.

"We're going for a drink," he called to Sergei. "The battle is over." They were withdrawing from the fight considerably richer than they were before it had begun.

— — —

Ben and Cassy waited for a full five minutes before they descended to the ground floor, and then he was cautious leaving.

Outside he kept a 360 watch as they walked to where he'd parked the car, but he didn't breathe easy until they were out of the neighborhood and heading back to the Best Western.

"Jesus Christ, you scared the living shit out of me," Chip's voice came over Ben's cell phone.

Cassy laughed so hard that Ben thought she had lost it, but then he started to laugh as well.

"It's over," he said.

"Not quite," Cassy told him.

106

It was well after one, and the gala was winding down, when Treadwell's cell phone vibrated in his pocket. It was Dammerman.

"Hardy just told me that we have the flash drive."

"That's fantastic," Treadwell said. Finally things were getting back on track. "How'd he come up with it?"

"The prick wouldn't tell me. I want to fire his ass."

"He may be a prick, but we should give him a raise."

"You're the boss."

"Yes, I am. Where are you?"

"I'm at the office to see that we don't run into any more shit."

"You're right. I'm going to break free here and come in soon as I get Bernice home."

Dammerman hung up.

Treadwell pocketed his cell phone. They were a go for opening bell.

Bernice came up behind him. "I'm ready to leave," she said.

He turned to her. "I need to get back to the office, but I'll drop you off at home first."

Her left eyebrow rose. "You're spending the night with that tramp of yours?"

"It's a thought," Treadwell said, smiling. "But we're going to have a big day when the market opens in the morning, and I have work to do to get ready for it."

"I'll get my own ride," she said. She started to leave, but then turned back. "And, Reid, don't bother coming back to the apartment. Ever. I'm done with you and your little girlfriends."

He watched her march across the room with a feeling

of relief and regret. Relief that he wouldn't have to put up with her bullshit again, and regret that he would be losing her money. But in a few hours he'd have plenty of money of his own.

He called Lawson to have the car brought around, and then left the party the same way he'd come in, with his head up, but with an odd feeling of power he'd never had before. Actually killing someone was a rush.

Outside, the Maybach was just gliding up to the curb. Lawson jumped out and opened the rear door for Treadwell, the sounds of sirens in the distance.

– – –

At the firm, Treadwell told Lawson that he wouldn't be needing him until just before opening bell.

Inside, the lobby was busy with Hardy's security people, the outlines of shoulder holsters visible through their blazers.

They nodded politely as he walked down the hall and boarded the executive elevator. Hardy hadn't been there, but it was enough that he'd managed to get the flash drive and have his people standing by to keep Levin and her boyfriend from getting into the building.

The overnight traders would be busy working the foreign markets, but they'd be even busier when everything went to hell after the opening bell in eight hours or so. And it would be the same downstairs in DCSS when the techies realized that somehow they'd missed something bigger than even they could imagine had happened, right under their noses.

No one else was on the top floor except for Dammerman, who sat at his desk watching the Asian trades on his Bloomberg monitor.

He looked up when Treadwell came in. "It's ugly over there, especially in Shanghai," he said. That market was where China did a majority of its trades, and it had been feeling the brunt of the country's banking crisis for some time now.

"Everything is in position, right?"

Once more Dammerman laid out the plan. It was reassuring, like listening to a familiar prayer. "As the market opens, Abacus is triggered in our system. It won't do much damage to us, just enough so we can claim later that we got hit too. We can say that our defenses were better than everyone else's. The SEC and others will never find where it originated. All trading networks are linked worldwide. Abacus spreads to the NYSE, and then to the rest of the exchanges and investment firms all over the map. They'll be out of operation for days, weeks even, who knows? Meanwhile the financial system's gears are stripped. No one can raise capital, trade stocks or bonds or anything."

Treadwell cast his absurd straw boater aside. "We have hours to wait for this, and it's already driving me nuts."

"Makes two of us," Dammerman said casually, talking almost as if he were describing a ballgame, not a financial apocalypse. "This will be like dominos falling. When the Russians blow up the NYSE's backup computer, the world will think terrorists were behind the market meltdown. With the system shattered, people will panic."

Treadwell nodded. "Everyone will want their debts repaid right away. And once trading does resume, the system will clog with sell orders. Utter chaos. And guess who'll be left to dig civilization out of the crash?"

"Neither Washington, nor any other government will know what to do. We come out of it on top."

"For a price."

"A sweet price," Dammerman said. "Abacus is unstoppable."

"Where's the flash drive?" Treadwell asked.

Dammerman pulled it out of his shirt pocket and handed it over.

Treadwell couldn't help but smile. "We might as well get rid of most of the security guys in the lobby. We don't need them now."

"I wouldn't be so fast, Mr. T."

"Isn't this thing encrypted?"

"Like nuclear launch orders. None of the nerds downstairs could figure it out, and when I called Masters in to take a quick peek, all he could do was shake his head."

"What about Julia? She might be able to figure it out."

"I haven't been able to get ahold of her," Dammerman said. "I called, emailed, texted, and told her to get her geeky ass back here on the double. But she doesn't answer. Do you want me to send one of Butch's people to her apartment to bring her here?"

"She recognizes your number, and right now you're not one of her favorite people," Treadwell said. He called her on his cell phone and put it on speaker mode.

On the third ring she picked up. "It's a little late to be calling, isn't it, Reid?"

"What's going on, Julia?" Treadwell asked. "Are you okay?"

It took her a moment to answer, and when she did it sounded as if she was on the verge of tears. "I've had time to do some thinking. I just can't go on with this. I mean, killing a young woman who only thought that she was doing her job? Cassy was helping us, for God's sake. And now we're going to push the world into the second Great Depression?"

"You weren't bothered about any of this from the beginning. Abacus was your idea."

"I wanted to believe you," she replied. "I set up Abacus as an experiment, and I went along with what Clyde wanted to do. But I was blinded by the money I'd make.

I was foolish. But now I'm willing to tell the authorities just that."

"Can't you see beyond the end of your nose?" Treadwell said, trying to keep his voice even, though he could feel the panic rising in his gut.

"I didn't sign on for murder," Julia said.

Treadwell had had enough. "Get up here immediately, because if you don't, I'll have some of Butch's boys drag you here. Do I make myself clear?"

"I'm sick of your games," Dammerman bellowed.

"Go fuck yourself, you ape," Julia shouted back. "And for the record, Reid, I quit. My cousin will be pleased to hear it."

"You're a part of this. If we go down, you go down."

"Betty will stand behind me."

"If you even think about going to her, I'll make sure that you end up like Cassy Levin! I swear to Christ I will!"

"It's a done deal, and she's primed to hack your balls off," Julia said. "Do I make *myself* clear?" She hung up.

Treadwell stood holding the phone in his hand, not knowing what to say for the moment.

"Did she say what I thought she said?" Dammerman asked.

"Get Hardy up here. We have to do some major damage control."

Dammerman looked up. "Here he comes."

107

Hardy stalked into Dammerman's office, and he didn't look happy. "They said downstairs that both of you were here," he said. "What's going on?"

"I need you to add two people to the Levin list," Treadwell said.

"People you want dead."

"Levin's a done deal, but we need Nast and O'Connell gone. I don't want them testifying against us."

"That's not going to be so easy."

"What are you talking about?" Treadwell demanded. "I want it done."

"That won't look good, Mr. Treadwell," Hardy said. "One BP executive plus the president's economic adviser—himself a former BP exec—suddenly go down. The cops would come snooping around, and so would the FBI."

"Nast lost his job today because he's an idiot, and no one would care if he got run over by a bus. And we're staring down the barrel of a possible catastrophe to our entire computer system that Julia was supposed to prevent. It could cost this firm million, perhaps even billions. Not to mention our good name."

Hardy shook his head. "Why bother to off them? Nast has been fired, so go ahead and fire O'Connell. Two unemployed bozos."

"Maybe we'll just fire your ass, and hire someone who knows how to follow orders," Dammerman shouted.

Hardy was angry, but he held his silence.

"Leave it like this, Butch," Treadwell said. "They can make allegations about us that we don't want people with badges to hear."

"Well, I came up here to tell you something else that you're not going to like," Hardy said. "My friends downtown said there was a big shootout in Brighton Beach a few hours ago. A lot of Russians with criminal associations are dead."

"The guys you hired," Treadwell asked.

Hardy nodded. "The ones who took Levin. A witness supposedly told the badges investigating that they saw a man and woman leaving the house and driving off." He glanced at Dammerman. "Could be Levin and her boyfriend—the ex-SEAL."

Treadwell sat down heavily in the chair in front of Dammerman's desk. It felt as if the bottom had just dropped out.

"If you're worried about them coming back here, don't," Hardy said. "My security is tight."

"You damn well better have it right this time," Dammerman shouted. "You chose the Russians. Sounds like it was Whalen, Levin's SEAL boyfriend, who slaughtered your pals. One guy offed them all? Christ, how incompetent can you get?"

Hardy made a fist. "Tell you what, fat boy, one more out of you and I'll cave in your fucking face!"

Dammerman jumped up. "You're fired, asshole! I want you out of here now!"

Treadwell had been staring out the window at the Empire State Building all lit up, but he pulled himself out of his funk. "I want both of you to calm down. Butch is going nowhere, because we need him. Some big stuff is coming down the road this morning, and we need to circle the wagons."

Dammerman sat down.

"There's more," Hardy said.

"Go ahead," Treadwell said.

"My friends uptown told me that a woman named Heather Rockingham was found shot to death in a stairwell at the Metropolitan Museum earlier this morning. Some preliminary testimony from witnesses had you and her having an argument before she disappeared, and you left."

"Who knows how many people she's slept with," Treadwell said. "I wouldn't be a bit surprised if some jealous wife murdered her."

"Possibly. But they want to interview you ASAP."

"Maybe later, after the opening bell," Treadwell said, rising. "I'm going to my office now."

"Duke told me to ask you if you disposed of the gloves."

Treadwell missed a step, but continued out the door and down the hall.

108

In his office he made sure that neither Hardy nor Dammerman had followed him and might be watching through the glass walls before he put his pistol and the flash drive in a drawer. The police would need a warrant to search his office, which they might get, so he made a note to himself to find a better hiding place.

But when the NYSE opened in a few hours, and markets around the world were turned upside down, no one would pay much attention to the murder of a minor executive in a nothing outdoor apparel company from the Midwest.

Even though the hour was late, he phoned Rupert Leland, one of his alternative brokers, this one in Panama City. Leland had been on the bad side of the law for most of his life, finally escaping to Panama, where money bought anything you might need—including immunity from extradition to the U.K.

"Top of the morning to you, then, Mr. Treadwell," Leland said, his fake British accent high-born.

"We're good with our trades?"

"Yes, sir. We closed the ten million short position, took out your fat profits, and wired the two million to your account in this lovely country."

"Just checking to make sure."

"Ta ta," Leland said and rang off.

Treadwell sat back and stared out the window at the dark harbor. Some of his maneuvers were going through, but he wished the opening bell would hurry.

109

It was very late, and all of Hardy's people were in place. He moved through the ground floor talking with his people, one-on-one, where they were stationed. He didn't want to call them together and leave any possible entrance unguarded. Not this late in the game.

His first responsibility, as he saw it, was to protect the firm. It was what he was getting paid for. But his second, even more important responsibility was protecting himself. Because he sure as hell wasn't going down because of whatever crap Treadwell and Dammerman had cooked up.

"You guys have the pictures of Whalen and Levin," he told Jack McGowan and the other three guys stationed at the Nassau Street entrance.

"Whalen the ex-SEAL," McGowan said. "Word is he was the shooter tonight out in Brighton Beach. That right?"

"Could be, but I'm calling in some guys," Hardy said, referring to his friends on the force. "You just keep him and the girl from getting in, and the guys will take care of the rest. But no matter what happens, the bottom line is neither of them gets downstairs to the DCSS. And that's the order from the brass."

"That's the word from Dammerman?" one of the other ex-cops asked. No one on the security staff had much use for BP's COO, who treated them like garbage.

"No. Treadwell himself."

"Fair enough," McGowan said. The big man knew most of their names, and he was usually friendly, though sometimes distant, and he saw that they all got regular pay raises and a Christmas bonus.

Hardy had his own opinion, which he kept to himself. Fact is, he'd never liked anyone on the top floor, especially not Dammerman, but definitely not Treadwell either. BP's CEO was nothing but a slick-talking con artist who would screw over the little guy any chance he got.

There were stories about how Treadwell had dodged trouble more times than once, walking over people on his way to the top, some of the time with Dammerman's help.

He looked through the glass doors as a blue-and-white, the roof mount unlit, slid up to the curb and stopped. He went outside as Roger Adams climbed out of the passenger side.

They shook hands, and Hardy moved his friend down the empty street away from the front doors. "I've got all hands on deck, but I'm glad you're here, Rog," he said.

"I'll do what I can. But you have to know that Young will probably spring Whalen if we take him in again. It'd only be a matter of time before we'd have to let him walk out the door." Adams's view of Mayor Bill Young was not positive. "Apparently he's pals with Whalen's boss, some big-time admiral down in D.C."

"Five will get you ten that Whalen's prints are going to be all over the place in Brighton Beach. Makes him a mass murderer."

"The Russians were scumbags, and no one is going to shed a tear if someone wiped them out. Anyway, it looks like they kidnapped his girlfriend, and he went out there to rescue her. Single-handed. Lots of extenuating circumstances that the press would love to get ahold of. And I'm already in deep shit."

"Look, all I need is for you to help keep him and Levin out of circulation for the rest of the morning, maybe till noon. I mean with the shooting, he's at least a material witness. And how do you know he was a white knight saving his lady? Maybe he had a drug deal that went bad, and he and the Russians had a falling-out. Shit like that happens all the time. Just saying."

"I'll take major flak from Voight, because if Young tells my commander to jump, Voight will ask how high."

Hardy stepped in closer. "Okay, I gotta tell you some heavy shit. Maybe save your ass, save both of us if it comes to that. But just remember you didn't hear this from me. A little bird whispered in your ear with a promise of secrecy."

"Fine. What is the little bird whispering?" Adams said.

"A lot of bad shit is going down upstairs. The brass were the ones who ordered Levin to be kidnapped, and they paid big money for it to happen. I'm not sure exactly why, but it has to do with some computer program, or something on a flash drive they wanted back."

Adams looked stunned. "You mean your bosses? The head honchos of Burnham Pike? Holy crap."

"Treadwell and Dammerman are the perps. Whatever they cooked up had to do with enough money that they were willing to resort to kidnapping and murder."

"Okay."

Hardy spread his hands, palms up. "I'm clean. But this could be a big bust for you."

"I've always had your back, Butch."

"I know," Hardy said. "And it's a two-way street."

They shook hands, and Hardy went back to the front entrance, a slight smile on his lips. Getting back was sweet. But getting even was even better.

110

Ben stood guard while Cassy took a quick hot shower when they got back to the motel. Chip had found an all-night grocery store where he picked up some coffee and sweet rolls, which was all she'd said her stomach could handle for the moment.

Although she had to get dressed in dirty clothes, she insisted that Chip show her what he had downloaded to his computer from the flash drive. And as soon as it had come up she'd sat back, a deeply disappointed look on her face.

"What is it?" Ben asked.

"I've got some work to do before this can be used."

"Did I screw it up?" Chip asked.

"There was a onetime-use Burnham Pike security marker embedded in the program. If the flash drive had been downloaded to a BP computer it would have been recognized as being legitimate. Downloaded into a foreign computer—your laptop—the markers were erased."

"Your flash drive and my computer talked with each other?" Chip asked.

Cassy nodded.

"You need to show me how you did that."

"Later," Cassy said, bringing up the first page of the program. "I need to fix this before we can load it into BP's system to neutralize Abacus."

"How long will it take once you've downloaded the thing?" Chip asked.

"I don't know. Twenty, maybe thirty minutes."

"But it has to be done at the firm?"

Cassy nodded, but her fingers were flying over the keyboard and she didn't look up.

"It's one-thirty now, and it'll take maybe a half hour or more to get downtown, which leaves you six hours or so with a margin to get it done before opening bell," Chip said. "Plenty of time."

This time Cassy did look up. "You don't understand. The markers are embedded on *every* page of the program. And there are more than one thousand pages. So let me get to it."

"I'll get some more coffee and something else to eat," Chip said.

Ben took Chip aside. "That's not the only problem," he said. "We'll still have to get her inside the building."

"What do you want me to do?"

"Under ordinary circumstances, I'd tell you to take the plane back to Washington."

"But these aren't ordinary circumstances."

"I think that it's a safe bet we're going to get stopped trying to get in. We might get arrested again, and I'll need you to call the admiral."

"He's not going to be real happy about that, especially if it's in the middle of the night. Admirals tend to get cranky when someone interrupts their beauty sleep."

"Tell him if he springs me, I'll gladly come back and finish W for him."

"That, he'll understand," Chip said. "I'm going on another chow run. Want anything?"

"Something not sweet."

"I'll see if there's a McDonald's open somewhere."

"Watch your six," Ben said.

"Will do."

111

Chip was gone for forty-five minutes, and during that time Ben sat by the window looking down at the parking lot. Brighton Beach was a Russian village, and it was possible that the remaining crew at the house where Cassy had been kept would have eyes on them.

He had just finished disassembling the Beretta to check if the pistol's works had picked up any lint, and reloading it with the spare magazine, when Chip showed up with a big bag from McDonald's.

"Did you pick up a tail?" Ben asked.

"There's not a lot of traffic at this time of the morning,

and I went around the block a couple of times before I came in and didn't see anything."

Cassy was still working on the laptop, her fingers racing over the keyboard.

"Do you want to take a break and have something to eat?" Ben asked her.

She waved him off.

"You need something."

"Benjamin," Cassy said sharply.

Ben and Chip exchanged a glance, then sat down at the small table by the window and had their burgers, fries, and coffee.

Ben looked at his watch. It was 3:45 already, a little less than six hours before the opening bell at the New York Stock Exchange. They were running out of time, especially if they ran into interference at BP.

"Do you want me to call Huggard now, give him the heads-up?" Chip asked.

"Not until we need him," Ben said, when Cassy looked up.

"Done," she said, powering the computer down and closing it. "Let's get this to BP."

112

Chip was behind the wheel of the Chevy SUV, Ben was in front riding shotgun, and Cassy was in the backseat cradling the laptop, as they headed over the Brooklyn Bridge across the river to lower Manhattan. Traffic was nearly nonexistent at this hour, so they made good time.

They got off at Park Row and headed south on Broadway, switching over to Nassau a couple of blocks later.

One block up from the Burnham Pike building, Chip slowed down. Several police cars, their lights flashing, were

parked on the street in front of the bank, along with a plain
gray Ford sedan with U.S. government plates.

"They're expecting us," Ben said. "Keep going, don't
stop."

"We've got to get into the building. Downstairs to my station in DCSS," Cassy said, sitting forward.

"I'll try first, and if I'm arrested, which I think will happen, Chip can call the admiral," Ben said. "As soon as
some strings are pulled, and I'm released, you guys can
pick me up, and we'll go in together."

"We don't have a lot of time," Cassy said. "It's after four
already."

"It won't do us any good if they arrest you and take the
laptop," Ben said.

They passed the BP tower, and a half a block later Chip
turned left on John Street and pulled up.

"No matter what, stay here," Ben told Cassy.

He and Chip got out of the car and went back to the corner.

"I'm going on alone," Ben said. "If it's all clear, I'll wave
you guys in. But if I'm taken, get the hell away and call Huggard."

"Will do," Chip said.

"The clock is ticking," Ben said, and he crossed the street
and headed down Nassau to the building and the waiting
police and Bureau cars.

- - -

Sergeant Adams stood next to a police car talking to a uniformed cop and two men in blue nylon jackets with FBI
stenciled in yellow as Ben approached.

One of the Bureau agents said something to the sergeant,
who turned around and smiled.

"Here's the tough guy back for the second round," Adams said.

"I need to get inside and talk to Mr. Treadwell," Ben said. "He's expecting me."

"Turn around and give me your wrists," Adams said, pulling a set of handcuffs from a belt pouch.

Ben did as he was told. "Won't be long and the mayor will know you personally."

Adams leaned in close. "Careful that you're not shot while resisting arrest and trying to escape."

113

It was just coming up on 6:00 A.M., and Treadwell was sitting at his desk trying to figure a way out of the mess that was growing around him when Ashley arrived. She was a full two hours early, and when she came to his open door she looked concerned.

He looked up. "You're early," he said.

"I didn't get much sleep last night after all the hubbub around here yesterday," she said. "You okay, Reid?"

"A lot on my mind and a lot to do before opening bell."

"The market was down twenty percent near the close yesterday; what do you think will happen today?"

"Asia is worse. But that's no surprise with the Chinese commercial banks still in trouble. Plus the failure of our T-bond sale. Something that's never happened before. And given the mountain of debt that every country, including ours, is facing, it's a wonder how we'll ever dig ourselves out."

Ashley offered him a tentative smile. "If anyone can figure a way out of the mess, it's you," she said.

He returned her smile. There was no way he could tell her the real problems he was facing. Cassy Levin on the loose, Julia O'Connell talking to Betty, Spencer Nast fired from his White House post, and the cops wanting to question him about Heather's death.

The only good things were the flash drive he had in his desk, and Whalen back in custody. Plus Abacus was set to go off when trading started in less than three and a half hours.

That is if nothing went wrong with the program, or if the Russians succeeded in taking out the NYSE's backup computer in Jersey, which would shift the blame for the crashed market on to terrorism.

He glanced out the window. The sun was just coming up, and it promised to be a beautiful day. All he had to do was somehow get through it.

Ashley had turned to go to her desk, but she came back. "By the way, I think there must have been a bad accident or something right in front of our building."

"What do you mean?" Treadwell asked, something clutching at his heart.

"There are a lot of cop cars with their lights flashing blocking off the street."

Treadwell got up and went to the window. It was still dark fifty-four stories down, and the flashing lights reflected off the buildings across Nassau Street. There were a lot of cop cars, maybe eight or ten. But no ambulances. It wasn't an accident.

Treadwell turned around as Dammerman came to his office door, shoving Ashley aside. He didn't look happy. "Do you see what the hell is going on downstairs?"

"Yes, but where is Butch?" Treadwell demanded.

"I can't raise him. But Duke Lawson was downstairs when he says the cops appeared from all over the place, pulling our security people away from every entry to the building, including the loading dock and the side door down to DCSS."

"They can't do that to us," Treadwell said. He was on the verge of panic.

"I don't know what kind of show Butch is running, but it sure the hell looks to me like a royal clusterfuck!" Dammerman said, then noticed Ashley standing next to him. "Get the fuck out of here."

"What's happening?" Ashley said, confused.

Dammerman shoved her out the door and closed it when she was clear.

"I'll call Hank Serling and get him over here right now," Treadwell said.

"Not a chance in hell I'm going down for this. It's on you, you slippery son of a bitch. Every last bit of it."

"We'll see how that turns out, you fat fuck," Treadwell said, finally getting his back up. "This is Burnham Pike, one of the largest investment banks in the world, and I'm the chief executive officer."

"I made you, starting when you had to cheat on that college exam. And I've been doing your dirty laundry ever since. But now you're Mr. High and Mighty, strutting his stuff with the bigwigs. High society hot shit. The toast of the town. The great Casanova who wouldn't be shit without me and without his wife's money and position."

"Let me remind you of something, Clyde. Abacus was your idea in the first place. You and Butch hired the Russians, and Julia designed the worm with help from her pals in Amsterdam. And you guys told me nothing about it."

Ashley, her eyes wide, opened the door.

"Not now, Ash," Treadwell said.

"The front desk just called and said some police officers and FBI agents are on their way up. Betty Ladd and Ms. O'Connell are with them."

Dammerman turned without a word, bolted out of the office, and disappeared down the stairs as the elevator opened.

Several men, some of them in police uniforms, others in plain business suits, a couple of whom Treadwell recognized, emerged and headed down the corridor. Trailing them were Betty Ladd in a stylish suit and trademark pearl earrings, and Julia O'Connell in a wrinkled white blouse and jeans.

"I'll take care of this, Ash," Treadwell said. "Just sit at your desk."

She was frightened, but she did as she was told.

The lead plainclothes, his badge held up, came into Treadwell's outer office. "Captain Harold Cohen," he said.

"I know who you are, Harry. In fact, BP and I personally give generously to the First Precinct's charity drives every year."

The FBI agent held up his credentials. "I'm Richard Mendoza, assistant agent in charge of the New York Division."

Treadwell forced a smile, even though he was bleeding inside. "I know you too, Richie. We've played golf a couple of times at Burning Tree."

Betty Ladd stepped forward. "I don't need an introduction either, Reid," she said. "I'm here in my capacity as a regulator of Burnham Pike. And because I want to see you led away in handcuffs, I've called the news media, who are waiting downstairs on the street."

"Mr. Treadwell, things will go much better for you if you volunteer to stop Abacus before the opening bell," Mendoza said. "I've been given reliable evidence that it could cause irreparable damage to the stock market if it's implemented."

"Never heard of it, Richie."

"You're lying," Julia shouted.

"Why on earth would I want to sabotage the market?" Treadwell said. His heart was hammering. "Burnham Pike's bread and butter is the stock market. So what you're saying makes no sense."

Betty broke in. "For one thing you shorted the S&P in a ten-million-dollar off-market trade in Hong Kong. You knew what was coming. Front-running. I've heard that you were using Rupert Leland for your sleazy trades. We had the Hong Kong authorities lean on him, and he gave you up like yesterday's garbage."

"Sounds like a frame-up to me," Treadwell said. Sweat was forming on his upper lip, something that never happened.

"The first priority is stopping Abacus," the FBI agent said.

"What exactly am I being charged with here?" Treadwell asked, working hard to maintain his composure.

"How about the murder of Heather Rockingham?" Betty said. "You shot her in a stairwell outside the gala last night."

Treadwell held out his hands. "You may have me tested for powder residue, if you'd like. But you'll find none."

"They found a pair of white gloves in the trash," Betty said. "I was there. You showed up wearing them, but left without."

Mendoza tried to interrupt her, but Cohen held him off. "Let her continue."

"By all means," Treadwell said.

"I gave Heather a recorder, which was keyed to my cell phone and hidden in her clutch," Betty said. "You thought that you were clever removing the battery in her phone." She pulled her own phone out and hit *play*.

They all heard Treadwell trying to bribe Heather by cutting her in on the deal. Then they talked about Abacus. No trading anywhere for at least a week, maybe longer, he said. Systems would be fried. The financial world would be on its knees. But Burnham Pike would be standing tall, helping society recover.

And trust me, my dear, it'll be a gold mine.

There were sounds of a scuffle, and then a single pistol shot.

Treadwell was staggered. It was over. Everything he'd ever worked for was done. His life, his position, all because of some little greedy bitch. It wasn't fair.

"Julia has agreed to testify that she was a part of the Abacus scheme, but so were you. Right in the middle of it. Plus you gave the order to have Cassy Levin kidnapped and killed."

Treadwell stepped back.

"You're nothing but scum, Reid," Betty said.

Treadwell swiveled on his heel, and before anyone could stop him, got into his office and closed and locked the heavy, shatterproof-glass door.

Mendoza and Cohen were at the door, pounding.

Treadwell opened his desk drawer, took out the flash drive, and threw it, sending the thing bouncing off the glass.

Nothing was fair.

He pulled out his father's .45. Maybe it would have been better if he'd used it that day in college.

Cohen had pulled out his pistol and was aiming it at the door.

Treadwell locked eyes with Betty, brought the muzzle to his temple, and pulled the trigger.

114

This time when Ben was taken to the Midtown South Precinct on West Thirty-fifth, he'd surrendered his clothes down to his underwear and gotten dressed in an orange jumpsuit before being locked in a windowless isolation cell.

The last time he'd managed to get a look at a clock it was five-thirty, and lying awake now on a cot, he had to figure it was at least eight or eight-thirty.

Cassy had told them that once she got to her workstation in DCSS with Chip's laptop, it would take her at least ten minutes to download the antidote program into BP's system, and another ten or maybe twenty for it to find the worm and neutralize it.

It meant that they would have to get there no later than nine to beat the opening bell at nine-thirty. They were running out of time.

A key grated in the lock, and Ben jumped up as the door opened.

A uniformed cop with a ring of keys in one hand and a mesh bag in the other came in and handed the bag to Ben, then went back out into the corridor.

Adams, a deep scowl on his face, appeared in the doorway. "Get dressed, you son of a bitch. You've got company waiting for you, and I don't have all morning to babysit you."

Ben took his dirty khaki slacks, light blue pullover, boat shoes, and wallet out of the bag and quickly got dressed.

Out of the cell, he followed Adams and the uniform back to the lobby, where Cassy, Chip, and a stern-looking man he didn't recognize in a business suit, no tie, his eyes bloodshot, were waiting.

"You are making a lot of people in this town unhappy, Mr. Whalen," the man said. "Including me."

Adams and the uniform disappeared, and another man in civilian clothes showed up. "Sorry to drag you away like this, Mr. Mayor."

"You're Voight, the precinct commander here?"

"Yes, sir."

"I don't want another call from Washington. This matter is concluded, unless Mr. Whalen shoots somebody, and then it'll depend on who he shoots."

"Yes, sir."

The mayor turned back to Ben. "Whatever you and your friends have come here to do, get it over with and go home."

"Yes, sir," Ben said. "And thank you."

The mayor turned and left.

"You heard the man," Voight said. "Get the hell out of my station."

The clock on the wall behind the booking desk was at fifteen minutes before nine as Ben, Chip, and Cassy raced outside to where the Chevy SUV was parked.

– – –

Workday morning traffic was heavy, and Chip drove as fast as was possible, blasting through red lights whenever he had the chance.

"Are we going to run into any trouble at BP?" Ben asked.

"The cops and Bureau people are all over the place, but with any luck, the mess will be cleared up by the time we get there, and we'll have a free ticket inside, or at least downstairs to where Cassy needs to go," Chip said.

"What mess?"

"There's a big shake-up. I saw them carting a body out the front door."

"Just get me inside before it's too late," Cassy said. She was cradling the laptop like it was a sick child as they sped down Ninth.

After threading through rush hour traffic exiting the Holland Tunnel, Chip clipped the rear end of a Yellow Cab on Varick, sending it crashing into the side of a garbage truck, and a half block later a police car, its lights flashing, and siren on, came from behind them.

"We can't be stopped," Ben said.

"I know, I know," Chip said.

He hauled the Chevy down Varick and managed to put a little distance between them and the cop car, switching down side streets whenever the lights and traffic permitted it, and reached Broadway. At City Hall they were completely bogged down.

The cop car was less than a half block behind them now.

"Get the hell out, this is the best I can do," Chip shouted.

Ben and Cassy jumped out and sprinted the few blocks to Nassau as fast as they could run. A dozen police cars, unmarked sedans, and SUVs were blocking the street before the next corner in front of the Burnham Pike tower.

"Is there a back way?" Ben asked, not breaking stride.

"A side door on John Street," Cassy said. "Follow me."

– – –

They slowed their pace so as to go unnoticed as they passed by the police cordon. Around the corner, the side door was locked but unmanned, so Cassy used her pass card to get inside. It was a bit of luck they badly needed.

Instead of taking the elevator down to DCSS, they took the stairs.

The cybersecurity room was filled with the usual people, except for Butch Hardy's watchdogs. Masters jumped up from behind his desk when they came through the door. Everyone else stopped what they were doing.

"What the hell is going on?" he demanded.

"Not now, Francis," Cassy said, racing across to her workstation. It was just nine.

Masters came around from behind his desk, but Ben blocked him.

"Who do you think you are?"

"Let it be," Ben said.

Cassy powered up Chip's laptop, plugged it into her center console, and once the connection was recognized and the antidote program came up on both screens, she hit *Enter* on the laptop, and the program began to run.

Ben came over. "Are we on time?"

"I think so," Cassy said, looking up at him. "I don't know."

"In twenty minutes, at opening bell, we'll all know," Ben said.

115

The white Mercedes transit van pulled over in front of the World Wide Destinations Travel Agency in Union City, New Jersey, a minute or two before nine-thirty. Viktor had gotten lucky with a parking spot, but didn't look over as Alexei, behind the wheel of the Mercedes C300, passed them and got lucky with another parking spot just half a block down the street.

"The gods are with us this morning," Alexei said.

Bykov, in the passenger seat, nodded, but something didn't feel right to him. He didn't know what it was, maybe a sixth sense, but his gut said *get out now*.

Traffic through the Lincoln Tunnel had been heavy, which they'd expected at that hour. But right here, Union City seemed almost deserted.

Only one car cruised past, the woman driver looking straight ahead. But there were no pedestrians on the sidewalks. No one waiting at the corner for the light to change so they could cross. Even the travel agency, the beauty salon, and the liquor store across the street from where they were parked seemed deserted.

"What's the matter?" Alexei, sensing something of Bykov's mood, asked.

"I don't know."

"It's quiet."

"Hold fast," Bykov said. He got out of the car and walked across the street to the liquor store.

The door was open and a clerk, an older man, came from the back. He looked bored.

"Good morning," Bykov said. "Stoli?"

"End of the aisle."

Bykov went down the aisle, found a liter bottle of Stolichnaya vodka, and back at the counter he paid cash for it.

The clerk made change and bagged the bottle. "Have a nice day."

"You too."

Taking the bottle, Bykov walked back across the street and got in the car. "We're leaving now."

Alexei looked up in the rearview mirror. "Something wrong?"

"Da," Bykov said, "But I don't know what." He got on the phone and tried Butch Hardy's number. He let it ring ten times, but Hardy didn't answer.

"Okay, what the hell is going on, Yuri?"

"It is a setup, and I think Hardy has turned us in."

"Pizdec."

Bykov phoned Viktor, who answered on the first ring. "Arkadi is just finishing. Stand by."

"Drop it and get up here right now, we're leaving."

"Wait, wait."

"Nyet!" Bykov said.

Viktor shouted something Bykov couldn't quite catch, and Arkadi's reply was equally as garbled.

Everything was wrong.

Bykov opened his door and was about to run back to the van, when he heard the sounds of a lot of sirens maybe a couple of blocks away, closing in.

He closed the door.

"What's the matter?" Alexei demanded.

"We're leaving right now."

"What about Viktor and Arkadi?" Alexei shouted.

"Drive to the airport."

Alexei pulled away from the curb. Turned left and sped back the way they had come.

"Slow down," Bykov said. "We can't be stopped for speeding."

— — —

Viktor couldn't believe his eyes watching Alexi and Yuri driving off. *"Yeb vas,"* he said. *Fuck off.*

"We need to get out of here now," Arkadi shouted, climbing over the seat.

"Shut the bomb off! Something's wrong."

Viktor opened his door and started to get out.

— — —

Around the corner a block and a half away, a tremendous explosion behind them split the air with an unbelievable roar. Seconds later, the concussion from the blast blew out windows on the left side of the street.

"Mother of God," Alexei said, crossing himself.

THIRTEEN

OPENING BELL DAY TWO

116

It was nearly a half hour after the opening bell when Cassy and Ben were cleared through security outside the New York Stock Exchange and got to the visitors waiting area.

In the middle of everything Betty Ladd had called down to Cassy's station in the DCSS to find out what progress was being made.

"My program has loaded," Cassy had told her.

"And my fingers are crossed," Betty had said. "If the cops will let you come over, we can watch what happens together."

"May I bring Ben and his friend along?"

"Absolutely. Love to meet them."

But Chip had begged off. "I have to talk to Huggard and let him know we ran into another delay," he'd said.

"Like helping save the world's free enterprise system," Cassy had told him. She stood up on tiptoes and gave him a kiss on the cheek.

"You know I do outrank Ben. And I'm making a lot more money than he does."

"I make it a rule never to date married men, especially happily married ones," Cassy had said and they all laughed.

A pretty young woman appeared with a smile. "I'm Jennifer, Ms. Ladd's assistant. Follow me, please."

Down the hall and around the corner they came to the trading floor, which was fairly calm, though there was some commotion at the post where BP's stock was traded.

Betty came over and gave Cassy a big hug. The older woman looked tired and worried, but she smiled. "Thank God you're okay," she said, and she turned to Ben and held out her hand. "The savior of the day."

They shook hands.

"She's worth it," Ben said. "But I thought there'd be more action here."

"It'll come if Cassy's program doesn't work, because on top of that I just learned that there was an explosion in Union City across the river that took out our backup computer and killed as many as a half dozen people."

"The Russians?" Ben asked.

Betty shrugged. "Unknown." She glanced at a monitor showing the numbers. The Dow was down only a few points, as were some of the other indicators. But it was nothing catastrophic. "We're about where I expected we would be," she said. "But we should have a better idea in the next half hour or so, because if Abacus does kick in, there'll be an all-out free fall that our automatic systems won't be able to stop."

A bearded man in a gray suit and knitted red tie walked up. "Sorry to interrupt, Betty. We're putting together a follow-up to our news story about Reid Treadwell. Any comment?"

"Reid was a giant of Wall Street," Betty said. "No one was smarter, more charismatic, or more visionary than he." She smiled faintly. "Considering everything else that's been happening this morning it's all I have for now, Tony. We'll talk later."

He returned her smile and walked away.

"Tony Langley of *The Wall Street Journal*," Betty said. "I'll give him the truth about Reid's suicide later."

"And the explosion?" Ben asked.

"I knew nothing about it until I heard it on the news this morning."

They glanced at the monitors again. The Dow and S&P were still falling but not dramatically.

"So far so good," Betty said. "But is there any chance your program didn't completely wipe out Abacus?"

"From my diagnostics in DCSS it looked as if we neutralized it," Cassy said.

"But the chance still exists?"

Cassy nodded uncomfortably. "There's always a chance. Whoever designed the thing knew what they were doing," she said. "But if it were going to kick in, it would have started by now."

"Good enough," Betty said, and she hugged Cassy again. "If you're looking for a job, say the word, and you can come here and work for the exchange as my director of cybersecurity."

A man in a blue trader's jacket who Cassy recognized as Seymour Schneider, Burnham Pike's legendary and always prescient floor trader, came over. He nodded to Ben and Cassy, but then turned to Betty. "A word with you?"

"Sure," she said. "Be right back," she told Ben and Cassy and went with Schneider off to the side of the floor.

"What's on your mind, Seymour?"

"I heard something of what went on overnight, but not everything. With Reid gone, what's going to happen on fifty-four?"

"That's up to your board."

"I meant, what's the exchange's next step?"

"We're not started with the inquiry yet, and even if we were you know I couldn't discuss it, except to say that the firm has been doing some seriously bad things."

"My question is, what about our leadership team? Reid is gone. Spence was arrested just an hour ago, and Julia was taken into FBI custody until whatever happened is unraveled."

"As I said, that'll be up to your board. And as much as I

don't like the man, you still have Dammerman if his hands are clean."

"I heard that he's all lawyered up. Says he had no real idea what Reid was up to, and that he needs to take over at least as interim CEO."

"I'll tell you this much, Seymour. Whatever my personal opinion is of the man, I think he was up to his neck in the scheme to cause a crash. I suspect that Julia might be able to provide some links."

"I wouldn't count him out," Schneider said. "Reid was a sneaky bastard, and Dammerman is three times worse. But he knows how to run the firm." He glanced over at a monitor. "Maybe we'll get through today better than yesterday, but the threat is still there."

"And what threat is that?" Betty asked, though she knew the answer, and it wasn't Abacus.

"The worldwide debt. We're on the rim of the abyss."

— — —

Cassy was sad. "I'm going to miss Donni. He was a bright kid and a really good friend. If it wasn't for me, he'd still be alive."

"If it wasn't for you giving him the flash drive, the Russians who took you would have gotten it, and this place would be a shambles right now. And if you're right, so would the entire world economy."

She nodded. "He did it."

"You and he did it," Ben said

Cassy smiled wistfully. "Maybe it's finally over," she said. "But you mentioned something about going to Paris. Is that still on?"

"You bet," Ben said.

"Then let's go."

"The admiral is going to have a fit, but what the hell."

"And wasn't there something you were going to ask me when we got there?" Cassy said.

"Why wait," Ben said, "Cassy Levin, I'm in love with you. Will you marry me?"

AFTERWORD

THE DEBT BOMB

Lawrence Light

How serious is the problem of too much debt in our world, an ever-growing burden that will crush us? Very serious. In *Crash,* our character Spencer Nast, the chief White House economist, aptly dubs the situation the "debt bomb." As a financial journalist who has covered the economy and Wall Street for many years, I know that forecasting holds perils. As the great Yankees player and all-around sage Yogi Berra put it: "I never make predictions, especially about the future." But odds are strong that a debt bomb is set to go off in the U.S. in just a few years.

It's built of a combustible mixture of obligations owed by the federal government, corporate America, public pension plans, and households. When will it go off? A good bet is when the next recession arrives. A downturn is inevitable: The economy moves in cycles. Then watch the whole cursed concoction go kerblooey, as the revenue to pay interest and principal dwindles.

Economics is like physics. Nothing can last forever. Like debt. A limit exists on how much public and private borrowers can go into hock. At some point, for instance, fixed-income buyers will grow leery of Treasury paper, even though now federally backed bonds are in great demand. But once Washington's debts reach an unsustainable level, that sentiment likely will change, and with a vengeance.

People don't want to face this, and Congress's attempts to cap federal spending always end in abject failure. Think of the Road Runner cartoon where the clever bird maneuvers Wile E. Coyote's shack onto railroad tracks. Coyote, busy inside fussing with dynamite to blow up the Road Runner, looks up and sees outside his window the locomotive bearing down on him. His response: Draw the blinds. This doesn't end well for the hapless canine.

FEDERAL DEBT. Right now the national debt is slightly higher than the gross domestic product, thanks to escalating federal spending to fight two wars and two recessions, and large tax cuts enacted under the Trump administration.

When Social Security was enacted in the 1930s, the system had forty-two workers for every recipient, hence a lot of taxpayers funded benefits for the elderly. Now the ratio is 3 to 1, and in another ten years that will be almost 2 to 1. A similar scary math governs Medicare. People are living longer, which means they will need more medical care. And health-care prices are burgeoning with no end in sight.

CORPORATE DEBT. This has exploded, as nonfinancial companies took advantage of low interest rates to expand their bond debt to a record $6.4 trillion, by the St. Louis Fed's count, a 75 percent increase. When it comes due, a reckoning will occur. The companies will have to dig deep to pay off the debt or attempt to refinance at much higher rates than today's. While corporations in general have ample cash, some $2.6 trillion, to service that debt, the problem is that the cash is concentrated among a few behemoths, like Apple.

There also has been a surge of speculative bonds, issued

by companies carrying an abundance of debt. These securities, known as junk bonds, are 20 percent of the corporate bond market. Those on the brink of junk, rated BBB, are twice that size, meaning they are at risk of being downgraded.

Time and again, recessions have amped up defaults among junk issues. While today only 3 percent of junk bonds default, that figure typically more than triples in an economic downturn. At the same time, investors eager for a yield in a low-interest-rate time—junk pays higher interest than investment-grade bonds due to its elevated risk—have fewer protections. Bonds normally carry covenants, restrictions that prevent issuing companies from doing investor-unfriendly things like adding yet more debt. Not anymore; in the land of junk, "covenant-light" bonds are the rule.

PENSION OBLIGATIONS. Years ago, states and municipalities pleased their workforces by promising nice retirement benefits. This is, in effect, debt these governments owe to their workers. The upshot is that a lot of them can't meet their obligations.

The average funding ratio, the amount in their investment portfolios compared to what they must give to pensioners, is around a third. Put another way, using unfunded liabilities as a percent of state revenues, the picture is even more frightening. The worst off is Illinois, whose unfunded liability is seven times the state government's annual revenue.

HOUSEHOLD DEBT. Consumer debt is back. After the financial crisis of '08, household borrowing declined sharply, especially for mortgages as home buying ebbed. But lately it has rebounded, and then some. By 2018, loans—for credit cards, homes, autos, college, etc.—had exceeded even the bloated total of 2008, now standing at $13.7 trillion.

Student loans, for example, have doubled over the past

ten years to stand at $1.5 trillion, with an average at just under $40,000. Many young people, who start out in low-paying jobs, can't afford to pay them, and the ninety-day-plus delinquency rate is at 11 percent.

Making matters worse, after a brief postrecession spate of thrift, Americans are back to their precrisis habit of saving very little, in favor of running up debt. The personal savings rate (savings as a percent of disposable personal income) is back to near precrisis levels at 2.4 percent. A big reason for all the borrowing is not a heedless orgy of spendthrift purchasing; rather it's that wages have been stagnant for years when adjusted for inflation. A growing economy has disproportionately shoveled its bounty to the upper tenth of the population.

While low interest rates have made carrying the extra debt bearable for more Americans, these days will end eventually. The Federal Reserve has nudged them up from near zero in a bid to reach the old levels, despite a pushback from the White House. A chilling statistic from a Federal Reserve survey found that 35 percent of U.S. adults couldn't pay their bills if faced with a $400 emergency.

WHAT'S NEXT? Either massive defaults occur—think of the chaos if Washington can't pay interest and principal on Treasury bonds—or Americans see their taxes double. Or both. The doubling of taxes is predicted by the former U.S. comptroller general, David Walker.

If companies, states, and individuals go bust, the nation has a big problem. And America has an even bigger problem if the federal government can't cover its obligations. The United States, its full faith and credit, and its universally used currency, underpin the entire world's economy.

That's the nightmare scenario we explore in *Crash*.